"I write what people want to read."

—Mickey Spillane

The muzzle of the gun was a pair of yawning chasms but there was no depth to their mouths. Down the length of the blued steel the blood crimson of her nails made a startling and symbolic contrast.

Death red, I thought. The fingers behind them should have been tan but weren't. They were a tense, drawing white and with another fraction of an inch the machinery of the gun would go into motion.

The Girl Hunters

Mike Hammer's voluptuous, long-lost love is alive—and targeted by the mastermind assassi~ ~~~~~ ~~ T~~ ~~~~~~

Playing protector to a run~ ~r trades barbs and lead witl d sex-hungry females.

The Twisted Thing

A kidnapping case leads Mike Hammer into a fourteen-year-old mystery and into the sights of the most venomous killer the two-fisted private eye has ever faced.

Also available:

The Mike Hammer Collection, Volume 1, featuring:

I, the Jury, My Gun Is Quick, and *Vengeance Is Mine!*
Introduction by Max Allan Collins

The Mike Hammer Collection, Volume 2, featuring:

One Lonely Night, The Big Kill, and *Kiss Me, Deadly*
Introduction by Lawrence Block

Mike Hammer Novels by Mickey Spillane

I, the Jury
My Gun Is Quick
Vengeance Is Mine!
One Lonely Night
The Big Kill
Kiss Me, Deadly
The Girl Hunters
The Snake
The Twisted Thing
The Body Lovers
Survival . . . ZERO!
The Killing Man
Black Alley

MICKEY SPILLANE

THE MIKE HAMMER COLLECTION

VOLUME 3

THE GIRL HUNTERS
THE SNAKE
THE TWISTED THING

AN OBSIDIAN MYSTERY

OBSIDIAN
Published by New American Library, a division of
Penguin Group (USA) Inc., 375 Hudson Street,
New York, New York 10014, USA
Penguin Group (Canada), 90 Eglinton Avenue East, Suite 700, Toronto,
Ontario M4P 2Y3, Canada (a division of Pearson Penguin Canada Inc.)
Penguin Books Ltd., 80 Strand, London WC2R 0RL, England
Penguin Ireland, 25 St. Stephen's Green, Dublin 2,
Ireland (a division of Penguin Books Ltd.)
Penguin Group (Australia), 250 Camberwell Road, Camberwell, Victoria 3124,
Australia (a division of Pearson Australia Group Pty. Ltd.)
Penguin Books India Pvt. Ltd., 11 Community Centre, Panchsheel Park,
New Delhi - 110 017, India
Penguin Group (NZ), 67 Apollo Drive, Rosedale, North Shore 0632,
New Zealand (a division of Pearson New Zealand Ltd.)
Penguin Books (South Africa) (Pty.) Ltd., 24 Sturdee Avenue,
Rosebank, Johannesburg 2196, South Africa

Penguin Books Ltd., Registered Offices:
80 Strand, London WC2R 0RL, England

Published by Obsidian, an imprint of New American Library, a division of Penguin Group
(USA) Inc. Previously published individually in Signet and Dutton editions.

First Obsidian Printing, October 2010
10 9 8 7 6 5 4 3 2 1

The Girl Hunters copyright © Mickey Spillane, 1962
The Snake copyright © Mickey Spillane, 1964
The Twisted Thing copyright © Mickey Spillane, 1966
Introduction copyright © Max Allan Collins, 2010
All rights reserved

OBSIDIAN and logo are trademarks of Penguin Group (USA) Inc.

Library of Congress Cataloging-in-Publication Data:

Spillane, Mickey, 1918–2006.
   The Mike Hammer collection, volume 3/Mickey Spillane.
      p.   cm.—(An Obsidian mystery)
   ISBN 978-0-451-23124-6
1. Hammer, Mike (Fictitious character)—Fiction.   2. Private investigators—New York
(State)—New York—Fiction.   I. Title.
   PS3537.P652A6   2010
   813'.54—dc22   2010022362

Set in Bembo
Designed by Ginger Legato

Printed in the United States of America

CONTENTS

The Return of Mike Hammer

Among aficionados of tough crime fiction, few literary mysteries rival that of the disappearance in 1952 of fictional private eye Mike Hammer at the peak of his—and his creator Mickey Spillane's—powers.

The still-unrivaled publishing success of this Brooklyn-born bartender's son began inauspiciously in 1947 with the hardcover publication by E. P. Dutton of *I, the Jury*. A few reviewers noticed it as a particularly nasty example of hard-boiled detective fiction, a few praised it, most panned it, and sales were less than ten thousand copies. There was such little notice taken of Mike Hammer's first adventure that when the young writer submitted a second Hammer novel, *For Whom the Gods Would Destroy*, Dutton rejected it. Spillane returned to the comic book field where, among other things, he wrote love comics.

Then, in December 1948, New American Library's paperback edition of *I, the Jury* came out and started selling—and selling. In part thanks to a vivid cover portraying the now-famous denouement of the novel—a seated Mike Hammer's back to the camera as he trains his .45 on a disrobing femme fatale—the book attracted legions of readers. Spillane was asked to resubmit *For Whom the Gods Would Destroy*, which he declined to do (more on that subject later), and instead *My Gun Is Quick* appeared in 1950, the second of six Hammer novels that would top bestseller lists worldwide, making Spillane the first pop-lit superstar—so big, it well and truly pissed off Ernest Hemingway, who asked to have Spillane's picture removed from a barroom wall in Florida and got his own taken down for the trouble.

Sixty years later, to describe the impact of those six novels—and a seventh non-Hammer Spillane, *The Long Wait*—is to tempt credulity. The millions of copies the blue-collar writer sold unveiled an audience for franker, more violent popular fiction, and the mystery field in particular was riddled with his imitators. This went beyond just other writers copying Spillane—the first major publisher of paperback original fiction, Gold Medal Books, was created in 1950 to serve the market Spillane had uncovered. He was even their paid consultant, and provided a memorable blurb for one of their mainstays, John D. MacDonald ("I wish I had written this book!"). Gold Medal's major Hammer imitation was the Shell Scott series by Richard S. Prather, zany comedies that nonetheless worked in the extreme violence and sex Spillane had first trafficked.

The sixth Hammer novel, *Kiss Me, Deadly* (1952), became the first private eye novel to crack the *New York Times* bestseller list (the likes of Dashiell Hammett, Raymond Chandler, and Erle Stanley Gardner had never come close), and the paperback edition was as wildly successful as its predecessors. Hollywood, via British producer/director Victor Saville, came calling, and the new Spillane book and three others were headed for the silver screen.

In the midst of success and celebrity that the young writer could never have imagined came a similarly shocking barrage of attacks. Though often characterized as a right-wing writer, Spillane was—like Dashiell Hammett (but not serving jail time!)—a victim of the McCarthy era. The former comic book writer found himself (alone among popular fiction practitioners) caught up in a four-color witch hunt that started with well-meaning but misguided psychiatrist Dr. Fredric Wertham and ended with a farcical Senate hearing. Wertham's anticomics book *Seduction of the Innocent* (1954) detailed example after example of rampant violence, sexually suggestive content, and latent homosexuality in the superhero, crime, and horror "funnies" of the fifties. He singled out only one popular fiction author: Mickey Spillane.

Wertham was not alone in going after Spillane hammer and tongs—diatribes in countless publications from *The Atlantic* to *Par-*

ents magazine attacked Spillane as a purveyor of filth, the nadir of popular culture, and the illegitimate father of juvenile delinquency. In public, and even in private, Spillane laughed all this off. But he was secretly troubled and frustrated that what he had conceived as sheer entertainment would be taken so seriously, and that he had become a kind of household-name villain, a synonym for sex and sadism.

How much effect this had on Spillane's decision to stop writing Mike Hammer novels after his sixth one is unknown. I spoke to him about this many times, and got many answers (some elliptical, others disingenuous), and have come to feel there's no one solution to the mystery.

Similarly, it's hard to know whether Spillane's conversion to the conservative religious sect the Jehovah's Witnesses was in part a response to this over-the-top criticism. Did Spillane feel guilty, and were the Witnesses his redemption? He never said. He rarely spoke about his religious beliefs in public, and in private said only that he'd responded to what he'd been told by a couple of *Watchtower*-dispensing missionaries who came to his door in typical Witness fashion.

What can't be denied is the problem created by his conservative faith for the hard-hitting, sexually provocative fiction for which he'd become rich and famous. Throughout his career, Spillane would alternate prolific periods with fallow ones, going in and out of the church, taking criticism from his fellow Witnesses as late as *The Killing Man* (1989), when he was nearly sent packing from his South Carolina Kingdom Hall over the use of profanity.

The criticism he received, whether from the *New York Times* or his church, was surely not the only factor for his seeming dry spell from 1952–1961. Spillane liked to say he wrote only when he needed the money, and in the 1950s, money was pouring in—he was the bestselling writer in the world, and Hollywood was adding to the coffers, as well, though in ways that frustrated him.

He spent a lot of time dueling with producer Saville, who rejected Spillane's choice to play Mike Hammer, ex-Marine and cop Jack Stang. Spillane, playing himself, and Stang, essentially as Hammer, starred for producers John Wayne and Bob Fellows in the circus thriller *Ring of Fear* (1954). Stang, though physically impressive, didn't make the impact onscreen that natural actor Spillane did—the author was clearly the Mike Hammer audiences had been expecting when Saville instead gave them Biff Elliot in *I, the Jury.*

Throughout the fifties, the absence of a new Hammer mystery did not keep the first six books from selling and selling, although finally NAL did develop a sort of fill-in, a British author named Fleming said to be the Spillane of the UK. Spillane was having the time of his life, touring with the Clyde Beatty Circus, racing stock cars, and fiddling with Hollywood projects. Saville made three more Spillane films, notably the classic *Kiss Me Deadly* (1955), directed by Robert Aldrich and with a nicely nasty Hammer in Ralph Meeker. A good, tough TV series starring Darren McGavin ran for two syndicated seasons in the late fifties; there was a radio show and, for a while, even a Hammer comic strip, with Spillane himself writing the Sunday stories.

During his bookless near decade, Spillane did keep his hand in the business—he wrote non-Hammer short stories and novellas for surprisingly low-end markets, usually dealing with editors and publishers he knew from his comic book days. The most successful writer in the world was selling his once- or twice-a-year short fiction to lower-tier publications such as *Cavalier, Male, Saga,* and *Manhunt.*

He stayed in contact with his book publishers, however, and may have been angling for an improved contract before getting back to work. He was notoriously casual about the business end of things, despite his workingman's pride in his craft, and made a number of bad decisions toward the start of his run of success that he spent much of his life trying to correct. He may have been on a kind of informal strike with Dutton and Signet.

Whatever the case, his return in 1960 with the non-Hammer novel *The Deep* earned him mixed reviews (actually a big step up) and the expected blockbuster sales, particularly in paperback. But readers and reviewers alike were asking the same question: *Where is Mike Hammer?*

This collection answers that question, beginning with the novel that signaled the end of the long wait between Hammer books— *The Girl Hunters* (1961). Few Hammer fans would rate any of the later novels above the initial very famous six (*I, The Jury; My Gun*

Is Quick; *Vengeance is Mine!*; *One Lonely Night*; *The Big Kill*; *Kiss Me, Deadly*). Most, however, would place *The Girl Hunters* next on that esteemed list.

Spillane is seldom credited with the innovative brand of continuity he developed in the Hammer series. Most mystery series have interchangeable parts—only the first and last of Agatha Christie's Poirot novels have any real sense of continuity; Archie Goodwin and Nero Wolfe remain ageless as Rex Stout indicates the changing times around them; and—once Erle Stanley Gardner got his cast and format in place—Perry Mason, Della Street, and Paul Drake span four decades or more behaving exactly the same.

Spillane, however, explored the impact of events on his character, so that the shocking conclusion of *I, the Jury* haunts the detective, with his guilt coming to a head in the fourth Hammer book, the surreal nightmare *One Lonely Night*. Even in 1961's *The Girl Hunters*, Hammer cops to feeling guilty over the "easy" decision he made on the last page of his 1947 debut novel.

The Girl Hunters answers the question of Hammer's disappearance, literally—the detective, guilt-ridden for causing the seeming death of his partner-secretary, Velda, has been on a seven-year drunk, as evidenced by the famous first line: "They found me in the gutter." Further, Spillane reveals that Hammer's best friend, Captain Pat Chambers of homicide, is now his worst enemy, as Chambers too is revealed to have been in love with Velda. When word comes that Velda may be alive, Hammer the alcoholic goes cold turkey (well, beers don't count, apparently) and soon is back on the mean streets.

But Spillane has a great time exploring his hero's new frailties. This Hammer is weak and uncertain after having been out of the game for a long time, and must now coast on his old reputation—and Spillane seems almost puckishly aware of the parallel between himself and Hammer. Whether his religious conversion or the sex-and-sadism critical blasts were factors, it's hard to say, but Spillane's technique has changed—he is more sparing with the sex and violence, although both are present, used, as the writer liked to say, "as exclamation points." *The Girl Hunters* signals a Hammer less likely to fire away with his .45 at the drop of a fedora, and shows a move to surprise endings that will often have Hammer tricking the bad guys into killing themselves so he doesn't have to bear the direct guilt.

The body count is high, but Hammer himself isn't responsible, although the vicious climatic fight with the Russian agent called The Dragon concludes with one of the most casually brutal acts Hammer ever perpetrated. With surprising ease, Spillane moves his fifties detective into the sixties, espionage substituting for the Mob and other more conventional villains. Hammer had fought "Commies" before (in *One Lonely Night*), but here he's entered the world of his British offspring, James Bond. There's a showbiz element connected to Spillane's own celebrity, including the use of real-life columnist Hy Gardner, a rival and contemporary of Walter Winchell and Earl Wilson.

Spillane is at his best in *The Girl Hunters*, his storytelling fast-moving, consistently entertaining, and with crisp, tough dialogue and action that shocks when it comes, plus mood-setting descriptions that show off his gift for noir poetry. Spillane employs a surprising narrative technique, the absence of Velda from the story—she is the girl being hunted, but she does not appear.

Spillane saves her reappearance for *The Snake*, the eighth Mike Hammer and a direct sequel to *The Girl Hunters*. Readers should understand, however, that *The Girl Hunters* and *The Snake* were never intended to be one book, one continuous story, and are advised to keep in mind that three years separated the publication of the two. Those fresh from spending time with a drunk Mike Hammer who was struggling to get back to his old self will need a grain of salt, at least, to accept Hammer in *The Snake*—which begins perhaps an hour after *The Girl Hunters* ends. Improbably, Hammer is not only his old self again, but is accepted around Manhattan by his cronies as if he'd been away for seven weeks, not seven years.

Still, *The Snake* is a first-rate tough mystery, with Spillane abandoning espionage for more traditional Mob concerns. Hammer and Velda are instantly the team of old as they help a damsel in distress and wade into the murky waters of big-time politics. In some respects, this is as close to a "standard" Mike Hammer mystery as you're likely to find. Had Spillane—like Stout, Christie, Gardner, and so many others—chosen to write dozens of Hammer novels rather than just *a* dozen (well, a baker's dozen), *The Snake* might have been the template. Moving around Manhattan with ease, Hammer works his contacts among journalists and reestablishes a working relationship, if not quite his friendship, with Pat Chambers. Even Spillane's old enemy Anthony Boucher praised the novel's craft, calling it "certainly Mike Hammer's best case."

The ending is (as they used to say) a corker, although the ambiguous nature of what happens next—i.e., do Velda and Mike consummate their love?—remains unresolved, at least as far as Spillane was concerned. This piece of continuity bedeviled Spillane, who, post-*Snake*, went back and forth on whether Hammer and Velda were intimate.

Clearly Spillane intended to write another batch of books about Mike Hammer, but several things interfered. He was sidetracked for a while working as screenwriter and star of the British-American production *The Girl Hunters* (1963). Last-minute funding problems caused the film to be shot in black-and-white, making it look shabby next to the early Bond films with which it was in direct competition (sharing Bond girl Shirley Eaton, who costarred in *The Girl Hunters* and had the small but memorable golden-girl role in *Goldfinger*).

Spillane received raves for his portrayal of his hero, a remarkable accomplishment—after all, it's not as though Edgar Rice Burroughs could have pulled off Tarzan onscreen, although Agatha Christie would have made a pretty fair Marple. The high concept of mystery writer playing his own detective attracted lots of media, in particular a witty *Esquire* magazine piece by Terry Southern. But Bond's emergence, and frankly dominance, screwed things up for Spillane—Ian Fleming, the Brit used by Signet to fill in for Spillane during "the long wait," was now on top of publishing and movies.

The Snake had been intended to be the basis for the second Spillane-as-Hammer film, and the Lolita-ish Sue was written as a role for his then wife, Broadway starlet Sherri Malinou. But *The Girl Hunters* didn't do well enough to justify a second film, and discouraged Spillane from focusing on his most famous character. Instead, he developed the Hammer clone Tiger Mann, a hard-boiled secret agent whose four adventures sold in the millions but did not generate TV shows or films despite the surrounding spy craze.

xvi • *The Return of Mike Hammer*

A brief aside—*The Girl Hunters* title was derived from the "Girl Hunt" ballet in the classic 1953 Fred Astaire film *The Band Wagon*, which overtly and beautifully spoofed Spillane and Mike Hammer. This gave the mystery writer great satisfaction, because Fred Astaire and Ginger Rogers movies were Mickey Spillane's cinema of choice.

Spillane wound up publishing only four Hammer novels in the sixties, although he began a number that were set aside for various reasons; over the remainder of his career, he began and set aside even more Hammer novels that he never published. After *The Snake*, Spillane developed a Hammer story that pitted his hero against the drug racket in a context of the swinging sixties. But he found himself up against a deadline to Dutton and Signet for a new Hammer novel, and rather than finish what would eventually become *The Big Bang* (published in 2010 as "the lost Mike Hammer sixties novel"), he pulled down a certain old, unpublished manuscript from his shelf—*For Whom the Gods Would Destroy*—and sent that instead, under the title *The Twisted Thing*.

This was, of course, the rejected novel he'd written right after selling *I, the Jury* (1947) to E. P. Dutton, making it chronologically the second Mike Hammer mystery. When Signet had a huge success with the paperback reprint of *I, the Jury*, however, the editor at Dutton came back to Spillane requesting *For Whom the Gods Would Destroy*, but (as indicated earlier) Spillane said no.

He chose to write *My Gun Is Quick* (1950) instead. The response from readers to the sex and violence of *I, the Jury* dictated a different Mike Hammer novel to follow the first. *For Whom the Gods Would Destroy* went onto a shelf in the writer's upstate New York home, where the sole manuscript was nearly lost in a fire. The retrieved pages lacked only the final one, which had been burned black; Spillane wrote a replacement last page for it in 1966, though a restoration of the charred page revealed he had remembered the original ending almost word for word.

Spillane's noir universe was so timeless that very little revision was required for publication in 1966 of a novel written in 1948. A small passage with Hammer's cop friend, Pat Chambers, makes reference to the events of *The Girl Hunters* and *The Snake*, and *The Twisted Thing* fits in well with the 1960s Hammer novels, which were tough and sexy but eased up on the emotional fire and extremes of violence and passion that had made *I, the Jury* (and the five Hammer novels that quickly followed it) such icons of controversy in the early 1950s.

Ironically, critics—again including *New York Times* stalwart Anthony Boucher—greeted this "new" Hammer mystery with accolades. "I suggest," said Boucher, "that [Mike Hammer's] creator is one of the last of the great storytellers in the pulp tradition, as he amply demonstrates in *The Twisted Thing.*"

Boucher, in terming the novel "vintage" Spillane, didn't know how right he was—or that he was responding enthusiastically to a novel written in the very period during which the critic had been (in his words) "one of the leaders in the attacks on Spillane."

Looking at *The Twisted Thing* in that context, Spillane's shelving it and substituting *My Gun Is Quick* is easy to understand: the latter novel plays off the violence and vengeance of *I, the Jury* with sexual passages that were frank for the day, and exhibits a generally seamy, sordid feel, beginning with Hammer's encountering a friendly hooker in a diner.

The Twisted Thing, however, implies the vengeful Hammer of the *first* novel was not envisioned by the writer as the Hammer of *all* the novels—rather, *I, the Jury* appears intended to tell just that one tale of murdered-friend retribution. In *The Twisted Thing* there is casual sex and vintage Spillane rough stuff, but the dominant theme is a father-son relationship between Mike Hammer and fourteen-year-old child genius Ruston York.

The Twisted Thing takes place in a small town where Hammer is initially involved with rescuing young Ruston from kidnappers—both Velda and Manhattan are largely absent from the novel. A tough, corrupt local cop—the evocatively named Dilwick—provides the initial conflict, but the young genius's wealthy father is soon murdered, and away Hammer goes. Hoods and a casino right out of *The Big Sleep* provide the toughest of tough dicks with further fun and games, but his detective work is right out of Christie, a search for missing documents more typical of Hercule Poirot than Mike Hammer.

The Girl Hunters is likely the best of the sixties Hammers, but *The Twisted Thing* isn't a sixties Hammer at all, but rather a late forties one. The ending, revealing the identity of the murderer, comes in typical abrupt, shocking Spillane style, and makes a lot of sense as the second such ending Spillane wrote, a huge surprise in 1966 that still has power today. The small-town setting, the classic pulp cast—troubled millionaire, willing wench, crooked cops, casino thugs—represent classic pulp at its liveliest. But the father-son relationship at the novel's core makes *The Twisted Thing* unique among Hammer novels.

Mike Hammer has come to be synonymous with tough private eyes, as has Mickey Spillane with hard-boiled mystery fiction. We may not know for a certainty why Spillane withdrew Mike Hammer, temporarily, from the public stage; but reading these, you'll say it's easy to understand why that public welcomed back both Spillane and Hammer so enthusiastically.

—Max Allan Collins
Summer 2010

Max Allan Collins has earned an unprecedented fifteen Private Eye Writers of America Shamus nominations, winning twice for novels in his historical Nathan Heller series. His graphic novel *Road to Perdition* is the basis of the Academy Award–winning Tom Hanks film. Shortly before Mickey Spillane's passing, the writer asked Collins to complete various unfinished works, including the Mike Hammer novel *The Big Bang* (begun 1964, published 2010). Both Spillane and Collins are recipients of the Eye, the Private Eye Writers life achievement award.

THE
GIRL
HUNTERS

This one is for Elliott Graham
who sweated more waiting for Mike than he did as a dog face
waiting for us brown-shoes fly-boys to give him aerial cover.
So here we go again, E.G., with more to come.
But this one is for you.

CHAPTER 1

They found me in the gutter. The night was the only thing I had left and not much of it at that. I heard the car stop, the doors open and shut and the two voices talking. A pair of arms jerked me to my feet and held me there.

"Drunk," the cop said.

The other one turned me around into the light. "He don't smell bad. That cut on his head didn't come from a fall either."

"Mugged?"

"Maybe."

I didn't give a damn which way they called it. They were both wrong anyhow. Two hours ago I was drunk. Not now. Two hours ago I was a roaring lion. Then the bottle sailed across the room. No lion left now.

Now was a time when I wasn't anything. Nothing was left inside except the feeling a ship must have when it's torpedoed, sinks and hits bottom.

A hand twisted into my chin and lifted my face up. "Ah, the guy's a bum. Somebody messed him up a little bit."

"You'll never make sergeant, son. That's a hundred-buck suit and it fits too good to be anything but his own. The dirt is fresh, not worn on."

"Okay, Daddy, let's check his wallet, see who he is and run him in."

The cop with the deep voice chuckled, patted me down and came up with my wallet. "Empty," he said.

Hell, there had been two bills in it when I started out. It must have been a pretty good night. Two hundred bucks' worth of night.

I heard the cop whistle between his teeth. "We got ourselves a real fish."

"Society boy? He don't look so good for a society boy. Not with his face. He's been splashed."

"Uh-uh. Michael Hammer, it says here on the card. He's a private jingle who gets around."

"So he gets tossed in the can and he won't get around so much."

The arm under mine hoisted me a little straighter and steered me toward the car. My feet moved; lumps on the end of a string that swung like pendulums.

"You're only joking," the cop said. "There are certain people who wouldn't like you to make such noises with your mouth."

"Like who?"

"Captain Chambers."

It was the other cop's turn to whistle.

"I told you this jingle was a fish," my pal said. "Go buzz the station. Ask what we should do with him. And use a phone—we don't want this on the air."

The cop grunted something and left. I felt hands easing me into the squad car, then shoving me upright against the seat. The hands went down and dragged my feet in, propping them against the floorboard. The door shut and the one on the other side opened. A heavy body climbed in under the wheel and a tendril of smoke drifted across my face. It made me feel a little sick.

The other cop came back and got in beside me. "The captain wants us to take him up to his house," he said. "He told me thanks."

"Good enough. A favor to a captain is like money in the bank, I always say."

"Then how come you ain't wearing plainclothes then?"

"Maybe I'm not the type, son. I'll leave it to you young guys."

The car started up. I tried to open my eyes but it took too much effort and I let them stay closed.

You can stay dead only so long. Where first there was nothing, the pieces all come drifting back together like a movie of an exploding shell run in reverse.

The fragments come back slowly, grating together as they seek a matching part and painfully jar into place. You're whole again, finally, but the scars and the worn places are all there to remind you that once you were dead. There's life once more and, with it, a dull pain that pulsates at regular intervals, a light that's too bright to look into and sound that's more than you can stand. The flesh is weak and crawly, slack from the disuse that is the death, sensitive with the agonizing fire that is life. There's memory that makes you want to crawl back into the void but the life is too vital to let you go.

The terrible shattered feeling was inside me, the pieces having a hard time trying to come together. My throat was still raw and cottony; constricted, somehow, from the tensed-up muscles at the back of my neck.

When I looked up Pat was holding out his cigarettes to me. "Smoke?"

I shook my head.

His voice had a callous edge to it when he said, "You quit?"

"Yeah."

I felt his shrug. "When?"

"When I ran out of loot. Now knock it off."

"You had loot enough to drink with." His voice had a real dirty tone now.

There are times when you can't take anything at all, no jokes, no rubs—nothing. Like the man said, you want nothing from nobody never. I propped my hands on the arms of the chair and pushed myself to my feet. The inside of my thighs quivered with the effort.

"Pat—I don't know what the hell you're pulling. I don't give a damn either. Whatever it is, I don't appreciate it. Just keep off my back, old buddy."

A flat expression drifted across his face before the hardness came back. "We stopped being buddies a long time ago, Mike."

"Good. Let's keep it like that. Now where the hell's my clothes?"

He spit a stream of smoke at my face and if I didn't have to hold the back of the chair to stand up I would have belted him one. "In the garbage," he said. "It's where you belong too but this time you're lucky."

"You son of a bitch."

I got another faceful of smoke and choked on it.

"You used to look a lot bigger to me, Mike. Once I couldn't have taken you. But now you call me things like that and I'll belt you silly."

"You son of a bitch," I said.

I saw it coming but couldn't move, a blurred white open-handed smash that took me right off my feet into the chair that turned over and left me in a sprawled lump against the wall. There was no pain to it, just a taut sickness in the belly that turned into a wrenching dry heave that tasted of blood from the cut inside my mouth. I could feel myself twitching spasmodically with every contraction of my stomach and when it was over I lay there with relief so great I thought I was dead.

He let me get up by myself and half fall into the chair. When I could focus again, I said, "Thanks, buddy. I'll keep it in mind."

Pat shrugged noncommittally and held out a glass. "Water. It'll settle your stomach."

"Drop dead."

He put the glass down on an end table as the bell rang. When he came back he threw a box down on the sofa and pointed to it. "New clothes. Get dressed."

"I don't have any new clothes."

"You have now. You can pay me later."

"I'll pay you up the guzukus later."

He walked over, seemingly balancing on the balls of his feet. Very quietly he said, "You can get yourself another belt in the kisser without trying hard, mister."

I couldn't let it go. I tried to swing coming up out of the chair and like the last time I could see it coming but couldn't get out of the way. All I heard was a meaty smash that had a familiar sound to it and my stomach tried to heave again but it was too late. The beautiful black had come again.

My jaws hurt. My neck hurt. My whole side felt like it was coming out. But most of all my jaws hurt. Each tooth was an independent source of silent agony while the pain in my head seemed to center just behind each ear. My tongue was too thick to talk and when I got my eyes open I had to squint them shut again to make out the checkerboard pattern of the ceiling.

When the fuzziness went away I sat up, trying to remember

what happened. I was on the couch this time, dressed in a navy blue suit. The shirt was clean and white, the top button open and the black knitted tie hanging down loose. Even the shoes were new and in the open part of my mind it was like the simple wonder of a child discovering the new and strange world of the ants when he turns over a rock.

"You awake?"

I looked up and Pat was standing in the archway, another guy behind him carrying a small black bag.

When I didn't answer Pat said, "Take a look at him, Larry."

The one he spoke to pulled a stethoscope from his pocket and hung it around his neck. Then everything started coming back again. I said, "I'm all right. You don't hit that hard."

"I wasn't half trying, wise guy."

"Then why the medic?"

"General principles. This is Larry Snyder. He's a friend of mine."

"So what?" The doc had the stethoscope against my chest but I couldn't stop him even if I had wanted to. The examination was quick, but pretty thorough. When he finished he stood up and pulled out a prescription pad.

Pat asked, "Well?"

"He's been around. Fairly well marked out. Fist fights, couple of bullet scars—"

"He's had them."

"Fist marks are recent. Other bruises made by some blunt instrument. One rib—"

"Shoes," I interrupted. "I got stomped."

"Typical alcoholic condition," he continued. "From all external signs I'd say he isn't too far from total. You know how they are."

"Damn it," I said, "quit talking about me in the third person."

Pat grunted something under his breath and turned to Larry. "Any suggestions?"

"What can you do with them?" the doctor laughed. "They hit the road again as soon as you let them out of your sight. Like him— you buy him new clothes and as soon as he's near a swap shop he'll turn them in on rags with cash to boot and pitch a big one. They go back harder than ever once they're off awhile."

"Meanwhile I can cool him for a day."

"Sure. He's okay now. Depends upon personal supervision."

Pat let out a terse laugh. "I don't care what he does when I let him loose. I want him sober for one hour. I need him."

When I glanced up I saw the doctor looking at Pat strangely, then me. "Wait a minute. This is that guy you were telling me about one time?"

Pat nodded. "That's right."

"I thought you were friends."

"We were at one time, but nobody's friends with a damn drunken bum. He's nothing but a lousy lush and I'd as soon throw his can in the tank as I would any other lush. Being friends once doesn't mean anything to me. Friends can wear out pretty fast sometimes. He wore out. Now he's part of a job. For old times' sake I throw in a few favors on the side but they're strictly for old times' sake and only happen once. Just once. After that he stays bum and I stay cop. I catch him out of line and he's had it."

Larry laughed gently and patted him on the shoulder. Pat's face was all tight in a mean grimace and it was a way I had never seen him before. "Relax," Larry told him. "Don't *you* get wound up."

"So I hate slobs," he said.

"You want a prescription too? There are economy-sized bottles of tranquilizers nowadays."

Pat sucked in his breath and a grin pulled at his mouth. "That's all I need is a problem." He waved a thumb at me. "Like him."

Larry looked down at me like he would at any specimen. "He doesn't look like a problem type. He probably plain likes the sauce."

"No, he's got a problem, right?"

"Shut up," I said.

"Tell the man what your problem is, Mikey boy."

Larry said, "Pat—"

He shoved his hand away from his arm. "No, go ahead and tell him, Mike. I'd like to hear it again myself."

"You son of a bitch," I said.

He smiled then. His teeth were shiny and white under tight lips and the two steps he took toward me were stiff-kneed. "I told you what I'd do if you got big-mouthed again."

For once I was ready. I wasn't able to get up, so I kicked him right smack in the crotch and once in the mouth when he started to fold up and I would have gotten one more in if the damn doctor hadn't laid me out with a single swipe of his bag that almost took my head off.

It was an hour before either one of us was any good, but from now on I wasn't going to get another chance to lay Pat up with a sucker trick. He was waiting for me to try it and if I did he'd have my guts all over the floor.

The doctor had gone and come, getting his own prescriptions filled. I got two pills and a shot. Pat had a fistful of aspirins, but he needed a couple of leeches along the side of his face where he was all black and blue.

But yet he sat there with the disgust and sarcasm still on his face whenever he looked at me and once more he said, "You didn't tell the doctor your problem, Mike."

I just looked at him.

Larry waved his hand for him to cut it out and finished repacking his kit.

Pat wasn't going to let it alone, though. He said, "Mike lost his girl. A real nice kid. They were going to get married."

That great big place in my chest started to open up again, a huge hole that could grow until there was nothing left of me, only that huge hole. "Shut up, Pat."

"He likes to think she ran off, but he knows all the time she's dead. He sent her out on too hot a job and she never came back, right, Mikey boy? She's dead."

"Maybe you'd better forget it, Pat," Larry told him softly.

"Why forget it? She was my friend too. She had no business playing guns with hoods. But no, wise guy here sends her out. His secretary. She has a P.I. ticket and a gun, but she's nothing but a girl and she never comes back. You know where she probably is, Doc? At the bottom of the river someplace, that's where."

And now the hole was all I had left. I was all nothing, a hole that could twist and scorch my mind with such incredible pain that even relief was inconceivable because there was no room for anything except that pain. Out of it all I could feel some movement. I knew I was watching Pat and I could hear his voice but nothing made sense at all.

His voice was far away saying, "Look at him, Larry. His eyes are all gone. And look at his hand. You know what he's doing. He's trying to kill me. He's going after a gun that isn't there anymore because he hasn't got a license to carry one. He lost that and his business and everything else when he shot up the people he thought got Velda. Oh, he knocked off some goodies and got away with it because they were all hoods caught in the middle of an armed robbery. But that was it for our tough boy there. Then what does he do? He cries his soul out into a whiskey bottle. Damn—look at his hand. He's pointing a gun at me he doesn't even have anymore and his finger's pulling the trigger. Damn, he'd kill me right where I sit."

Then I lost sight of Pat entirely because my head was going from side to side and the hole was being filled in again from the doctor's wide-fingered slaps until once more I could see and feel as much as I could in the half life that was left in me.

This time the doctor had lost his disdainful smirk. He pulled the skin down under my eyes, stared at my pupils, felt my pulse and did things to my earlobe with his fingernail that I could barely feel. He stopped, stood up and turned his back to me. "This guy is shot down, Pat."

"It couldn't've happened to a better guy."

"I'm not kidding. He's a case. What do you expect to get out of him?"

"Nothing. Why?"

"Because I'd say he couldn't stay rational. That little exhibition was a beauty. I'd hate to see it if he was pressed further."

"Then stick around. I'll press him good, the punk."

"You're asking for trouble. Somebody like him can go off the deep end anytime. For a minute there I thought he'd flipped. When it happens they don't come back very easily. What is it you wanted him to do?"

I was listening now. Not because I wanted to, but because it was something buried too far in my nature to ignore. It was something from way back like a hunger that can't be ignored.

Pat said, "I want him to interrogate a prisoner."

For a moment there was silence, then: "You can't be serious."

"The hell I'm not. The guy won't talk to anybody else *but* him."

"Come off it, Pat. You have ways to make a person talk."

"Sure, under the right circumstances, but not when they're in the hospital with doctors and nurses hovering over them."

"Oh?"

"The guy's been shot. He's only holding on so he can talk to this slob. The doctors can't say what keeps him alive except his determination to make this contact."

"But—"

"But nuts, Larry!" His voice started to rise with suppressed rage. "We use any means we can when the chips are down. This guy was shot and we want the one who pulled the trigger. It's going to be a murder rap any minute and if there's a lead we'll damn well get it. I don't care what it takes to make this punk sober, but that's the way he's going to be and I don't care if the effort kills him, he's going to do it."

"Okay, Pat. It's your show. Run it. Just remember that there are plenty of ways of killing a guy."

I felt Pat's eyes reach out for me. "For him I don't give a damn."

Somehow I managed a grin and felt around for the words. I couldn't get a real punch line across, but to me they sounded good enough.

Just two words.

Pat had arranged everything with his usual methodical care. The years hadn't changed him a bit. The great arranger. Mr. Go, Go, Go himself. I felt the silly grin come back that really had no meaning, and someplace in the back of my mind a clinical voice told me softly that it could be a symptom of incipient hysteria. The grin got sillier and I couldn't help it.

Larry and Pat blocked me in on either side, a hand under each arm keeping me upright and forcing me forward. As far as anybody was concerned I was another sick one coming in the emergency entrance and if he looked close enough he could even smell the hundred-proof sickness.

I made them take me to the men's room so I could vomit again, and when I sluiced down in frigid water I felt a small bit better. Enough so I could wipe off the grin. I was glad there was no mirror over the basin. It had been a long time since I had looked at myself and I didn't want to start now.

Behind me the door opened and there was some hurried medical chatter between Larry and a white-coated intern who had come in with a plainclothesman. Pat finally said, "How is he?"

"Going fast," Larry said. "He won't let them operate either. He knows he's had it and doesn't want to die under ether before he sees your friend here."

"Damn it, don't call him my friend."

The intern glanced at me critically, running his eyes up and down then doing a quickie around my face. His fingers flicked out to spread my eyelids open for a look into my pupils and I batted them away.

"Keep your hands off me, sonny," I said.

Pat waved him down. "Let him be miserable, Doctor. Don't try to help him."

The intern shrugged, but kept looking anyway. I had suddenly become an interesting psychological study for him.

"You'd better get him up there. The guy hasn't long to live. Minutes at the most."

Pat looked at me. "You ready?"

"You asking?" I said.

"Not really. You don't have a choice."

"No?"

Larry said, "Mike—go ahead and do it."

I nodded. "Sure, why not. I always did have to do half his work for him anyway." Pat's mouth went tight and I grinned again. "Clue me on what you want to know."

There were fine white lines around Pat's nostrils and his lips were tight and thin. "Who shot him. Ask him that."

"What's the connection?"

Now Pat's eyes went half closed, hating my guts for beginning to think again. After a moment he said, "One bullet almost went through him. They took it out yesterday. A ballistics check showed it to be from the same gun that killed Senator Knapp. If this punk upstairs dies we can lose our lead to a murderer. Understand? You find out who shot him."

"Okay," I said. "Anything for a friend. Only first I want a drink."

"No drink."

"So drop dead."

"Bring him a shot," Larry told the intern.

The guy nodded, went out and came back a few seconds later with a big double in a water glass. I took it in a hand that had the shakes real bad, lifted it and said, "Cheers."

The guy on the bed heard us come in and turned his head on the pillow. His face was drawn, pinched with pain and the early glaze of death was in his eyes.

I stepped forward and before I could talk he said, "Mike? You're—Mike Hammer?"

"That's right."

He squinted at me, hesitating. "You're not like—"

I knew what he was thinking. I said, "I've been sick."

From someplace in back Pat sucked in his breath disgustedly.

The guy noticed them for the first time. "Out. Get them out."

I waved my thumb over my shoulder without turning around. I knew Larry was pushing Pat out the door over his whispered protestations, but you don't argue long with a medic in his own hospital.

When the door clicked shut I said, "Okay, buddy, you wanted to see me and since you're on the way out it has to be important. Just let me get some facts straight. I never saw you before. Who are you?"

"Richie Cole."

"Good. Now who shot you?"

"Guy they call . . . The Dragon. No name . . . I don't know his name."

"Look . . ."

Somehow he got one hand up and waved it feebly. "Let me talk."

I nodded, pulled up a chair and sat on the arm. My guts were all knotted up again and beginning to hurt. They were crying out for some bottle love again and I had to rub the back of my hand across my mouth to take the thought away.

The guy made a wry face and shook his head. "You'll . . . never do it."

My tongue ran over my lips without moistening them. "Do what?"

"Get her in time."

"Who?"

"The woman." His eyes closed and for a moment his face relaxed. "The woman Velda."

I sat there as if I were paralyzed; for a second totally immobilized, a suddenly frozen mind and body that had solidified into one great silent scream at the mention of a name I had long ago consigned to a grave somewhere. Then the terrible cold was drenched with an even more terrible wash of heat and I sat there with my hands bunched into fists to keep them from shaking.

Velda.

He was watching me closely, the glaze in his eyes momentarily gone. He saw what had happened to me when he said the name and there was a peculiar expression of approval in his face.

Finally I said, "You knew her?"

He barely nodded. "I *know* her."

And again that feeling happened to me, worse this time because I knew he wasn't lying and that she was alive someplace. *Alive!*

I kept a deliberate control over my voice. "Where is she?"

"Safe for . . . the moment. But she'll be killed unless . . . you find her. The one called The Dragon . . . he's looking for her too. You'll have to find her first."

I was damn near breathless. *"Where?"* I wanted to reach over and shake it out of him but he was too close to the edge of the big night to touch.

Cole managed a crooked smile. He was having a hard time to talk and it was almost over. "I gave . . . an envelope to Old Dewey. Newsy on Lexington by the Clover Bar . . . for you."

"Damn it, where is she, Cole?"

"No . . . you find The Dragon . . . before he gets her."

"Why me, Cole? Why that way? You had the cops?"

The smile still held on. "Need someone . . . ruthless. Someone very terrible." His eyes fixed on mine, shiny bright, mirroring one last effort to stay alive. "She said . . . you could . . . if someone could find you. You had been missing . . . long time." He was fighting hard now. He only had seconds. "No police . . . unless necessary. You'll see . . . why."

"Cole . . ."

His eyes closed, then opened and he said, "Hurry." He never closed them again. The gray film came and his stare was a lifeless one, hiding things I would have given an arm to know.

I sat there beside the bed looking at the dead man, my thoughts groping for a hold in a brain still soggy from too many bouts in too many bars. I couldn't think, so I simply looked and wondered where and when someone like him had found someone like her.

Cole had been a big man. His face, relaxed in death, had hard planes to it, a solid jawline blue with beard and a nose that had been broken high on the bridge. There was a scar beside one eye running into the hairline that could have been made by a knife. Cole had been a hard man, all right. In a way a good-looking hardcase whose business was trouble.

His hand lay outside the sheet, the fingers big and the wrist thick. The knuckles were scarred, but none of the scars was fresh. They were old scars from old fights. The incongruous part was the nails. They were thick and square, but well cared for. They reflected all the care a manicurist could give with a treatment once a week.

The door opened and Pat and Larry came in. Together they looked at the body and stood there waiting. Then they looked at me and whatever they saw made them both go expressionless at once.

Larry made a brief inspection of the body on the bed, picked up a phone and relayed the message to someone on the other end. Within seconds another doctor was there with a pair of nurses verifying the situation, recording it all on a clipboard.

When he turned around he stared at me with a peculiar expression and said, "You feel all right?"

"I'm all right," I repeated. My voice seemed to come from someone else.

"Want another drink?"

"No."

"You'd better have one," Larry said.

"I don't want it."

Pat said, "The hell with him." His fingers slid under my arm. "Outside, Mike. Let's go outside and talk."

I wanted to tell him what he could do with his talk, but the numbness was there still, a frozen feeling that restricted thought and movement, painless but effective. So I let him steer me to the small waiting room down the hall and took the seat he pointed out.

There is no way to describe the immediate aftermath of a sudden shock. If it had come at another time in another year it would have been different, but now the stalk of despondency was withered and brittle, refusing to bend before a wind of elation.

All I could do was sit there, bringing back his words, the tone of his voice, the way his face crinkled as he saw me. Somehow he had expected something different. He wasn't looking for a guy who had the earmarks of the Bowery and every slop chute along the avenues etched into his skin.

I said, "Who was he, Pat?" in a voice soggy and hollow.

Pat didn't bother to answer my question. I could feel his eyes crawl over me until he asked, "What did he tell you?"

I shook my head. Just once. My way could be final too.

With a calm, indifferent sincerity Pat said, "You'll tell me. You'll get worked on until talking won't even be an effort. It will come out of you because there won't be a nerve ending left to stop it. You know that."

I heard Larry's strained voice say, "Come off it, Pat. He can't take much."

"Who cares. He's no good to anybody. He's a louse, a stinking, drinking louse. Now he's got something I have to have. You think I'm going to worry about him? Larry, buddy, you just don't know me very well anymore."

I said, "Who was he?"

The wall in front of me was a friendly pale green. It was blank from one end to the other. It was a vast, meadowlike area, totally unspoiled. There were no foreign markings, no distracting pictures. Unsympathetic. Antiseptic.

I felt Pat's shrug and his fingers bit into my arm once more. "Okay, wise guy. Now we'll do it my way."

"I told you, Pat—"

"Damn it, Larry, you knock it off. This bum is a lead to a killer. He learned something from that guy and I'm going to get it out of him. Don't hand me any pious crap or medical junk about what can happen. I know guys like this. I've been dealing with them all my life. They go on getting banged around from saloon to saloon, hit by cars, rolled by muggers and all they ever come up with are fresh scars. I can beat the hell out of him and maybe he'll talk. Maybe he won't, but man, let me tell you this—I'm going to have my crack at him and when I'm through the medics can pick up the pieces for their go. Only first me, understand?"

Larry didn't answer him for a moment, then he said quietly. "Sure, I understand. Maybe you could use a little medical help yourself."

I heard Pat's breath hiss in softly. Like a snake. His hand relaxed on my arm and without looking I knew what his face was like. I had seen him go like that before and a second later he had shot a guy.

And this time it was me he listened to when I said, "He's right, old buddy. You're real sick."

I knew it would come and there wouldn't be any way of getting away from it. It was quick, it was hard, but it didn't hurt a bit. It was like flying away to never-never land where all is quiet and peaceful and awakening is under protest because then it will really hurt and you don't want that to happen.

Larry said, "How do you feel now?"

It was a silly question. I closed my eyes again.

"We kept you here in the hospital."

"Don't do me any more favors," I told him.

"No trouble. You're a public charge. You're on the books as an acute alcoholic with a D and D to boot and if you're real careful you might talk your way out on the street again. However, I have my doubts about it. Captain Chambers is pushing you hard."

"The hell with him."

"He's not the only one."

"So what's new?" My voice was raspy, almost gone.

"The D.A., his assistant and some unidentified personnel from higher headquarters are interested in whatever statement you'd care to make."

"The hell with them too."

"It could be instrumental in getting you out of here."

"Nuts. It's the first time I've been to bed in a long time. I like it here."

"Mike—" His voice had changed. There was something there now that wasn't that of the professional medic at a bedside. It was worried and urgent and I let my eyes slit open and looked at him.

"I don't like what's happening to Pat."

"Tough."

"A good word, but don't apply it to him. You're the tough one. You're not like him at all."

"He's tough."

"In a sense. He's a pro. He's been trained and can perform certain skills most men can't. He's a policeman and most men aren't that. Pat is a normal sensitive human. At least he was. I met him after you went to pot. I heard a lot about you, mister. I watched Pat change character day by day and what caused the change was you and what you did to Velda."

The name again. In one second I lived every day the name was alive and with me. Big, Valkyrian and with hair as black as night.

"Why should he care?"

"He says she was his friend."

Very slowly I squeezed my eyes open. "You know what she was to me?"

"I think so."

"Okay."

"But it could be he was in love with her too," he said.

I couldn't laugh like I wanted to. "She was in love with me, Doc."

"Nevertheless, *he* was in love with *her*. Maybe you never realized it, but that's the impression I got. He's still a bachelor, you know."

"Ah! He's in love with his job. I know him."

"Do you?"

I thought back to that night and couldn't help the grin that tried to climb up my face. "Maybe not, Doc, maybe not. But it's an interesting thought. It explains a lot of things."

"He's after you now. To him, you killed her. His whole personality, his entire character has changed. You're the focal point. Until now he's never had a way to get to you to make you pay for what happened. Now he has you in a nice tight bind and, believe me, you're going to be racked back first class."

"That's G.I. talk, Doc."

"I was in the same war, buddy."

I looked at him again. His face was drawn, his eyes searching and serious. "What am I supposed to do?"

"He never told me and I never bothered to push the issue, but since I'm his friend rather than yours, I'm more interested in him personally than you."

"Lousy bedside manner, Doc."

"Maybe so, but he's my friend."

"He used to be mine."

"No more."

"So?"

"What happened?"

"What would you believe coming from an acute alcoholic and a D and D?"

For the first time he laughed and it was for real. "I hear you used to weigh in at two-o-five?"

"Thereabouts."

"You're down to one sixty-eight, dehydrated, undernourished. A bum, you know?"

"You don't have to remind me."

"That isn't the point. You missed it."

"No I didn't."

"Oh?"

"Medics don't talk seriously to D and D's. I know what I was. Now *there* is a choice of words if you can figure it out."

He laughed again. "*Was.* I caught it."

"Then talk."

"Okay. You're a loused-up character. There's nothing to you anymore. Physically, I mean. Something happened and you tried to drink yourself down the drain."

"I'm a weak person."

"Guilt complex. Something you couldn't handle. It happens to the hardest nuts I've seen. They can take care of anything until the irrevocable happens and then they blow. Completely."

"Like me?"

"Like you."

"Keep talking."

"You were a lush."

"So are a lot of people. I even know some doctors who—"

"You came out of it pretty fast."

"At ease, Doc."

"I'm not prying," he reminded me.

"Then talk right."

"Sure," he said. "Tell me about Velda."

CHAPTER 3

"It was a long time ago," I said.

And when I had said it I wished I hadn't because it was something I never wanted to speak about. It was over. You can't beat time. Let the dead stay dead. If they can. But was she dead? Maybe if I told it just once I could be sure.

"Tell me," Larry asked.

"Pat ever say anything?"

"Nothing."

So I told him.

"It was a routine job," I said.

"Yes?"

"A Mr. Rudolph Civac contacted me. He was from Chicago, had plenty of rocks and married a widow named Marta Singleton who inherited some kind of machine-manufacturing fortune. Real social in Chicago. Anyway, they came to New York, where she wanted to be social too and introduce her new husband around."

"Typical," Larry said.

"Rich bitches."

"Don't hold it against them," he told me.

"Not me, kid," I said.

"Then go on."

I said, "She was going to sport all the gems her dead husband gave her, which were considerable and a prime target for anybody in the field, and her husband wanted protection."

Larry made a motion with his hand. "A natural thought."

"Sure. So he brought me in. Big party. He wanted to cover the gems."

"Any special reason?"

"Don't be a jerk. They were worth a half a million. Most of my business is made of stuff like that."

"Trivialities."

"Sure, Doc, like unnecessary appendectomies."

"Touché."

"Think nothing of it."

He stopped then. He waited seconds and seconds and watched and waited, then: "A peculiar attitude."

"You're the psychologist, Doc, not me."

"Why?"

"You're thinking that frivolity is peculiar for a D and D."

"So go on with the story."

"Doc," I said, "later I'm going to paste you right in the mouth. You know this?"

"Sure."

"That's *my* word."

"So sure."

"Okay, Doc, ask for it. Anyway, it was a routine job. The target was a dame. At that time a lot of parties were being tapped by a fat squad who saw loot going to waste around the neck of a big broad who never needed it—but this was a classic. At least in our business."

"How?"

"Never mind. At least she called us in. I figured it would be better if we changed our routine. That night I was on a homicide case. Strictly insurance, but the company was paying off and there would be another grand in the kitty. I figured it would be a better move to let Velda cover the affair since she'd be able to stay with the client at all times, even into the ladies' room."

Larry interrupted with a wave of his hand. "Mind a rough question?"

"No."

"Was this angle important or were you thinking, rather, of the profit end—like splitting your team up between two cases."

I knew I had started to shake and pressed my hands against my sides hard. After a few seconds the shakes went away and I could answer him without wanting to tear his head off. "It was an important angle," I said. "I had two heists pulled under my nose when they happened in a powder room."

"And—the woman. How did she feel about it?"

"Velda was a pro. She carried a gun and had her own P.I. ticket."

"And she could handle any situation?"

I nodded. "Any we presumed could happen here."

"You were a little too presumptuous, weren't you?"

The words almost choked me when I said, "You know, Doc, you're asking to get killed."

He shook his head and grinned. "Not you, Mike. You aren't like you used to be. I could take you just as easy as Pat did. Almost anybody could."

I tried to get up, but he laid a hand on my chest and shoved me back and I couldn't fight against him. Every nerve in me started to jangle and my head turned into one big round blob of pain.

Larry said, "You want a drink?"

"No."

"You'd better have one."

"Stuff it."

"All right, suffer. You want to talk some more or shall I take off?"

"I'll finish the story. Then you can work on Pat. When I get out of here I'm going to make a project of rapping you and Pat right in the mouth."

"Good. You have something to look forward to. Now talk."

I waited a minute, thinking back years and putting the pieces in slots so familiar they were worn smooth at the edges. Finally I said, "At eleven o'clock Velda called me at a prearranged number. Everything was going smoothly. There was nothing unusual, the guests were all persons of character and money, there were no suspicious or unknown persons present including the household staff. At that time they were holding dinner awaiting the arrival of Mr. Rudolph Civac. That was my last connection with Velda."

"There was a police report?"

"Sure. At 11:15 Mr. Civac came in and after saying hello to the guests, went upstairs with his wife for a minute to wash up. Velda went along. When they didn't appear an hour and a half later a maid went up to see if anything was wrong and found the place empty.

She didn't call the police, thinking that they had argued or something, then went out the private entrance to the rear of the estate. She served dinner with a lame excuse for the host's absence, sent the guests home and cleaned up with the others.

"The next day Marta Civac was found in the river, shot in the head, her jewels gone and neither her husband nor Velda was ever seen again."

I had to stop there. I didn't want to think on the next part anymore. I was hoping it would be enough for him, but when I looked up he was frowning with thought, digesting it a little at a time like he was diagnosing a disease, and I knew it wasn't finished yet.

He said, "They were abducted for the purpose of stealing those gems?"

"It was the only logical way they could do it. There were too many people. One scream would bring them running. They probably threatened the three of them, told them to move on out quietly where the theft could be done without interruption and allow the thieves to get away."

"Would Velda have gone along with them?"

"If they threatened the client that's the best way. It's better to give up insured gems than get killed. Even a rap on the head can kill if it isn't done right and, generally speaking, jewel thieves aren't killers unless they're pushed."

I felt a shudder go through my shoulders. "No. The body—showed why." I paused and he sat patiently, waiting. "Marta was a pudgy dame with thick fingers. She had crammed on three rings worth a hundred grand combined and they weren't about to come off normally. To get the rings they had severed the fingers."

Softly, he remarked, "I see."

"It was lousy."

"What do you think happened, Mike?"

I was going to hate to tell him, but it had been inside too long. I said, "Velda advised them to go along thinking it would be a heist without any physical complications. Probably when they started to take the rings off the hard way the woman started to scream and was shot. Then her husband and Velda tried to help her and that was it."

"Was what?"

I stared at the ceiling. Before it had been so plain, so simple. Totally believable because it had been so totally terrible. For all those years I had conditioned myself to think only one way because in my job you got to know which answers were right.

Now, suddenly, maybe they weren't right anymore.

Larry asked, "So they killed the man and Velda too and their bodies went out to sea and were never found?"

My tired tone was convincing. I said, "That's how the report read."

"So Pat took it all out on you."

"Looks that way."

"Uh-huh. You let her go on a job you should have handled yourself."

"It didn't seem that way at first."

"Perhaps, but you've been taking it out on yourself too. It just took that one thing to make you a bum."

"Hard words, friend."

"You realize what happened to Pat?"

I glanced at him briefly and nodded. "I found out."

"The hard way."

"So I didn't think he cared."

"You probably never would have known if that didn't happen."

"Kismet, buddy. Like your getting punched in the mouth."

"But there's a subtle difference now, Mikey boy, isn't there?"

"Like how?" I turned my head and watched him. He was the type who could hide his thoughts almost completely, even to a busted-up pro like me, but it didn't quite come off. I knew what he was getting to.

"Something new has been added, Mike."

"Oh?"

"You were a sick man not many hours ago."

"I'm hurting right now."

"You know what I'm talking about. You were a drunk just a little while back."

"So I kicked the habit."

"Why?"

"Seeing old friends helped."

He smiled at me, leaned forward and crossed his arms. "What did that guy tell you?"

"Nothing," I lied.

"I think I know. I think I know the only reason that would turn you from an acute alcoholic to a deadly sober man in a matter of minutes."

I had to be sure. I had to see what he knew. I said, "Tell me, Doc."

Larry stared at me a moment, smiled smugly and sat back, enjoying every second of the scene. When he thought my reaction would be just right he told me, "That guy mentioned the name of the killer."

So he couldn't see my face I turned my head. When I looked at him again he was still smiling, so I looked at the ceiling without answering and let him think what he pleased.

Larry said, "Now you're going out on your own, just like in the old days Pat used to tell me about."

"I haven't decided yet."

"Want some advice?"

"No."

"Nevertheless, you'd better spill it to Pat. He wants the same one."

"Pat can go drop."

"Maybe."

This time there was a peculiar intonation in his voice. I half turned and looked up at him. "Now what's bugging you?"

"Don't you think Pat knows you have something?"

"Like the man said, frankly, buddy, I don't give a damn."

"You won't tell me about it then?"

"You can believe it."

"Pat's going to lay charges on you."

"Good for him. When you clear out I'm going to have a lawyer ready who'll tear Pat apart. So maybe you'd better tell him."

"I will. But for your own sake, reconsider. It might be good for both of you."

Larry stood up and fingered the edge of his hat. A change came over his face and he grinned a little bit.

"Tell you something, Mike. I've heard so much about you it's like we're old friends. Just understand something. I'm really trying to help. Sometimes it's hard to be a doctor and a friend."

I held out my hand and grinned back. "Sure, I know. Forget that business about a paste in the mouth. You'd probably tear my head off."

He laughed and nodded, squeezed my hand and walked out. Before he reached the end of the corridor I was asleep again.

They make them patient in the government agencies. There was no telling how long he had been there. A small man, quiet, plain-looking—no indication of toughness unless you knew how to read it in his eyes. He just sat there as if he had all the time in the world and nothing to do except study me.

At least he had manners. He waited until I was completely awake before he reached for the little leather folder, opened it and said, "Art Rickerby, Federal Bureau of Investigation."

"No," I said sarcastically.

"You've been sleeping quite a while."

"What time is it?"

Without consulting his watch he said, "Five after four."

"It's pretty late."

Rickerby shrugged noncommittally without taking his eyes from my face. "Not for people like us," he told me. "It's never too late, is it?" He was smiling a small smile, but behind his glasses his eyes weren't smiling at all.

"Make your point, friend," I said.

He nodded thoughtfully, never losing his small smile. "Are you—let's say, capable of coherent discussion?"

"You've been reading my chart?"

"That's right. I spoke to your doctor friend too."

"Okay," I said, "forget the AA tag. I've had it, you know?"

"I know."

"Then what do we need the Feds in for? I've been out of action for how many years?"

"Seven."

"Long time, Art, long time, feller. I got no ticket, no rod. I haven't even crossed the state line in all that time. For seven years I cool myself off the way I want to and then all of a sudden I have a Fed on my neck." I squinted at him, trying to find the reason in his face. "Why?"

"Cole, Richie Cole."

"What about him?"

"Suppose you tell me, Mr. Hammer. He asked for you, you came and he spoke to you. I want to know what he said."

I reached way back and found a grin I thought I had forgotten how to make. "Everybody wants to know that, Rickeyback."

"Rickerby."

"So sorry." A laugh got in behind the grin. "Why all the curiosity?"

"Never mind why, just tell me what he said."

"Nuts, buddy."

He didn't react at all. He sat there with all the inbred patience of years of this sort of thing and simply looked at me tolerantly because I was in a bed in the funny ward and it might possibly be an excuse for anything I had to say or do.

Finally he said, "You *can* discuss this, can't you?"

I nodded. "But I won't."

"Why not?"

"I don't like anxious people. I've been kicked around, dragged into places I didn't especially want to go, kicked on my can by a cop who used to be a friend and suddenly faced with the prospects of formal charges because I object to the police version of the hard sell."

"Supposing I can offer you a certain amount of immunity?"

After a few moments I said, "This is beginning to get interesting."

Rickerby reached for words, feeling them out one at a time. "A long while ago you killed a woman, Mike. She shot a friend of yours and you said no matter who it was, no matter where, that killer would die. You shot her."

"Shut up, man," I said.

He was right. It was a very long time ago. But it could have been yesterday. I could see her face, the golden tan of her skin, the incredible whiteness of her hair and eyes that could taste and devour you with one glance. Yet, Charlotte was there still. But dead now.

"Hurt, Mike?"

There was no sense trying to fool him. I nodded abruptly. "I try not to think of it." Then I felt that funny sensation in my back and saw what he was getting at. His face was tight and the little lines around his eyes had deepened so that they stood out in relief, etched into his face.

I said, "You knew Cole?"

It was hard to tell what color his eyes were now. "He was one of us," he said.

I couldn't answer him. He had been waiting patiently a long time to say what he had to say and now it was going to come out. "We were close, Hammer. I trained him. I never had a son and he was as close as I was ever going to get to having one. Maybe now you know exactly why I brought up your past. It's mine who's dead now and it's me who has to find who did it. This should make sense to you. It should also tell you something else. Like you, I'll go to any extremes to catch the one who did it. I've made promises of my own, Mr. Hammer, and I'm sure you know what I'm talking about. Nothing is going to stop me and you are my starting point." He paused, took his glasses off, wiped them, put them back on and said, "You understand this?"

"I get the point."

"Are you sure?" And now his tone had changed. Very subtly, but changed nevertheless. "Because as I said, there are no extremes to which I won't go."

When he stopped I watched him, and the way he sat, the way he looked, the studied casualness became the poised kill-crouch of a cat, all cleverly disguised by clothes and the innocent aspect of rimless bifocals.

Now he was deadly. All too often people have the preconceived notion that a deadly person is a big one, wide in the shoulders with a face full of hard angles and thickset teeth and a jawline that would be a challenge too great for anyone to dare. They'd be wrong. Deadly people aren't all like that. Deadly people are determined people who will stop at nothing at all, and those who are practiced in the arts of the kill are the most deadly of all. Art Rickerby was one of those.

"That's not a very official attitude," I said.

"I'm just trying to impress you," he suggested.

I nodded. "Okay, kid, I'm impressed."

"Then what about Cole?"

"There's another angle."

"Not with me there isn't."

"Easy, Art, I'm not that impressed. I'm a big one too."

"No more, Hammer."

"Then you drop dead, too."

Like a large gray cat, he stood up, still pleasant, still deadly, and said, "I suppose we leave it here?"

"You pushed me, friend."

"It's a device you should be familiar with."

I was getting tired again, but I grinned a little at him. "Cops. Damn cops."

"You were one once."

After a while I said, "I never stopped being one."

"Then cooperate."

This time I turned my head and looked at him. "The facts are all bollixed up. I need one day and one other little thing you might be able to supply."

"Go ahead."

"Get me the hell out of here and get me that day."

"Then what?"

"Maybe I'll tell you something, maybe I won't. Just don't do me any outsized favors because if you don't bust me out of here I'll go out on my own. You can just make it easier. One way or another, I don't care. Take your pick."

Rickerby smiled. "I'll get you out," he said. "It won't be hard. And you can have your day."

"Thanks."

"Then come to me so I won't have to start looking for you."

"Sure, buddy," I said. "Leave your number at the desk."

He said something I didn't quite catch because I was falling asleep again, and when the welcome darkness came in I reached for it eagerly and wrapped it around me like a soft, dark suit of armor.

He let me stay there three days before he moved. He let me have the endless bowls of soup and the bed rest and shot series before the tall thin man showed up with my clothes and a worried nurse whose orders had been countermanded somehow by an authority she neither understood nor could refuse.

When I was dressed he led me downstairs and outside to an unmarked black Ford and I got in without talking. He asked, "Where to?" and I told him anyplace midtown and in fifteen minutes he dropped me in front of the Taft. As I was getting out his hand closed on my arm and very quietly he said, "You have one day. No more."

I nodded. "Tell Rickerby thanks."

He handed me a card then, a simple business thing giving the address and phone of Peerage Brokers located on Broadway only two blocks off. "You tell him," he said, then pulled away from the curb into traffic.

For a few minutes I waited there, looking at the city in a strange sort of light I hadn't seen for too long. It was morning, and quiet because it was Sunday. Overhead, the sun forced its way through a haze that had rain behind it, making the day sulky, like a woman in a pout.

The first cabby in line glanced up once, ran his eyes up and down me, then went back to his paper. Great picture, I thought. I sure must cut a figure. I grinned, even though nothing was funny, and shoved my hands in my jacket pockets. In the right-hand one somebody had stuck five tens, neatly folded, and I said, "Thanks,

Art Rickerby, old buddy," silently, and waved for the cab first in line to come over.

He didn't like it, but he came, asked me where to in a surly voice and when I let him simmer a little bit I told him Lex and Forty-ninth. When he dropped me there I let him change the ten, gave him two bits and waited some more to see if anyone had been behind me.

No one had. If Pat or anyone else had been notified I had been released, he wasn't bothering to stick with me. I gave it another five minutes then turned and walked north.

Old Dewey had held the same corner down for twenty years. During the war, servicemen got their paper free, which was about as much as he could do for the war effort, but there were those of us who never forgot and Old Dewey was a friend we saw often so that we were friends rather than customers. He was in his eighties now and he had to squint through his glasses to make out a face. But the faces of friends, their voices and their few minutes' conversation were things he treasured and looked forward to. Me? Hell, we were old friends from long ago, and back in the big days I never missed a night picking up my pink editions of the *News* and *Mirror* from Old Dewey, even when I had to go out of my way to do it. And there were times when I was in business that he made a good intermediary. He was always there, always dependable, never took a day off, never was on the take for a buck.

But he wasn't there now.

Duck-Duck Jones, who was an occasional swamper in the Clover Bar, sat inside the booth picking his teeth while he read the latest *Cavalier* magazine and it was only after I stood there a half minute that he looked up, scowled, then half recognized me and said, "Oh, hello, Mike."

I said, "Hello, Duck-Duck. What are you doing here?"

He made a big shrug under his sweater and pulled his eyebrows up. "I help Old Dewey out alla time. Like when he eats. You know?"

"Where's he now?"

Once again, he went into an eloquent shrug. "So he don't show up yesterday. I take the key and open up for him. Today the same thing."

"Since when does Old Dewey miss a day?"

"Look, Mike, the guy's gettin' old. I take over maybe one day every week when he gets checked. Doc says he got something inside him, like. All this year he's been hurtin'."

"You keep the key?"

"Sure. We been friends a long time. He pays good. Better'n swabbing out the bar every night. This ain't so bad. Plenty of books with pictures. Even got a battery radio."

"He ever miss two days running?"

Duck-Duck made a face, thought a second and shook his head. "Like this is the first time. You know Old Dewey. He don't wanna miss nothin'. Nothin' at all."

"You check his flop?"

"Nah. You think I should? Like he could be sick or somethin'?"

"I'll do it myself."

"Sure, Mike. He lives right off Second by the diner, third place down in the basement. You got to—"

I nodded curtly. "I've been there."

"Look, Mike, if he don't feel good and wants me to stay on a bit I'll do it. I won't clip nothin'. You can tell him that."

"Okay, Duck."

I started to walk away and his voice caught me. "Hey, Mike."

"What?"

He was grinning through broken teeth, but his eyes were frankly puzzled. "You look funny, man. Like different from when I seen you last down at the Chink's. You off the hop?"

I grinned back at him. "Like for good," I said.

"Man, here we go again," he laughed.

"Like for sure," I told him.

Old Dewey owned the building. It wasn't much, but that and the newsstand were his insurance against the terrible thought of public support, a sure bulwark against the despised welfare plans of city and state. A second-rate beauty shop was on the ground floor and the top two were occupied by families who had businesses in the neighborhood. Old Dewey lived in humble quarters in the basement, needing only a single room in which to cook and sleep.

I tried his door, but the lock was secure. The only windows were those facing the street, the protective iron bars imbedded in the brick-work since the building had been erected. I knocked again, louder this time, and called out, but nobody answered.

Then again I had that funny feeling I had learned not to ignore, but it had been so long since I had felt it that it was almost new and once more I realized just how long it had been since I was in a dark place with a kill on my hands.

Back then it had been different. I had the gun. I was big.

Now was—how many years later? There was no gun. I wasn't big anymore.

I was what was left over from being a damn drunken bum, and if there were anything left at all it was sheer reflex and nothing else.

So I called on the reflex and opened the door with the card the tall thin man gave me because it was an old lock with a wide gap in the doorframe. I shoved it back until it hit the door, standing there where anybody inside could target me easily, but knowing that it was safe because I had been close to death too many times not to recognize the immediate sound of silence it makes.

He was on the floor face down, arms outstretched, legs spread, his head turned to one side so that he stared at one wall with the universal expression of the dead. He lay there in a pool of soup made from his own blood that had gouted forth from the great slash in his throat. The blood had long ago congealed and seeped into the cracks in the flooring, the coloring changed from scarlet to brown and already starting to smell.

Somebody had already searched the room. It hadn't taken long, but the job had been thorough. The signs of the expert were there, the one who had time and experience, who knew every possible hiding place and who had overlooked none. The search had gone around the room and come back to the body on the floor. The seams of the coat were carefully torn open, the pockets turned inside out, the shoes ripped apart.

But the door had been locked and this was not the sign of some-one who had found what he wanted. Instead, it was the sign of he who hadn't and wanted time to think on it—or wait it out—or pos-sibly study who else was looking for the same thing.

I said, "Don't worry, Dewey, I'll find him," and my voice was strangely hushed like it came from years ago. I wiped off the light switch, the knob, then closed the door and left it like I found it and felt my way to the back through the labyrinth of alleys that is New York over on that side and pretty soon I came out on the street again and it had started to rain.

His name was Nat Drutman. He owned the Hackard Building where I used to have my office and now, seven years later, he was just the same—only a little grayer and a little wiser around the eyes and when he glanced up at me from his desk it was as if he had seen me only yesterday.

"Hello, Mike."

"Nat."

"Good to see you."

"Thanks," I said.

This time his eyes stayed on me and he smiled, a gentle smile that had hope in it. "It has been a long time."

"Much too long."

"I know." He watched me expectantly.

I said, "You sell the junk from my office?"

"No."

"Store it?"

He shook his head, just once. "No."

"No games, kid," I said.

He made the Lower East Side gesture with his shoulders and let his smile stay pat. "It's still there, Mike."

"Not after seven years, kid," I told him.

"That's so long?"

"For somebody who wants their loot it is."

"So who needs loot?"

"Nat—"

"Yes, Mike?"

His smile was hard to understand.

"No games."

"You still got a key?" he asked.

"No. I left to stay. No key. No nothing anymore."

He held out his hand, offering me a shiny piece of brass. I took it automatically and looked at the number stamped into it, a fat 808. "I had it made special," he said.

As best I could, I tried to be nasty. "Come off it, Nat."

He wouldn't accept the act. "Don't thank me. I knew you'd be back."

I said, "Shit."

There was a hurt look on his face. It barely touched his eyes and the corners of his mouth, but I knew I had hurt him.

"Seven years, Nat. That's a lot of rent."

He wouldn't argue. I got that shrug again and the funny look that went with it. "So for you I dropped the rent to a dollar a year while you were gone."

I looked at the key, feeling my shoulders tighten. "Nat—"

"Please—don't talk. Just take. Remember when you gave? Remember Bernie and those men? Remember—"

"Okay, Nat."

The sudden tension left his face and he smiled again. I said, "Thanks, kid. You'll never know."

A small laugh left his lips and he said, "Oh I'll know, all right. That'll be seven dollars. Seven years, seven dollars."

I took out another ten and laid it on his desk. With complete seriousness he gave me back three ones, a receipt, then said, "You got a phone too, Mike. Same number. No 'thank yous,' Mike. Augie Strickland came in with the six hundred he owed you and left it with me so I paid the phone bill from it. You still got maybe a couple bucks coming back if we figure close."

"Save it for service charges," I said.

"Good to see you, Mike."

"Good to see you, Nat."

"You look pretty bad. Is everything going to be like before, Mike?"

"It can never be like before. Let's hope it's better."

"Sure, Mike."

"And thanks anyway, kid."

"My pleasure, Mike."

I looked at the key, folded it in my fist and started out. When I reached the door Nat said, "Mike—"

I turned around.

"Velda . . .?"

He watched my eyes closely.

"That's why you're back?"

"Why?"

"I hear many stories, Mike. Twice I even saw you. Things I know that nobody else knows. I know why you left. I know why you came back. I even waited because I knew someday you'd come. So you're back. You don't look like you did except for your eyes. They never change. Now you're all beat up and skinny and far behind. Except for your eyes, and that's the worst part."

"Is it?"

He nodded. "For somebody," he said.

I put the key in the lock and turned the knob. It was like coming back to the place where you had been born, remembering, yet without a full recollection of all the details. It was a drawing, wanting power that made me swing the door open because I wanted to see how it used to be and how it might have been.

Her desk was there in the anteroom, the typewriter still covered, letters from years ago stacked in a neat pile waiting to be answered, the last note she had left for me still there beside the phone some itinerant spider had draped in a nightgown of cobwebs.

The wastebasket was where I had kicked it, dented almost double from my foot; the two captain's chairs and antique bench we used for clients were still overturned against the wall where I had thrown them. The door to my office swung open, tendrils of webbing seeming to tie it to the frame. Behind it I could see my desk and chair outlined in the gray shaft of light that was all that was left of the day.

I walked in, waving the cobwebs apart, and sat down in the chair. There was dust, and silence, and I was back to seven years ago, all of a sudden. Outside the window was another New York— not the one I had left, because the old one had been torn down and rebuilt since I had looked out that window last. But below on the street the sounds hadn't changed a bit, nor had the people. Death and destruction were still there, the grand overseers of life toward the great abyss, some slowly, some quickly, but always along the same road.

For a few minutes I just sat there swinging in the chair, recalling the feel and the sound of it. I made a casual inspection of the desk drawers, not remembering what was there, yet enjoying a sense of familiarity with old things. It was an old desk, almost antique, a relic from some solid, conservative corporation that supplied its executives with the best.

When you pulled the top drawer all the way out there was a niche built into the massive framework, and when I felt in the shallow recess the other relic was still there.

Calibre .45, Colt Automatic, U.S. Army model, vintage of 1914. Inside the plastic wrapper it was still oiled, and when I checked the action it was like a thing alive, a deadly thing that had but a single fundamental purpose.

I put it back where it was beside the box of shells, inserted the drawer and slid it shut. The day of the guns was back there seven years ago. Not now.

Now I was one of the nothing people. One mistake and Pat had me, and where I was going, one mistake and *they* would have me.

Pat. The slob really took off after me. I wondered if Larry had been right when he said Pat had been in love with Velda too.

I nodded absently, because he had changed. And there was more to it, besides. In seven years Pat should have moved up the ladder. By now he should have been an Inspector. Maybe whatever it was he had crawling around in his guts got out of hand and he never made the big try for promotion, or, if he did, he loused up.

The hell with him, I thought. Now he was going wide open to nail a killer and a big one. Whoever killed Richie Cole had killed Senator Knapp in all probability, and in all probability, too, had killed Old Dewey. Well, I was one up on Pat. He'd have another kill in his lap, all right, but only I could connect Dewey and the others.

Which put me in the middle all around.

So okay, Hammer, I said. *You've been a patsy before. See what you'll do with this one and do it right. Someplace she's alive. Alive! But for how long? And where? There are killers loose and she must be on the list.*

Absently, I reached for the phone, grinned when I heard the dial tone, then fingered the card the thin man gave me from my pocket and called Peerage Brokers.

He was there waiting and when I asked, "Rickerby?" a switch clicked.

Art answered, "You still have a little more time."

"I don't need time. I need now. I think we should talk."

"Where are you?"

"My own office through courtesy of a friend. The Hackard Building."

"Stay there. I'll be up in ten minutes."

"Sure. Bring me a sandwich."

"A drink too?"

"None of that. Maybe a couple of Blue Ribbons, but nothing else."

Without answering, he hung up. I glanced at my wrist, but there was no watch there anymore. Somehow, I vaguely remembered hocking it somewhere and called myself a nut because it was a good Rolex and I probably drank up the loot in half a day. Or got rolled for it.

Damn!

From the window I could see the clock on the Paramount Building and it was twenty past six. The street was slick from the drizzle that had finally started to fall and the crosstown traffic was like a giant worm trying to eat into the belly of the city. I opened the window and got supper smells in ten languages from the restaurants below and for the first time in a long time it smelled good. Then I switched on the desk lamp and sat back again.

Rickerby came in, put a wrapped sandwich and two cans of Blue Ribbon in front of me and sat down with a weary smile. It was a very peculiar smile, not of friendliness, but of anticipation. It was one you didn't smile back at, but rather waited out.

And I made him wait until I had finished the sandwich and a can of beer, then I said, "Thanks for everything."

Once again, he smiled. "Was it worth it?"

His eyes had that flat calm that was nearly impenetrable. I said, "Possibly. I don't know. Not yet."

"Suppose we discuss it."

I smiled some too. The way his face changed I wondered what I looked like. "It's all right with me, Rickety."

"Rickerby."

"Sorry," I said. "But let's do it question-and-answer style. Only I want to go first."

"You're not exactly in a position to dictate terms."

"I think I am. I've been put upon. You know?"

He shrugged, and looked at me again, still patient. "It really doesn't matter. Ask me what you want to."

"Are you officially on this case?"

Rickerby didn't take too long putting it in its proper category. It would be easy enough to plot out if you knew how, so he simply made a vague motion with his shoulders. "No. Richie's death is at this moment a local police matter."

"Do they know who he was?"

"By now, I assume so."

"And your department won't press the matter?"

He smiled, nothing more.

I said, "Suppose I put it this way—if his death resulted in the line of duty he was pursuing—because of the case he was on, then your department would be interested."

Rickerby looked at me, his silence acknowledging my statement.

"However," I continued, "if he was the victim of circumstances that could hit anybody, it would remain a local police matter and his other identity would remain concealed from everyone possible. True?"

"You seem familiar enough with the machinations of our department, so draw your own conclusions," Rickerby told me.

"I will. I'd say that presently it's up in the air. You're on detached duty because of a personal interest in this thing. You couldn't be ordered off it, otherwise you'd resign and pursue it yourself."

"You know, Mike, for someone who was an alcoholic such a short time ago, your mind is awfully lucid." He took his glasses off and wiped them carefully before putting them back on. "I'm beginning to be very interested in this aspect of your personality."

"Let me clue you, buddy. It was shock. I was brought back to my own house fast, and suddenly meeting death in a sober condition really rocked me."

"I'm not so sure of that," he said. "Nevertheless, get on with your questions."

"What was Richie Cole's job?"

After a moment's pause he said, "Don't be silly. I certainly don't know. If I did I wouldn't reveal it."

"Okay, what was his cover?"

All he did was shake his head and smile.

I said, "You told me you'd do anything to get the one who killed him."

This time a full minute passed before he glanced down at his hands, then back to me again. In that time he had done some rapid mental calculations. "I—don't see how it could matter now," he said. When he paused a sadness creased his mouth momentarily, then he went on. "Richie worked as a seaman."

"Union man?"

"That's right. He held a full card."

CHAPTER 5

The elevator operator in the Trib Building looked at me kind of funny like when I told him I wanted to find Hy. But maybe Hy had all kinds of hooples looking for him at odd hours. At one time the guy would never have asked questions, but now was now. The old Mike wasn't quite there anymore.

In gold, the letters said, HY GARDNER. I knocked, opened the door and there he was, staring until recognition came, and with a subtle restraint he said, "Mike—" It was almost a question.

"A long time, Hy."

But always the nice guy, this one. Never picking, never choosing. He said, "Been too long. I've been wondering."

"So have a lot of people."

"But not for the same reasons."

We shook hands, a couple of old friends saying hello from a long while back; we had both been big, but while he had gone ahead and I had faded, we were still friends, and good ones.

He tried to cover the grand hiatus of so many years with a cigar stuck in the middle of a smile and made it all the way, without words telling me that nothing had really changed at all since the first time we had played bullets in a bar and he had made a column out of it the next day.

Hell, you've read his stuff. You know us.

I sat down, waved the crazy blond bouffant he used as a secretary now out of the room and leaned back enjoying myself. After seven years it was a long time to enjoy anything. Friends.

I still had them.

"You look lousy," Hy said.

"So I've been told."

"True what I hear about you and Pat?"

"Word gets around fast."

"You know this business, Mike."

"Sure, so don't bother being kind."

"You're a nut," he laughed.

"Aren't we all. One kind or another."

"Sure, but you're on top. You know the word that's out right now?"

"I can imagine."

"The hell you can. You don't even know. What comes in this office you couldn't imagine. When they picked you up I heard about it. When you were in Pat's house I knew where you were. If you really want to know, whenever you were in the drunk tank, unidentified, I knew about it."

"Cripes, why didn't you get me out?"

"Mike," he laughed around the stogie, "I got problems of my own. When you can't solve yours, who can solve anything? Besides, I thought it would be a good experience for you."

"Thanks."

"No bother." He shifted the cigar from one side to the other. "But I was worried."

"Well, that's nice anyway," I said.

"Now it's worse."

Hy took the cigar away, studied me intently, snuffed the smoke out in a tray and pulled his eyes up to mine.

"Mike—"

"Say it, Hy."

He was honest. He pulled no punches. It was like time had never been at all and we were squaring away for the first time. "You're poison, Mike. The word's out."

"To you?"

"No." He shook his head. "They don't touch the Fourth Estate, you know that. They tried it with Joe Ungermach and Victor Reisel and look what happened to them. So don't worry about me."

"You worried about me?"

Hy grunted, lit another cigar and grinned at me. He had his

glasses up on his head and you'd never think he could be anything but an innocuous slob, but then you'd be wrong. When he had it lit, he said, "I gave up worrying about you a long time ago. Now what did you want from me? It has to be big after seven years."

"Senator Knapp," I said.

Sure, he was thinking, *after seven years who the hell would think you'd come back with a little one? Mike Hammer chasing ambulances? Mike Hammer suddenly a reformer or coming up with a civic problem? Hell, anybody would have guessed. The Mike doesn't come back without a big one going. This a kill, Mike? What's the scoop? Story there, isn't there? You have a killer lined up just like in the old days and don't lie to me because I've seen those tiger eyes before. If they were blue or brown like anybody else's maybe I couldn't tell, but you got tiger eyes, friend, and they glint. So tell me. Tell me hard. Tell me now.*

He didn't have to say it. Every word was there in his face, like when he had read it out to me before. I didn't have to hear it now. Just looking at him was enough.

I said, "Senator Knapp. He died when I was—away."

Quietly, Hy reminded me, "He didn't die. He was killed."

"Okay. The libraries were closed and besides, I forgot my card."

"He's been dead three years."

"More."

"First why?"

"Because."

"You come on strong, man."

"You know another way?"

"Not for you."

"So how about the Senator?"

"Are we square?" he asked me. "It can be my story?"

"All yours, Hy. I don't make a buck telling columns."

"Got a few minutes?"

"All right," I said.

He didn't even have to consult the files. All he had to do was light that damn cigar again and sit back in his chair, then he sucked his mouth full of smoke and said, "Leo Knapp was another McCarthy. He was a Commie-hunter but he had more prestige and more power. He was on the right committee and, to top it off, he was this country's missile man.

"That's what they called him, the *Missile Man*. Mr. America. He pulled hard against the crap we put up with like the Cape Canaveral strikes when the entire program was held up by stupid jerks who went all that way for unionism and—hell, read *True* or the factual accounts and see what happened. The Reds are running us blind. Anyway, Knapp was the missile pusher."

"Big," I said.

Hy nodded. "Then some louse shoots him. A simple burglary and he gets killed in the process."

"You sure?"

Hy looked at me, the cigar hard in his teeth. "You know me, Mike, I'm a reporter. I'm a Commie-hater. You think I didn't take this one right into the ground?"

"I can imagine what you did."

"Now fill me in."

"Can you keep your mouth shut?"

He took the cigar away and frowned, like I had hurt him. "Mike—"

"Look," I said, "I know, I know. But I may feed you a hot one and I have to be sure. Until it's ended, it can't come out. There's something here too big to mess with and I won't even take a little chance on it."

"So tell me. I know what you're angling for. Your old contacts are gone or poisoned and you want me to shill for you."

"Natch."

"So I'll shill. Hell, we've done it before. It won't be like it's a new experience."

"And keep Marilyn out of it. To her you're a new husband and a father and she doesn't want you going down bullet alley anymore."

"Aw, shut up and tell me what's on your mind."

I did.

I sat back and told it all out and let somebody else help carry the big lid. I gave it to him in detail from seven years ago and left out nothing. I watched his face go through all the changes, watched him let the cigar burn itself out against the lip of the ashtray, watched him come alive with the crazy possibilities that were inherent in this one impossibility and when I finished I watched him sit back, light another cigar and regain his usual composure.

When he had it back again he said, "What do you want from me?"

"I don't know. It could be anything."

Like always, Hy nodded. "Okay, Mike. When it's ready to blow let me light the fuse. Hell, maybe we can do an interview with the about-to-be-deceased on the TV show ahead of time."

"No jokes, kid."

"Ah, cheer up. Things could be worse."

"I know," I quoted, " 'So I cheered up and sure enough things got worse.' "

Hy grinned and knocked the ash off the stogie. "Right now—anything you need?"

"Senator Knapp—"

"Right now his widow is at her summer place upstate in Phoenicia. That's where the Senator was shot."

"You'd think she'd move out."

Hy shrugged gently. "That's foolishness, in a way. It was the Senator's favorite home and she keeps it up. The rest of the year she stays at the residence in Washington. In fact, Laura is still one of the capital's favorite hostesses. Quite a doll."

"Oh?"

He nodded sagely, the cigar at an authoritative tilt. "The Senator was all man and what he picked was all woman. They were a great combination. It'll be a long time before you see one like that again."

"Tough."

"That's the way it goes. Look, if you want the details, I'll have a package run out from the morgue."

"I'd appreciate that."

Two minutes after he made his call a boy came through with a thick manila envelope and laid it on the desk. Hy hefted it, handed it over and said: "This'll give you all the background on the murder. It made quite a story."

"Later there will be more."

"Sure," he agreed, "I know how you work."

I got up and put on my hat. "Thanks."

"No trouble, Mike." He leaned back in his chair and pulled his glasses down. "Be careful, Mike. You look lousy."

"Don't worry."

"Just the same, don't stick your neck out. Things can change in a few years. You're not like you were. A lot of people would like to catch up with you right now."

I grinned back at him. "I think most already have."

You drive up the New York Thruway, get off at Kingston and take the mountain route through some of the most beautiful country in the world. At Phoenicia you turn off to the north for five or six miles until you come to The Willows and there is the chalet nestling in the upcurve of the mountain, tended by blue spruces forty feet high and nursed by a living stream that dances its way in front of it.

It was huge and white and very senatorial, yet there was a lived-in look that took away any pretentiousness. It was a money house and it should have been because the Senator had been a money man. He had made it himself and had spent it the way he liked and this had been a pet project.

I went up through the gentle curve of the drive and shut off the motor in front of the house. When I touched the bell I could hear it chime inside, and after a minute of standing there, I touched it again. Still no one answered.

Just to be sure, I came down off the open porch, skirted the house on a flagstone walk that led to the rear and followed the S turns through the shrubbery arrangement that effectively blocked off all view of the back until you were almost on top of it.

There was a pool on one side and a tennis court on the other. Nestling between them was a green-roofed cottage with outside shower stalls that was obviously a dressing house.

At first I thought it was deserted here too, then very faintly I heard the distance-muffled sound of music. A hedgerow screened the southeast corner of the pool and in the corner of it the multi-color top of a table umbrella showed through the interlocking branches.

I stood there a few seconds, just looking down at her. Her hands were cradled behind her head, her eyes were closed and she was stretched out to the sun in taut repose. The top of the two-piece bathing suit was filled to overflowing with a matured ripeness that was breathtaking; the bottom half turned down well below her dimpled navel in a bikini effect, exposing the startling whiteness of untanned flesh against that which had been sun-kissed. Her breathing shallowed her stomach, then swelled it gently, and she turned slightly, stretching, pointing her toes so that a sinuous ripple of muscles played along her thighs.

I said, "Hello."

Her eyes came open, focused sleepily and she smiled at me. "Oh." Her smile broadened and it was like throwing a handful of beauty in her face. "Oh, hello."

Without being asked I handed her the terry-cloth robe that was thrown across the tabletop. She took it, smiled again and threw it around her shoulders. "Thank you."

"Isn't it a little cold for that sort of thing?"

"Not in the sun." She waved to the deck chair beside her. "Please?" When I sat down she rearranged her lounge into a chair and settled back in it. "Now, Mr.—"

"Hammer. Michael Hammer." I tried on a smile for her too. "And you are Laura Knapp?"

"Yes. Do I know you from somewhere, Mr. Hammer?"

"We've never met."

"But there's something familiar about you."

"I used to get in the papers a lot."

"Oh?" It was a full-sized question.

"I was a private investigator at one time."

She frowned, studying me, her teeth white against the lushness of her lip as she nibbled at it. "There was an affair with a Washington agency at one time—"

I nodded.

"I remember it well. My husband was on a committee that was affected by it." She paused. "So you're Mike Hammer." Her frown deepened.

"You expected something more?"

Her smile was mischievous. "I don't quite know. Perhaps."

"I've been sick," I said, grinning.

"Yes," she told me, "I can believe that. Now, the question is, what are you doing here? Is this part of your work?"

There was no sense lying to her. I said, "No, but there's a possibility you can help me."

"How?"

"Do you mind going over the details of your husband's murder, or is it too touchy a subject?"

This time her smile took on a wry note. "You're very blunt, Mr. Hammer. However, it's something in the past and I'm not afraid to discuss it. You could have examined the records of the incident if you wanted to. Wouldn't that have been easier?"

I let my eyes travel over her and let out a laugh. "I'm glad I came now."

Laura Knapp laughed back. "Well, thank you."

"But in case you're wondering, I did go over the clips on the case."

"And that wasn't enough?"

I shrugged. "I don't know. I'd rather hear it firsthand."

"May I ask why?"

"Sure," I said. "Something has come up that might tie in your husband's killer with another murder."

Laura shook her head slowly. "I don't understand—"

"It's a wild supposition, that's all, a probability I'm trying to chase down. Another man was killed with the same gun that shot your husband. Details that seemed unimportant then might have some bearing now."

"I see." She came away from the chair, leaning toward me with her hands hugging her knees, a new light of interest in her eyes. "But why aren't the police here instead of you?"

"They will be. Right now it's a matter of jurisdiction. Very shortly you'll be seeing a New York City officer, probably accompanied by the locals, who will go over the same ground. I don't have any legal paperwork to go through so I got here first."

Once again she started a slow smile and let it play around her mouth a moment before she spoke. "And if I don't talk—will you belt me one?"

"Hell," I said, "I never hit dames."

Her eyebrows went up in mock surprise.

"I always kick 'em."

The laugh she let out was pleasant and throaty and it was easy to see why she was still queen of the crazy social whirl at the capital. Age never seemed to have touched her, though she was in the loveliest early forties. Her hair shimmered with easy blond highlights, a perfect shade to go with the velvety sheen of her skin.

"I'll talk," she laughed, "but do I get a reward if I do?"

"Sure, I won't kick you."

"Sounds enticing. What do you want to know?"

"Tell me what happened."

She reflected a moment. It was evident that the details were there, stark as ever in her mind, though the thought didn't bring the pain back any longer. She finally said, "It was a little after two in the morning. I heard Leo get up but didn't pay any attention to it since he often went down for nighttime snacks. The next thing I heard was his voice shouting at someone, then a single shot. I got up, ran downstairs and there he was on the floor, dying."

"Did he say anything?"

"No—he called out my name twice, then he died." She looked down at her feet, then glanced up. "I called the police. Not immediately. I was—stunned."

"It happens."

She chewed at her lip again. "The police were inclined to—well, they were annoyed. They figured the person had time to get away." Her eyes clouded, then drifted back in time. "But it couldn't have been more than a few minutes. No more. In fact, there could have been no time at all before I called. It's just that I don't remember those first few moments."

"Forget it anyway," I said. "That part doesn't count anymore."

Laura paused, then nodded in agreement. "You're right, of course. Well, then the police came, but there was nothing they could do. Whoever it was had gone through the French windows in the den, then had run across the yard, gone through the gate and driven away. There were no tire tracks and the footprints he left were of no consequence."

"What about the house?"

She wrinkled her forehead as she looked over at me. "The safe was open and empty. The police believe Leo either surprised the burglar after he opened the safe or the burglar made him open the safe and when Leo went for him, killed him. There were no marks on the safe at all. It had been opened by using the combination."

"How many people knew the combination?"

"Just Leo, as far as I know."

I said, "The papers stated that nothing of importance was in the safe."

"That's right. There couldn't have been over a few hundred dollars in cash, a couple of account books, Leo's insurance policies, some legal papers and some jewelry of mine. The books and legal papers were on the floor intact so—"

"What jewelry?" I interrupted.

"It was junk."

"The papers quoted you as saying about a thousand dollars' worth."

She didn't hesitate and there was no evasion in her manner. "That's right, a thousand dollars' worth of paste. They were replicas of the genuine pieces I keep in a vault. That value is almost a hundred thousand dollars."

"A false premise is as good a reason for robbery as any."

Her eyes said she didn't agree with me. "Nobody knew I kept that paste jewelry in there."

"Two people did."

"Oh?"

I said, "Your husband and his killer."

The implication of it finally came to her. "He wouldn't have mentioned it to anyone. No, you're wrong there. It wasn't that important to him at all."

"Then why put it in the safe?"

"It's a natural place for it. Besides, as you mentioned, it could be a strong come-on to one who didn't know any better."

"Why didn't you have the combination?"

"I didn't need it. It was the only safe in the house, in Leo's private study—and, concerning his affairs, I stayed out completely."

"Servants?"

"At that time we had two. Both were very old and both have since died. I don't think they ever suspected that there were two sets of jewels anyway."

"Were they trustworthy?"

"They had been with Leo all his life. Yes, they were trustworthy."

I leaned back in the chair, reaching hard for any possibility now. "Could anything else have been in that safe? Something you didn't know about?"

"Certainty."

I edged forward now, waiting.

"Leo *could* have kept anything there, but I doubt that he did. I believe you're thinking of what could be termed state secrets?"

"It's happened before. The Senator was a man pretty high in the machinery of government."

"And a smart one," she countered. "His papers that had governmental importance were all intact in his safe-deposit box and were recovered immediately after his death by the FBI, according to a memo he left with his office." She waited a moment then, watching me try to fasten on some obscure piece of information. Then she asked, "May I know what you're trying to get at?"

This time there was no answer. Very simply the whole thing broke down to a not unusual coincidence. One gun had been used for two kills. It happens often enough. These kills had been years apart, and from all the facts, totally unrelated.

I said, "It was a try, that's all. Nothing seems to match."

Quietly, she stated, "I'm sorry."

"Couldn't be helped." I stood up, not quite wanting to terminate our discussion. "It might have been the jewels, but a real pro would have made sure of what he was going after, and this isn't exactly the kind of place an amateur would hit."

Laura held out her hand and I took it, pulling her to her feet. It was like an unwinding, like a large fireside cat coming erect, yet so naturally that you were never aware of any artifice, but only the similarity. "Are you sure there's nothing further . . .?"

"Maybe one thing," I said. "Can I see the den?"

She nodded, reaching out to touch my arm. "Whatever you want."

While she changed she left me alone in the room. It was a man's place, where only a man could be comfortable, a place designed and used by a man used to living. The desk was an oversized piece of deep-colored wood, almost antique in style, offset by dark leather chairs and original oil seascapes. The walnut paneling was hand carved, years old and well polished, matching the worn Oriental rug that must have come over on a Yankee clipper ship.

The wall safe was a small circular affair that nestled behind a two-by-three-foot picture, the single modern touch in the room. Laura had opened the desk drawer, extracted a card containing the combination and handed it to me. Alone, I dialed the seven numbers and swung the safe out. It was empty.

That I had expected. What I hadn't expected was the safe itself. It was a Grissom 914A and was not the type you installed to keep junk jewelry or inconsequential papers in. This safe was more than a fireproof receptacle and simple safeguard for trivia. This job had been designed to be burglar-proof and had a built-in safety factor on the third number that would have been hooked into the local police PBX at the very least. I closed it, dialed it once again using the secondary number, opened it and waited.

Before Laura came down the cops were there, two excited young fellows in a battered Ford who came to the door with Police Specials out and ready, holding them at my gut when I let them in and looking able to use them.

The taller of the pair went around me while the other looked at me carefully and said, "Who're you?"

"I'm the one who tuned you in."

"Don't get smart."

"I was testing the wall safe out."

His grin had a wicked edge to it. "You don't test it like that, buddy."

"Sorry. I should have called first."

He went to answer, but his partner called in from the front room and he waved me ahead with the nose of the .38. Laura and the cop were there, both looking puzzled.

Laura had changed into a belted black dress that accented the sweeping curves of her body and when she stepped across the room toward me it was with the lithe grace of an athlete. "Mike—do you know what—"

"Your safe had an alarm number built into it. I checked it to see if it worked. Apparently it did."

"That right, Mrs. Knapp?" the tall cop asked.

"Well, yes. I let Mr. Hammer inspect the safe. I didn't realize it had an alarm on it."

"It's the only house around here that has that system, Mrs. Knapp. It's more or less on a commercial setup."

Beside me the cop holstered his gun with a shrug. "That's that," he said. "It was a good try."

The other one nodded, adjusted his cap and looked across at me. "We'd appreciate your calling first if it happens again."

"Sure thing. Mind a question?"

"Nope."

"Were you on the force when the Senator was killed?"

"We both were."

"Did the alarm go off then?"

The cop gave me a long, deliberate look, his face wary, then, "No, it didn't."

"Then if the killer opened the safe he knew the right combination."

"Or else," the cop reminded me, "he forced the Senator to open it, and knowing there was nothing of real value in there, and not willing to jeopardize his own or his wife's life by sudden interference, the Senator didn't use the alarm number."

"But he was killed anyway," I reminded him.

"If you had known the Senator you could see why."

"Okay, why?" I asked him.

Softly, the cop said: "If he was under a gun he'd stay there, but given one chance to jump the guy and he'd have jumped. Apparently he thought he saw the chance and went for the guy after the safe was open and just wasn't fast enough."

"Or else surprised the guy when the safe was already opened."

"That's the way it still reads." He smiled indulgently. "We had those angles figured out too, you know. Now do you mind telling me where you fit in the picture?"

"Obscurely. A friend of mine was killed by a bullet from the same gun."

The two cops exchanged glances. The one beside me said, "We didn't hear about that part yet."

"Then you will shortly. You'll be speaking to a Captain Chambers from New York sometime soon."

"That doesn't explain you."

I shrugged. "The guy was a friend."

"Do you represent a legal investigation agency?"

"No longer," I told him. "There was a time when I did."

"Then maybe you ought to leave the investigation up to authorized personnel."

His meaning was obvious. If I hadn't been cleared by Laura Knapp and tentatively accepted as her friend, we'd be doing our talking in the local precinct house. It was a large Keep Off sign he was pointing out and he wasn't kidding about it. I made a motion with my hand to let him know I got the message, watched them tip their caps to Laura and walk out.

When they had pulled away Laura said, "Now what was *that* all about?" She stood balanced on one foot, her hands on her hips in an easy, yet provocative manner, frowning slightly as she tried to sift through the situation.

I said, "Didn't you know there was an alarm system built into that box?"

She thought for a moment, then threw a glance toward the wall. "Yes, now that you mention it, but that safe hasn't been opened since—then, and I simply remember the police discussing an alarm system. I didn't know how it worked at all."

"Did your husband always keep that combination card in his desk?"

"No, the lawyer found it in his effects. I kept it in the desk just in case I ever wanted to use the safe again. However, that never happened." She paused, took a step toward me and laid a hand on my arm. "Is there some significance to all this?"

I shook my head. "I don't know. It was a thought and not a very new one. Like I told you, this was only a wild supposition at best. All I can say is that it might have established an M.O."

"What?"

"A technique of operation," I explained. "Your husband's killer really could have gone after those jewels. The other man he killed was operating—well, was a small-time jewel smuggler. There's a common point here."

For a moment I was far away in thought. I was back in the hospital with a dying man, remembering the reason why I wanted to find that link so badly. I could feel claws pulling at my insides and a fierce tension ready to burst apart like an overwound spring.

It was the steady insistence of her voice that dragged me back to the present, her "Mike—Mike—please, Mike."

When I looked down I saw my fingers biting into her forearm and the quiet pain in her eyes. I let her go and sucked air deep into my lungs. "Sorry," I said.

She rubbed her arm and smiled gently. "That's all right. You left me there for a minute, didn't you?"

I nodded.

"Can I help?"

"No. I don't think there's anything more here for me."

Once again, her hand touched me. "I don't like finalities like that, Mike."

It was my turn to grin my thanks. "I'm not all that sick. But I appreciate the thought."

"You're lonely, Mike. That's a sickness."

"Is it?"

"I've had it so long I can recognize it in others."

"You loved him very much, didn't you?"

Her eyes changed momentarily, seeming to shine a little brighter, then she replied, "As much as you loved her, Mike, whoever she was." Her fingers tightened slightly. "It's a big hurt. I eased mine by all the social activity I could crowd in a day."

"I used a bottle. It was a hell of a seven years."

"And now it's over. I can still see the signs, but I can tell it's over."

"It's over. A few days ago I was a drunken bum. I'm still a bum but at least I'm sober." I reached for my hat, feeling her hand fall away from my arm. She walked me to the door and held it open. When I stuck out my hand she took it, her fingers firm and cool inside mine. "Thanks for letting me take up your time, Mrs. Knapp."

"Please—make it Laura."

"Sure."

"And can you return the favor?"

"My pleasure."

"I told you I didn't like finalities. Will you come back one day?"

"I'm nothing to want back, Laura."

"Maybe not to some. You're big. You have a strange face. You're very hard to define. Still, I hope you'll come back, if only to tell me how you're making out."

I pulled her toward me gently. She didn't resist. Her head tilted up, she watched me, she kissed me as I kissed her, easily and warm in a manner that said hello rather than good-bye, and that one touch awakened things I thought had died long ago.

She stood there watching me as I drove away. She was still there when I turned out of sight at the roadway.

CHAPTER 6

The quiet voice at Peerage Brokers told me I would be able to meet with Mr. Rickerby in twenty minutes at the Automat on Sixth and Forty-fifth. When I walked in he was off to the side, coffee in front of him, a patient little gray man who seemingly had all the time in the world.

I put down my own coffee, sat opposite him and said, "You have wild office hours."

He smiled meaninglessly, a studied, yet unconscious gesture that was for anyone watching. But there was no patience in his eyes. They seemed to live by themselves, being held in check by some obscure force. The late edition of the *News* was folded back to the center spread where a small photo gave an angular view of Old Dewey dead on the floor. The cops had blamed it on terrorists in the neighborhood.

Rickerby waited me out until I said, "I saw Laura Knapp today," then he nodded.

"We covered that angle pretty thoroughly."

"Did you know about the safe? It had an alarm system."

Once again, he nodded. "For your information, I'll tell you this. No connection has been made by any department between Senator Knapp's death and that of Richie. If you're assuming any state papers were in that safe you're wrong. Knapp had duplicate listings of every paper he had in his possession and we recovered everything."

"There were those paste jewels," I said.

"I know. I doubt if they establish anything, even in view of

Richie's cover. It seems pretty definite that the gun was simply used in different jobs. As a matter of fact, Los Angeles has since come up with another murder in which the same gun was used. This was a year ago and the victim was a used-car dealer."

"So it wasn't a great idea."

"Nor original." He put down his coffee and stared at me across the table. "Nor am I interested in others besides Richie." He paused, let a few seconds pass, then added, "Have you decided to tell me what Richie really told you?"

"No."

"At least I won't have to call you a liar again."

"Knock it off."

Rickerby's little smile faded slowly and he shrugged. "Make your point then."

"Cole. I want to know about him."

"I told you once—"

"Okay, so it's secret. But now he's dead. You want a killer, I want a killer and if we don't get together someplace nobody gets nothing. You know?"

His fingers tightened on the cup, the nails showing the strain. He let a full minute pass before he came to a decision. He said, "Can you imagine how many persons are looking for this—killer?"

"I've been in the business too, friend."

"All right. I'll tell you this. I know nothing of Richie's last mission and I doubt if I'll find out. But this much I do know—he wasn't supposed to be back here at all. He disobeyed orders and would have been on the carpet had he not been killed."

I said, "Cole wasn't a novice."

And for the first time Rickerby lost his composure. His eyes looked puzzled, bewildered at this sudden failure of something he had built himself. "That's the strange part about it."

"Oh?"

"Richie was forty-five years old. He had been with one department or another since '41 and his record was perfect. He was a book man through and through and wouldn't bust a reg for any reason. He could adapt if the situation necessitated it, but it would conform to certain regulations." He stopped, looked across his cup at me and shook his head slowly. "I—just can't figure it."

"Something put him here."

This time his eyes went back to their bland expression. He had allowed himself those few moments and that was all. Now he was on the job again, the essence of many years of self-discipline, nearly emotionless to the casual observer. "I know," he said.

And he waited and watched for me to give him the one word that might send him out on a kill chase. I used my own coffee cup to cover what I thought, ran through the possibilities until I knew what I wanted and leaned back in my chair. "I need more time," I told him.

"Time isn't too important to me. Richie's dead. Time would be important only if it meant keeping him alive."

"It's important to me."

"How long do you need before telling me?"

"Telling what?"

"What Richie thought important enough to tell you."

I grinned at him. "A week, maybe."

His eyes were deadly now. Cold behind the glasses, each one a deliberate ultimatum. "One week, then. No more. Try to go past it and I'll show you tricks you never thought of when it comes to making a man miserable."

"I could turn up the killer in that time."

"You won't."

"There were times when I didn't do so bad."

"Long ago, Hammer. Now you're nothing. Just don't mess anything up. The only reason I'm not pushing you hard is because you couldn't take the gaff. If I thought you could, my approach would be different."

I stood up and pushed my chair back. "Thanks for the consideration. I appreciate it."

"No trouble at all."

"I'll call you."

"Sure. I'll be waiting."

The same soft rain had come in again, laying a blanket over the city. It was gentle and cool, not heavy enough yet to send the sidewalk crowd into the bars or running for cabs. It was a good rain to walk in if you weren't in a hurry, a good rain to think in.

So I walked to Forty-fourth and turned west toward Broadway, following a pattern from seven years ago I had forgotten, yet still existed. At the Blue Ribbon I went into the bar, had a stein of Prior's dark beer, said hello to a few familiar faces, then went back toward the glow of lights that marked the Great White Way.

The night man in the Hackard Building was new to me, a sleepy-looking old guy who seemed to just be waiting time out so he could leave life behind and get comfortably dead. He watched me sign the night book, hobbled after me into the elevator and let me out where I wanted without a comment, anxious for nothing more than to get back to his chair on the ground floor.

I found my key, turned the lock and opened the door.

I was thinking of how funny it was that some things could transcend all others, how from the far reaches of your mind something would come, an immediate reaction to an immediate stimulus. I was thinking it and falling, knowing that I had been hit, but not hard, realizing that the cigarette smoke I smelled meant but one thing, that it wasn't mine, and if somebody was still there he had heard the elevator stop, had time to cut the lights and wait—and act. But time had not changed habit and my reaction was quicker than his act.

Metal jarred off the back of my head and bit into my neck. Even as I fell I could sense him turn the gun around in his hand and heard the click of a hammer going back. I hit face down, totally limp, feeling the warm spill of blood seeping into my collar. The light went on and a toe touched me gently. Hands felt my pockets, but it was a professional touch and the gun was always there and I couldn't move without being suddenly dead, and I had been dead too long already to invite it again.

The blood saved me. The cut was just big and messy enough to make him decide it was useless to push things any further. The feet stepped back, the door opened, closed, and I heard the feet walk away.

I got to the desk as fast as I could, fumbled out the .45, loaded it and wrenched the door open. The guy was gone. I knew he would be. He was long gone. Maybe I was lucky, because he was a real pro. He could have been standing there waiting, just in case, and his first shot would have gone right where he wanted it to. I looked at my hand and it was shaking too hard to put a bullet anywhere near a target. Besides, I had forgotten to jack a shell into the chamber. So some things did age with time, after all.

Except luck. I still had some of that left.

I walked around the office slowly, looking at the places that had been ravaged in a fine search for something. The shakedown had been fast, but again, in thoroughness, the marks of the complete professional were apparent. There had been no time or motion lost in the wrong direction and had I hidden anything of value that could have been tucked into an envelope, it would have been found. Two places I once considered original with me were torn open expertly, the second, and apparently last, showing a touch of annoyance.

Even Velda's desk had been torn open and the last thing she had written to me lay discarded on the floor, ground into a twisted sheet by a turning foot and all that was left was the heading.

It read, *Mike Darling*—and that was all I could see.

I grinned pointlessly, and this time I jacked a shell into the chamber and let the hammer ease down, then shoved the .45 into my belt on the left side. There was a sudden familiarity with the weight and the knowledge that here was life and death under my hand, a means of extermination, of quick vengeance, and of remembrance of the others who had gone down under that same gun.

Mike Darling—

Where was conscience when you saw those words?

Who *really* were the dead: those killing, or those already killed?

Then suddenly I felt like myself again and knew that the road back was going to be a long one alive or a short one dead and there wasn't even time enough to count the seconds.

Downstairs an old man would be dead in his chair because he alone could identify the person who came up here. The name in the night book would be fictitious and cleverly disguised if it had even been written there, and unless a motive were proffered, the old man's killing would be another one of those unexplainable things that happen to lonely people or alone people who stay too close to a terroristic world and are subject to the things that can happen by night.

I cleaned up the office so that no one could tell what had happened, washed my head and mopped up the blood spots on the floor, then went down the stairwell to the lobby.

The old man was lying dead in his seat, his neck broken neatly by a single blow. The night book was untouched, so his deadly visitor had only faked a signing. I tore the last page out, made sure I was unobserved and walked out the door. Someplace near Eighth Avenue I ripped up the page and fed the pieces into the gutter, the filthy trickle of rainwater swirling them into the sewer at the corner.

I waited until a cab came along showing its top light, whistled it over and told the driver where to take me. He hit the flag, pulled away from the curb and loafed his way down to the docks until he found the right place. He took his buck with another silent nod and left me there in front of Benny Joe Grissi's bar where you could get a program for all the trouble shows if you wanted one or a kill arranged or a broad made or anything at all you wanted just so long as you could get in the place.

But best of all, if there was anything you wanted to know about the stretch from the Battery to Grant's Tomb that constitutes New York's harbor facilities on either side of the river, or the associated unions from the NMU to the Teamsters, or wanted a name passed around the world, you could do it here. There was a place like it in London and Paris and Casablanca and Mexico City and Hong Kong and, if you looked hard enough, a smaller, more modified version would be in every city in the world. You just had to know where to look. And this was my town.

At the table near the door the two guys scrutinizing the customers made their polite sign which meant stay out. Then the little one got up rather tiredly and came over and said, "We're closing, buddy. No more customers."

When I didn't say anything he looked at my face and threw a finger toward his partner. The other guy was real big, his face suddenly ugly for having been disturbed. We got eye to eye and for a second he followed the plan and said, "No trouble, pal. We don't want trouble."

"Me either, kid."

"So blow."

I grinned at him, teeth all the way. "Scram."

My hand hit his chest as he swung and he went on his can

swinging like an idiot. The little guy came in low, thinking he was pulling a good one, and I kicked his face all out of shape with one swipe and left him whimpering against the wall.

The whole bar had turned around by then, all talk ended. You could see the excitement in their faces, the way they all thought it was funny because somebody had nearly jumped the moat—but not quite. They were waiting to see the rest, like when the big guy got up off the floor and earned his keep and the big guy was looking forward to it too.

Out of the sudden quiet somebody said, "Ten to one on Sugar Boy," and, just as quietly, another one said, "You're on for five."

Again it was slow motion, the bar looking down at the funny little man at the end, wizened and dirty, but liking the odds, regardless of the company. Somebody laughed and said, "Pepper knows something."

"That I do," the funny little man said.

But by then the guy had eased up to his feet, his face showing how much he liked the whole deal, and just for the hell of it he let me have the first swing.

I didn't hurt him. He let me know it and came in like I knew he would and I was back in that old world since seven years ago, tasting floor dirt and gagging on it, feeling my guts fly apart and the wild wrenching of bones sagging under even greater bones and while they laughed and yelled at the bar, the guy slowly killed me until the little bit of light was there like I knew that would be too and I gave him the foot in the crotch and, as if the world had collapsed on his shoulders, he crumpled into a vomiting heap, eyes bulging, hating, waiting for the moment of incredible belly pain to pass, and when it did, reached for his belt and pulled out a foot-long knife and it was all over, all over for everybody because I reached too and no blade argues with that great big bastard of a .45 that makes the big boom so many times, and when he took one look at my face his eyes bulged again, said he was sorry, Mac, and to deal him out, I was the wrong guy, he knew it and don't let the boom go off. He was close for a second and knew it, then I put the gun back without letting the hammer down, stepped on the blade and broke it and told him to get up.

The funny little guy at the bar said, "That's fifty I got coming."

The one who made the bet said, "I told you Pepper knew something."

The big guy got up and said, "No offense, Mac, it's my job."

The owner came over and said, "Like in the old days, hey Mike?"

I said, "You ought to clue your help, Benny Joe."

"They need training."

"Not from me."

"You did lousy tonight. I thought Sugar Boy had you."

"Not when I got a rod."

"So who knew? All this time you go clean? I hear even Gary Moss cleaned you one night. You, even. Old, Mike."

Around the bar the eyes were staring at me curiously, wondering. "They don't know me, Benny Joe."

The little fat man shrugged. "Who would? You got skinny. Now how about taking off."

"Not you, Benny Joe," I said. "Don't tell me you're pushing too."

"Sure. Tough guys I got all the time. Old tough guys I don't want. They always got to prove something. So with you I call the cops and you go down. So blow, okay?"

I hadn't even been looking at him while he talked, but now I took the time to turn around and see the little fat man, a guy I had known for fifteen years, a guy who should have known better, a guy who was on the make since he began breathing but a guy who had to learn the hard way.

So I looked at him, slow, easy, and in his face I could see my own face and I said, "How would you like to get deballed, Benny Joe? You got nobody to stop me. You want to sing tenor for that crib you have keeping house for you?"

Benny Joe almost did what he started out to do. The game was supposed to have ended in the Old West, the making of a reputation by one man taking down a big man. He almost took the .25 out, then he went back to being Benny Joe again and he was caught up in something too big for him. I picked the .25 out of his fingers, emptied it, handed it back and told him, "Don't die without cause, Benny Joe."

The funny little guy at the bar with the new fifty said, "You don't remember me, do you, Mike?"

I shook my head.

"Ten, fifteen years ago—the fire at Carrigan's?"

Again, I shook my head.

"I was a newspaperman then. Bayliss Henry of the *Telegram*. Pepper, they call me now. You had that gunfight with Cortez Johnson and his crazy bunch from Red Hook."

"That was long ago, feller."

"Papers said it was your first case. You had an assignment from Aliet Insurance."

"Yeah," I told him, "I remember the fire. Now I remember you too. I never did get to say thanks. I go through the whole damn war without a scratch and get hit in a lousy heist and almost burn to death. So thanks!"

"My pleasure, Mike. You got me a scoop bonus."

"Now what's new?"

"Hell, after what guys like us saw, what else *could* be new?"

I drank my beer and didn't say anything.

Bayliss Henry grinned and asked, "What's with you?"

"What?" I tried to sound pretty bored.

It didn't take with him at all. "Come on, Big Mike. You've always been my favorite news story. Even when I don't write, I follow the columns. Now you just don't come busting in this place anymore without a reason. How long were you a bum, Mike?"

"Seven years."

"Seven years ago you never would have put a gun on Sugar Boy."

"I didn't need it then."

"Now you need it?"

"Now I need it," I repeated.

Bayliss took a quick glance around. "You got no ticket for that rod, Mike."

I laughed, and my face froze him. "Neither had Capone. Was he worried?"

The others had left us. The two guys were back at their table by the door watching the rain through the windows, the music from the overlighted juke strangely soft for a change, the conversation a subdued hum above it.

A rainy night can do things like that. It can change the entire course of events. It seems to rearrange time.

I said, "What?"

"Jeez, Mike, why don't you listen once? I've been talking for ten minutes."

"Sorry, kid."

"Okay, I know how it is. Just one thing."

"What?"

"When you gonna ask it?"

I looked at him and took a pull of the beer.

"The big question. The one you came here to ask somebody."

"You think too much, Bayliss, boy."

He made a wry face. "I can think more. You got a big one on your mind. This is a funny place, like a thieves' market. Just anybody doesn't come here. It's a special place for special purposes. You want something, don't you?"

I thought a moment, then nodded. "What can you supply?"

His wrinkled face turned up to mine with a big smile. "Hell, man, for you just about anything."

"Know a man named Richie Cole?" I asked.

"Sure," he said, casually, "he had a room under mine. He was a good friend. A damn smuggler who was supposed to be small-time, but he was better than that because he had loot small smugglers never get to keep. Nice guy, though."

And that is how a leech line can start in New York if you know where to begin. The interweaving of events and personalities can lead you to a crossroad eventually where someone stands who, with one wave of a hand, can put you on the right trail—if he chooses to. But the interweaving is not a simple thing. It comes from years of mingling and mixing and kneading, and although the answer seems to be an almost casual thing, it really isn't at all.

I said, "He still live there?"

"Naw. He got another place. But he's no seaman."

"How do you know?"

Bayliss grunted and finished his beer. "Now what seaman will keep a furnished room while he's away?"

"How do you know this?"

The little guy shrugged and waved the bartender over. "Mike—

I've been there. We spilled plenty of beer together." He handed me a fresh brew and picked up his own. "Richie Cole was a guy who made plenty of bucks, friend, and don't you forget it. You'd like him."

"Where's his place?"

Bayliss smiled broadly, "Come on, Mike. I said he was a friend. If he's in trouble I'm not going to make it worse."

"You can't," I told him. "Cole's dead."

Slowly, he put the beer down on the bar, turned and looked at me with his forehead wrinkling in a frown. "How?"

"Shot."

"You know something, Mike? I thought something like that would happen to him. It was in the cards."

"Like how?"

"I saw his guns. He had three of them in a trunk. Besides, he used me for a few things."

When I didn't answer, he grinned and shrugged.

"I'm an old-timer, Mike. Remember? Stuff I know hasn't been taught some of the fancy boys on the papers yet. I still got connections that get me a few bucks here and there. No trouble, either. I did so many favors that now it pays off and, believe me, this retirement pay business isn't what it looks like. So I pick up a few bucks with some well chosen directions or clever ideas. Now, Cole, I never did figure just what he was after, but he sure wanted some peculiar information."

"How peculiar?"

"Well, to a thinking man like me, it was peculiar because no smuggler the size he was supposed to be would want to know what he wanted."

"Smart," I told him. "Did you mention it to Cole?"

"Sure," Bayliss grinned, "but we're both old at what we were doing and could read eyes. I wouldn't pop on him."

"Suppose we go see his place."

"Suppose you tell me what he really was first."

Right then he was real roostery, a Bayliss Henry from years ago before retirement and top dog on the news beat, a wizened little guy, but one who wasn't going to budge an inch. I wasn't giving a damn for national security as the book describes it, at all, so I said,

"Richie Cole was a Federal agent and he stayed alive long enough to ask me in on this."

He waited, watched me, then made a decisive shrug with his shoulders and pulled a cap down over his eyes. "You know what you could be getting into?" he asked me.

"I've been shot before," I told him.

"Yeah, but you haven't been dead before," he said.

The place was a brownstone building in Brooklyn that stood soldier-fashion shoulder to shoulder in place with fifty others, a row of face-like oblongs whose windows made dull, expressionless eyes of the throttled dead, the bloated tongue of a stone stoop hanging out of its gaping mouth.

The rest wasn't too hard, not when you're city-born and have nothing to lose anyway. Bayliss said the room was ground-floor rear so we simply got into the back through a cellarway three houses down, crossed the slatted fences that divided one pile of garbage from another until we reached the right window, then went in. Nobody saw us. If they did, they stayed quiet about it. That's the kind of place it was.

In a finger-thick beam of the pencil flash I picked out the sofa bed, an inexpensive contour chair, a dresser and a desk. For a furnished room it had a personal touch that fitted in with what Bayliss suggested. There were times when Richie Cole had desired a few more of the creature comforts than he could normally expect in a neighborhood like this.

There were a few clothes in the closet: a military raincoat, heavy dungaree jacket and rough-textured shirts. An old pair of hip boots and worn high shoes were in one corner. The dresser held changes of underwear and a few sports shirts, but nothing that would suggest that Cole was anything he didn't claim to be.

It was in the desk that I found the answer. To anyone else it would have meant nothing, but to me it was an answer. A terribly cold kind of answer that seemed to come at me like a cloud that could squeeze and tear until I thought I was going to burst wide open.

Cole had kept a simple, inexpensive photo album. There were the usual pictures of everything from the Focking Distillery to the San Francisco Bridge with Cole and girls and other guys and girls and just girls alone the way a thousand other seamen try to maintain a visual semblance of life.

But it was in the first few pages of the album that the fist hit me in the gut because there was Cole a long time ago sitting at a table in a bar with some RAF types in the background and a couple of American GI's from the 8th Air Force on one side and with Richie Cole was Velda.

Beautiful, raven hair in a long pageboy, her breasts swelling tautly against the sleeveless gown, threatening to free themselves. Her lips were wet with an almost deliberate gesture and her smile was purposely designing. One of the GIs was looking at her with obvious admiration.

Bayliss whispered, "What'd you say, Mike?"

I shook my head and flipped a page over. "Nothing."

She was there again, and a few pages further on. Once they were standing outside a pub, posing with a soldier and a WREN, and in another they stood beside the bombed-out ruins of a building with the same soldier, but a different girl.

There was nothing contrived about the album. Those pictures had been there a long time. So had the letters. Six of them dated in 1944, addressed to Cole at a P.O. box in New York, and although they were innocuous enough in content, showed a long-standing familiarity between the two of them. And there was Velda's name, the funny "V" she made, the green ink she always used and, although I hadn't even known her then, I was hating Cole so hard it hurt. I was glad he was dead but wished I could have killed him, then I took a fat breath, held it once and let it out slowly and it wasn't so bad anymore.

I felt Bayliss touch my arm and he said, "You okay, Mike?"

"Sure."

"You find anything?"

"Nothing important."

He grunted under his breath. "You're full of crap."

"A speciality of mine," I agreed. "Let's get out of here."

"What about those guns? He had a trunk some place."

"We don't need them. Let's go."

"So you found something. You could satisfy my curiosity."

"Okay," I told him, "Cole and I had a mutual friend."

"It means something?"

"It might. Now move."

He went out first, then me, and I let the window down. We took the same route back, going over the fences where we had crossed earlier, me boosting Bayliss up then following him. I was on top of the last one when I felt the sudden jar of wood beside my hand, then a tug at my coat between my arm and rib cage and the instinct and reaction grabbed me again and I fell on top of Bayliss while I hauled the .45 out and, without even knowing where the silenced shots were coming from, I let loose with a tremendous blast of that fat musket that tore the night wide open with a rolling thunder that let the world know the pigeon was alive and had teeth.

From a distance came a clattering of cans, of feet, then windows slammed open and voices started yelling and the two of us got out fast. We were following the same path of the one who had followed us, but his start was too great. Taillights were already diminishing down the street and in another few minutes a prowl car would be turning the corner.

We didn't wait for it.

Six blocks over we picked up a cab, drove to Ed Dailey's bar and got out. I didn't have to explain a thing to Bayliss. He had been through it all too often before. He was shaking all over and couldn't seem to stop swallowing. He had two double ryes before he looked at me with a peculiar expression and said softly, "Jeez, I'll never learn to keep my mouth shut."

Peerage Brokers could have been anything. The desks and chairs and filing cabinets and typewriters represented nothing, yet represented everything. Only the gray man in the glasses sitting alone in the corner drinking coffee represented something.

Art Rickerby said, "Now?" and I knew what he meant.

I shook my head. He looked at me silently a moment, then sipped at the coffee container again. He knew how to wait, this one. He wasn't in a hurry now, not rushing to prevent something. He was simply waiting for a moment of vengeance because the thing was done and sooner or later time would be on his side.

I said, "Did you know Richie pretty well?"

"I think so."

"Did he have a social life?"

For a moment his face clouded over, then inquisitiveness replaced anger and he put the coffee container down for a reason, to turn his head away. "You'd better explain."

"Like girls," I said.

When he turned back he was expressionless again. "Richie had been married," he told me. "In 1949 his wife died of cancer."

"Oh? How long did he know her?"

"They grew up together."

"Children?"

"No. Both Richie and Ann knew about the cancer. They married after the war anyway but didn't want to leave any children a difficult burden."

"How about before that?"

"I understood they were both pretty true to each other."

"Even during the war?"

Again there was silent questioning in his eyes. "What are you getting at, Mike?"

"What was Richie during the war?"

The thought went through many channels before it was properly classified. Art said, "A minor O.S.I. agent. He was a Captain then based in England. With mutual understanding, I never asked, nor did he offer, the kind of work he did."

"Let's get back to the girls."

"He was no virgin, if that's what you mean."

He knew he reached me with that one but didn't know why. I could feel myself tighten up and had to relax deliberately before I could speak to him again.

"Who did he go with when he was here? When he wasn't on a job."

Rickerby frowned and touched his glasses with an impatient gesture. "There were—several girls. I really never inquired. After Ann's death—well, it was none of my business, really."

"But you knew them?"

He nodded, watching me closely. Once more he thought quickly, then decided. "There was Greta King, a stewardess with American Airlines that he would see occasionally. And there was Pat Bender over at the Craig House. She's a manicurist there and they had been friends for years. Her brother, Lester, served with Richie but was killed just before the war ended."

"It doesn't sound like he had much fun."

"He didn't look for fun. Ann's dying took that out of him. All he wanted was an assignment that would keep him busy. In fact, he rarely ever got to see Alex Bird, and if—"

"Who's he?" I interrupted.

"Alex, Lester and Richie were part of a team throughout the war. They were great friends in addition to being experts in their work. Lester got killed, Alex bought a chicken farm in Marlboro, New York, and Richie stayed in the service. When Alex went civilian he and Richie sort of lost communication. You know the code in this work—no friends, no relatives—it's a lonely life."

When he paused I said, "That's all?"

Once again, he fiddled with his glasses, a small flicker of annoyance showing in his eyes. "No. There was someone else he used to see on occasions. Not often, but he used to look forward to the visit."

My voice didn't sound right when I asked, "Serious?"

"I—don't think so. It didn't happen often enough and generally it was just a supper engagement. It was an old friend, I think."

"You couldn't recall the name?"

"It was never mentioned. I never pried into his business."

"Maybe it's about time."

Rickerby nodded sagely. "It's about time for you to tell me a few things too."

"I can't tell you what I don't know."

"True." He looked at me sharply and waited.

"If the information isn't classified, find out what he really did during the war, who he worked with and who he knew."

For several seconds he ran the thought through his mental file, then: "You think it goes back that far?"

"Maybe." I wrote my number down on a memo pad, ripped off the page and handed it to him. "My office. I'll be using it from now on."

He looked at it, memorized it and threw it down. I grinned, told him so-long and left.

Over in the west Forties I got a room in a small hotel, got a box, paper and heavy cord from the desk clerk, wrapped my .45 up, addressed it to myself at the office with a buck's worth of stamps and dropped it in the outgoing mail, then sacked out until it was almost noon in a big new tomorrow.

Maybe I still had that look because they thought I was another cop. Nobody wanted to talk, and if they had, there would have been little they could have said. One garrulous old broad said she saw a couple of men in the back court and later a third. No, she didn't know what they were up to and didn't care as long as they weren't in *her* yard. She heard the shot and would show me the place, only she didn't know why I couldn't work with the rest of the cops instead of bothering everybody all over again.

I agreed with her, thanked her and let her take me to where I almost had it going over the fence. When she left, wheezing and muttering, I found where the bullet had torn through the slats and jumped the fence, and dug it out of the two-by-four frame in the section on the other side of the yard. There was still enough of it to show the rifling marks, so I dropped it in my pocket and went back to the street.

Two blocks away I waved down a cab and got in. Then I felt the seven years, and the first time back I had to play it hard and almost stupid enough to get killed. There was a time when I never would have missed with the .45, but now I was happy to make a noise with it big enough to start somebody running. For a minute I felt skinny and shrunken inside the suit and cursed silently to myself.

If she was alive, I was going to have to do better than I was doing now. Time, damn it. There wasn't any. It was like when the guy in the porkpie hat had her strung from the rafters and the whip in his hand had stripped her naked flesh with bright red welts, the force of each lash stroke making her spin so that the lush beauty of her body and the deep-space blackness of her hair and the wide sweep of her breasts made an obscene kaleidoscope and then I shot his arm off with the tommy gun and it dropped with a wet thud in the puddle of clothes around her feet like a pagan sacrifice and while he was dying I killed the rest of them, all of them, twenty of them, wasn't it? And they called me those terrible names, the judge and the jury did.

Damn. Enough.

CHAPTER 7

The body was gone, but the police weren't. The two detectives interrogating Nat beside the elevators were patiently listening to everything he said, scanning the night book one held open. I walked over, nodded and said, "Morning, Nat."

Nat's eyes gave me a half-scared, half-surprised look followed by a shrug that meant it was all out of his hands.

"Hello, Mike." He turned to the cop with the night book. "This is Mr. Hammer. In 808."

"Oh?" The cop made me in two seconds. "Mike Hammer. Didn't think you were still around."

"I just got back."

His eyes went up and down, then steadied on my face. He could read all the signs, every one of them. "Yeah," he said sarcastically. "Were you here last night?"

"Not me, buddy. I was out on the town with a friend."

The pencil came into his hand automatically. "Would you like to—"

"No trouble. Bayliss Henry, an old reporter. I think he lives—"

He put the pencil away with a bored air. "I know where Bayliss lives."

"Good," I said. "What's the kick here?"

Before the pair could tell him to shut up, Nat blurted, "Mike—it was old Morris Fleming. He got killed."

I played it square as I could. "Morris Fleming?"

"Night man, Mike. He started working here after—you left."

The cop waved him down. "Somebody broke his neck."

"What for?"

He held up the book. Ordinarily he never would have answered, but I had been around too long in the same business. "He could have been identified. He wanted in the easy way so he signed the book, killed the old man later and ripped the page out when he left." He let me think it over and added, "Got it figured yet?"

"You don't kill for fun. Who's dead upstairs?"

Both of them threw a look back and forth and stared at me again. "Clever boy."

"Well?"

"No bodies. No reported robberies. No signs of forcible entry. You're one of the last ones in. Maybe you'd better check your office."

"I'll do that," I told him.

But I didn't have to bother. My office had already been checked. Again. The door was open, the furniture pushed around, and in my chair behind the desk was Pat, his face cold and demanding, his hands playing with the box of .45 shells he had found in the niche in the desk.

Facing him with her back to me, the light from the window making a silvery halo around the yellow of her hair, was Laura Knapp.

I said, "Having fun?"

Laura turned quickly, saw me and a smile made her mouth beautiful. "Mike!"

"Now how did you get here?"

She took my hand, held it tightly a moment with a grin of pleasure and let me perch on the end of the desk. "Captain Chambers asked me to." She turned and smiled at Pat, but the smile was lost on him. "He came to see me not long after you did."

"I told you that would happen."

"It seems that since you showed some interest in me he did too, so we just reviewed all—the details of what happened—to Leo." Her smile faded then, her eyes seeming to reflect the hurt she felt.

"What's the matter, Pat, don't you keep files anymore?"

"Shut up."

"The manual says to be nice to the public." I reached over and picked up the box of .45's. "Good thing you didn't find the gun."

"You're damn right. You'd be up on a Sullivan charge right now."

"How'd you get in, Pat?"

"It wasn't too hard. I know the same tricks you do. And don't get snotty." He flipped a paper out of his pocket and tossed it on the desk. "A warrant, mister. When I heard there was a kill in this particular building I took this out first thing."

I laughed at the rage in his face and rubbed it in a little. "Find what you were looking for?"

Slowly, he got up and walked around the desk, and though he stood there watching me it was to Laura that he spoke. "If you don't mind, Mrs. Knapp, wait out in the other room. And close the door."

She looked at him, puzzled, so I nodded to her and she stood up with a worried frown creasing her eyes and walked out. The door made a tiny *snick* as it closed and we had the place all to ourselves. Pat's face was still streaked with anger, but there were other things in his eyes this time. "I'm fed up, Mike. You'd just better talk."

"And if I don't?"

The coldness took all the anger away from his face now. "All right, I'll tell you the alternative. You're trying to do something. Time is running against you. Don't give me any crap because I know you better than you know yourself. This isn't the first time something like this cropped up. You pull your connections on me, you try to play it smart—okay—I'll make time run out on you. I'll use every damn regulation I know to harass you to death. I'll keep a tail on you all day, and every time you spit I'll have your ass hauled into the office. I'll hold you on every pretext possible and if it comes to doing a little high-class framing I can do that too."

Pat wasn't lying. Like he knew me, I knew him. He was real ready to do everything he said and time was one thing I didn't have enough of. I got up and walked around the desk to my chair and sat down again. I pulled out the desk drawer, stowed the .45's back in the niche without trying to be smug about what I did with the gun. Then I sat there groping back into seven years, knowing that instinct went only so far, realizing that there was no time to relearn and that every line had to be straight across the corners.

I said, "Okay, Pat. Anything you want. But first a favor."

"No favors."

"It's not exactly a favor. It's an or else." I felt my face go as cold as his was. "Whether you like it or not I'm ready to take my chances."

He didn't answer. He couldn't. He was ready to throw his fist at my face again and would have, only he was too far away. Little by little he relaxed until he could speak, then all those years of being a cop took over and he shrugged, but he wasn't fooling me any. "What is it?"

"Nothing I couldn't do if I had the time. It's all a matter of public record."

He glanced at me shrewdly and waited.

"Look up Velda's P.I. license."

His jaw dropped open stupidly for a brief second, then snapped shut and his eyes followed suit. He stood there, knuckles white as they gripped the edge of the desk and he gradually leaned forward so that when he swung he wouldn't be out of reach this time.

"What kind of crazy stunt are you pulling?" His voice was almost hoarse.

I shook my head. "The New York State law says that you must have served three or more years in an accredited police agency, city, state, or federal in a rating of sergeant or higher to get a Private Investigator's license. It isn't easy to get and takes a lot of background work."

Quietly, Pat said, "She worked for you. Why didn't you ask?"

"One of the funny things in life. Her ticket was good enough for me at first. Later it never occurred to me to ask. I was always a guy concerned with the present anyway and you damn well know it."

"You bastard. What are you trying to pull?"

"Yes or no, Pat."

His grin had no humor in it. Little cords in his neck stood out against his collar and the pale blue of his eyes was deadly. "No," he said. "You're a wise guy, punk. Don't pull your tangents on me. You got this big feeling inside you that you're coming back at me for slapping you around. You're using *her* now as a pretty little oblique switch—but, mister, you're pulling your crap on the wrong soldier. You've just about had it, boy."

Before he could swing I leaned back in my chair with as much insolence as I could and reached in my pocket for the slug I had dug out of the fence. It was a first-class gamble, but not quite a bluff. I had the odds going for me and if I came up short, I'd still have a few hours ahead of him.

I reached out and laid the splashed-out bit of metal on the desk. "Don't *punk* me, man. Tell ballistics to go after that and tell me what I want and I'll tell you where that came from."

Pat picked it up, his mind putting ideas together, trying to make one thing fit another. It was hard to tell what he was thinking, but one thing took precedence over all others. He was a cop. First-rate. He wanted a killer. He had to play his own odds too.

"All right," he told me, "I can't take any chances. I don't get your point, but if it's a phony, you've had it."

I shrugged. "When will you know about the license?"

"It won't take long."

"I'll call you," I said.

He straightened up and stared out the window over my head, still half in thought. Absently, he rubbed the back of his neck. "You do that," he told me. He turned away, putting his hat on, then reached for the door.

I stopped him. "Pat—"

"What?"

"Tell me something."

His eyes squinted at my tone. I think he knew what I was going to ask.

"Did you love Velda too?"

Only his eyes gave the answer, then he opened the door and left.

"May I come in?"

"Oh, Laura—please."

"Was there—trouble?"

"Nothing special." She came back to the desk and sat down in the client's chair, her face curious. "Why?"

With a graceful motion, she crossed her legs and brushed her skirt down over her knees. "Well, when Captain Chambers was with me—well, he spoke constantly of you. It was as if you were right in the middle of everything." She paused, turning her head toward me. "He hates you, doesn't he?"

I nodded. "But we were friends once."

Very slowly, her eyebrows arched. "Aren't most friendships only temporary at best?"

"That's being pretty cynical."

"No—only realistic. There are childhood friendships. Later those friends from school, even to the point of nearly blood brother-hood fraternities, but how long do they last? Are your Army or Navy friends still your friends or have you forgotten their names?"

I made a motion with my shoulders.

"Then your friends are only those you have at the moment. Either you outgrow them or something turns friendship into hatred."

"It's a lousy system," I said.

"But there it is, nevertheless. In 1945 Germany and Japan were our enemies and Russia and the rest our allies. Now our former enemies are our best friends and the former allies the direct enemies."

She was so suddenly serious I had to laugh at her. "Beautiful blondes aren't generally philosophers."

But her eyes didn't laugh back. "Mike—it really isn't that funny. When Leo was—alive, I attended to all his affairs in Washington. I still carry on, more or less. It's something he would have wanted me to do. I *know* how people who run the world think. I served cocktails to people making decisions that rocked the earth. I saw wars start over a drink and the friendship of generations between nations wiped out because one stupid, pompous political appointee wanted to do things his way. Oh, don't worry, I *know* about friendships."

"So this one went sour."

"It hurts you, doesn't it?"

"I guess so. It never should have happened that way."

"Oh?" For a few moments she studied me, then she knew. "The woman—we talked about—you both loved her?"

"I thought only I did." She sat there quietly then, letting me finish. "We both thought she was dead. He still thinks so and blames me for what happened."

"Is she, Mike?"

"I don't know. It's all very strange, but if there is even the most remote possibility that some peculiar thing happened seven years ago and that she is still alive somewhere, I want to know about it."

"And Captain Chambers?"

"He could never have loved her as I did. She was mine."

"If—you are wrong—and she is dead, maybe it would be better not to know."

My face was grinning again. Not me, just the face part. I stared at the wall and grinned idiotically. "If she is alive, I'll find her. If she is dead, I'll find who killed her. Then slowly, real slowly, I'll take him apart, inch by inch, joint by joint, until dying will be the best thing left for him."

I didn't realize that I was almost out of the chair, every muscle twisted into a monstrous spasm of murder. Then I felt her hands pulling me back and I let go and sat still until the hate seeped out of me.

"Thanks."

"I know what you feel like, Mike."

"You do?"

"Yes." Her hand ran down the side of my face, the fingers tracing a warm path along my jaw. "It's the way I felt about Leo. He was a great man, then suddenly for no reason at all he was dead."

"I'm sorry, Laura."

"But it's not over for me anymore, either."

I swung around in the chair and looked up at her. She was magnificent then, a study in symmetry, each curve of her wonderful body coursing into another, her face showing the full beauty of maturity, her eyes and mouth rich with color.

She reached out her hand and I stood up, tilted her chin up with my fingers and held her that way. "You're thinking, kitten."

"With you I have to."

"Why?"

"Because somehow you know Leo's death is part of her, and I feel the same way you do. Whoever killed Leo is going to die too."

I let go of her face, put my hands on her shoulders and pulled her close to me. "If he's the one I want I'll kill him for you, kid."

"No, Mike. I'll do it myself." And her voice was as cold and as full of purpose as my own when she said it. Then she added, "You just find that one for me."

"You're asking a lot, girl."

"Am I? After you left I found out all about you. It didn't take long. It was very fascinating information, but nothing I didn't know the first minute I saw you."

"That was me of a long time ago. I've been seven years drunk and I'm just over the bum stage now. Maybe I could drop back real easy. I don't know."

"I know."

"Nobody knows. Besides, I'm not authorized to pursue investigations."

"That doesn't seem to stop you."

A grin started to etch my face again. "You're getting to a point, kid."

She laughed gently, a full, quiet laugh. Once again her hand came up to my face. "Then I'll help you find your woman, Mike, if you'll find who killed Leo."

"Laura—"

"When Leo died the investigation was simply routine. They were more concerned about the political repercussions than in locating his killer. *They* forgot about that one, but I haven't. I thought I had, but I really hadn't. Nobody would look for me—they all promised and turned in reports, but they never really cared about finding that one. But you do, Mike, and somehow I know you will. Oh, you have no license and no authority, but I have money and it will put many things at your disposal. You take it. You find your woman, and while you're doing it, or before, or after, whatever you like, you find the one I want. Tomorrow I'll send you five thousand dollars in cash. No questions. No paperwork. No reports. Even if nothing comes of it there is no obligation on you."

Under my hands she was trembling. It didn't show on her face, but her shoulders quivered with tension. "You loved him very much," I stated.

She nodded. "As you loved her."

We were too close then, both of us feeling the jarring impact of new and sudden emotions. My hands were things of their own, leaving her shoulders to slide down to her waist, then reaching behind her to bring her body close to mine until it was touching, then pressing until a fusion was almost reached.

She had to gasp to breathe, and fingers that were light on my face were suddenly as fierce and demanding as my own as she brought me down to meet her mouth and the scalding touch of her tongue that worked serpentlike in a passionate orgy that screamed of release after so long a time.

She pulled away, her breasts moving spasmodically against my chest. Her eyes were wet and shimmering with a glow of disbelief that it could ever happen again and she said softly: "You, Mike—I want a man. It could never be anybody but—a man." She turned her eyes on mine, pleading. "Please, Mike."

"You never have to say please," I told her, then I kissed her again and we found our place in time and in distance, lost people who didn't have to hurry or be cautious and who could enjoy the sensual discomfort of a cold leather couch on naked skin and take pleasure in the whispering of clothing and relish the tiny sounds of a bursting seam; two whose appetites had been stifled for much too long, yet who loved the food of flesh enough not to rush through the first offering, but to taste and become filled course by course until in an explosion of delight, the grand finale of the whole table, was served and partaken.

We were gourmets, the body satisfied, but the mind knowing that it was only a momentary filling and that there would be other meals, each different, each more succulent than the last in a never-ending progression of enjoyment. The banquet was over so we kissed and smiled at each other, neither having been the guest, but rather, one the host, the other the hostess, both having the same startling thought of *Where was the past now? Could the present possibly be more important?*

When she was ready I said, "Let's get you home now, Laura."

"Must I?"

"You must."

"I could stay in town."

"If you did it would be a distraction I can't afford."

"But I live a hundred and ten miles from your city."

"That's only two hours up the Thruway and over the hills."

She grinned at me. "Will you come?"

I grinned back. "Naturally."

I picked up my hat and guided her to the outer office. For a single, terrible moment I felt a wash of shame drench me with guilt. There on the floor where it had been squashed underfoot by the one who killed old Morris Fleming and who had taken a shot at me was the letter from Velda that began, "*Mike Darling—*"

We sat at the corner of the bar in P. J. Moriarty's steak and chop house on Sixth and Fifty-second and across the angle his eyes were terrible little beads, magnified by the lenses of his glasses. John, the Irish bartender, brought us each a cold Blue Ribbon, leaving without a word because he could feel the thing that existed there.

Art Rickerby said, "How far do you think you can go?"

"All the way," I said.

"Not with me."

"Then alone."

He poured the beer and drank it as if it were water and he was thirsty, yet in a perfunctory manner that made you realize he wasn't a drinker at all, but simply doing a job, something he had to do.

When he finished he put the glass down and stared at me blandly. "You don't realize just how alone you really are."

"I know. Now do we talk?"

"Do you?"

"You gave me a week, buddy."

"Uh-huh." He poured the rest of the bottle into the glass and made a pattern with the wet bottom on the bar. When he looked up he said, "I may take it back."

I shrugged. "So you found something out."

"I did. About you too."

"Go ahead."

From overhead, the light bounced from his glasses so I couldn't see what was happening to his eyes. He said, "Richie was a little bigger than I thought during the war. He was quite important. Quite."

"At his age?"

"He was your age, Mike. And during the war age can be as much of a disguise as a deciding factor."

"Get to it."

"My pleasure." He paused, looked at me and threw the rest of the beer down. "He commanded the Seventeen Group." When I didn't give him the reaction he looked for he asked me, "Did you ever hear of Butterfly Two?"

I covered the frown that pulled at my forehead by finishing my own beer and waving to John for another. "I heard of it. I don't know the details. Something to do with the German system of total espionage. They had people working for them ever since the First World War."

There was something like respect in his eyes now. "It's amazing that you even heard of it."

"I have friends in amazing places."

"Yes, you had."

As slowly as I could I put the glass down. "What's that supposed to mean?"

And then his eyes came up, fastened on my face so as not to lose sight of even the slightest expression and he said, "It was your girl, the one called Velda, that he saw on the few occasions he was home. She was something left over from the war."

The glass broke in my hand and I felt a warm surge of blood spill into my hand. I took the towel John offered me and held it until the bleeding stopped. I said, "Go on."

Art smiled. It was the wrong kind of smile, with a gruesome quality that didn't match his face. "He last saw her in Paris just before the war ended and at that time he was working on Butterfly Two."

I gave the towel back to John and pressed on the Band-Aid he gave me.

"Gerald Erlich was the target then. At the time his name wasn't known except to Richie—and the enemy. Does it make sense now?"

"No." My guts were starting to turn upside down. I reached for the beer again, but it was too much. I couldn't do anything except listen.

"Erlich was the head of an espionage ring that had been instituted in 1920. Those agents went into every land in the world to get ready for the next war and even raised their children to be agents. Do you think World War II was simply the result of a political turnover?"

"Politics are not my speciality."

"Well, it wasn't. There was another group. It wasn't part of the German General Staff's machinations either. They utilized this group and so did Hitler—or better still, let's say vice versa."

I shook my head, not getting it at all.

"It was a world conquest scheme. It incorporated some of the greatest military and corrupt minds this world has ever known and is using global wars and brushfire wars to its own advantage until one day when everything is ready *they* can take over the world for their own."

"You're nuts!"

"I am?" he said softly. "How many powers were involved in 1918?"

"All but a few."

"That's right. And in 1945?"

"All of them were—"

"Not quite. I mean, who were the major powers?"

"We were. England, Germany, Russia, Japan—"

"That narrows it down a bit, doesn't it? And now, right now, how many *major powers* are there really?"

What he was getting at was almost inconceivable. "Two. Ourselves and the Reds."

"Ah—now we're getting to the point. And they hold most of the world's land and inhabitants in their hands. They're the antagonists. They're the ones pushing and we're the ones holding."

"Damn it, Rickerby—"

"Easy, friend. Just think a little bit."

"Ah, think my ass. What the hell are you getting to? Velda's part of that deal? You have visions, man, you got the big bug! Damn, I can get better than that from them at a jag dance in the Village. Even the bearded idiots make more sense."

His mouth didn't smile. It twisted. "Your tense is unusual. You spoke as if she were alive."

I let it go. I deliberately poured the beer into the glass until the head was foaming over the rim, then drank it off with a grimace of pleasure and put the glass down.

When I was ready I said, "So now the Reds are going to take over the world. They'll bury us. Well, maybe they will, buddy, but there won't be enough Reds around to start repopulating again, that's for sure."

"I didn't say that," Art told me.

His manner had changed again. I threw him an annoyed look and reached for the beer.

"I think the world conquest parties changed hands. The conqueror has been conquered. The Reds have located and are using this vast fund of information, this great organization we call Butterfly Two, and that's why the free world is on the defensive."

John asked me if I wanted another Blue Ribbon and I said yes.

He brought two, poured them, put the bar check in the register and returned it with a nod. When he had gone I half swung around, no longer so filled with a crazy fury that I couldn't speak. I said, "You're lucky, Rickerby. I didn't know whether to belt you in the mouth or listen."

"You're fortunate you listened."

"Then finish it. You think Velda's part of Butterfly Two." Everything, yet nothing, was in his shrug. "I didn't ask that many questions. I didn't care. All I want is Richie's killer."

"That doesn't answer my question. What do you *think*?"

Once again he shrugged. "It looks like she was," he told me.

So I thought my way through it and let the line cut all the corners off because there wasn't that much time and I asked him, "What was Richie working on when he was killed?"

Somehow, he knew I was going to ask that one and shook his head sadly. "Not that at all. His current job had to do with illegal gold shipments."

"You're sure."

"I'm sure."

"Then what about this Erlich?"

Noncommittally, Art shrugged. "Dead or disappeared. Swallowed up in the aftermath of war. Nobody knows."

"Somebody does," I reminded him. "The Big Agency boys don't give up their targets that easily. Not if the target is so big it makes a lifetime speciality of espionage."

He reflected a moment and nodded. "Quite possible. However, it's more than likely Erlich is dead at this point. He'd be in his sixties now if he escaped the general roundup of agents after the war. When the underground organizations of Europe were free of restraint they didn't wait on public trials. They knew who their targets were and how to find them. You'd be surprised at just how many people simply disappeared, big people and little people, agents and collaborators both. Many a person we wanted badly went into a garbage pit somewhere."

"Is that an official attitude?"

"Don't be silly. We don't reflect on attitudes to civilians. Occasionally it becomes necessary—"

"Now, for instance," I interrupted.

"Yes, like now. And believe me, they're better off knowing nothing."

Through the glasses his eyes tried to read me, then lost whatever expression they had. There was a touch of contempt and disgust in the way he sat there, examining me like a specimen under glass, then the last part of my line cut across the last corner and I asked him casually, "Who's The Dragon?"

Art Rickerby was good. Damn, but he was good. It was as if I had asked what time it was and he had no watch. But he just wasn't that good. I saw all the little things happen to him that nobody else would have noticed and watched them grow and grow until he could contain them no longer and had to sluff them off with an aside remark. So with an insipid look that didn't become him at all he said, "Who?"

"Or is it whom? Art?"

I had him where the hair was short and he knew it. He had given me all the big talk but this one was one too big. It was even bigger than he was and he didn't quite know how to handle it. You could say this about him: he was a book man. He put all the facts through the machine in his head and took the risk alone. He couldn't tell what I knew, yet he couldn't tell what I didn't know. Neither could he take a chance on having me clam up.

Art Rickerby was strictly a statesman. A federal agent, true, a cop, a dedicated servant of the people, but foremost he was a statesman. He was dealing with big security now and all the wraps were off. We were in a bar drinking beer and somehow the world was at our feet. What was it Laura had said—*"I saw wars start over a drink"*—and now it was almost the same thing right here.

"You didn't answer me," I prodded.

He put his glass down, and for the first time his hand wasn't steady. "How did you know about that?"

"Tell me, is it a big secret?"

His voice had an edge to it. *"Top secret."*

"Well, whatta you know."

"Hammer—"

"Nuts, Rickerby. You tell me."

Time was on my side now. I could afford a little bit of it. He couldn't. He was going to have to get to a phone to let someone bigger than he was know that The Dragon wasn't a secret any longer. He flipped the mental coin and that someone lost. He turned slowly and took his glasses off, wiping them on a handkerchief. They were all fogged up. "The Dragon is a team."

"So is Rutgers."

The joke didn't go across. Ignoring it, he said, "It's a code name for an execution team. There are two parts, Tooth and Nail."

I turned the glass around in my hand, staring at it, waiting. I asked, "Commies?"

"Yes." His reluctance was almost tangible. He finally said, "I can name persons throughout the world in critical positions in government who have died lately, some violently, some of natural causes apparently. You would probably recognize their names."

"I doubt it. I've been out of circulation for seven years."

He put the glasses on again and looked at the backbar. "I wonder," he mused to himself.

"The Dragon, Rickerby, if it were so important, how come the name never appeared? With a name like that it was bound to show."

"Hell," he said, "it was *our* code name, not theirs." His hands made an innocuous gesture, then folded together. "And now that you know something no one outside our agency knows, perhaps you'll tell *me* a little something about The Dragon."

"Sure," I said, and I watched his face closely. "The Dragon killed Richie."

Nothing showed.

"Now The Dragon is trying to kill Velda."

Still nothing showed, but he said calmly, "How do you know?"

"Richie told me. That's what he told me before he died. So she couldn't be tied up with the other side, could she?"

Unexpectedly, he smiled, tight and deadly and you really couldn't tell what he was thinking. "You never know," Art answered. "When their own kind slip from grace, they too become targets. We have such in our records. It isn't even unusual."

"You bastard."

"You know too much, Mr. Hammer. You might become a target yourself."

"I wouldn't be surprised."

He took a bill from his pocket and put it on the bar. John took it, totaled up the check and hit the register. When he gave the change back Art said, "Thanks for being so candid. Thank you for The Dragon."

"You leaving it like that?"

"I think that's it, don't you?"

"Sucker," I said.

He stopped halfway off his stool.

"You don't think I'd be that stupid, do you? Even after seven years I wouldn't be that much of a joker."

For a minute he was the placid little gray man I had first met, then almost sorrowfully he nodded and said, "I'm losing my insight. I thought I had it all. What else do you know?"

I took a long pull of the Blue Ribbon and finished the glass. When I put it down I said to him, "Richie told me something else that could put his killer in front of a gun."

"And just what is it you want for this piece of information?"

"Not much." I grinned. "Just an official capacity in some department or another so that I can carry a gun."

"Like in the old days," he said.

"Like in the old days," I repeated.

CHAPTER 8

Hy Gardner was taping a show and I didn't get to see him until it was over. We had a whole empty studio to ourselves, the guest chairs to relax in and for a change a quiet that was foreign to New York.

When he lit his cigar and had a comfortable wreath of smoke over his head he said, "How's things going, Mike?"

"Looking up. Why, what have you heard?"

"A little here and there." He shrugged. "You've been seen around." Then he laughed with the cigar in his teeth and put his feet up on the coffee table prop. "I heard about the business down in Benny Joe Grissi's place. You sure snapped back in a hurry."

"Hell, I don't have time to train. Who put you on the bit?"

"Old Bayliss Henry still has his traditional afternoon drink at Ted's with the rest of us. He knew we were pretty good friends."

"What did he tell you?"

Hy grinned again. "Only about the fight. He knew that would get around. I'd sooner hear the rest from you anyway."

"Sure."

"Should I tape notes?"

"Not yet. It's not that big yet, but you can do something for me."

"Just say it."

"How are your overseas connections?"

Hy took the cigar out, studied it and knocked off the ash. "I figure the next question is going to be a beauty."

"It is."

"Okay," he nodded. "In this business you have to have friends.

Reporters aren't amateurs, they have sources of information and almost as many ways of getting what they want as Interpol has."

"Can you code a request to your friends and get an answer back the same way?"

After a moment he nodded.

"Swell. Then find out what anybody knows about The Dragon."

The cigar went back, he dragged on it slowly and let out a thin stream of smoke.

I said, "That's a code name too. Dragon is an execution team. Our side gave it the tag and it's a top secret bit, but that kind of stew is generally the easiest to stir once you take the lid off the kettle."

"You don't play around, do you?"

"I told you, I haven't got time."

"Damn, Mike, you're really sticking it out, aren't you?"

"You'll get the story."

"I hope you're alive long enough to give it to me. The kind of game you're playing has put a lot of good men down for keeps."

"I'm not exactly a patsy," I said.

"You're not the same Mike Hammer you were either, friend."

"When can you get the information off?" I asked him.

"Like now," he told me.

There was a pay phone in the corridor outside. The request went through Bell's dial system to the right party and the relay was assured. The answer would come into Hy's office at the paper coded within a regular news transmission and the favor was expected to be returned when needed.

Hy hung up and turned around. "Now what?"

"Let's eat, then take a run down to the office of a cop who used to be a friend."

I knocked and he said to come in and when he saw who it was his face steeled into an expression that was so noncommittal it was pure betrayal. Behind it was all the resentment and animosity he had let spew out earlier, but this time it was under control.

Dr. Larry Snyder was sprawled out in a wooden desk chair left over from the gaslight era, a surprised smile touching the corner of his mouth as he nodded to me.

I said, "Hy Gardner, Dr. Larry Snyder. I think you know Pat Chambers."

"Hi, Larry. Yes, I know Captain Chambers."

They nodded all around, the pleasantries all a fat fake, then Hy took the other chair facing the desk and sat down. I just stood there looking down at Pat so he could know that I didn't give a damn for him either if he wanted it that way.

Pat's voice had a cutting edge to it and he took in Hy with a curt nod. "Why the party?"

Hy's got an interest in the story end."

"We have a procedure for those things."

"Maybe you have, but I don't and this is the way it's going to be, old buddy."

"Knock it off."

Quietly, Larry said, "Maybe it's a good thing I brought my medical bag, but if either one of you had any sense you'd keep it all talk until you find the right answers."

"Shut up, Larry," Pat snarled, "you don't know anything about this."

"You'd be surprised at what I know," he told him. Pat let his eyes drift to Larry's and he frowned. Then all his years took hold and his face went blank again.

I said, "What did ballistics come up with?"

He didn't answer me and didn't have to. I knew by his silence that the slug matched the others. He leaned on the desk, his hands folded together and when he was ready he said, "Okay, where did you get it?"

"We had something to trade, remember?"

His grin was too crooked. "Not necessarily."

But my grin was just as crooked. "The hell it isn't. Time isn't working against me anymore, kiddo. I can hold out on you as long as I feel like it."

Pat half started to rise and Larry said cautioningly, "Easy, Pat."

He let out a grunt of disgust and sat down again. In a way he was like Art, always thinking, but covering the machinery of his mind with clever little moves. But I had known Pat too long and too well. I knew his play and could read the signs. When he handed me the photostat I was smiling even dirtier and he let me keep on with it until I felt the grin go tight as a drum, then pull into a harsh grimace. When I looked at Pat his face mirrored my own, only his had hate in it.

"Read it out loud," he said.

"Drop dead."

"No," he insisted, his voice almost paternal, a woodshed voice taking pleasure in the whipping, "go ahead and read it."

Silently, I read it again. Velda had been an active agent for the O.S.I. during the war, certain code numbers in the Washington files given for reference, and her grade and time in that type of service had qualified her for a Private Investigator's ticket in the State of New York.

Pat waited, then finally, "Well?"

I handed back the photostat. It was my turn to shrug, then I gave him the address in Brooklyn where Cole had lived and told him where he could find the hole the slug made. I wondered what he'd do when he turned up Velda's picture.

He let me finish, picked up the phone and dialed an extension. A few minutes later another officer laid a folder on his desk and Pat opened it to scan the sheet inside. The first report was enough. He closed the folder and rocked back in the chair. "There were two shots. They didn't come from the same gun. One person considered competent said the second was a large-bore gun, most likely a .45."

"How about that," I said.

His eyes were tight and hard now. "You're being cute, Mike. You're playing guns again. I'm going to catch you at it and then your ass is going to be hung high. You kill anybody on this prod and I'll be there to watch them strap you in the hot squat. I could push you a little more on this right now and maybe see you take a fall, but if I do it won't be enough to satisfy me. When you go down, I want to see you fall all the way, a six-foot fall like the man said."

"Thanks a bunch."

"No trouble," he smiled casually.

I glanced at Larry, then nodded toward Pat. "He's a sick man, Doctor. He won't admit it, but he *was* in love with her too."

Pat's expression didn't change a bit.

"Weren't you?" I asked him.

He waited until Hy and I were at the door and I had turned around to look at him again and this time I wasn't going to leave until he had answered me. He didn't hesitate. Softly, he said, "Yes, damn you."

On the street Hy steered me toward a bar near the Trib Building. We picked a booth in the back, ordered a pair of frigid Blue Ribbons and toasted each other silently when they came. Hy said, "I'm thinking like Alice in Wonderland now, that things keep getting curiouser and curiouser. You've given me a little bit and now I want more. It's fun writing a Broadway column and throwing out squibs about famous people and all that jazz, but essentially I'm a reporter and it wouldn't feel bad at all to do a little poking and prying again for a change."

"I don't know where to start, Hy."

"Well, give it a try."

"All right. How about this one? *Butterfly Two, Gerald Erlich.*"

The beer stopped halfway to his mouth. "How did you know about Butterfly Two?"

"How did *you* know about it?"

"That's war stuff, friend. Do you know what I was then?"

"A captain in special services, you told me."

"That's right. I was. But it was a cover assignment at times too. I was also useful in several other capacities besides."

"Don't tell me you were a spy."

"Let's say I just kept my ear to the ground regarding certain activities. But what's this business about Butterfly Two and Erlich? That's seventeen years old now and out of style."

"Is it?"

"Hell, Mike, when that Nazi war machine—" Then he got the tone of my voice and put the glass down, his eyes watching me closely. "Let's have it, Mike."

"Butterfly Two isn't as out of style as you think."

"Look—"

"And what about Gerald Erlich?"

"Presumed dead."

"Proof?"

"None, but damn it, Mike—"

"Look, there are too many suppositions."

"What are you driving at, anyway? Man, don't tell me about Gerald Erlich. I had contact with him on three different occasions. The first two I knew him only as an allied officer, the third time I saw him in a detention camp after the war but didn't realize who he was until I went over it in my mind for a couple of hours. When I went back there the prisoners had been transferred and the truck they were riding in had hit a land mine taking a detour around a bombed bridge. It was the same truck Giesler was on, the SS Colonel who had all the prisoners killed during the Battle of the Bulge."

"You saw the body?"

"No, but the survivors were brought in and he wasn't among them."

"Presumed dead?"

"What else do you need? Listen, I even have a picture of the guy I took at that camp and some of those survivors when they were brought back. He wasn't in that bunch at all."

I perched forward on my chair, my hands flat on the table. "You have *what?*"

Surprised at the edge in my voice, he pulled out another one of those cigars. "They're in my personal stuff upstairs." He waved a thumb toward the street.

"Tell me something, Hy," I said. "Are you cold on these details?"

He caught on quick. "When I got out of the army, friend, I got out. All the way. I was never that big that they called me back as a consultant."

"Can we see those photos?"

"Sure. Why not?"

I picked up my beer, finished it, waited for him to finish his, then followed him out. We went back through the press section of the paper, took the service elevator up and got out at Hy's floor. Except for a handful of night men, the place was empty, a gigantic echo chamber that magnified the sound of our feet against the tiled floor. Hy unlocked his office, flipped on the light and pointed to a chair.

It took him five minutes of rummaging through his old files, but he finally came up with the photos. They were 120 contact sheets still in a military folder that was getting stiff and yellow around the edges and when he laid them out he pointed to one in the top left-hand corner and gave me an enlarging glass to bring out the image.

His face came in loud and clear, chunky features that bore all the physical traits of a soldier with overtones of one used to command. The eyes were hard, the mouth a tight slash as they looked contemptuously at the camera.

Almost as if he knew what was going to happen, I thought.

Unlike the others, there was no harried expression, no trace of fear. Nor did he have the stolid composure of a prisoner. Again, it was as if he were not really a prisoner at all.

Hy pointed to the shots of the survivors of the accident. He wasn't in any of those. The mangled bodies of the dead were unrecognizable.

Hy said, "Know him?"

I handed the photos back. "No."

"Sure?"

"I never forget faces."

"Then that's one angle out."

"Yeah," I said.

"But where did you ever get hold of that bit?"

I reached for my hat. "Have you ever heard of a red herring?"

Hy chuckled and nodded. "I've dropped a few in my life."

"I think I might have picked one up. It stinks."

"So drop it. What are you going to do now?"

"Not drop it, old buddy. It stinks just a little too bad to be true. No, there's another side to this Erlich angle I'd like to find out about."

"Clue me."

"Senator Knapp."

"The Missile Man, Mr. America. Now how does he come in?"

"He comes in because he's dead. The same bullet killed him as Richie Cole and the same gun shot at me. That package on Knapp that you gave me spelled out his war record pretty well. He was a light colonel when he went in and a major general when he came out. I'm wondering if I could tie his name in with Erlich's anyplace."

Hy's mouth came open and he nearly lost the cigar. *"Knapp working for another country?"*

"Hell no," I told him. "Were you?"

"But—"

"He could have had a cover assignment too."

"For Pete's sake, Mike, if Knapp had a job other than what was known he could have made political capital of it and—"

"Who knew about yours?"

"Well—nobody, naturally. At least, not until now," he added.

"No friends?"

"No."

"Only authorized personnel."

"Exactly. And they were mighty damn limited."

"Does Marilyn know about it now?"

"Mike—"

"Does she?"

"Sure, I told her one time, but all that stuff is seventeen years old. She listened politely like a wife will, made some silly remark and that was it."

"The thing is, she knows about it."

"Yes. So what?"

"Maybe Laura Knapp does too."

Hy sat back again, sticking the cigar in his mouth. "Boy," he said, "you sure are a cagey one. You'll rationalize anything just to see that broad again, won't you?"

I laughed back at him. "Could be," I said. "Can I borrow that photo of Erlich?"

From his desk Hy pulled a pair of shears, cut out the shot of the Nazi agent and handed it to me. "Have fun, but you're chasing a ghost now."

"That's how it goes. But at least if you run around long enough something will show up."

"Yeah, like a broad."

"Yeah," I repeated, then reached for my hat and left.

———

Duck-Duck Jones told me that they had pulled the cop off Old Dewey's place. A relative had showed up, some old dame who claimed to be his half sister and had taken over Dewey's affairs. The only thing she couldn't touch was the newsstand which he had left to Duck-Duck in a surprise letter held by Bucky Harris who owned the Clover Bar. Even Duck-Duck could hardly believe it, but now pride of ownership had taken hold and he was happy to take up where the old man left off.

When I had his ear I said, "Listen, Duck-Duck, before Dewey got bumped a guy left something with him to give to me."

"Yeah? Like what, Mike?"

"I don't know. A package or something. Maybe an envelope. Anyway, did you see anything laying around here with my name on it? Or just an unmarked thing."

Duck folded a paper and thrust it at a customer, made change and turned back to me again. "I don't see nuttin', Mike. Honest. Besides, there ain't no place to hide nuttin' here. You wanna look around?"

I shook my head. "Naw, you would have found it by now."

"Well what you want I should do if somethin' shows up?"

"Hang onto it, Duck. I'll be back." I picked up a paper and threw a dime down.

I started to leave and Duck stopped me. "Hey, Mike, you still gonna do business here? Dewey got you down for some stuff."

"You keep me on the list, Duck. I'll pick up everything in a day or two."

I waved, waited for the light and headed west across town. It was a long walk, but at the end of it was a guy who owed me two hundred bucks and had the chips to pay off on the spot. Then I hopped a cab to the car rental agency on Forty-ninth, took my time about picking out a Ford coupé and turned toward the West Side Drive.

It had turned out to be a beautiful day, it was almost noon, the sun was hot, and once on the New York Thruway I had the wide concrete road nearly to myself. I stayed at the posted sixty and occasionally some fireball would come blasting by, otherwise it was a smooth run with only a few trucks to pass. Just before I reached Harriman I saw the other car behind me close to a quarter mile and hold there. Fifteen miles further at the Newburgh entrance it was still there so I stepped it up to seventy. Momentarily, the distance widened, then closed and we stayed like that. Then just before the New Paltz exit the car began to close the gap, reached me, passed and kept on going. It was a dark blue Buick Special with a driver lazing behind the wheel and as he went by all the tension left my shoulders. What he had just pulled was a typical tricky habit of a guy who had driven a long way—staying behind a car until boredom set in, then running for it to find a new pacer for a while. I eased off back to sixty, turned through the toll gate at Kingston, picked up Route 28 and loafed my way up to the chalet called The Willows and when I cut the motor of the car I could hear music coming through the trees from behind the house and knew that she was waiting for me.

She was lying in the grass at the edge of the pool, stretched out on an oversized towel with her face cradled in her intertwined fingers. Her hair spilled forward over her head, letting the sun tan her neck, her arms pulled forward so that lines of muscles were in gentle bas-relief down her back into her hips. Her legs were stretched wide in open supplication of the inveterate sun worshipper and her skin glistened with a fine, golden sweat.

Beside her the shortwave portable boomed in a symphony, the thunder of it obliterating any sound of my feet. I sat there beside her, quietly, looking at the beauty of those long legs and the pert way her breasts flattened against the towel, and after long minutes passed the music became muted and drifted off into a finale of silence.

I said, "Hello, Laura," and she started as though suddenly awakened from sleep, then realizing the state of affairs, reached for the edge of the towel to flip it around her. I let out a small laugh and did it for her.

She rolled over, eyes wide, then saw me and laughed back. "Hey, you."

"You'll get your tail burned lying around like that."

"It's worse having people sneak up on you."

I shrugged and tucked my feet under me. "It was worth it. People like me don't get to see such lovely sights very often."

Her eyes lit up impishly. "That's a lie. Besides, I'm not that new to you," she reminded me.

"Out in the sunlight you are, kitten. You take on an entirely new perspective."

"Are you making love or being clinical?" she demanded.

"I don't know. One thing could lead into another."

"Then maybe we should just let nature take its course."

"Maybe."

"Feel like a swim?"

"I didn't bring a suit."

"Well . . ." and she grinned again.

I gave her a poke in the ribs with my forefinger and she grunted. "There are some things I'm prudish about, baby."

"Well I'll be damned," she whispered in amazement. "You never can tell, can you?"

"Sometimes never."

"There are extra suits in the bathhouse."

"That sounds better."

"Then let me go get into one first. I'm not going to be all skin while you play coward."

I reached for her but she was too fast, springing to her feet with the rebounding motion of a tumbler. She swung the towel sari-fashion around herself and smiled, knowing she was suddenly more desirable then than when she was naked. She let me eat her with my eyes for a second, then ran off boyishly, skirting the pool, and disappeared into the dressing room on the other side.

She came back out a minute later in the briefest black bikini I had ever seen, holding up a pair of shorts for me. She dropped them on a chair, took a run for the pool and dove in. I was a nut for letting myself feel like a colt, but the day was right, the woman was right and those seven years had been a long, hard grind. I walked over, picked up the shorts and without bothering to turn on the overhead light got dressed and went back out to the big, big day.

Underwater she was like an eel, golden brown, the black of the bikini making only the barest slashes against her skin. She was slippery and luscious and more tantalizing than a woman had a right to be. She surged up out of the water and sat on the edge of the pool with her stomach sucked in so that a muscular valley ran from her navel up into the cleft of her breasts, whose curves arched up in proud nakedness a long way before feeling the constraint of the miniature halter.

She laughed, stuck her tongue out at me and walked to the grass by the radio and sat down. I said, "Damn," softly, waited a bit, then followed her.

When I was comfortable she put her hand out on mine, making me seem almost prison-pale by comparison. "Now we can talk, Mike. You didn't come all the way up here just to see me, did you?"

"I didn't think so before I left."

She closed her fingers over my wrist. "Can I tell you something very frankly?"

"Be my guest."

"I like you, big man."

I turned my head and nipped at her forearm. "The feeling's mutual, big girl. It shouldn't be though."

"Why not?" Her eyes were steady and direct, deep and warm as they watched and waited for the answer.

"Because we're not at all alike. We're miles apart in the things we do and the way we think. I'm a trouble character, honey. It's always been that way and it isn't going to change. So be smart. Don't encourage me because I'll only be too anxious to get in the game. We had a pretty hello and a wonderful beginning and I came up here on a damn flimsy pretext because I was hungry for you and now that I've had a taste again I feel like a pig and want it all."

"Ummmm," Laura said.

"Don't laugh," I told her. "White eyes is not speaking with forked tongue. This old soldier has been around."

"There and back?'

"All the way, buddy."

Her grin was the kind they paint on pixie dolls. "Okay, old soldier, so kill me."

"It'll take days and days."

"Ummm," she said again. "But tell me your pretext for coming in the first place."

I reached out and turned the radio down. "It's about Leo."

The smile faded and her eyes crinkled at the corners. "Oh?"

"Did he ever tell you about his—well, job let's say, during the war?"

She didn't seem certain of what I asked. "Well, he was a general. He was on General Stoeffler's staff."

"I know that. But what did he *do*? Did he ever speak about what his job was?"

Again, she looked at me, puzzled. "Yes. Procurement was their job. He never went into great detail and I always thought it was because he never saw any direct action. He seemed rather ashamed of the fact."

I felt myself make a disgusted face.

"Is there—anything specific—like—"

"No," I said bluntly, "it's just that I wondered if he could possibly have had an undercover job."

"I don't understand, Mike." She propped herself up on one elbow and stared at me. "Are you asking if Leo was part of the cloak-and-dagger set?"

I nodded.

The puzzled look came back again and she moved her head in easy negative. "I think I would have known. I've seen all his old personal stuff from the war, his decorations, his photos, his letters of commendation and heard what stories he had to tell. But as I said, he always seemed to be ashamed that he wasn't on the front line getting shot at. Fortunately, the country had a better need for him."

"It was a good try," I said and sat up.

"I'm sorry, Mike."

Then I thought of something, told her to wait and went back to the bathhouse. I got dressed and saw the disappointment in her eyes from all the way across the pool when I came out, but the line had to be drawn someplace.

Laura gave me a look of mock disgust and patted the grass next to her. When I squatted down I took out the photo of Gerald Erlich and passed it over. "Take a look, honey. Have you ever seen that face in any of your husband's effects?"

She studied it, her eyes squinting in the sun, and when she had made sure she handed it back. "No, I never have. Who is he?"

"His name used to be Gerald Erlich. He was a trained espionage agent working for the Nazis during the war."

"But what did he have to do with Leo?"

"I don't know," I told her. "His name has been coming up a little too often to be coincidental."

"Mike—" She bit her lip, thinking, then: "I have Leo's effects in the house. Do you think you might find something useful in them? They might make more sense to you than they do to me."

"It sure won't hurt to look." I held out my hand to help her up and that was as far as I got. The radio between us suddenly burst apart almost spontaneously and slammed backward into the pool.

I gave her a shove that threw her ten feet away, rolled the other way and got to my feet running like hell for the west side of the house. It had to have been a shot and from the direction the radio skidded I could figure the origin. It had to be a silenced blast from a pistol because a rifle would have had either Laura or me with no trouble at all. I skirted the trees, stopped and listened, and from almost directly ahead I heard a door slam and headed for it wishing I had kept the .45 on me and to hell with Pat. The bushes were too thick to break through so I had to cut down the driveway, the gravel crunching under my feet. I never had a chance. All I saw was the tail end of a dark blue Buick Special pulling away to make a turn that hid it completely.

And now the picture was coming out a little clearer. It hadn't been a tired driver on the Thruway at all. The bastard had picked me up at Duck's stand, figured he had given me something when he had handed me the paper, probably hired a car the same time I did with plenty of time to do it in since I wasn't hurrying at all. He followed me until he was sure he knew where I was headed and waited me out.

Damn. It was too close. But what got me was, how many silenced shots had he fired before hitting that radio? He had been too far away for accurate shooting apparently, but he could have been plunking them all around us hoping for a hit until he got the radio. Damn!

And I was really important. He knew where I was heading. Even since I had started to operate I had had a tail on me and it had almost paid off for him. But if I were important dead, so was Laura, because now that killer could never be sure I hadn't let her in on the whole business. Another damn.

She stood over the wreckage of the portable she had fished from the pool, white showing at the corners of her mouth. Her hands trembled so that she clasped them in front of her and she breathed as though she had done the running, not me. Breathlessly, she said, "Mike—what was it? Please, Mike—"

I put my arm around her shoulder and with a queer sob she buried her face against me. When she looked up she had herself under control. "It was a shot, wasn't it?"

"That's right. A silenced gun."

"But—"

"It's the second time he's tried for me."

"Do you think—"

"He's gone for now," I said.

"But who was he?"

"I think he was The Dragon, sugar."

For a few seconds she didn't answer, then she turned her face up toward mine. "Who?"

"Nobody you know. He's an assassin. Up until now his record has been pretty good. He must be getting the jumps."

"My gracious, Mike, this is crazy! It's absolutely crazy."

I nodded in agreement. "You'll never know, but now we have a real problem. You're going to need protection."

"Me!"

"Anybody I'm close to is in trouble. The best thing we can do is call the local cops."

She gave me a dismayed glance. "But I can't—I have to be in Washington— Oh, Mike!"

"It won't be too bad in the city, kid, but out here you're too alone."

Laura thought about it, then shrugged. "I suppose you're right. After Leo was killed the police made me keep several guns handy. In fact, there's one in each room."

"Can you use them?"

Her smile was wan. "The policeman you met the last time showed me."

"Swell, but what about out here?"

"There's a shotgun in the corner of the bathhouse."

"Loaded?"

"Yes."

"A shotgun isn't exactly a handgun."

"Leo showed me how to use it. We used to shoot skeet together at the other end of the property."

"Police protection would still be your best bet."

"Can it be avoided?"

"Why stick your neck out?"

"Because from now on I'm going to be a very busy girl, Mike. Congress convenes this week and the race is on for hostess of the year."

"That stuff is a lot of crap."

"Maybe, but that's what Leo wanted."

"So he's leaving a dead hand around."

There was a hurt expression on her face. "Mike—I did love him. Please . . .?"

"Sorry, kid. I don't have much class. We bat in different leagues."

She touched me lightly, her fingers cool. "Perhaps not. I think we are really closer than you realize."

I grinned and squeezed her hand, then ran my palm along the soft swell of her flanks.

Laura smiled and said, "Are you going to—do anything about that shot?"

"Shall I?"

"It's up to you. This isn't my league now."

I made the decision quickly. "All right, we'll keep it quiet. If that slob has any sense he'll know we won't be stationary targets again. From now on I'll be doing some hunting myself."

"You sure, Mike?"

"I'm sure."

"Good. Then let's go through Leo's effects."

Inside she led me upstairs past the bedrooms to the end of the hall, opened a closet and pulled out a small trunk. I took it from her, carried it into the first bedroom and dumped the contents out on the dresser.

When you thought about it, it was funny how little a man actually accumulated during the most important years of his life. He could go through a whole war, live in foreign places with strange people, be called upon to do difficult and unnatural work, yet come away from those years with no more than he could put in a very small trunk.

Leo Knapp's 201 file was thick, proper and as military as could be. There was an attempt at a diary that ran into fifty pages, but the last third showed an obvious effort being made to overcome boredom, then the thing dwindled out. I went through every piece of paperwork there was, uncovering nothing, saving the photos until last.

Laura left me alone to work uninterruptedly, but the smell of her perfume was there in the room and from somewhere downstairs I could hear her talking on the phone. She was still tense from the experience outside and although I couldn't hear her conversation I could sense the strain in her voice. She came back in ten minutes later and sat on the edge of the bed, quiet, content just to be there, then she sighed and I knew the tension had gone out of her.

I don't know what I expected, but the results were a total negative. Of the hundreds of photos, half were taken by G.I. staff photogs and the rest an accumulation of camp and tourist shots that every soldier who ever came home had tucked away in his gear. When you were old and fat you could take them out, reminisce over the days when you were young and thin and wonder what had happened to all the rest in the picture before putting them back in storage for another decade.

Behind me Laura watched while I began putting things back in the trunk and I heard her ask, "Anything, Mike?"

"No." I half threw his medals in the pile. "Everything's as mundane as a mud pie."

"I'm sorry, Mike."

"Don't be sorry. Sometimes the mundane can hide some peculiar things. There's still a thread left to pull. If Leo had anything to do with Erlich I have a Fed for a friend who just might come up with the answer." I snapped the lock shut on the trunk. "It just gives me a pain to have everything come up so damn hard."

"Really?" Her voice laughed.

I glanced up into the mirror on the dresser and felt that wild warmth steal into my stomach like an ebullient catalyst that pulled me taut as a bowstring and left my breath hanging in my throat.

"Something should be made easy for you then," she said.

Laura was standing there now, tall and lovely, the sun still with her in the rich loamy color of her skin, the nearly bleached white tone of her hair.

At her feet the bikini made a small puddle of black like a shadow, then she walked away from it to me and I was waiting for her.

CHAPTER 9

Night and the rain had come back to New York, the air musty with dust driven up by the sudden surge of the downpour. The bars were filled, the sheltered areas under marquees crowded and an empty taxi a rare treasure to be fought over.

But it was a night to think in. There is a peculiar anonymity you can enjoy in the city on a rainy night. You're alone, yet not alone. The other people around you are merely motion and sound and the sign of life whose presence averts the panic of being truly alone, yet who observe the rules of the city and stay withdrawn and far away when they are close.

How many times had Velda and I walked in the rain? She was big and our shoulders almost touched. We'd deliberately walk out of step so that our inside legs would touch rhythmically and if her arm wasn't tucked underneath mine we'd hold hands. There was a ring I had given her. I'd feel it under my fingers and she'd look at me and smile because she knew what that ring meant.

Where was she now? What had really happened? Little hammers would go at me when I thought of the days and hours since they had dragged me into Richie Cole's room to watch him die, but could it have been any other way?

Maybe not seven years ago. Not then. I wouldn't have had a booze-soaked head then. I would have had a gun and a ticket that could get me in and out of places and hands that could take care of anybody.

But now. Now I was an almost-nothing. Not quite, because I still had years of experience going for me and a reason to push. I was coming back little by little, but unless I stayed cute about it all I could be a pushover for any hardcase.

What I had to do now was think. I still had a small edge, but how long it would last was anybody's guess. So think, Mike, old soldier. Get your head going the way it's supposed to. You know who the key is. You've known it all along. Cole died with her name on his lips and ever since then she's been the key. But why? But why?

How could she still be alive?

Seven years is a long time to hide. Too long. Why? Why?

So think, old soldier. Go over the possibilities.

The rain came down a little harder and began to run off the brim of my hat. In a little while it seeped through the top of the cheap trench coat and I could feel the cold of it on my shoulders. And then I had the streets all alone again and the night and the city belonged only to me. I walked, so I was king. The others who huddled in the doorways and watched me with tired eyes were the lesser ones. Those who ran for the taxis were the scared ones. So I walked and I was able to think about Velda again. She had suddenly become *a case* and it had to be that way. It had to be cold and logical, otherwise it would vaporize into incredibility and there would be nothing left except to go back to where I had come from.

Think.

Who saw her die? No one. It was an assumption. Well assumed, but an assumption nevertheless.

Then, after seven years, who saw her alive? Richie Cole.

Sure, he had reason to know her. They were friends. War buddies. They had worked together. Once a year they'd meet for supper and a show and talk over old times. Hell, I'd done it myself with George and Earle, Ray, Mason and the others. It was nothing you could talk about to anybody else, though. Death and destruction you took part in could be shared only with those in range of the same enemy guns. With them you couldn't brag or lie. You simply recounted and wondered that you were still alive and renewed a friendship.

Cole couldn't have made a mistake. *He knew her.*

And Cole had been a pro. Velda was a pro. He had come looking for me because she had told him I was a pro and he had been disappointed at what he had seen. He had taken a look at me and his reason for staying alive died right then. Whatever it was, he didn't think I could do it. He saw a damned drunken bum who had lost every bit of himself years before and he died thinking she was going to die too and he was loathing me with eyes starting to film over with the nonexistence of death.

Richie Cole just didn't know me very well at all.

He had a chance to say the magic word and that made all the difference.

Velda.

Would it still be the same? How will *you* look after seven years? Hell, you should see me. You should see the way *I* look. And what's inside *you* after a time span like that? Things happen in seven years; things build, things dissolve. What happens to people in love? Seven years ago that's the way we were. In Love. Capital *L*. Had we stayed together time would only have lent maturity and quality to that which it served to improve.

But my love, my love, how could you look at me, me after seven years? You knew what I had been and called for me at last, but I wasn't what you expected at all. That big one you knew and loved is gone, kid, long gone, and you can't come back that big anymore. Hell, Velda, you know that. You can't come back . . . you should have known what would happen to me. Damn, you knew me well enough. And it happened. So how can you yell for me now? *I know you knew what I'd be like, and you asked for me anyway.*

I let out a little laugh and only the rain could enjoy it with me. She knew, all right. You can't come back just as big. Either lesser or bigger. There was no other answer. She just didn't know the odds against the right choice.

There was a new man on the elevator now. I signed the night book, nodded to him and gave him my floor. I got off at eight and went down the hall, watching my shadow grow longer and longer from the single light behind me.

I had my keys in my hand, but I didn't need them at all. The door to 808 stood wide open invitingly, the lights inside throwing a warm glow over the dust and the furniture and when I closed it behind me I went through the anteroom to my office where Art

Rickerby was sitting and picked up the sandwich and Blue Ribbon beer he had waiting for me and sat down on the edge of the couch and didn't say a word until I had finished both.

Art said, "Your friend Nat Drutman gave me the key."

"It's okay."

"I pushed him a little."

"He's been pushed before. If he couldn't read you right you wouldn't have gotten the key. Don't sell him short."

"I figured as much."

I got up, took off the soggy coat and hat and threw them across a chair. "What's with the visit? I hope you're not getting too impatient."

"No. Patience is something inbred. Nothing I can do will bring Richie back. All I can do is play the angles, the curves, float along the stream of time, then, my friend, something will bite, even on an unbaited hook."

"Shit."

"You know it's like that. You're a cop."

"A long time ago."

He watched me, a funny smile on his face. "No. *Now.* I know the signs. I've been in this business too long."

"So what do you want here?"

Rickerby's smile broadened. "I told you once. I'll do anything to get Richie's killer."

"Oh?"

He reached in his pocket and brought out an envelope. I took it from him, tore it open and read the folded card it contained on all four of its sides, then slid it into my wallet and tucked it away.

"Now I can carry a gun," I said.

"Legally. In any state."

"Thanks. What did you give up to get it?"

"Not a thing. Favors were owed me too. Our department is very—wise."

"They think it's smart to let me carry a rod again?"

"There aren't any complaints. You have your—ticket."

"It's a little different from the last one this state gave me."

"Don't look a gift horse in the mouth, my friend."

"Okay. Thanks."

"No trouble. I'm being smug."

"Why?"

He took off his glasses again, wiped them and put them back on. "Because I have found out all about you a person could find. You're going to do something I can't possibly do because you have the key to it all and won't let it go. Whatever your motives are, they aren't mine, but they encompass what I want and that's enough for me. Sooner or later you're going to name Richie's killer and that's all I want. In the meantime, rather than interfere with your operation, I'll do everything I can to supplement it. Do you understand?"

"I think so," I said.

"Good. Then I'll wait you out." He smiled, but there was nothing pleasant in his expression. "Some people are different from others. You're a killer, Mike. You've always been a killer. Somehow your actions have been justified and I think righteously so, but nevertheless, you're a killer. You're on a hunt again and I'm going to help you. There's just one thing I ask."

"What?"

"If you do find Richie's murderer before me, don't kill him."

I looked up from the fists I had made. "Why?"

"I want him, Mike. Let him be mine."

"What will you do with him?"

Rickerby's grin was damn near inhuman. It was a look I had seen before on other people and never would have expected from him. "A quick kill would be too good, Mike," he told me slowly. "But the law—this supposedly just, merciful provision—this is the most cruel of all. It lets you rot in a death cell for months and deteriorate slowly until you're only an accumulation of living cells with the consciousness of knowing you are about to die; then the creature is tied in a chair and jazzed with a hot shot that wipes him from the face of the earth with one big jolt and that's that."

"Pleasant thought," I said.

"Isn't it, though? Too many people think the sudden kill is the perfect answer for revenge. Ah, no, my friend. It's the waiting. It's the knowing beforehand that even the merciful provisions of a public trial will only result in what you already know—more waiting and further contemplation of that little room where you spend your last days with death in an oaken chair only a few yards away.

And do you know what? I'll see that killer every day. I'll savor his anguish like a fine drink and be there as a witness when he burns and he'll see me and know why I'm there and when he's finished I'll be satisfied."

"You got a mean streak a yard wide, Rickerby."

"But it doesn't quite match yours, Mike."

"The hell it doesn't."

"No—you'll see what I mean some day. You'll see yourself express the violence of thought and action in a way I'd never do. True violence isn't in the deed itself. It's the contemplation and enjoyment of the deed."

"Come off it."

Rickerby smiled, the intensity of hatred he was filled with a moment ago seeping out slowly. If it had been me I would have been shaking like a leaf, but now he casually reached out for the can of beer, sipped at it coolly and put it down.

"I have some information you requested," he told me.

While I waited I walked behind the desk, sat down and pulled open the lower drawer. The shoulder holster was still supple although it had lain there seven years. I took off my jacket, slipped it on and put my coat back.

Art said, "I—managed to find out about Gerald Erlich."

I could feel the pulse in my arm throb against the arm of the chair. I still waited.

"Erlich is dead, my friend."

I let my breath out slowly, hoping my face didn't show how I felt.

"He died five years ago and his body was positively identified."

Five years ago! But he was supposed to have died during the war!

"He was found shot in the head in the Eastern Zone of Germany. After the war he had been fingerprinted and classified along with other prisoners of note so there was no doubt as to his identity." Art stopped a moment, studied me, then went on. "Apparently this man was trying to make the Western Zone. On his person were papers and articles that showed he had come out of Russia, there were signs that he had been under severe punishment and if you want to speculate, you might say that he had escaped from a prison and was tracked down just yards from freedom."

"That's pretty good information to come out of the Eastern Zone," I said.

Rickerby nodded sagely. "We have people there. They purposely investigate things of this sort. There's nothing coincidental about it.

"There's more."

His eyes were funny. They had an oblique quality as if they watched something totally foreign, something they had never realized could exist before. They watched and waited. Then he said, "Erlich had an importance we really didn't understand until lately. He was the nucleus of an organization of espionage agents the like of which had never been developed before and whose importance remained intact even after the downfall of the Third Reich. It was an organization so ruthless that its members, in order to pursue their own ends, would go with any government they thought capable of winning a present global conflict and apparently they selected the Reds. To oppose them and us meant fighting two battles, so it would be better to support one until the other lost, then undermine that one until it could take over."

"Crazy," I said.

"Is it?"

"They can't win."

"But they can certainly bring on some incredible devastation."

"Then why kill Erlich?"

Art sat back and folded his hands together in a familiar way. "Simple. He defected. He wanted out. Let's say he got smart in his late years and realized the personal futility of pushing this thing any further. He wanted to spend a few years in peace."

It was reasonable in a way. I nodded.

"But he had to die," Art continued. "There was one thing he knew that was known only to the next in line in the chain of command, the ones taking over the organization."

"Like what?"

"He knew every agent in the group. He could bust the whole shebang up if he spilled his guts to the West and the idea of world conquest by the Reds or the others would go smack down the drain."

"This you know?" I asked.

He shook his head. "No. Let's say I'm sure of it, but I don't *know* it. At this point I really don't care. It's the rest of the story I pulled out of the hat I'm interested in." And now his eyes cocked themselves up at me again. "He was tracked down and killed by one known to the Reds as their chief assassin agent, Gorlin, but to us as The Dragon."

If he could have had his hand on my chest, or even have touched me anywhere, he would have known what was happening. My guts would knot and churn and my head was filled with a wild flushing sensation of blood almost bursting through their walls. But he didn't touch me and he couldn't tell from my face so his eyes looked at me even a little more obliquely, expecting even the slightest reaction and getting none. None at all.

"You're a cold-blooded bastard," he nearly whispered.

"You said that before."

He blinked owlishly behind his glasses and stood up, his coat over his arm. "You know where to reach me."

"I know."

"Do you need anything?"

"Not now. Thanks for the ticket."

"No trouble. Will you promise me something?"

"Sure."

"Just don't use that gun on The Dragon."

"I won't kill him, Art."

"No. Leave that for me. Don't spoil my pleasure or yours either."

He went out, closing the door softly behind him. I pulled the center desk drawer out, got the extra clip and the box of shells from the niche and closed the drawer.

The package I had mailed to myself was on the table by the door where Nat always put my packages when he had to take them from the mailman. I ripped it open, took out the .45, checked the action and dropped it in the holster.

Now it was just like old times.

I turned off the light in my office and went outside. I was reaching for the door when the phone on Velda's desk went off with a sudden jangling that shook me for a second before I could pick it up.

Her voice was rich and vibrant when she said hello and I wanted her right there with me right then. She knew it too, and her laugh rippled across the miles. She said, "Are you going to be busy tonight, Mike?"

Time was something I had too little of, but I had too little of her too. "Well—why?"

"Because I'm coming into your big city."

"Isn't it kind of late?"

"No. I have to be there at ten p.m. to see a friend of yours and since I see no sense of wasting the evening I thought that whatever you have to do you can do it with me. Or can you?"

"It takes two to dance, baby."

She laughed again. "I didn't mean it *that* way."

"Sure, come on in. If I said not to I'd be lying. Who's my friend you have a date with?"

"An old friend and new enemy. Captain Chambers."

"What is this?"

"I don't know. He called and asked if I could come in. It would simplify things since his going out of his jurisdiction requires a lot of work."

"For Pete's sake—"

"Mike—I don't mind, really. If it has to do with Leo's death, well, I'll do anything. You know that."

"Yeah, but—"

"Besides, it gives me an excuse to see you even sooner than I hoped. Okay?"

"Okay."

"See you in a little while, Mike. Any special place?"

"Moriarty's at Sixth and Fifty-second. I'll be at the bar."

"Real quick," she said and hung up.

I held the disconnect bar down with my finger. Time. Seven years' worth just wasted and now there was none left. I let the bar up and dialed Hy Gardner's private number at the paper, hoping I'd be lucky enough to catch him in. I was.

He said, "Mike, if you're not doing anything, come on up here. I have to get my column out and I'll be done before you're here. I have something to show you."

"Important?"

"Brother, one word from you and everybody flips. Shake it up."

"Fifteen minutes."

"Good."

I hung up and pushed the phone back. When I did I uncovered a heart scratched in the surface with something sharp. Inside it was a *V* and an *M. Velda and Mike.* I pulled the phone back to cover it, climbed into my coat and went outside. Just to be sure I still had the night to myself I walked down, out the back way through the drugstore then headed south on Broadway toward Hy's office.

Marilyn opened the door and hugged me hello, a pretty grin lighting her face up. She said, "Hy's inside waiting for you. He won't tell me what it's all about."

"You're his wife now, not his secretary anymore. You don't work for him."

"The heck I don't. But he still won't tell me."

"It's man talk, sugar."

"All right, I'll let you be. I'll get some coffee—and Mike—" I turned around.

"It's good to have you back."

When I winked she blew me a kiss and scurried out the door.

Hy was at his desk inside with his glasses up on his forehead, frowning at some sheets in his hand. They were covered with penciled notations apparently culled from another batch beside his elbow.

I pulled up a chair, sat down and let Hy finish what he was doing. Finally he glanced up, pulling his glasses down. "I got your message across."

"So?"

"So it was like I dropped a bomb in HQ. Over there they seem to know things we don't read in the paper here." He leaned forward and tapped the sheets in his hand. "This bit of The Dragon is the hottest item in the cold war, buddy. Are you sure you know what you're up to?"

"Uh-huh."

"Okay, I'll go along with you. The Reds are engaged in an operation under code name REN. It's a chase thing. Behind the Iron Curtain there has been a little hell to pay the last few years. Somebody was loose back there who could rock the whole Soviet system and that one had to be eliminated. That's where The Dragon came in. This one has been on that chase and was close to making his hit. Nobody knows what the score really is." He stopped then, pushed his glasses back up and said seriously, "Or do they, Mike?"

"They?"

I should have been shaking. I should have been feeling some emotion, some wildness like I used to. What had happened? But maybe it was better this way. I could feel the weight of the .45 against my side and tightened my arm down on it lovingly. "They're after Velda," I said. "It's her. They're hunting her."

Hy squeezed his mouth shut and didn't say anything for a full minute. He laid the papers down and leaned back in his chair. "Why, Mike?"

"I don't know, Hy. I don't know why at all."

"If what I heard is true she doesn't have a chance."

"She has a chance," I told him softly.

"Maybe it really isn't her at all, Mike."

I didn't answer him. Behind us the door opened and Marilyn came in. She flipped an envelope on Hy's desk and set down the coffee container. "Here's a picture that just came off the wires. Del said you requested it."

Hy looked at me a little too quickly, opened the envelope and took out the photo. He studied it, then passed it across.

It really wasn't a good picture at all. The original had been fuzzy to start with and transmission electrically hadn't improved it any. She stood outside a building, a tall girl with seemingly black hair longer than I remembered it, features not quite clear and whose shape and posture were hidden under bulky Eastern European style clothing. Still, there was that indefinable something, some subtlety in the way she stood, some trait that came through the clothing and poor photography that I couldn't help but see.

I handed the photo back. "It's Velda."

"My German friend said the picture was several years old."

"Who had it?"

"A Red agent who was killed in a skirmish with some West German cops. It came off his body. I'd say he had been assigned to REN too and the picture was for identification purposes."

"Is this common information?"

Hy shook his head. "I'd say no. Rather than classify this thing government sources simply refuse to admit it exists. We came on it separately."

I said, "The government knows it exists."

"You know too damn much, Mike."

"No, not enough. I don't know where she is now."

"I can tell you one thing," Hy said.

"Oh?"

"She isn't in Europe any longer. The locale of REN has changed. The Dragon has left Europe. His victim got away somehow and all indications point to them both being in this country."

Very slowly, I got up, put my coat and hat on and stretched the dampness out of my shoulders. I said, "Thanks, Hy."

"Don't you want your coffee?"

"Not now."

He opened a drawer, took out a thick manila envelope and handed it to me. "Here. You might want to read up a little more on Senator Knapp. It's confidential stuff. Gives you an idea of how big he was. Save it for me."

"Sure." I stuck it carelessly in my coat pocket. "Thanks."

Marilyn said, "You all right, Mike?"

I grinned at her a little crookedly. "I'm okay."

"You don't look right," she insisted.

Hy said, "Mike—"

And I cut him short. "I'll see you later, Hy." I grinned at him too. "And thanks. Don't worry about me." I patted the gun under my coat. "I have a friend along now. Legally."

While I waited, I read about just how great a guy Leo Knapp had been. His career had been cut short at a tragic spot because it was evident that in a few more years he would have been the big man on the political scene. It was very evident that he had been one of the true powers behind the throne, a man initially responsible for military progress and missile production in spite of opposition from the knotheaded liberals and "better-Red-than-dead" slobs.

He had thwarted every attack and forced through the necessary programs and in his hands had been secrets of vital importance that made him a number-one man in the Washington setup. His death came at a good time for the enemy. The bullet that killed him came from the gun of The Dragon. A bullet from the same gun killed Richie Cole and almost killed me twice. A bullet from that same gun was waiting to kill Velda.

She came in then, the night air still on her, shaking the rain from her hair, laughing when she saw me. Her hand was cool when she took mine and climbed on the stool next to me. John brought her a martini and me another Blue Ribbon. We raised the glasses in a toast and drank the top off them.

"Good to see you," I said.

"You'll never know," she smiled.

"Where are you meeting Pat?"

She frowned, then, "Oh, Captain Chambers. Why, right here." She glanced at her watch. "In five minutes. Shall we sit at a table?"

"Let's." I picked up her glass and angled us across the room to the far wall. "Does Pat know I'll be here?"

"I didn't mention it."

"Great. Just great."

Pat was punctual, as usual. He saw me but didn't change expression. When he said hello to Laura he sat beside her and only then looked at me. "I'm glad you're here too."

"That's nice."

He was a mean, cold cop if ever there was one, his face a mask you couldn't penetrate until you looked into his eyes and saw the hate and determination there. "Where do you find your connections, Mike?"

"Why?"

"It's peculiar how a busted private dick, a damn drunken pig in trouble up to his ears can get a gun-carrying privilege we can't break. How do you do it, punk?"

I shrugged, not feeling like arguing with him. Laura looked at the two of us, wondering what was going on.

"Well, you might need it at that if you keep getting shot at. By the way, I got a description of your back alley friend. He was seen by a rather observant kid in the full light of the streetlamp. Big guy, about six-two with dark curly hair and a face with deep lines in the cheeks. His cheekbones were kind of high so he had kind of an Indian look. Ever see anybody like that?"

He was pushing me now, doing anything to set me off so he'd have a reason to get at me but sure, I saw a guy like that. He drove past me on the Thruway and I thought he was a tired driver, then he shot at me later and now I know damn well who he is. You call him The Dragon. He had a face I'd see again someday, a face I couldn't miss.

I said, "No, I don't know him." It wasn't quite a lie.

Pat smiled sardonically. "I have a feeling you will."

"So okay, I'll try to catch up with him for you."

"You do that, punk. Meanwhile I'll catch up with you. I'm putting you into this thing tighter than ever."

"Me?"

"That's right. That's why I'm glad you're here. It saves seeing you later." He had me curious now and knew it, and he was going to pull it out all the way. "There is a strange common denominator running throughout our little murder puzzle here. I'm trying to find out just what it all means."

"Please go on," Laura said.

"Gems. For some reason I can't get them out of my mind. Three times they cross in front of me." He looked at me, his eyes narrowed. "The first time when my old friend here let a girl die because of them, then when Senator Knapp was killed a batch of paste jewels were taken from the safe, and later a man known for his gem smuggling was killed with the same gun. It's a recurrent theme, isn't it, Mike? You're supposed to know about these things. In fact, it must have occurred to you too. You were quick enough about getting upstate to see Mrs. Knapp here."

"Listen, Pat."

"Shut up. There's more." He reached in his pocket and tugged at a cloth sack. "We're back to the gems again." He pulled the top open, spilled the sack upside down and watched the flood of rings, brooches and bracelets make a sparkling mound of brilliance on the table between us.

"Paste, pure paste, Mrs. Knapp, but I think they are yours."

Her hand was shaking when she reached out to touch them. She picked up the pieces one by one, examining them, then shaking her head. "Yes—they're mine! But where—"

"A pathetic old junkman was trying to peddle them in a pawnshop. The broker called the cops and we grabbed the guy. He said he found them in a garbage can a long time ago and kept them until now to sell. He figured they were stolen, all right, but didn't figure he'd get picked up like he did."

"Make your connection, Pat. So far all you showed was that a smart crook recognized paste jewelry and dumped it."

His eyes had a vicious cast to them this time. "I'm just wondering about the original gem robbery, the one your agency was hired to prevent. The name was Mr. and Mrs. Rudolph Civac. I'm wondering what kind of a deal was really pulled off there. You sent in Velda but wouldn't go yourself. I'm thinking that maybe you turned sour way back there and tried for a big score and fouled yourself up in it somehow."

His hands weren't showing so I knew one was sitting on a gun butt. I could feel myself going around the edges but hung on anyway. "You're nuts," I said, "I never even saw Civac. He made the protection deal by phone. I never laid eyes on him."

Pat felt inside his jacket and came out with a four-by-five glossy photo. "Well take a look at what your deceased customer looked like. I've been backtracking all over that case, even as cold as it is. Something's going to come up on it, buddy boy, and I hope you're square in the middle of it." He forgot me for a moment and turned to Laura. "Do you positively identify these, Mrs. Knapp?"

"Oh, yes. There's an accurate description of each piece on file and on the metal there's—"

"I saw the hallmarks."

"This ring was broken—see here where this prong is off—yes, these are mine."

"Fine. You can pick them up at my office tomorrow if you want to. I'll have to hold them until then though."

"That's all right."

He snatched the picture out of my fingers and put it back in his pocket. "You I'll be seeing soon," he told me.

I didn't answer him. I nodded, but that was all. He looked at me a moment, scowled, went to say something and changed his mind. He told Laura good-bye and walked to the door.

Fresh drinks came and I finished mine absently. Laura chuckled once and I glanced up. "You've been quiet a long time. Aren't we going to do the town?"

"Do you mind if we don't?"

She raised her eyebrows, surprised, but not at all unhappy. "No, do you want to do something else?"

"Yes. Think."

"Your place?" she asked mischievously.

"I don't have a place except my office."

"We've been there before," she teased.

But I had kissed Velda there too many times before too. "No," I said.

Laura leaned forward, serious now. "It's important, isn't it?"

"Yes."

"Then let's get out of the city entirely. Let's go back upstate to where it's cool and quiet and you can think right. Would you like to do that?"

"All right."

I paid the bill and we went outside to the night and the rain to flag down a cab to get us to the parking lot. She had to do it for me because the only thing I could think of was the face in that picture Pat had showed me.

Rudolph Civac was the same as Gerald Erlich.

CHAPTER 10

I couldn't remember the trip at all. I was asleep before we reached the West Side Drive and awakened only when she shook me. Her voice kept calling to me out of a fog and for a few seconds I thought it was Velda, then I opened my eyes and Laura was smiling at me. "We're home, Mike."

The rain had stopped, but in the stillness of the night I could hear the soft dripping from the shadows of the blue spruces around the house. Beyond them a porch and inside light threw out a pale yellow glow. "Won't your servants have something to say about me coming in?"

"No, I'm alone at night. The couple working for me come only during the day."

"I haven't seen them yet."

"Each time you were here they had the day off."

I made an annoyed grimace. "You're nuts, kid. You should keep somebody around all the time after what happened."

Her hand reached out and she traced a line around my mouth. "I'm trying to," she said. Then she leaned over and brushed me with lips that were gently damp and sweetly warm, the tip of her tongue a swift dart of flame, doing it too quickly for me to grab her to make it last.

"Quit brainwashing me," I said.

She laughed at me deep in her throat. "Never, Mister Man. I've been too long without you."

Rather than hear me answer she opened the door and slid out of the car. I came around from the other side and we went up the steps into the house together. It was a funny feeling, this coming home sensation. There was the house and the woman and the mutual desire, an instinctive demanding passion we shared, one for the other, yet realizing that there were other things that came first and not caring because there was always later.

There was a huge couch in the living room of soft, aged leather, a hidden hi-fi that played Dvořák, Beethoven and Tchaikovsky and somewhere in between Laura had gotten into yards of flowing nylon that did nothing to hide the warmth of her body or restrain the luscious bloom of her thighs and breasts. She lay there in my arms quietly, giving me all of the moment to enjoy as I pleased, only her sometimes-quickened breathing indicating her pleasure as I touched her lightly, caressing her with my fingertips. Her eyes were closed, a small satisfied smile touched the corners of her mouth and she snuggled into me with a sigh of contentment.

How long I sat there and thought about it I couldn't tell. I let it drift through my mind from beginning to end, the part I knew and the part I didn't know. Like always, a pattern was there. You can't have murder without a pattern. It weaves in and out, fabricating an artful tapestry, and while the background colors were apparent from the beginning it is only at the last that the picture itself emerges. But who was the weaver? Who sat invisibly behind the loom with shuttles of death in one hand and skeins of lives in the other? I fell asleep trying to peer behind the gigantic framework of that murder factory, a sleep so deep, after so long, that there was nothing I thought about or remembered afterward.

I was alone when the bright shaft of sunlight pouring in the room awakened me. I was stretched out comfortably, my shoes off, my tie loose and a light Indian blanket over me. I threw it off, put my shoes back on and stood up. It took me a while to figure out what was wrong, then I saw the .45 in the shoulder holster draped over the back of a chair with my coat over it and while I was reaching for it she came in with all the exuberance of a summer morning, a tray of coffee in her hands, and blew me a kiss.

"Well hello," I said.

She put the tray down and poured the coffee. "You were hard to undress."

"Why bother?"

Laura looked up laughing. "It's not easy to sleep with a man wearing a gun." She held out a cup. "Here, have some coffee. Sugar and milk?"

"Both. And I'm glad it's milk and not cream."

She fixed my cup, stirring it too. "You're a snob, Mike. In your own way you're a snob." She made a face at me and grinned. "But I love snobs."

"You should be used to them. You travel in classy company."

"They aren't snobs like you. They're just scared people putting on a front. You're the real snob. Now kiss me good morning—or afternoon. It's one o'clock." She reached up offering her mouth and I took it briefly, but even that quick touch bringing back the desire again.

Laura slid her hand under my arm and walked me through the house to the porch and out to the lawn by the pool. The sun overhead was brilliant and hot, the air filled with the smell of the mountains. She said, "Can I get you something to eat?"

I tightened my arm on her hand. "You're enough for right now."

She nuzzled my shoulder, wrinkled her nose and grinned. We both pulled out aluminum and plastic chairs, and while she went inside for the coffeepot I settled down in mine.

Now maybe I could think.

She poured another cup, knowing what was going through my mind. When she sat down opposite me she said, "Mike, would it be any good to tell me about it? I'm a good listener. I'll be somebody you can aim hypothetical questions at. Leo did this with me constantly. He called me his sounding board. He could think out loud, but doing it alone he sounded foolish to himself so he'd do it with me." She paused, her eyes earnest, wanting to help. "I'm yours for anything if you want me, Mike."

"Thanks, kitten."

I finished the coffee and put the cup down.

"You're afraid of something," she said.

"Not of. *For.* Like for you, girl. I told you once I was a trouble character. Wherever I am there's trouble and when you play guns there are stray shots and I don't want you in the way of any."

"I've already been there, remember?"

"Only because I wasn't on my toes. I've slowed up. I've been away too damn long and I'm not careful."

"Are you careful now?"

My eyes reached hers across the few feet that separated us. "No. I'm being a damn fool again. I doubt if we were tailed here, but it's only a doubt. I have a gun in the house, but we could be dead before I reached it."

She shrugged unconcernedly. "There's the shotgun in the bathhouse."

"That's still no good. It's a pro game. There won't be any more second chances. You couldn't reach the shotgun either. It's around the pool and in the dark."

"So tell me about it, Mike. Think to me and maybe it will end even faster and we can have ourselves to ourselves. If you want to think, or be mad or need a reaction, think to me."

I said, "Don't you like living?"

A shadow passed across her face and the knuckles of her hand on the arms of the chair went white. "I stopped living when Leo died. I thought I'd never live again."

"Kid—"

"No, it's true, Mike. I know all the objections you can put up about our backgrounds and present situations but it still doesn't make any difference. It doesn't alter a simple fact that I knew days ago. I fell in love with you, Mike. I took one look at you and fell in love, knowing then that objections would come, troubles would be a heritage and you might not love me at all."

"Laura—"

"Mike—I started to live again. I thought I was dead and I started to live again. Have I pushed you into anything?"

"No."

"And I won't. You can't push a man. All you can do is try, but you just can't push a man and a woman should know that. If she can, then she doesn't have a man."

She waved me to be quiet and went on. "I don't care how you feel toward me. I hope, but that is all. I'm quite content knowing I can live again and no matter where you are you'll know that I love you. It's a peculiar kind of courtship, but these are peculiar times and I don't care if it has to be like this. Just be sure of one thing.

You can have anything you want from me, Mike. Anything. There's nothing you can ask me to do that I won't do. Not one thing. That's how completely yours I am. There's a way to be sure. Just ask me. But I won't push you. If you ask me never to speak of it again, then I'll do that too. You see, Mike, it's a sort of hopeless love, but I'm living again, I'm loving, and you can't stop me from loving you. It's the only exception to what you can ask—I won't stop loving you.

"But to answer your question, yes, I like living. You brought me alive. I was dead before."

There was a beauty about her then that was indescribable. I said, "Anything you know can be too much. You're a target now. I don't want you to be an even bigger one."

"I'll only die if you die," she said simply.

"Laura—"

She wouldn't let me finish. "Mike—do you love me—at all?"

The sun was a honeyed cloud in her hair, bouncing off the deep brown of her skin to bring out the classic loveliness of her features. She was so beautifully deep-breasted, her stomach molding itself hollow beneath the outline of her ribs, the taut fabric of the sleeveless playsuit accentuating the timeless quality that was Laura.

I said, "I think so, Laura. I don't know for sure. It's just that I—can't tell anymore."

"It's enough for now," she said. "That little bit will grow because it has to. You were in love before, weren't you?"

I thought of Charlotte and Velda and each was like being suddenly shot low down when knowledge precedes breathlessness and you know it will be a few seconds before the real pain hits.

"Yes," I told her.

"Was it the same?"

"It's never the same. You are—different."

She nodded. "I know, Mike. I know." She waited, then added, "It will be—the other one—or me, won't it?"

There was no sense lying to her. "That's right."

"Very well. I'm satisfied. So now do you want to talk to me? Shall I listen for you?"

I leaned back in the chair, let my face look at the sun with my eyes closed and tried to start at the beginning. Not the beginning the way it happened, but the beginning the way I thought it could have happened. It was quite a story. Now I had to see if it made sense.

I said:

"There are only principals in this case. They are odd persons, and out of it entirely are the police and the Washington agencies. The departments only know results, not causes, and although they suspect certain things they are not in a position to be sure of what they do. We eliminate them and get to basic things. They may be speculative, but they are basic and lead to conclusions.

"The story starts at the end of World War I with an espionage team headed by Gerald Erlich who, with others, had visions of a world empire. Oh, it wasn't a new dream. Before him there had been Alexander and Caesar and Napoleon so he was only picking up an established trend. So Erlich's prime mover was nullified and he took on another—Hitler. Under that regime he became great and his organization became more nearly perfected, and when Hitler died and the Third Reich became extinct this was nothing too, for now the world was more truly divided. Only two parts remained, the East and the West, and he chose, for the moment, to side with the East. Gerald Erlich picked the Red Government as his next prime mover. He thought they would be the ultimate victors in the conquest of the world, then, when the time was right, he would take over from them.

"Ah, but how time and circumstances can change. He didn't know that the Commies were equal to him in *their* dreams of world empire. He didn't realize that they would find *him* out and use *him* while he thought they were in *his* hands. They took over his organization. Like they did the rest of the world they control, they took his corrupt group and corrupted it even further. But an organization they could control. The leader of the organization, a fanatical one, they knew they couldn't. He had to go. Like dead.

"However, Erlich wasn't quite that stupid. He saw the signs and read them right. He wasn't young any longer and his organization had been taken over. His personal visions of world conquest didn't seem quite so important anymore and the most important thing was to stay alive as best he could and the place to do it was in the States. So he came here. He married well under the assumed name of Rudy Civac to a rich widow and all was well in his private world for a time.

"Then, one day, they found him. His identity was revealed. He scrambled for cover. It was impossible to ask for police protection so he did the next best thing, he called a private detective agency and as a subterfuge, used his wife's jewels as the reason for needing security. Actually, he wanted guns around. He wanted shooting protection.

"Now here the long arm of fate struck a second time. Not co-incidence—but fate, pure unblemished fate. I sent Velda. During the war she had been young, beautiful, intelligent, a perfect agent to use against men. She was in the O.S.S., the O.S.I. and another highly secretive group and assigned to Operation Butterfly Two, which was nailing Gerald Erlich and breaking down his organiza-tion. The war ended before it could happen, she was discharged, came with me into the agency because it was a work she knew and we stayed together until Rudy Civac called for protection. He ex-pected me. He got her.

"Fate struck for sure when she saw him. She knew who he was. She knew that a man like that had to be stopped because he might still have his purposes going for him. There was the one thing she knew that made Gerald Elrich the most important man in the world right then. He knew the names and identities of every major agent he ever had working for him and these were such dedicated people they never stopped working—and now they were working for the Reds.

"Coincidence here. Or Fate. Either will do. This was the night the Red agents chose to act. They hit under the guise of burglars. They abducted Rudy Civac, his wife and Velda. They killed the wife, but they needed Rudy to find out exactly what he knew.

"And Velda played it smart. She made like she was part of Civac's group just to stay alive and it was conceivable that she had things they must know too. This we can't forget—Velda was a trained op-erative—she had prior experience even I didn't know about. What-ever she did she made it stick. They got Civac and her back into Europe and into Red territory and left the dead wife and the stolen jewels as a red herring that worked like a charm, and while Velda was in the goddamn Russian country I was drinking myself into a lousy pothole—"

She spoke for the first time. She said, "Mike—" and I squeezed open my eyes and looked at her.

"Thanks."

"It's all right. I understand."

I closed my eyes again and let the picture form.

"The Commies aren't the greatest brains in the world, though. Those stupid peasants forgot one thing. Both Civac—or Erlich—and Velda were pros. Someplace along the line they slipped and both of them cut out. They got loose inside the deep Iron Curtain and from then on the chase was on.

"Brother, I bet heads rolled after that. Anyway, when they knew two real hotshots were on the run they called in the top man to make the chase. *The Dragon*. Comrade Gorlin. But I like The Dragon better. I'll feel more like St. George when I kill him." *And won't Art hate me for that*, I thought.

"The chase took seven years. I think I know what happened during that time. Civac and Velda had to stay together to pool their escape resources. One way or another Velda was able to get things from Civac—or Erlich—and the big thing was those names. I'll bet she made him recount every one and she committed them to memory and carried them in her head all the way through so that she was fully as important now as Civac was.

"Don't underplay the Reds. They're filthy bastards, every one, but they're on the ball when it comes to thinking out the dirty work. They're so used to playing it themselves that it's second nature to them. Hell, they knew what happened. They knew Velda was as big as Erlich now—perhaps even bigger. Erlich's dreams were on the decline . . . what Velda knew would put us on the upswing again, so above all, she had to go.

"So The Dragon in his chase concentrated on those two. Eventually he caught up with Erlich and shot him. That left Velda. Now he ran into a problem. During her war years she made a lot of contacts. One of them was Richie Cole. They'd meet occasionally when he was off assignment and talk over the old days and stayed good friends. She knew he was in Europe and somehow or other made contact with him. There wasn't time enough to pass on what she had memorized and it wasn't safe to write it down, so the answer was to get

Velda back to the States with her information. There wasn't even time to assign the job to a proper agency.

"Richie Cole broke orders and took it upon himself to protect Velda and came back to the States. He knew he was followed. He knew The Dragon would make him a target—he knew damn well there wouldn't be enough time to do the right thing, but Velda had given him a name. She gave him me and a contact to make with an old newsie we both knew well.

"Sure, Cole tried to make the contact, but The Dragon shot him first. Trouble was, Cole didn't die. He held off until they got hold of me because Velda told him I was so damn big I could break the moon apart in my bare hands and he figured if she said it I really could. Then he saw me."

I put my face in my hands to rub out the picture. *"Then he saw me!"*

"Mike—"

"Let's face it, kid. I was a drunk."

"Mike—"

"Shut up. Let me talk."

Laura didn't answer, but her eyes hoped I wasn't going off the deep end, so I stopped a minute, poured some coffee, drank it, then started again.

"Once again those goddamn Reds were smart. They back-tracked Velda and found out about me. They knew what Richie Cole was trying to do. Richie knew where Velda was and wanted to tell me. He died before he did. They thought he left the information with Old Dewey and killed the old man. They really thought I knew and they put a tail on me to see if I made a contact. They tore Dewey's place and my place apart looking for information they thought Cole might have passed to me. Hell, The Dragon even tried to kill me because he thought I wasn't really important at all and was better out of the way."

I leaned back in the chair, my insides feeling hollow all of a sudden. Laura asked, "Mike, what's the matter?"

"Something's missing. Something big."

"Please don't talk any more."

"It's not that. I'm just tired, I guess. It's hard to come back to normal this fast."

"If we took a swim it might help."

I opened my eyes and looked at her and grinned. "Sick of hearing hard luck stories?"

"No."

"Any questions?"

She nodded. "Leo. Who shot him?"

I said, "In this business guns can be found anywhere. I'm never surprised to see guns with the same ballistics used in different kills. Did you know the same gun that shot your husband and Richie Cole was used in some small kill out West?"

"No, I didn't know that."

"There seemed to be a connection through the jewels. Richie's cover was that of a sailor and smuggler. Your jewels were missing. Pat made that a common factor. I don't believe it."

"Could Leo's position in government—well, as you intimated—"

"There is a friend of mine who says no. He has reason to know the facts. I'll stick with him."

"Then Leo's death is no part of what you are looking for?"

"I don't think so. In a way I'm sorry. I wish I could help avenge him too. He was a great man."

"Yes, he was."

"I'll take you up on that swim."

"The suits are in the bathhouse."

"That should be fun," I said.

In the dim light that came through the ivy-screened windows we turned our backs and took off our clothes. When you do that deliberately with a woman, it's hard to talk and you are conscious only of the strange warmth and the brief, fiery contact when skin meets skin and a crazy desire to turn around and watch or to grab and hold or do anything except what you said you'd do when the modest moment was in reality a joke—but you didn't quite want it to be a joke at all.

Then before we could turn it into something else and while we could still treat it as a joke, we had the bathing suits on and she grinned as she passed by me. I reached for her, stopped her, then turned because I saw something else that left me cold for little *ticks* of time.

Laura said, "What is it, Mike?"

I picked the shotgun out of the corner of the room. The building had been laid up on an extension of the tennis court outside and the temporary floor was clay. Where the gun rested by the door water from the outside shower had seeped in and wet it down until it was a semi-firm substance, a blue putty you could mold in your hand.

She had put the shotgun down muzzle first and both barrels were plugged with clay and when I picked it up it was like somebody had taken a bite out of the blue glop with a cookie cutter two inches deep!

Before I opened it I asked her, "Loaded?"

"Yes."

I thumbed the lever and broke the gun. It fell open and I picked out the two twelve-guage Double O shells, then slapped the barrels against my palm until the cores of clay emerged far enough for me to pull them out like the deadly plugs they were.

She saw the look on my face and frowned, not knowing what to say. So I said it instead. "Who put the gun here?"

"I did."

"I thought you knew how to handle it?" There was a rasp in my voice you could cut with a knife.

"Leo—showed me how to shoot it."

"He didn't show you how to handle it, apparently."

"Mike—"

"Listen, Laura, and you listen good. You play with guns and you damn well better *know* how to handle them. You went and stuck this baby's nose down in the muck and do you know what would happen if you ever tried to shoot it?"

Her eyes were frightened at what she saw in my face and she shook her head. "Well, damn it, you listen then. Without even thinking you stuck this gun in heavy clay and plugged both barrels. It's loaded with high-grade sporting ammunition of the best quality and if you ever pulled the trigger you would have had one infinitesimal span of life between the big then and the big now because when you did the back blast in that gun would have wiped you right off the face of the earth."

"Mike—"

"No—keep quiet and listen. It'll do you good. You won't make the mistake again. That barrel would unpeel like a tangerine and you'd get that whole charge right down your lovely throat and if ever you want to give a police medical examiner a job to gag a maggot, that's the way to do it. They'd have to go in and scrape your brains up with a silent butler and pick pieces of your skull out of the woodwork with needle-nosed pliers. I saw eyeballs stuck to a wall one time and if you want to *really* see a disgusting sight, try that. They're bigger than you would expect them to be and they leak fluid all the time they look at you trying to lift them off the boards and then you have no place to put them except in your hand and drop them in the bucket with the rest of the pieces. They float on top and keep watching you until you put on the lid."

"*Mike!*"

"Damn it, shut up! Don't play guns stupidly around me! You did it, now listen!"

Both hands covered her mouth and she was almost ready to vomit.

"The worst of all is the neck because the head is gone and the neck spurts blood for a little bit while the heart doesn't know its vital nerve center is gone—and do you know how high the blood can squirt? No? Then let me tell you. It doesn't just ooze. It goes up under pressure for a couple of feet and covers everything in the area and you wouldn't believe just how much blood the body has in it until you see a person suddenly become headless and watch what happens. I've been there. I've had it happen. *Don't let it happen to you!*"

She let her coffee go on the other side of the door and I didn't give a damn because anybody that careless with a shotgun or any other kind of a gun needs it like that to make them remember. I wiped the barrels clean, reloaded the gun and put it down in place, butt first.

When I came out Laura said, "Man, are you mean."

"It's not a new saying." I still wasn't over my mad.

Her smile was a little cockeyed, but a smile nevertheless. "Mike—I understand. Please?"

"Really?"

"Yes."

"Then you watch it. I play guns too much. It's my business. I hate to see them abused."

"Please, Mike?"

"Okay. I made my point."

"Nobly, to say the least. I usually have a strong stomach."

"Go have some coffee."

"Oh, Mike."

"So take a swim," I told her and grinned. It was the way I felt and the grin was the best I could do. She took a run and a dive and hit the water, came up stroking for the other side, then draped her arms on the edge of the drain and waited for me.

I went in slowly, walking up to the edge, then I dove in and stayed on the bottom until I got to the other side. The water made her legs fuzzy, distorting them to Amazonian proportions, enlarging the cleft and swells and declivities of her belly, then I came up to where all was real and shoved myself onto the concrete surface and reached down for Laura.

She said, "Better?" when I pulled her to the top.

I was looking past her absently. "Yes. I just remembered something."

"Not about the gun, Mike."

"No, not about the gun."

"Should I know?"

"It doesn't matter. I don't really know myself yet. It's just a point."

"Your eyes look terribly funny."

"I know."

"Mike—"

"What?"

"Can I help?"

"No."

"You're going to leave me now, aren't you?"

"Yes, I am."

"Will you come back?"

I couldn't answer her.

"It's between the two of us, isn't it?"

"The girl hunters are out," I said.

"But will you come back?"

My mind was far away, exploring the missing point. "Yes," I said, "I have to come back."

"You loved her."

"I did."

"Do you love me at all?"

I turned around and looked at this woman. She was mine now, beautiful, wise, the way a woman should be formed for a man like I was, lovely, always naked in my sight, always incredibly blond and incredibly tanned, the difference in color—or was it comparison—a shocking, sensual thing. I said, "I love you, Laura. Can I be mistaken?"

She said, "No, you can't be mistaken."

"I have to find her first. She's being hunted. Everybody is hunting her. I loved her a long time ago so I owe her that much. She asked for me."

"Find her, Mike."

I nodded. I had the other key now. "I'll find her. She's the most important thing in this old world today. What she knows will decide the fate of nations. Yes, I'll find her."

"Then will you come back?"

"Then I'll come back," I said.

Her arms reached out and encircled me, her hands holding my head, her fingers tight in my hair. I could feel every inch of her body pressed hard against mine, forcing itself to meet me, refusing to give at all.

"I'm going to fight her for you," she said.

"Why?"

"Because you're mine now."

"Girl," I said, "I'm no damn good to anybody. Look good and you'll see a corn ear husked, you know?"

"I know. So I eat husks."

"Damn it, don't fool around!"

"Mike!"

"Laura—"

"You say it nice, Mike—but there's something in your voice that's terrible and I can sense it. If you find her, what will you do?"

"I can't tell."

"Will you still come back?"

"Damn it, I don't know."

"Why don't you know, Mike?"

I looked down at her. "Because I don't know what I'm really

like anymore. Look—do you know what I *was*? Do you know that a judge and jury took me down and the whole world once ripped me to little bits? It was only Velda who stayed with me then."

"That was then. How long ago was it?"

"Nine years maybe."

"Were you married?"

"No."

"Then I can claim part of you. I've had part of you." She let go of me and stood back, her eyes calm as they looked into mine. "Find her, Mike. Make your decision. Find her and take her. Have you ever had her at all?"

"No."

"You've had *me*. Maybe you're more mine than hers."

"Maybe."

"Then find her." She stepped back, her hands at her side. "If what you said was true then she deserves this much. You find her, Mike. I'm willing to fight anybody for you—but not somebody you think is dead. Not somebody you think you owe a debt to. Let me love you my own way. It's enough for me at least. Do you understand that?"

For a while we stood there. I looked at her. I looked away. I said, "Yes, I understand."

"Come back when you've decided."

"You have all of Washington to entertain."

Laura shook her head. Her hair was a golden swirl and she said, "The hell with Washington. I'll be waiting for you."

Velda, Laura. The names were so similar. Which one? After seven years of nothingness, which one? Knowing what I did, which one? Yesterday was then. Today was now. Which one?

I said, "All right, Laura, I'll find out, then I'll come back."

"Take my car."

"Thanks."

And now I had to take her. My fingers grabbed her arms and pulled her close to where I could kiss her and taste the inside of her mouth and feel the sensuous writhing of her tongue against mine because this was the woman I knew I was coming back to.

The *Girl Hunters*. We all wanted the same one and for reasons of a long time ago. We would complete the hunt, but what would we do with the kill?

She said, "After that you shouldn't leave."

"I have to," I said.

"Why?"

"She had to get in this country someway. I think I know how."

"You'll find her, then come back?"

"Yes," I said, and let my hands roam over her body so that she knew there could never be anybody else, and when I was done I held her off and made her stay there while I went inside to put on the gun and the coat and go back to the new Babylon that was the city.

CHAPTER 11

And once again it was night, the city coming into its nether life like a minion of Count Dracula. The bright light of day that could strip away the facade of sham and lay bare the coating of dirt was gone now, and to the onlooker the unreal became real, the dirt had changed into subtle colors under artificial lights and it was as if all of that vast pile of concrete and steel and glass had been built only to live at night.

I left the car at the Sportsmen's Parking Lot on the corner of Eighth and Fifty-second, called Hy Gardner and told him to meet me at the Blue Ribbon on Forty-fourth, then started my walk to the restaurant thinking of the little things I should have thought of earlier.

The whole thing didn't seem possible, all those years trapped in Europe. You could walk around the world half a dozen times in seven years. But you wouldn't be trapped then. The thing was, they *were* trapped. Had Velda or Erlich been amateurs they would have been captured without much trouble, but being pros they edged out. Almost. That made Velda even better than he had been.

Somehow, it didn't seem possible.

But it was.

Hy had reached the Blue Ribbon before me and waited at a table sipping a stein of rich, dark beer. I nodded at the waiter and he went back for mine. We ordered, ate, and only then did Hy bother to give me his funny look over the cigar he lit up. "It's over?"

"It won't be long now."

"Do we talk about it here?"

"Here's as good as any. It's more than you can put in your column."

"You let me worry about space."

So he sat back and let me tell him what I had told Laura, making occasional notes, because now was the time to make notes. I told him what I knew and what I thought and where everybody stood, and every minute or so he'd glance up from his sheets with an expression of pure incredulity, shake his head and write some more. When the implications of the total picture began really to penetrate, his teeth clamped down on the cigar until it was half hanging out of his mouth unlit, then he threw it down on his plate and put a fresh one in its place.

When I finished he said, "Mike—do you realize what you have hold of?"

"I know."

"How can you stay so damn calm?"

"Because the rough part has just started."

"Ye gods, man—"

"You know what's missing, don't you?"

"Sure. You're missing something in the head. You're trying to stand off a whole political scheme that comes at you with every force imaginable no matter where you are. Mike, you don't fight these guys alone!"

"Nuts. It looks like I have to. I'm not exactly an accredited type character. Who would listen to me?"

"Couldn't this Art Rickerby—"

"He has one purpose in mind. He wants whoever killed Richie Cole."

"That doesn't seem likely. He's a trained federal agent."

"So what? When something hits you personally, patriotism can go by the boards awhile. There are plenty of other agents. He wants a killer and knows I'll eventually come up with him. Like Velda's a key to one thing, I'm a key to another. They think that I'm going to stumble over whatever it was Richie Cole left for me. I know what it was now. So do you, don't you?"

"Yes," Hy said. "It was Velda's location, wherever she is."

"That's right. They don't know if I know or if I'll find out. You can damn well bet that they know he stayed alive waiting for me to show. They can't even be sure if he just clued me. They can't be sure of anything, but they know that I have to stay alive if they want to find Velda too."

Hy's eyes went deep in thought. "Alive? They tried to shoot you twice, didn't they?"

"Fine, but neither shot connected and I can't see a top assassin missing a shot. Both times I was a perfect target."

"Why the attempt then?"

"I'll tell you why," I said. I leaned on the table feeling my hands go open and shut wanting to squeeze the life out of somebody. "Both tries were deliberately sour. They were pushing me. They wanted me to move fast, and if anything can stir a guy up it's getting shot at. If I had anything to hide or to work at, it would come out in a hurry."

"But you didn't bring anything out?"

I grinned at him and I could see my reflection in the glass facing of the autographed pictures behind his head. It wasn't a pretty face at all, teeth and hate and some wildness hard to describe. "No, I didn't. So now I'm a real target because I know too much. They know I *don't* have Velda's location and from now on I can only be trouble to them. I'll bet you that right now a hunt is on for me."

"Mike—if you called Pat—"

"Come off it. He's no friend anymore. He'll do anything to nail my ass down and don't you forget it."

"Does he know the facts?"

"No. The hell with him."

Hy pushed his glasses up on his head, frowning. "Well, what are you going to do?"

"Do, old buddy? I'll tell you what I'm going to do. I'm going after the missing piece. If I weren't so damn slow after all those years I would have caught it before. I'm going after the facts that can wrap up the ball game and you're going with me."

"But you said—"

"Uh-uh. I didn't say anything. I *don't* know where she is, but I do know a few other things. Richie Cole came blasting back into this country when he shouldn't have and ducked out to look for me. That had a big fat meaning and I muffed it. Damn it, I muffed it!"

"But how?"

"Come on, Hy—Richie was a sailor—he smuggled her on the ship he came in on. *He never left her in Europe! He got her back in this country!*"

He put the cigar down slowly, getting the implication.

I said, "He had to smuggle her out, otherwise they would have killed her. If they took a plane they would have blown it over the ocean, or if she sailed under an assumed name and cover identity they would have had enough time to locate her and a passenger would simply fall overboard. No, he smuggled her out. He got her on that ship and got her into this country."

"You make it sound easy."

"Sure it's easy! You think there wasn't some cooperation with others in the crew! Those boys love to outfox the captain and the customs. What would they care as long as it was on Cole's head? He was on a tramp steamer and they can do practically anything on those babies if they know how and want to. Look, you want me to cite you examples?"

"I know it could be done."

"All right, then here's the catch. Richie realized how close The Dragon was to Velda when they left. He had no time. He had to act on his own. This was a project bigger than any going in the world at the time, big enough to break regulations for. He got her out—but he didn't underestimate the enemy either. He knew they'd figure it and be waiting.

"They were, too," I continued. "The Dragon was there all right, and he followed Cole thinking he was going to an appointed place where he had already hidden Velda, but when he realized that Cole wasn't doing anything of the kind he figured the angles quickly. He shot Cole, had to leave because of the crowd that collected and didn't have a chance until later to reach Old Dewey, then found out about me. Don't ask me the details about *how* they can do it—they have resources at their fingertips everywhere. Later he went back, killed Dewey, didn't find the note Cole left and had to stick with me to see where I led him."

Hy was frowning again.

I said, "I couldn't lead him to Velda. I didn't know. But before long he'll figure out the same thing I did. Somebody else helped Cole get her off that boat and knows where she is!"

"What are you going to do?" His voice was quietly calm next to mine.

"Get on that ship and see who else was in on the deal."

"How?"

"Be my guest and I'll show you the seamier side of life."

"You know me," Hy said, standing up.

I paid the cabbie outside Benny Joe Grissi's bar and when Hy saw where we were he let out a low whistle and said he hoped I knew what I was doing. We went inside and Sugar Boy and his smaller friend were still at their accustomed places and when Sugar Boy saw me he got a little pasty around the mouth and looked toward the bar with a quick motion of his head.

Benny Joe gave the nod and we walked past without saying a word, and when I got to the bar I held out the card Art Rickerby had given me and let Benny Joe take a long look at it. "In case you get ideas like before, mister. I'll shoot this place apart and you with it."

"Say, Mike, I never—"

"Tone it down," I said. "Bayliss Henry here?"

"Pepper? Yeah. He went in the can."

"Wait here, Hy."

I went down to the end with the door stenciled MEN and pushed on in. Old Bayliss was at the washstand drying his hands and saw me in the mirror, his eyes suddenly wary at the recognition. He turned around and put his hands on my chest. "Mike, my boy, no more. Whatever it is, I want none of it. The last time out taught me a lesson I won't forget. I'm old, I scare easy, and what life is left to me I want to enjoy. Okay?"

"Sure."

"Then forget whatever you came in here to ask me. Don't let me talk over my head about the old days or try and make like a reporter again."

"You won't get shot at."

Bayliss nodded and shrugged. "How can I argue with you? What do you want to know?"

"What ship was Richie Cole on?"

"The *Vanessa*."

"What pier?"

"She was at number twelve, but that won't do you any good now."

"Why not?"

"Hell, she sailed the day before yesterday."

What I had to say I did under my breath. Everything was right out the window because I thought too slow and a couple of days had made all the difference.

"What was on it, Mike?"

"I wanted to see a guy."

"Oh? I thought it was the ship. Well maybe you can still see some of the guys. You know the *Vanessa* was the ship they had the union trouble with. Everybody complained about the chow and half the guys wouldn't sign back on. The union really laid into 'em."

Then suddenly there was a chance again and I had to grab at it. "Listen, Bayliss—who did Cole hang around with on the ship?"

"Jeepers, Mike, out at sea—"

"Did he have any friends on board?"

"Well, no, I'd say."

"Come on, damn it, a guy doesn't sail for months and not make some kind of an acquaintance!"

"Yeah, I know—well, Cole was a chess player and there was this one guy—let's see, Red Markham—yeah, that's it, Red Markham. They'd have drinks together and play chess together because Red sure could play chess. One time—"

"Where can I find this guy?"

"You know where Annie Stein's pad is?"

"The flophouse?"

"Yeah. Well, you look for him there. He gets drunk daytimes and flops early."

"Suppose you go along."

"Mike, I told you—"

"Hy Gardner's outside."

Bayliss looked up and grinned. "Well, shoot. If he's along I'll damn well go. He was still running copy when I did the police beat."

———

Annie Stein's place was known as the Harbor Hotel. It was a dollar a night flop, pretty expensive as flops go, so the trade was limited to occasional workers and itinerant seamen. It was old and dirty and smelled of disinfectant and urine partially smothered by an old-man odor of defeat and decay.

The desk clerk froze when we walked in, spun the book around without asking, not wanting any trouble at all. Red Markham was in the third room on the second floor, his door half open, the sound and smell of him oozing into the corridor.

I pushed the door open and flipped on the light. Overhead a sixty-watt bulb turned everything yellow. He was curled on the cot, an empty pint bottle beside him, breathing heavily through his mouth. On the chair with his jacket and hat was a pocket-sized chessboard with pegged chessmen arranged in some intricate move.

It took ten minutes of cold wet towels and a lot of shaking to wake him up. His eyes still had a whiskey glassiness and he didn't know what we wanted at all. He was unintelligible for another thirty minutes, then little by little he began to come around, his face going through a succession of emotions. Until he saw Bayliss he seemed scared, but one look at the old man and he tried on a drunken grin, gagged and went into a spasm of dry heaves. Luckily, there was nothing in his stomach, so we didn't have to go through that kind of mess.

Hy brought in a glass of water and I made him sip at it. I said, "What's your name, feller?"

He hiccoughed. "You—cops?"

"No, a friend."

"Oh." His head wobbled, then he looked back to me again. "You play chess?"

"Sorry, Red, but I had a friend who could. Richie Cole."

Markham squinted and nodded solemnly, remembering. "He— pretty damn good. Yessir. Good guy."

I asked him, "Did you know about the girl on the ship?"

Very slowly, he scowled, his lips pursing out, then a bit of clarity returned to him and he leered with a drunken grimace. "Sure.

Hell of—joke." He hiccoughed and grinned again. "Joke. Hid—her in—down in—hold."

We were getting close now. His eyes drooped sleepily and I wanted him to hang on. I said, "Where is she now, Red?"

He just looked at me foggily.

"Damn it, think about it!"

For a second he didn't like the way I yelled or my hand on his arm and he was about to balk, then Bayliss said, "Come on, Red, if you know where she is, tell us."

You'd think he was seeing Bayliss for the first time. "Pepper," he said happily, his eyes coming open.

"Come on, Red. The girl on the *Vanessa*. Richie's girl."

"Sure. Big—joke. You know?"

"We know, but tell us where she is."

His shrug was the elaborate gesture of the sodden drunk. "Dunno. I—got her—on deck."

Bayliss looked at me, not knowing where to go. It was all over his head and he was taking the lead from me. Then he got the pitch and shook Red's shoulder. "Is she on shore?"

Red chuckled and his head weaved. "On—shore. Sure—on shore." He laughed again, the picture coming back to his mind. "Dennis—Wallace packed her—in crate. Very funny."

I pushed Bayliss away and sat on the edge of the cot. "It sure was a good joke all right. Now where did the crate go?"

"Crate?"

"She was packed in the crate. This Dennis Wallace packed her in the crate, right?"

"Right!" he said assuredly, slobbering on himself.

"Then who got the crate?"

"Big joke."

"I know, now let us in on it. Who got the crate?"

He made another one of those shrugs. "I—dunno."

"Somebody picked it up," I reminded him.

Red's smile was real foolish, that of the drunk trying to be secretive. "Richie's—joke. He called—a friend. Dennis gave him—the crate." He laughed again. "Very funny."

Hy said, "Cute."

I nodded. "Yeah. Now we have to find this Dennis guy."

"He's got a place not far from here," Bayliss said.

"You know everybody?"

"I've been around a long time, Mike."

We went to leave Red Markham sitting there, but before we could reach the door he called out, "Hey, you."

Bayliss said, "What, Red?"

"How come—everybody wants—old Dennis?"

"I don't—"

My hand stopped the old guy and I walked back to the cot. "Who else wanted Dennis, Red?"

"Guy—gimme this pint." He reached for the bottle, but was unable to make immediate contact. When he did he sucked at the mouth of it, swallowed as though it was filled and put the bottle down.

"What did he look like, Red?"

"Oh—" he lolled back against the wall. "Big guy. Like you."

"Go on."

"Mean. Son of a—he was mean. You ever see—mean ones? Like a damn Indian. Something like Injun Pete on the *Darby Standard*—he—"

I didn't bother to hear him finish. I looked straight at Hy and felt cold all over. "The Dragon," I said. "He's one step up."

Hy had a quiet look on his face. "That's what I almost forgot to tell you about, Mike."

"What?"

"The Dragon. I got inside the code name from our people overseas. There may be two guys because The Dragon code breaks down to *tooth* and *nail*. When they operate as a team they're simply referred to as The Dragon."

"Great," I said. "Swell. That's all we need for odds." My mouth had a bad taste in it. "Show us Dennis's place, Bayliss. We can't stay here any longer."

"Not me," he said. "You guys go it alone. Whatever it is that's going on, I don't like it. I'll tell you where, but I'm not going in any more dark places with you. Right now I'm going back to Benny Joe Grissi's bar and get stinking drunk where you can't get at me and if anything happens I'll read about it in the papers tomorrow."

"Good enough, old-timer. Now where does Dennis live?"

The rooming house was a brownstone off Ninth Avenue, a firetrap like all the others on the block, a crummy joint filled with cubicles referred to as furnished rooms. The landlady came out of the front floor flat, looked at me and said, "I don't want no cops around here," and when Hy handed her the ten-spot her fat face made a brief smile and she added, "So I made a mistake. Cops don't give away the green. What're you after?"

"Dennis Wallace. He's a seaman and—"

"Top floor front. Go on up. He's got company."

I flashed Hy a nod, took the stairs with him behind me while I yanked the .45 out and reached the top floor in seconds. The old carpet under our feet puffed dust with every step but muffled them effectively and when I reached the door there was no sound from within and a pencil-thin line of light seeped out at the sill. I tried the knob, pushed the door open and was ready to cut loose at anything that moved wrong.

But there was no need for any shooting, if the little guy on the floor with his hands tied behind him and his throat slit wide open was Dennis Wallace, for his killer was long gone.

The fat landlady screeched when she saw the body and told us it was Dennis all right. She waddled downstairs again and pointed to the wall phone and after trying four different numbers I got Pat and told him I was with another dead man. It wasn't anything startling. He was very proper about getting down the details and told me to stay right there. His voice had a fine tone of satisfaction to it that said he had me where he could make me sweat and maybe even break me like he had promised.

Hy came down as I hung up and tapped my shoulder. "You didn't notice something on the guy up there."

"What's that?"

"All that blood didn't come from his throat. His gut is all carved up and his mouth is taped shut. The blood obscures the tape."

"Tortured?"

"It sure looks that way."

The landlady was in her room taking a quick shot for her nerves and seemed to hate us for causing all the trouble. I asked her when Dennis' guest had arrived and she said a couple of hours ago. She hadn't heard him leave so she assumed he was still there. Her description was brief, but enough. He was a big mean-looking guy who reminded her of an Indian.

There was maybe another minute before a squad car would come along and I didn't want to be here when that happened. I pulled Hy out on the stoop and said, "I'm going to take off."

"Pat won't like it."

"There isn't time to talk about it. You can give him the poop."

"All of it?"

"Every bit. Lay it out for him."

"What about you?"

"Look, you saw what happened. The Dragon put it together the same way I did. He was here when the boat docked and Richie Cole knew it. So Richie called for a friend who knew the ropes, told him to pick up the crate with Velda in it and where to bring it. He left and figured right when he guessed anybody waiting would follow him. He pulled them away from the boat and tried to make contact with Old Dewey at the newstand and what he had for Dewey was the location of where that friend was to bring the crate."

"Then there's one more step."

"That's right. The friend."

"You can't trace that call after all this time."

"I don't think I have to."

Hy shook his head. "If Cole was a top agent then he didn't have any friends."

"He had one," I said.

"Who?"

"Velda."

"But—"

"So he could just as well have another. Someone who was in the same game with him during the war, someone he knew would realize the gravity of the situation and act immediately and someone he knew would be capable of fulfilling the mission."

"Who, Mike?"

I didn't tell him. "I'll call you when it's over. You tell Pat."

Down the street a squad car turned the corner. I went down the steps and went in the other direction, walking casually, then when I reached Ninth, I flagged a cab and gave him the parking lot where I had left Laura's car.

CHAPTER 12

If I was wrong, the girl hunters would have Velda. She'd be dead. They wanted nothing of her except that she be dead. Damn their stinking hides anyway. Damn them and their philosophies! Death and destruction were the only things the Kremlin crowd was capable of. They knew the value of violence and death and used it over and over in a wild scheme to smash everything flat but their own kind.

But there was one thing they didn't know. They didn't know how to handle it when it came back to them and exploded in their own faces. *Let her be dead*, I thought, and I'll start a hunt of my own. They think *they* can hunt? Shit. They didn't know how to be *really* violent. Death? I'd get them, every one, no matter how big or little, or wherever they were. I'd cut them down like so many grapes in ways that would scare the living crap out of them and those next in line for my kill would never know a second's peace until their heads went flying every which way.

So I'd better not be wrong.

Dennis Wallace had known who was to pick up the crate. There wouldn't have been time for elaborate exchanges of coded recognition signals and if Dennis had known it was more than just a joke he might conceivably have backed out. No, it had to be quick and simple and not at all frightening. He had turned the crate over to a guy whose name had been given him and since it was big enough a truck would have been used in the delivery. He would have seen lettering on the truck, he would have been able to identify both it and the driver, and with some judicious knife work on his belly he would have had his memory jarred into remembering every single detail of the transaction.

I had to be right.

Art Rickerby had offered the clue.

The guy's name had to be Alex Bird, Richie's old war buddy in the O.S.S. who had a chicken farm up in Marlboro, New York, and who most likely had a pickup truck that could transport a crate. He would do the favor, keep his mouth shut and forget it the way he had been trained to, and it was just as likely he missed any newspaper squibs about Richie's death and so didn't show up to talk to the police when Richie was killed.

By the time I reached the George Washington Bridge the stars were wiped out of the night sky and you could smell the rain again. I took the Palisades Drive and where I turned off to pick up the Thruway the rain came down in fine slanting lines that laid a slick on the road and whipped in the window.

I liked a night like this. It could put a quiet on everything. Your feet walked softer and dogs never barked in the rain. It obscured visibility and overrode sounds that could give you away otherwise and sometimes was so soothing that you could be lulled into a death sleep. Yeah, I remembered other nights like this too. Death nights.

At Newburgh I turned off the Thruway, drove down 17K into town and turned north on 9W. I stopped at a gas station when I reached Marlboro and asked the attendant if he knew where Alex Bird lived.

Yes, he knew. He pointed the way out and just to be sure I sketched out the route then picked up the blacktop road that led back into the country.

I passed by it the first time, turned around at the crossroad cursing to myself, then eased back up the road looking for the mailbox. There was no name on it, just a big wooden cutout of a bird. It was in the shadow of a tree before, but now my lights picked it out and when they did I spotted the drive, turned in, angled off into a cut in the bushes and killed the engine.

The farmhouse stood an eighth of a mile back off the road, an old building restored to more modern taste. In back of it, dimly lit by the soft glow of night lights, were two long chicken houses, the manure odor of them hanging in the wet air. On the right, a hundred feet away, a two-story boxlike barn stood in deep shadow, totally dark.

Only one light was on in the house when I reached it, downstairs on the chimney side and obviously in a living room. I held there a minute, letting my eyes get adjusted to the place. There were no cars around, but that didn't count since there were too many places to hide one. I took out the .45, jacked a shell in the chamber and thumbed the hammer back.

But before I could move another light went on in the opposite downstairs room. Behind the curtains a shadow moved slowly, purposefully, passed the window several times then disappeared altogether. I waited, but the light didn't go out. Instead, one top-floor light came on, but too dimly to do more than vaguely outline the form of a person on the curtains.

Then it suddenly made sense to me and I ran across the distance to the door. Somebody was searching the house.

The door was locked and too heavy to kick in. I hoped the rain covered the racket I made, then laid my trench coat against the window and pushed. The glass shattered inward to the carpeted floor without much noise, I undid the catch, lifted the window and climbed over the sill.

Alex Bird would be the thin, balding guy tied to the straight-back chair. His head slumped forward, his chin on his chest and when I tilted his head back his eyes stared at me lifelessly. There was a small lumpy bruise on the side of his head where he had been hit, but outside of a chafing of his wrists and ankles, there were no other marks on him. His body had the warmth of death only a few minutes old and I had seen too many heart-attack cases not to be able to diagnose this one.

The Dragon had reached Alex Bird, all right. He had him right where he could make him talk and the little guy's heart exploded on him. That meant just one thing. He hadn't talked. The Dragon was still searching. *He didn't know where she was yet!*

And right then, right that very second he was upstairs tearing the house apart!

The stairs were at a shallow angle reaching to the upper landing and I hugged the wall in the shadows until I could definitely place him from the sounds. I tried to keep from laughing out loud because

I felt so good, and although I could hold back the laugh I couldn't suppress the grin. I could feel it stretch my face and felt the pull across my shoulders and back, then I got ready to go.

I knew when he felt it. When death is your business you have a feeling for it; an animal instinct can tell when it's close even when you can't see it or hear it. You just know it's there. And like he knew suddenly that I was there, I realized he knew it too.

Upstairs the sounds stopped abruptly. There was the smallest of metallic *clicks* that could have been made by a gun, but that was all. Both of us were waiting. Both of us knew we wouldn't wait long.

You can't play games when time is so important. You take a chance on being hit and maybe living through it just so you get one clean shot in where it counts. You have to end the play knowing one must die and sometimes two and there's no other way. For the first time you both know it's pro against pro, two cold, calm killers facing each other down and there's no such thing as sportsmanship and if an advantage is offered it will be taken and whoever offered it will be dead.

We came around the corners simultaneously with the rolling thunder of the .45 blanking out the rod in his hand and I felt a sudden torch along my side and another on my arm. It was immediate and unaimed diversionary fire until you could get the target lined up and in the space of four rapid-fire shots I saw him, huge at the top of the stairs, his high-cheekboned face truly Indianlike, the black hair low on his forehead and his mouth twisted open in the sheer enjoyment of what he was doing.

Then my shot slammed the gun out of his hand and the advantage was his because he was up there, a crazy killer with a scream on his lips and like the animal he was he reacted instantly and dove headlong at me through the acrid fumes of the gunsmoke.

The impact knocked me flat on my back, smashing into a corner table so that the lamp shattered into a million pieces beside my head. I had my hands on him, his coat tore, a long tattered slice of it in my fingers, then he kicked free with a snarl and a guttural curse, rolling to his feet like an acrobat. The .45 had skittered out of my hand and lay up against the step. All it needed was a quick movement and it was mine. He saw the action, figured the odds and knew he couldn't reach me before I had the gun, and while

I grabbed it up he was into the living room and out the front door. The slide was forward and the hammer back so there was still one shot left at least and he couldn't afford the chance of losing. I saw his blurred shadow racing toward the drive and when my shadow broke the shaft of light coming from the door he swerved into the darkness of the barn and I let a shot go at him and heard it smash into the woodwork.

It was my last. This time the slide stayed back. I dropped the gun in the grass, ran to the barn before he could pull the door closed and dived into the darkness.

He was on me like a cat, but he made a mistake in reaching for my right hand thinking I had the gun there. I got the other hand in his face and damn near tore it off. He didn't yell. He made a sound deep in his throat and went for my neck. He was big and strong and wild mean, but it was my kind of game too. I heaved up and threw him off, got to my feet and kicked out to where he was. I missed my aim, but my toe took him in the side and he grunted and came back with a vicious swipe of his hand I could only partially block. I felt his next move coming and let an old-time reflex take over. The judo bit is great if everything is going for you, but a terrible right cross to the face can destroy judo or karate or anything else if it gets there first.

My hand smashed into bone and flesh and with the meaty impact I could smell the blood and hear the gagging intake of his breath. He grabbed, his arms like great claws. He just held on and I knew if I couldn't break him loose he could kill me. He figured I'd start the knee coming up and turned to block it. But I did something worse, I grabbed him with my hands, squeezed and twisted and his scream was like a woman's, so high-pitched as almost to be noiseless, and in his frenzy of pain he shoved me so violently I lost that fanatical hold of what manhood I had left him, and with some blind hate driving him he came at me as I stumbled over something and fell on me like a wild beast, his teeth tearing at me, his hands searching and ripping and I felt the shock of incredible pain and ribs break under his pounding and I couldn't get him off no matter what I did, and he was holding me down and butting me with his head while he kept up that whistlelike screaming and in another minute it would be me dead and him alive, then Velda dead.

And when I thought of her name something happened, that little thing you have left over was there and I got my elbow up, smashed his head back unexpectedly, got a short one to his jaw again, then another, and another, and another, then I was on top of him and hitting, hitting, smashing—and he wasn't moving at all under me. He was breathing, but not moving.

I got up and found the doorway somehow, standing there to suck in great breaths of air. I could feel the blood running from my mouth and nose, wetting my shirt, and with each breath my side would wrench and tear. The two bullet burns were nothing compared to the rest. I had been squeezed dry, pulled apart, almost destroyed, but I had won. Now the son of a bitch would die.

Inside the door I found a light switch. It only threw on a small bulb overhead, but it was enough. I walked back to where he lay face up and then spat down on The Dragon. Mechanically, I searched his pockets, found nothing except money until I saw that one of my fists had torn his hair loose at the side and when I ripped the wig off there were several small strips of microfilm hidden there.

Hell, I didn't know what they were. I didn't care. I even grinned at the slob because he sure did look like an Indian now, only one that had been half scalped by an amateur. He was big, big. Cheekbones high, a Slavic cast to his eyes, his mouth a cruel slash, his eyebrows thick and black. Half bald, though, he wouldn't have looked too much like an Indian. Not our kind, anyway.

There was an ax on the wall, a long-handled, double-bitted ax with a finely honed edge and I picked it from the pegs and went back to The Dragon.

Just how *did* you kill a dragon? I could bury the ax in his belly. That would be fun, all right. Stick it right in the middle of his skull and it would look at lot better. They wouldn't come fooling around after seeing pictures of that. How about the neck? One whack and his head would roll like the Japs used to do. But nuts, why be that kind?

This guy was *really* going to die.

I looked at the big pig, put the ax down and nudged him with my toe. What was it Art had said? Like about suffering? I thought he was nuts, but he could be right. Yeah, he sure could be right. Still, there had to be some indication that people were left who treat those Commie slobs like they liked to treat people.

Some indication.

He was Gorlin now, Comrade Gorlin. Dragons just aren't dragons anymore when they're bubbling blood over their chins.

I walked around the building looking for an *indication*.

I found it on a workbench in the back.

A twenty-penny nail and a ball-peen hammer. The nail seemed about four inches long and the head big as a dime.

I went back and turned Comrade Gorlin over on his face.

I stretched his arm out palm down on the floor.

I tapped the planks until I found a floor beam and put his hand on it.

It was too bad he wasn't conscious.

Then I held the nail in the middle of the back of his hand and slammed it in with the hammer and slammed and slammed and slammed until the head of that nail dimpled his skin and he was so tightly pinned to the floor like a piece of equipment he'd never get loose until he was pried out and he wasn't going to do it with a ball-peen. I threw the hammer down beside him and said, "Better'n handcuffs, buddy," but he didn't get the joke. He was still out.

Outside, the rain came down harder. It always does after a thing like that, trying to flush away the memory of it. I picked up my gun, took it in the house and dismantled it, wiped it dry and reassembled the piece.

Only then did I walk to the telephone and ask the operator to get me New York and the number I gave her was that of the Peerage Brokers. Art Rickerby answered the phone himself. He said, "Mike?"

"Yes."

For several seconds there was silence. "Mike—"

"I have him for you. He's still alive."

It was as though I had merely told him the time. "Thank you," he said.

"You'll cover for me on this."

"It will be taken care of. Where is he?"

I told him. I gave him the story then too. I told him to call Pat and Hy and let it all loose at once. Everything tied in. It was almost all wrapped up.

Art said, "One thing, Mike."

"What?"

"*Your* problem."

"No trouble. It's over. I was standing here cleaning my gun and it all was like snapping my fingers. It was simple. If I had thought of it right away Dewey and Dennis Wallace and Alex Bird would still be alive. It was tragically simple. I could have found out where Velda was days ago."

"Mike—"

"I'll see you, Art. The rest of The Dragon has yet to fall."

"What?" He didn't understand me.

"*Tooth and Nail.* I just got Tooth—Nail is more subtle."

"We're going to need a statement."

"You'll get it."

"How will—"

I interrupted him with, "I'll call you."

CHAPTER 13

At daylight the rain stopped and the music of sunlight played off the trees and grass at dawn. The mountains glittered and shone and steamed a little, and as the sun rose the sheen stopped and the colors came through. I ate at an all-night drive-in, parking between the semis out front. I sat through half a dozen cups of coffee before paying the bill and going out to the day, ignoring the funny looks of the carhop.

I stopped again awhile by the Ashokan Reservoir and did nothing but look at the water and try to bring seven years into focus. It was a long time, that. You change in seven years.

You change in seven days too, I thought.

I was a bum Pat had dragged into a hospital to look at a dying man. Pat didn't know it, but I was almost as dead as the one on the bed. It depends on where you die. My dying had been almost done. The drying up, the withering, had taken place. Everything was gone except hopelessness and that is the almost death of living.

Remember, Velda, when we were big together? You must have remembered or you would never have asked for me. And all these years I had spent trying to forget you while you were trying to remember me.

I got up slowly and brushed off my pants, then walked back across the field to the car. During the night I had gotten it all muddy driving aimlessly on the back roads, but I didn't think Laura would mind.

The sun had climbed high until it was almost directly overhead.

When you sit and think time can go by awfully fast. I turned the key, pulled out on the road and headed toward the mountains.

When I drove up, Laura heard me coming and ran out to meet me. She came into my arms with a rush of pure delight and did nothing for a few seconds except hold her arms around me, then she looked again, stepped back and said, "Mike—your face!"

"Trouble, baby. I told you I was trouble."

For the first time I noticed my clothes. My coat swung open and there was blood down my jacket and shirt and a jagged tear that was clotted with more blood at my side.

Her eyes went wide, not believing what she saw. "Mike! You're—you're all—"

"Shot down, kid. Rough night."

She shook her head. "It's not funny. I'm going to call a doctor!"

I took her hand. "No, you're not. It isn't that bad."

"Mike—"

"Favor, kitten. Let me lie in the sun like an old dog, okay? I don't want a damn medic. I'll heal. It's happened before. I just want to be left alone in the sun."

"Oh, Mike, you stubborn fool."

"Anybody home?" I asked her.

"No, you always pick an off day for the servants." She smiled again now. "You're clever and I'm glad."

I nodded. For some reason my side had started to ache and it was getting hard to breathe. There were other places that had pain areas all their own and they weren't going to get better. It had only just started. I said, "I'm tired."

So we went out back to the pool. She helped me off with my clothes and once more I put the trunks on, then eased down into a plastic contour chair and let the sun warm me. There were blue marks from my shoulders down and where the rib was broken a welt had raised, an angry red that arched from front to back. Laura found antiseptic and cleaned out the furrow where the two shots had grazed me and I thought back to the moment of getting them, realizing how lucky I was because the big jerk was too impatient, just like I had been, taking too much pleasure out of something that should have been strictly business.

I slept for a while. I felt the sun travel across my body from one side to the other, then I awoke abruptly because events had compacted themselves into my thoughts and I knew that there was still that one thing more to do.

Laura said, "You were talking in your sleep, Mike."

She had changed back into that black bikini and it was wet like her skin so she must have just come from the water. The tight band of black at her loins had rolled down some from the swim and fitted tightly into the crevasses of her body. The top half was like an artist's brush stroke, a quick motion of impatience at a critical sex-conscious world that concealed by reason of design only. She was more nearly naked dressed than nude.

How lovely.

Large, flowing thighs. Full, round calves. They blended into a softly concave stomach and emerged, higher, into proud, outthrust breasts. Her face and hair were a composite halo reaching for the perfection of beauty and she was smiling.

Lovely.

"What did I say, Laura?"

She stopped smiling then. "You were talking about dragons."

I nodded. "Today, I'm St. George."

"Mike—"

"Sit down, baby."

"Can we talk again?"

"Yes, we'll talk."

"Would you mind if I got dressed first? It's getting chilly out here now. You ought to get dressed yourself."

She was right. The sun was a thick red now, hanging just over the crest of a mountain. While one side was a blaze of green, the other was in the deep purple of the shadow.

I held out my hand and she helped me up, and together we walked around the pool to the bathhouse, touching each other, feeling the warmth of skin against skin, the motion of muscle against muscle. At the door she turned and I took her in my arms. "Back to back?" she said.

"Like prudes," I told her.

Her eyes grew soft and her lips wet her tongue. Slowly, with an insistent hunger, her mouth turned up to mine and I took it, tasting her again, knowing her, feeling the surge of desire go through me and through her too.

I let her go reluctantly and she went inside with me behind her. The setting sun threw long orange rays through the window, so there was no need of the overhead light. She went into the shower and turned on a soft drizzle while I got dressed slowly, aching and hurting as I pulled on my clothes.

She called out, "When will it all be over, Mike?"

"Today," I said quietly.

"Today?"

I heard her stop soaping herself in the shower. "Are you sure?"

"Yes."

"You were dreaming about dragons," she called out.

"About how they die, honey. They die hard. This one will die especially hard. You know, you wouldn't believe how things come about. Things that were planted long ago suddenly bear fruit now. Like what I told you. Remember all I told you about Velda?"

"Yes, Mike, I do."

"I had to revise and add to the story, Laura."

"Really?" She turned the shower off and stood there behind me soaping herself down, the sound of it so nice and natural I wanted to turn around and watch. I knew what she'd look like: darkly beautiful, blondly beautiful, the sun having turned all of her hair white.

I said, "Pat was right and I was right. Your jewels did come into it. They were like Mrs. Civac's jewels and the fact that Richie Cole was a jewel smuggler."

"Oh?" That was all she said.

"They were all devices. Decoys. Red herrings. How would you like to hear the rest of what I think?"

"All right, Mike."

She didn't see me, but I nodded. "In the government are certain key men. Their importance is apparent to critical eyes long before it is to the public. Your husband was like that. It was evident that he was going to be a top dog one day and the kind of top dog our Red enemy could hardly afford to have up there.

"That was Leo Knapp, your husband. Mr. Missile Man. Mr. America. He sure was a big one. But our wary enemy knew his stuff. Kill him off and you had a public martyr or a great investigation that might lead to even greater international stuff and those Reds just aren't the kind who can stand the big push. Like it or not, they're still a lousy bunch of peasants who killed to control but who can be knocked into line by the likes of us. They're shouting slobs who'll run like hell when class shows and they know this inside their feeble little heads. So they didn't want Leo Knapp put on a pedestal.

"Control comes other ways, however. For instance, he could marry a woman who would listen to him as a sounding board and relay his thoughts and secrets to the right persons so that whatever he did could be quickly annulled by some other action. He could marry a woman who, as his official Washington hostess, had the ear of respected persons and could pick up things here and there that were as important to enemy ears as any sealed documents. He could find his work being stymied at every turn.

"Then one day he figured it all out. He pinpointed the enemy and found it within his own house. He baited a trap by planting supposedly important papers in his safe and one night while the enemy, his wife, was rifling his safe with her compatriot who was to photograph the papers and transport the photos to higher headquarters, he came downstairs. He saw her, accused her, but blundered into a game bigger than he was.

"Let's say she shot him. It doesn't really matter. She was just as guilty even if it was the other one. At least the other one carried the gun off—a pickup rod traceable to no one if it was thrown away printless. His wife delayed long enough so she and her compatriot could fake a robbery, let the guy get away, then call in the cops.

"Nor does it end there. The same wife still acts as the big Washington hostess with her same ear to the same ground and is an important and inexhaustible supply of information to the enemy. Let's say that she is so big as to even be part of The Dragon team. He was Tooth, she was Nail, both spies, both assassins, both deadly enemies of this country."

Behind me the water went on again, a downpour that would rinse the bubbles of soap from her body.

"All went well until Richie Cole was killed. Tooth went and

used the same gun again. It tied things in. Like I told you when I let you be *my* sounding board—coincidence is a strange thing. I like the word 'fate' even better. Or is 'consequence' an even better one? Richie and Leo and Velda were all tied into the same big situation and for a long time I was too damn dumb to realize it.

"A guy like me doesn't stay dumb forever, though. Things change. You either die or smarten up. I had The Dragon on my back and when I think about it all the little things make sense too. At least I think so. Remember how when Gorlin shot the radio you shook with what I thought was fear? Hell, baby, that was rage. You were pissed off that he could pull such a stupid stunt and maybe put your hide in danger. Later you gave him hell on the phone, didn't you? That house is like an echo chamber, baby. Talk downstairs and you hear the tones all over. You were mad. I was too interested in going through your husband's effects to pay any attention, that was all.

"Now it's over. Tooth is nailed, but that's a joke you don't understand yet, baby. Let's just say that The Dragon is tethered. He'll sit in the chair and all the world will know why and nations will backtrack and lie and propaganda will tear up the knotheads in the Kremlin and maybe their satellite countries will wise up and blast loose and maybe we'll wise up and blast them, but however it goes, The Dragon is dead. It didn't find Velda. She'll talk, she'll open up the secrets of the greatest espionage organization the world has ever known and Communist philosophy will get the hell knocked out of it.

"You see, baby, I know where Velda is."

The shower stopped running and I could hear her hum as though she couldn't even hear me.

"The catch was this. Richie Cole did make his contact. He gave Old Dewey, the newsstand operator, a letter he had that told where Alex Bird would take Velda. It was a prepared place and she had orders to stay there until either he came for her or I came for her. He'll never come for her.

"Only me," I said. "Dewey put the letter in a magazine. Every month he holds certain magazines aside for me and to make sure I got it he put it inside my copy of *Cavalier*. It will be there when I go back to the city. I'll pick it up and it will tell me where Velda is."

I finished dressing, put on the empty gun and slid painfully into the jacket. The blood was crusty on my clothes, but it really didn't matter anymore.

I said, "It's all speculation, I might be wrong. I just can't take any chances. I've loved other women. I loved Velda. I've loved you and like you said, it's either you or her. I have to go for her, you know that. If she's alive I have to find her. The key is right there inside my copy of that magazine. It will have my name on it and Duck-Duck will hand it over and I'll know where she is."

She stopped humming and I knew she was listening. I heard her make a curious woman-sound like a sob.

"I may be wrong, Laura. I may see her and not want her. I may be wrong about you, and if I am I'll be back, but I have to find out." The slanting beam of the sun struck the other side of the bathhouse leaving me in the shadow then. I knew what I had to do. It had to be a test. They either passed it or failed it. No in-betweens. I didn't want it on my head again.

I reached for the shotgun in the corner, turned it upside down and shoved the barrels deep into the blue clay and twisted them until I was sure both barrels were plugged just like a cookie cutter and I left it lying there and opened the door.

The mountains were in deep shadow, the sun out of sight and only its light flickering off the trees. It was a hundred miles into the city, but I'd take the car again and it wouldn't really be very long at all. I'd see Pat and we'd be friends again and Hy would get his story and Velda—Velda? What would it be like now?

I started up the still wet concrete walk away from the bathhouse and she called out, "Mike—*Mike!*"

I turned at the sound of her voice and there she stood in the naked, glossy, shimmering beauty of womanhood, the lovely tan of her skin blossoming and swelling in all the vast hillocks and curves that make a woman, the glinting blond hair throwing tiny lights back into the sunset and over it all those incredible gray eyes.

Incredible.

They watched me over the elongated barrels of the shotgun and seemed to twinkle and swirl in the fanatical delight of murder they come up with at the moment of the kill, the moment of truth.

But for whom? Truth will out, but for whom?

The muzzle of the gun was a pair of yawning chasms but there was no depth to their mouths. Down the length of the blued steel the blood crimson of her nails made a startling and symbolic contrast.

Death red, I thought. The fingers behind them should have been tan but weren't. They were a tense, drawing white and with another fraction of an inch the machinery of the gun would go into motion.

She said, "*Mike—*" and in that one word there was hate and desire, revenge and regret, but above all the timbre of duty long ago instilled into a truly mechanical mind.

I said, "So long, baby."

Then I turned and walked toward the outside and Velda and behind me I heard the unearthly roar as she pulled both triggers at once.

THE
SNAKE

For Bob Fellows,
who knows Mike
from too many angles.
And Donna, who knows Bob
the same way.

CHAPTER 1

You walk down the street at night. It's raining out. The only sound is that of your own feet. There are city sounds too, but these you don't hear because at the end of the street is the woman you've been waiting for for seven long years and each muffled tread of your footsteps takes you closer and closer and the sound of them marks off seconds and days and months of waiting.

Then, suddenly, you're there, outside a dark-faced building, a brownstone anachronism that stares back dully with the defiant expression of the moronic and you have an impending sense of being challenged.

What would it be like? I thought. Was she still beautiful? Had seven years of hell changed her as it had me? And what did you say to a woman you loved and thought was killed because you pulled a stupid play? How do you go from seven years ago to now?

Only a little while ago a lot of other feet were pointing this way, searching for this one house on this one street, but now mine were the only ones left to find it because the rest belonged to dead men or those about to die.

The woman inside was important now. Perhaps the most important in the world. What she knew would help destroy an enemy when she told it. My hands in my pockets balled into hard knots to keep from shaking and for a moment the throbbing ache of the welts and cuts that laced my skin stopped.

And I took the first step.

There were five more, then the V code on the doorbell marked *Case*, the automatic clicking of the lock and I was in the vestibule of the building under a dim yellow light from a single overhead bulb and down the shadowed hallway to the rear was the big door. Behind it lay seven years ago.

I tapped out a Y on the panel and waited, then tapped a slow R and the bolt slid back and the knob turned and there she stood with the gun still ready if something had gone wrong.

Even in that pale light I could see that she was more beautiful than ever, the black shadow of her hair framing a face I had seen every night in the misery of sleep for so long. Those deep brown eyes still had that hungry look when they watched mine and the lush fullness of her mouth glistened with a damp warmth of invitation.

Then, as though there had never been those seven years, I said, "Hello, Velda."

For a long second she just stood there, somehow telling me that it was only the *now* that counted and with that same rich voice that could make music with a simple word, she answered, "Mike . . ."

She came into my arms with a rush and buried her face in my neck, barely able to whisper my name over and over because my arms were so tight around her. Even though I knew I was hurting her I couldn't stop and she didn't ask me to. It was like we were trying to get inside each other and in the frenzy of it found a way when our mouths met in a predatory coupling we had never known before. I tasted the fire and beauty of her, my fingers probing the flesh of her back and arms and shoulders, leaving marks wherever they touched. That familiar resiliency was still in her body, tightening gradually into a passionate tautness that rippled and quivered, crying out soundlessly for more, more, more.

I took the gun from her hand, dropped it in a chair, then pushed the door closed with my foot and felt for the light switch. A lamp on the table seemed to come alive with the unreal slowness of a movie prop, gradually highlighting the classic beauty of her face and the provocative thrust of her breasts.

There was a subtle leanness about her now, like you saw in those fresh from a battle area, every gesture a precision movement, every sense totally alert. And now she was just beginning to realize that it was over and she could be free again.

"Hello, kitten," I said, and watched her smile.

There wasn't much we could say. That would take time, but

now we had all the time in the world. She looked at me, talking through those crazy eyes, then her expression went soft and a frown made small creases across her forehead. Her fingers went out and touched my face and the white edge of her teeth went into her lip.

"Mike . . .?"

"It's okay, baby."

"You're not . . . hurt?"

I shook my head. "Not anymore."

"There's something about you now . . . I can't quite tell what . . ."

"Seven years, Velda," I interrupted. "It was downhill all the way until I found out you were still alive. It leaves marks, but none that can't be wiped out."

Her eyes blurred under tears that came too quickly to control. "Mike darling . . . I couldn't reach you. It was all too impossible and big . . ."

"I know it, kid. You don't have to explain."

Her hair swirled in a dark arc when she shook her head. "But I do."

"Later."

"Now." Her fingers touched my mouth to silence me and I let them. "It took seven years to learn a man's secret and escape Communist Europe with information that will keep us equal or better than they are. I know I could have . . . gotten away earlier . . . but I had to make a choice."

"You made the right one."

"There was no way to tell you."

"I know it."

"Truly . . ."

"I understand, kitten."

She wouldn't listen. Her voice was softly insistent, almost pleading. "I could have, Mike. I know I could have some way, but I couldn't afford the chance. There were millions of lives at stake." She paused a second, then pulled my cheek against hers. "I know how you must have felt, thinking you had me killed. I thought of it so often I nearly went out of my mind, but I still couldn't have changed things."

"Forget it," I told her.

"What did happen to you, Mike?"

She pushed away, holding me at arm's length to study me.

"I got to be a drunk," I said.

"You?"

"Me, kitten."

Her expression was one of curious bewilderment. "But when I told them . . . they had to find you . . . only you could do it . . ."

"One mentioned your name and I changed, honey. When you came alive again, so did I."

"Oh, Mike . . ."

As big as she was, I picked her up easily, kissed her again, and took her across the room to the gaudy mohair couch that nestled in the bay of an airshaft window. She quivered against me, smiled when I laid her down, then pulled my mouth to hers with a desperation that told me of the loneliness of seven years and the gnawing wanting inside her now.

Finally she said, "I'm a virgin, Mike."

"I know."

"I've always waited for you. It's been a pretty long wait."

I grinned down at her. "I was crazy to make you wait."

"And now?"

Then I wasn't grinning anymore. She was all mine whenever I wanted her, a big, beautiful animal of a woman who loved me and was ready to be taken *now, now*. Even touching was a painful emotion and the fire that had been dormant was one I didn't want to put out.

I said, "Can you wait a little bit more?"

"Mike?" There was a quick hurt in her eyes, then the question.

"Let's do it right, kitten. Always I do the wrong things. Let's make this one right." Before she could answer I said, "Don't argue. Don't even talk about it. We do it, that's all, then we can explode into a million pieces. We do the bit at City Hall with the license and do it right."

Velda smiled back impishly, the happiness of knowing what I wanted plain in her face. "That really doesn't matter," she told me. "First I want you. Now. More than ever."

"Crazy broad," I said, then fought her mouth with mine, knowing we were both going to win. My hand drifted across the satiny expanse of her naked shoulder, feeling the minute trembling throughout her body. She twisted so she pressed against me, moaning softly, demanding things we never had from each other.

"Pretty," he said from the door. *"Real pretty."*

I still had the .45 in my belt but I never could have made it. Velda's convulsive grip around my neck slowed the action enough so that I saw the Police Positive in his hand and didn't get killed after all. The hammer was back for faster shooting and the look on his face was one I had seen before on other cheap killers and knew that he'd drop me the second he thought I might be trouble.

"Go on, don't stop," he said. "I like good shows."

I made my grin as simpering as I could, rolling away from Velda until I sat perched on the edge of the couch. I was going wild inside and fought to keep my hands dangling at my sides while I tried to look like an idiot caught in the act until I could think my way past this thing.

"I didn't know there'd be two but it figures a babe like you'd have something going for her." He nudged the gun toward me. "But why grab off a mutt like this, baby?"

When she spoke from behind me her voice was completely changed. "When I could have had you?"

"That's the way, baby. I've been watching you through that window four days and right now I'm ready. How about that?"

I would have gone for the rod right then, but I felt the pressure of her knee against my back.

"How about that?" Velda repeated.

The guy let out a jerky laugh and looked at me through slitted eyes. "So maybe we'll make music after all, kid. Just as soon as I dump the mutt here."

Then I couldn't keep quiet any longer. "You're going to have to do it the hard way."

The gun shifted just enough so it pointed straight at my head. "That's the way I always do things, mutt."

He was ready. The gun was tight in his hand and the look was there and he was ready. Velda said, "Once that gun goes off you won't have me."

It wasn't enough. The guy laughed again and nodded. "That's okay too, baby. This is what I came for anyway."

"Why?" she asked him.

"Games, baby?" The gun swung gently toward her, then back to me, ready to take either or both of us when he wanted to. I tried to let fear bust through the hate inside me and hoped it showed like that when I slumped a little on the couch. My hand was an inch nearer the .45 now, but still too far away.

"I want the kid, baby, ya know?" he said. "So no games. Trot her out, I take off, and you stay alive."

"Maybe," I said.

His eyes roved over me. "Yeah, maybe." He grinned. "You know something, mutt? You ain't scared enough. You're thinking."

"Why not?"

"Sure, why not? But whatever you think it just ain't there for you, mutt. This ain't your day."

There were only seconds now. He was past being ready and his eyes said it was as good as done and I was dead and he started that final squeeze as Velda and I moved together.

We never would have made it if the door hadn't slammed open into him and knocked his arm up. The shot went into the ceiling and with a startled yell he spun around toward the two guys in the doorway, dropping as he fired, but the smaller guy got him first with two quick shots in the chest and he started to tumble backwards with the blood bubbling in his throat.

I was tangled in the raincoat trying to get at my gun when the bigger one saw me, streaked off a shot that went by my head, and in the light of the blast I knew they weren't cops because I recognized a face of a hood I knew a long time. It was the last shot he ever made. I caught him head-on with a .45 that pitched him back through the door. The other one tried to nail me while I was rolling away from Velda and forgot about the guy dying on the floor. The mug let one go from the Police Positive that ripped into the hood's belly and with a choking yell he tumbled out the door, tripped, and hobbled off out of sight, calling to someone that he'd been hit.

I kicked the gun out of the hand of the guy on the floor, stepped over him, and went out in the hall gun first. It was too late. The car was pulling away from the curb and all that was left was the peculiar silence of the street.

He was on his way out when I got back to him, the sag of death in his face. There were things I wanted to ask him, but I never got the chance. Through bloody froth he said, "You'll . . . get yours, mutt."

I didn't want him to die happy. I said, "No chance, punk. This is my day after all."

His mouth opened in a grimace of hate and frustration that was the last living thing he ever did.

From where to where? I thought. *Why are there always dead men around me? I came back, all right. Just like in the old days. Love and death going hand in hand.*

There was something familiar about his face. I turned his head with my toe, looked at him closely and caught it. Velda said, "Do you know him?"

"Yeah. His name is Basil Levitt. He used to be a private dick until he tried a shakedown on somebody who wouldn't take it, then he did time for second-degree murder."

"What about the other one?"

"They call him Kid Hand. He was a freelance gun that did muscle for small bookies on bettors who didn't want to pay off. He's had a fall before too."

I looked at Velda and saw the way she was breathing and the set expression on her face. There was a strange sort of wildness there you find on animals suddenly having to fight for their lives. I said, "They aren't from the other side, kitten. These are new ones. These want something different." I waited a moment, then: "Who's the kid, honey?"

"Mike . . ."

I pointed to the one on the floor. "He came for a kid. He came here ready to shoot you up. Now who's the kid?"

Again, she gave me an anguished glance. "A girl . . . she's only a young girl."

I snapped my fingers impatiently. "Come on, give me, damn it. You know where you stand! How many people have died because of what you know? And right now you haven't got rid of it. You want to get killed after everything that happened for some stupid reason?"

"All right, Mike." Anguish gave way to concern then and she glanced upward. "Right now she's in an empty room on the top floor. Directly over this one."

"Okay, who is she?"

"I . . . don't know. She came here the day after . . . I was brought here. I heard her crying outside and took her in."

"That wasn't very smart."

"Mike . . . there were times when I wish someone had done that to me."

"Sorry."

"She was young, desperate, in trouble. I took care of her. It was like taking in a scared rabbit. Whatever her trouble was, it was big enough. I thought I'd give her time to quiet down, then perhaps be able to help her."

"What happened?"

"She's scared, Mike. Terrified. She's all mixed up and I'm the only one she can hang on to."

"Good, I'll take your word for it. Now get me up to her before this place is crawling with cops. We have about five minutes before somebody is going to be curious enough to make a phone call."

From the third floor you could hear the rhythmic tap of her feet dancing a staccato number that made you think of an Eleanor Powell routine when prettylegs was queen of the boards. There was no music, yet you knew *she* heard some and was in a never-never land of her own.

Velda knocked but the dancing didn't stop. She turned the knob and pushed the door open and with a soft cry the girl in the middle of the room twisted around, her hand going to her mouth when she saw me, huge eyes darting from Velda's to mine. She threw one glance toward the window when Velda said, "It's all right, Sue. This is our friend."

It was going to take more than that to convince her and there wasn't enough time. "My name is Mike Hammer, Sue. I'm going to help you. Can you understand that?"

Whatever it was, it worked. The fear left her face and she tried on a tentative smile and nodded. "Will you . . . really?"

"Really," I nodded back. To Velda I said, "Can we get her out of here?"

"Yes. I know of a place I can take her."

"Where?"

"Do you remember Connie Lewis' restaurant on Forty-first?"

"Just off Ninth?"

"That's it. I'll be there. She has the upper three floors to herself."

"That was seven years ago."

"She'll be there," Velda told me.

"Okay," I said, "you get there with the kid. I'll do the talking on the bit downstairs, then in about an hour you show up at Pat's office. I'm being a damn fool for letting you out on the street again but I can't see any other way of doing it."

Her hand squeezed mine and she smiled. "It'll be all right, Mike."

Then the kid walked up and I looked into the face of the prettiest little Lolita-type I ever saw. She was a tiny blonde with enormous brown eyes and a lovely mouth in a pert pointed face that made you want to pick her up like a doll. Her hair was silk-soft and hung loosely to her shoulders and when she moved all you could see was girl-woman and if you weren't careful you'd feel the wrong kind of feel.

But I was an old soldier who had been there and back, so I said, "How old are you, chicken?"

She smiled and said, "Twenty-one."

I grinned at Velda. "She's not lying. You thought she was kidding when she told you that, didn't you?"

Velda nodded.

"We'll get straight on this later. Right now take off." I looked at Sue, reaching out to feel her hair. "I don't know what your trouble is, girl, but first things first. I'm going to lay something on the line with you though."

"Oh?"

"Downstairs there are two dead men because of you. So play it the way you're told and we'll make it. Try using your own little head and there may be more dead people. Me, I've had it. I'll help you all the way as long as you do it like I say, but go on your own and you're like out, kid, understand? There aren't any more people who can make this boy tumble again, big or little. I'm telling you this because you're not as little as you look. You can fool a lot of slobs, but not this slob, so we're starting off square, okay?"

"Okay, Mr. Hammer." There was no hesitation at all.

"Call me Mike."

"Sure, Mike."

"Get her out of here, Velda."

The sirens converged from both directions. They locked the street in on either end and two more took the street to the front of the house. The floods hit the doorway and the uniformed cops came in with .38's in their hands.

I had the door open, the lights lit, and both hands in view when the first pair stepped through the doorway. Before they asked I took the position, let them see my .45 on the table beside the other guns, and watched patiently while they flipped open my wallet with the very special ticket in the identification window.

The reaction was slow at first. They weren't about to take any chances with two dead men on the floor, but they couldn't go too far the other way either. Finally the older one handed my wallet back. "I knew you back in the old days, Mike."

"Times haven't changed much."

"I wonder." He nodded toward the two bodies. "I don't suppose you want to explain about all this now?"

"That's right."

"You got a big ticket there. When?"

"Call Captain Chambers. This is his baby."

"I guess it is."

"There's a new Inspector in the division. He might not like the action."

"No sweat, friend. Don't worry."

"I'm not worrying. I just remember you and Captain Chambers were friends."

"No more."

"I heard that too." He holstered his gun. Behind him another pair came in cautiously, ready. "This a big one?" he asked.

"Yeah. Can I make a call?"

"Mind if I make it for you?"

"Nope." I gave him a number that he already knew and watched his face go flat when I handed him the name. He went outside to the car, put the call through, and when he came back there was a subtle touch of deference in his attitude. Whatever he had said to the others took the bull off me and by the time the M.E. got there it was like someone had diplomatic immunity.

Pat came in five minutes later. He waited until the pictures were taken and the bodies removed, then waved everybody else out except the little man in gray whom nobody was big enough to wave out. Then he studiously examined my big fat .45 and said, "The same one, isn't it?"

"It's the only one I ever needed."

"How many men have you killed with it?"

"Nine," I said. Then added, "With that gun."

"Good score."

"I'm still alive."

"Sometimes I wonder."

I grinned at him. "You hate me, buddy, but you're glad, aren't you?"

"That you're still alive?"

"Uh-huh."

He turned slowly, his eyes searching for some obscure answer. "I don't know," he said. "Sometimes I can't tell who is the worse off. Right now I'm not sure. It's hard to kill friendships. I tried hard enough with you and I almost made it work. Even with a woman between us I can't be sure anymore. You crazy bastard, I watch what you do, see you get shot and beat to hell and wonder why it has to happen like that, and I'm afraid to tell myself the answer. I know it but I can't say it."

"So say it."

"Later."

"Okay."

"Now what happened?" He looked at Art Rickerby sitting in the chair.

I said, "Velda was here. I came for her. These two guys bust in, this one here first. The other came in time to break up the play."

"Nicely parlayed."

"Well put, buddy."

"For an ex-drunk you're doing all right." He glanced at Rickerby again.

"Some people have foresight," I reminded him.

"Do I leave now?" Pat said. "Do I go along with the Federal bit and take off?"

For the first time Art Rickerby spoke. He was quiet as always and I knew that there were no ends left untied in the past I had just left. He said, "Captain . . . there are times when . . . there are times. It was you who forced Mr. Hammer into circumstances he could hardly cope with. It was a dead man and me who made him stick to it. If he's anathema out of the past, then it's our fault. We brought a man back who should have died a long time ago. The present can't stand a man like that anymore. Now they want indecision and compromise and reluctance and fear . . . and we've dropped a hot iron in society's lap. We've brought a man back who almost shouldn't be here and now you and me and society are stuck with him."

"Thanks a bunch," I said.

"Sure," Pat said to Art, "he's always been in the special-privilege class, but now it's over my head. You got the pull, Rickerby. I don't get all the picture, but I've been around long enough to figure a few things out. Just clue me on this one."

"Pat . . ." I started.

"Not you, Mike. *Him*." He smiled with that gentle deceptiveness. "And make it good. We have two dead men here and I'm not writing that off for anybody. No more I'm not."

Art nodded and glanced at his watch. "The girl Velda," he said, "she was the crux. She has information this country depends upon. A team of assassins was assigned to kill her and nobody could get to that team we called 'The Dragon' but him because nobody could be as terrible as they were. It turned out that he was even worse. If that is a good word. For that information this country would pay any price and part of the cost was to rehabilitate this man in a sense and give him back his privilege and his gun.

"The Dragon team is gone now. There is only the girl Velda. There is still that price to pay and he can call the tune. You have no choice but to back him up. Is that clear?"

"No, but it's coming through," Pat said. "I know most of the story but I find it hard to believe."

I said, "Pat . . ."

"What?"

"Let's leave it, kid. We were both right. So she's still mine. If you want her then take her away, but you have to fight me for her and you haven't got a chance in the world of winning."

"Not as long as you're alive," he told me.

"Sure, Pat."

"And the law of averages is on my side."

"Why sure."

I didn't think he could do it, but he did. He grinned and stuck out his hand and instinctively I took it. "Okay, boy. It's like before now. We start fresh. Do I get the story or does he?"

"First him, buddy," I said, nodding toward Art, "then you. It's bigger than local and I'm not just a private cop anymore."

"They told me about your ticket. Smart."

"You know me. Never travel small."

"That's right. Somebody's got to be the hero."

"Nuts. If I'm on a dead play, then I want odds that will pay off."

"They did."

"Damn right they did. I stuck it up and broke it off. Everybody wanted me dead and instead it turned all the way around. So I got the payoff. A big ticket and the rod back and nobody puts the bull on me until I flub it royally . . . and this, friend, I'm not about to do again."

"No?"

"Watch."

"My pleasure, big buddy." He grinned. Again. "Mind if I leave and you talk it out with Mister Government here?"

"No. But be at your office soon. She'll be there and so will I."

"Soon?"

"An hour."

"I'll be waiting, hero."

When he left Art Rickerby said, "She has to talk right away. Where is she?"

"I told you . . . in an hour . . . at Pat's office."

"There were dead men here."

"So . . ."

"Don't piddle with me, Mike."

"Don't piddle with me, Art."

"Who were they?"

"I damn well don't know, but this you'll do and damn well do it right."

"Don't tell me what to do."

"No? I'll shove it up your tail if I want to, Art, and don't you forget it. You do this one my way. This is something else from your personal angle and leave it alone. Let those dead men be. As far as anybody is concerned they're part of The Dragon group and the last part at that. There ain't no more, the end, finis. They came for Velda and I was here to lay on the gravy like I did the rest and you go along with it. What's here is not part of your business at all, but for the moment you can cover me. Do it."

"Mike . . ."

"Just do it and shut up."

"Mike . . ."

I said softly, "I gave you The Dragon, didn't I?"

"Yes."

"I was dead. You exhumed me. You made me do things that were goddamned near impossible and when I didn't die doing them you were surprised. So be surprised now. Do like I tell you."

"Or . . .?'

"Or Velda won't come in."

"You're sure?"

"Positive, friend."

"It will be done."

"Thanks."

"No trouble."

And Velda told them the next day. She spelled it out in detail and a government organization collapsed. In Moscow thirty men died and in the East Zone of Berlin five more disappeared and in South America there was a series of accidents and several untimely deaths and across the face of the globe the living went to the dead in unaccountable numbers and codes and files were rearranged and meetings hastily brought about and summit conferences planned and in the U.N. buildings whole new philosophies were adopted and decisions brought about in a changed light and as suddenly as she had been a threat to a different world, she had become a person again. She had nothing more to give and in the world of politics there was no retribution as long as you knew nothing new and really didn't care at all.

But there *was* something new. There were two dead men to tell about it and somewhere in the city was another with a bullet in his gut looking for somebody to take it out and if the little blonde didn't tell, one of these would.

You just didn't lay dead men at your feet without someone coming looking for you.

And I had them at my feet.

I knew I had a tail on me when I left the D.A.'s office. It had been nicely set up even though Rickerby had put the fix in for me. No local police force likes to be queered out of a deal in their own backyard, and if they could move in, orders or not, they were going to give it the big try. If Pat had set the tail it would have been hard to spot, but the new D.A. was too ambitious to figure out there were civilian-type pros in the police business too.

For an hour I let him wait outside bars, fool around a department store while I picked up a few goodies, then went in one door of the Blue Ribbon Restaurant on Forty-fourth, around through the bar, and out that door while he was looking for me at the tables. I was back on Seventh Avenue before he knew I was gone, flagged down a cab, and had him cut over to Forty-ninth and Ninth.

Connie Lewis' place was called "La Sabre" and turned out to be a downstairs supper place for the neighborhood trade. It specialized in steaks and chops and seemed to be built around a huge charcoal grill that smoked and sizzled into a copper canopy. Connie was a round little woman with a perpetual smile and wrinkles at the corners of her eyes and mouth that said it was for real. It had been years since I had seen her and she hadn't changed a bit.

But me she didn't recognize at first. When it did come she beamed all over, tried to get me to drink, then eat, and when I wouldn't do either, showed me the way to the staircase going upstairs and told me Velda was on the second floor rear with her company.

I used the same VY knock and she opened the door. There was

no gun in her hand this time, but I knew it wasn't far out of reach. She pulled me in, closed the door, and locked it. I grinned at her, grabbed her by the shoulders, and touched her mouth with mine. Lightly. I couldn't afford any more. Her eyes laughed back at me and told me I could pick my own time and place. Any time, any place.

I said, "Hello, beautiful. Where's the kid?"

"Here I am, Mike."

She eased into the room impishly, hands clasped behind her back. She stood at the corner of the bedroom door watching, seemingly unafraid, but inside those huge brown eyes was a worm of fear that had been there too long to be plucked out easily.

I took Velda's arm, steered her to the table, and motioned the kid to come over too. Automatically, the kid slid closer to Velda, knowing she was protected there, never taking her eyes from my face.

"Let's have it," I said.

Velda nodded. "You can tell him."

"I . . . don't know."

For what it was worth I took out my new wallet and flipped it open. The blue and gold card with the embossed seal in the plastic window did the trick again. She studied it, frowned, then made up her mind.

"All right," she finally told me. "My name is Sue Devon." When she said it there was a challenge in her voice I couldn't ignore.

"Am I supposed to know you?"

She flicked her eyes to her hands, to Velda, then to me. "I have another name."

"Oh?"

"Torrence. I never use it. He had me legally adopted a long time ago but I never use his name. I hate it."

I shook my head. "Sorry, kid. I don't make you at all."

Velda reached out and touched my hand. "Sim Torrence. He was the District Attorney once; now he's running in the primaries for governor of the state."

"Win with Sim?"

"That's right."

"I remember seeing posters around but I never tied him up with the D.A.'s office." I let a grin ease out. "It's been a rough seven years. I didn't keep up with politics. Now let's hear the rest of this."

Sue nodded, her hair tumbling around her face. She bit at her lip with even white teeth, her hands clasped so tight the knuckles showed white. "I ran away from him."

"Why?"

The fear was a live thing in her eyes. "I think . . . he killed my mother. Now he wants to kill me."

When I glanced at Velda I knew she was thinking the same thing I was. I said, "People running for governor don't usually kill people."

"He killed my mother," she repeated.

"You said you *thought* he did." She didn't answer so I asked, "When was this supposed to have happened?"

"A long time ago."

"How long?"

"I . . . was a baby. Eighteen years ago."

"How do you know he did this?"

She wouldn't look at me. "I just know it, that's all."

"Honey," I said, "you can't accuse a man of murder with a reason like that."

She made a little shrug and worked her fingers together.

I said, "You have something else in your mind. What is it?"

Velda slipped her arm around her shoulders and squeezed. Sue looked at her gratefully and turned back to me again. "I remember Mama talking. Before she died. Whatever she said . . . is in my mind . . . but I can't pick out the words. I was terribly frightened. She was dying and she talked to me and told me something and I don't remember what it was!" She sucked her breath in and held it while the tears welled up in her eyes.

When she relaxed I said, "And what makes you think he wants to kill you?"

"I know . . . the way he looks at me. He . . . touches me."

"Better, baby. You'll have to do better than that."

"Very well. There was a car. It almost hit me."

"Did you recognize it?"

"No."

"Go on."

"There was a man one night. He followed me home from the theater. He tried to cut me off but I knew the roads and lost him not far from the house."

"Did you recognize him or his car?"

"No."

"Did you report the incidents?"

"No," she said softly.

"Okay, Sue, my turn. Do you know you're an exceptionally pretty girl?" She looked up at me. "Sure you do. Men are going to follow you, so get used to dodging. Nearly everybody has had a close call with a car, so don't put too much store in that. And so far as your stepfather is concerned, he'd look at you like any man would his daughter and touch you the same way. You haven't said anything concrete yet."

"Then what about that man you killed and the other one?"

"*Touché*," I said. But I couldn't let it lay there. She was waiting and she was scared. I looked at Velda. "Did you tell her where you've been for seven years and what happened?"

"She knows."

"And about me?"

"Everything."

"Then maybe this is an answer . . . those men were part of an enemy organization who had to destroy Velda before she talked. They moved in to get her, not you. And now it's over. Nobody's going to kill her because now she's said her piece and it's too late. What do you think about that?"

"I'm not going back," she said simply.

"Supposing I go see your stepfather. Suppose I can really find out the truth, even to what your mother told you. Would that help any?"

"Maybe." Her voice was a whisper.

"Okay, kid, I'll play Big Daddy."

Velda looked up with eyes so full of thanks I had to laugh at her. She scooted the kid off to the other end of the room, took my arm, and walked me to the door. "You'll do all you can?"

"You know, you'd think I'd know better by now."

"Mike . . . don't change."

"No chance, baby."

She opened the door. "Do you . . . believe that about . . . those men coming for me?"

After a few seconds I said, "No. Basil Levitt said he wanted both you and the kid so it wasn't anything to do with the last operation. She's in it someplace." I knew I was frowning.

"What are you thinking of?"

"Something he said, damn it." I wiped my face with my hand and grimaced. "I've been away too long. I'm not clicking."

"It will come."

"Sure, honey," I said. I touched her face lightly. "Later?"

"I'll be waiting."

"Put the kid to bed."

She made a face at me, grinned and nodded.

It was like there had never been those seven years at all.

There wasn't much trouble getting background material on Simpson Torrence. He had been making headlines since the '30s, was featured in several of the latest magazines, and was the subject of three editorials in opposition newspapers. I took two hours to go over the bits and pieces and what I came up with made him a likely candidate for governor. In fact, several of his high-ranking constituents were looking past the mansion at Albany to the White House in Washington.

But good points I wasn't looking for. If there was anything to the kid's story at all, then something would have to point to another side of the guy's character. People just don't come all good.

I called Hy Gardner and asked him to meet me at the Blue Ribbon with anything he might have on Torrence. All he said was, "Now what?" But it meant he'd be there.

He showed up with Pete Ladero, who did legwork for a political columnist, and over lunch I picked out all the information on Torrence I could get. Substantially, it was the same as the better magazines had reported. Sim Torrence was a product of New York schools, had graduated magna cum laude and gone into public service immediately afterward. He had a small inheritance that made him independent enough to be able to afford the work and a determination that took him from an assistant D.A. through the main office into the State Legislature and Senate, and now he was standing at the threshold of the governorship. I said, "What's wrong with the guy?"

"Nothing," Pete told me. "Find out something and I'll peddle it to the opposition for a million bucks."

"Didn't they try?"

"You kidding?"

Hy shoved his glasses up on his forehead. "So what's the business then, Mike? What are you laying into Torrence for?"

"Curiosity right now. His name came up in a little deal a while back."

"This for publication?"

"No. It's strictly for curiosity value."

"I wish to hell you'd say what you're going to say."

"Okay," I agreed. "What about his marriage?"

Pete and Hy looked at each other, shrugged, and Pete said, "His wife died years ago. He never remarried."

"Who was she?"

Pete thought a moment, then: "Her name was Devon, Sally Devon. If I remember right she was a fairly pretty showgirl when it was fashionable to marry showgirls. But hell, she died not long after the war. There was never any scandal connected with his marriage."

"What about the kid?" I asked.

Pete shook his head. "Nothing. I've met her several times. Torrence adopted her when her mother died, sent her to pretty good schools, and she's lived with him since."

"She ran away."

"You don't run away when you're over twenty-one," he reminded me. "Sim probably has given her a checking account that will keep her provided for wherever she goes." He paused a moment. "I don't get the angle there."

"Because I haven't got one," I said. "In my business names and people get dropped into funny places and no matter who they are they get checked out. Hell, it never hurts to prove a clean man clean."

Pete agreed with a nod, finished his coffee, and told us so-long. Hy said, "Satisfied?"

"I'm getting there."

"Do I get a hint at least?"

"Sure. The two dead men the night I found Velda."

Hy frowned and pulled his glasses off, his cigar working across his mouth. "The ones who followed you and tried to nail Velda at the last minute?"

"That's the story the papers got, friend."

He waited, staring at me.

I said, "They had nothing to do with the espionage bit. They were part of another story."

"Brother!" Hy poked the cigar out in the ashtray and reached for his pencil and scratch sheets.

"No story yet, Hy. Hold it back. I'll tell you when."

Reluctantly, he put them back. "Okay, I'll wait."

"Velda had Torrence's kid with her. She took her in like a stray cat. Strictly coincidence, but there we are. The kid said she was hiding out from her old man, but whether she's lying or not, we know one thing: two dead men and a possible third say trouble's there."

"How the hell can you suppress stuff like that!" Hy exploded.

"Angles, buddy."

"Boy, you sure come on like gangbusters. I hope you're protecting yourself."

"Don't worry about me."

"Don't worry, I won't."

Hy had to get back to his desk at the *Tribune* building so I dropped him off and went ahead to Pat's office. The uniformed sergeant at the desk waved to me, said Pat was upstairs in new quarters and to go ahead up.

He was eating at his desk as usual, too crammed with work to take time out at a lunch counter. But he wasn't too busy to talk to me. I was part of his work. He grinned and said, "How is Velda?"

"Fine, but not for you."

"Who knows?" He reached for the coffee container. "What's up?"

"What did you get on Levitt and the other guy?"

"Nothing new on Levitt. He'd been sporting some fresh money lately without saying where it came from. It was assumed that he picked up his old blackmail operations."

"And the other one?"

"Kid Hand. You knew him, didn't you?"

"I've seen him around. Small-time muscle."

"Then you haven't seen him lately. He's gone up in the world.

Word has it that he's been handling all the bookie operations on the Upper West Side."

"Tillson's old run?"

"Hell, Tillson was knocked off a year ago."

"So who's Hand working for?"

"I wish I knew. Mr. Big has been given the innocuous-sounding name of Mr. Dickerson, but nobody seems to know any more about him."

"Somebody's going to be taking over Hand's end. There'll be a shake-up somewhere."

"Mike . . . you just don't know the rackets anymore. It's all I.B.M.-style now. Business, purely business, and they're not being caught without a chain of command. No, there won't be a shake-up. It'll all happen nice and normally. Somebody else will be appointed to Kid Hand's job and that will be that."

"You guessed the bug, though, didn't you?"

Pat nodded. "Certainly. What's a wheel like Hand taking on a muscle job for anyway? You know the answer?"

"Sure. I'd say he was doing somebody a favor. Like somebody big."

"Yeah," Pat said sourly. "Now the question is, who was killing who? You nailed Hand, Levitt fired two shots, and we recovered one out of the ceiling."

"Another one got Hand's friend in the gut. You might check the hospitals."

"*Now* you tell me."

"Nuts, Pat. You figured it right after it happened."

He swung around idly in his chair, sipping at the coffee container. When he was ready he said, "What were they really after, Mike?"

I took my time too. "I don't know. Not yet I don't. But I'll find out."

"Great. And with all that top cover you got I have to sweat you out."

"Something like that."

"Let me clue you, Mike. We have a new Inspector. He's a tough nut and a smart one. Between him and the D.A., you're liable to find your tail in a jam. Right now they're trying hard to bust you loose for them to work over, so you'd better have pretty powerful friends in that office you seem to be working for."

I put my hat on and stood up. "Anything I come up with you'll get."

"Gee, thanks," he said sarcastically, then grinned.

Sim Torrence lived inside a walled estate in Westchester that reflected the quiet dignity of real wealth and importance. A pair of ornate iron gates were opened wide, welcoming visitors, and I turned my rented Ford up the drive.

The house, a brick colonial type, was surrounded by blue spruces that reached to the eaves. Two black Caddies were parked in front of one wing and I pulled up behind them, got out, touched the doorbell, and waited.

I had expected a maid or a butler, but not a stunning brunette with electric blue eyes that seemed to spark at you. She had an early season tan that made her eyes and the red of her mouth jump right at you and when she smiled and said quizzically, "Yes?" it was like touching a hot line.

I grinned crookedly. "My name is Hammer. I'm looking for Mr. Torrence."

"Is he expecting you?"

"No, but I think he'll see me. It's about his daughter."

The eyes sparked again with some peculiar fear. "Is she . . . all right?"

"Fine."

Then relief took over and she held out her hand to me. "Please come in, Mr. Hammer. I'm Geraldine King, Mr. Torrence's secretary. He's going to be awfully glad to see you. Since Sue ran off again he's been so upset he can't do a thing."

"Again?"

She glanced up at me and nodded. "She's gone off several times before. If she only knew what she does to Mr. Torrence when she gets in one of her peeves she'd be more considerate. In here, Mr. Hammer." She pointed into a large study that smelled of cigars and old leather. "Make yourself at home, please."

There wasn't much time for that. Before I had a chance to make a circuit of the room I heard the sound of hurried feet and Big Sim Torrence, the Man-Most-Likely-To-Succeed, came in looking not at all like a politician, but with the genuine worry of any distraught father.

He held out his hand, grabbed mine, and said, "Thanks for coming, Mr. Hammer." He paused, offered me a chair, and sat down. "Now, where is Sue? Is she all right?"

"Sure. Right now she's with a friend of mine."

"Where, Mr. Hammer?"

"In the city."

He perched on the edge of the chair and frowned. "She . . . *does* intend to come back here?"

"Maybe."

His face hardened then. It was a face that had an expression I had seen a thousand times in courtrooms. It became a prosecuting attorney's face who suddenly found himself with a hostile witness and was determined to drag out the right answers the hard way.

Torrence said, "Perhaps I don't understand your concern in this matter."

"Perhaps not. First, let me tell you that it's by accident that I'm here at all. Sue was sort of taken in hand by my secretary and I made a promise to look into things before letting her return."

"Oh?" He looked down into his hands. "You are . . . qualified for this matter then?"

The wallet worked its magic again and the hostility faded from his face. His expression was serious, yet touched with impatience. "Then please get to the point, Mr. Hammer. I've worried enough about Sue so . . ."

"It's simple enough. The kid says she's scared stiff of you."

A look of pain flitted across his eyes. He held up his hand to stop me, nodded, and looked toward the window. "I know, I know. She says I killed her mother."

He caught me a little off base. When he looked around once more I said, "That's right."

"May I explain something?"

"I wish somebody would."

Torrence settled back in his chair, rubbing his face with one hand. His voice was flat, as though he had gone through the routine countless times before. "I married Sally Devon six months after her husband died. Sue was less than a year old at the time. I had known Sally for years then and it was like . . . well, we were old friends. What I didn't know was that Sally had become an alcoholic. In the first years of our marriage she grew worse in spite of everything we tried to do. Sally took to staying at my place in the Catskills with an old lady for a housekeeper, refusing to come into the city, refusing any help . . . just drinking herself to death. She kept Sue with her although it was old Mrs. Lee who really took care of the child. One night she drank herself into a stupor, went outside into the bitter cold for something, and passed out. She was unconscious when Mrs. Lee found her and dead before either a doctor or I could get to her. For some reason the child thinks I had something to do with it."

"She says her mother told her something before she died."

"I know that too. She can't recall anything, but continues to make the charge against me." He paused and rubbed his temples. "Sue has been a problem. I've tried the best schools and let her follow her own desires but nothing seems to help matters any. She wants to be a showgirl like her mother was." He looked up at me slowly. "I wish I knew the answer."

This time I was pretty direct. "She says you're trying to kill her."

His reaction was one of amazement. *"What?"* Very slowly he came to the edge of his seat. *"What's that?"*

"A car tried to run her down, she was deliberately followed, and somebody took a shot at her."

"Are you sure?"

"I am about the last time. I was there when it happened." I didn't bother giving him any of the details.

"But . . . why haven't I heard . . .?"

"Because it involved another matter too. In time you'll hear about it. Not now. Just let's say it happened."

For the first time his courtroom composure left him. He waved his hands like a lost person and shook his head.

I said, "Mr. Torrence, do you have any enemies?"

"Enemies?"

"That's right."

"I . . . don't think so." He reflected a moment and went on. "Political enemies, perhaps. There are two parties and . . ."

"Would they want to kill you?" I interrupted.

"No . . . certainly not. Disagree, but that's all."

"What about women?" I asked bluntly.

He paid no attention to my tone. "Mr. Hammer . . . I haven't kept company with a woman since Sally died. This is a pretty well-known fact."

I looked toward the door meaningfully. "You keep pretty company."

"Geraldine King was assigned to me by our state chairman. She has been with me through three political campaigns. Between times she works with others in the party running for office."

"No offense," I said. "But how about other possibles? Could you have made any special enemies during your political career?"

"Again, none that I know of who would want to kill me."

"You were a D.A. once."

"That was twenty-some years ago."

"So go back that far."

Torrence shrugged impatiently. "There were a dozen threats, some made right in the courtroom. Two attempts that were unsuccessful."

"What happened?"

"Nothing," he said. "Police routine stopped the action. Both persons were apprehended and sent back to prison. Since then both have died, one of T.B., the other of an ulcer."

"You kept track of them?"

"No, the police did. They thought it best to inform me. I wasn't particularly worried."

"Particularly?"

"Not for myself. For Sue and anyone else, yes. Personally, my recourse is to the law and the police. But remember this, Mr. Hammer, it isn't unusual for a District Attorney to be a target. There was a man named Dewey the mobs could have used dead, but to kill him would have meant that such pressure would be brought on organized crime that when Dutch Schultz wanted to kill him the Mob killed Dutch instead. This is a precarious business and I realize it. At the same time,

I won't alter my own philosophies by conforming to standards of the scared."

"How often have you been scared?"

"Often. And you?"

"Too often, buddy." I grinned at him and he smiled back slowly, his eyes showing me he knew what I meant.

"Now about Sue."

"I'll speak to her."

"You'll bring her home?"

"That's up to Sue. I'll see what she says. Supposing she won't come?"

Torrence was silent a moment, thinking. "That's up to her then. She's a . . . child who isn't a child. Do you know what I mean?"

"Uh-huh."

He nodded. "She's well provided for financially and frankly, I don't see what else I can do for her. I'm at a point where I need advice."

"From whom?"

His eyes twinkled at me. "Perhaps from you, Mr. Hammer."

"Could be."

"May I ask your status first?"

"I hold a very peculiar legal authorization. At the moment it allows me to do damn near anything I want to. Within reason, of course."

"For how long?"

"You're quick, friend." He nodded and I said, "Until somebody cuts me out of it or I make a mistake."

"Oh?"

"And the day of mistakes is over."

"Then advise me. I need advice from someone who doesn't make mistakes anymore." There was no sarcasm in his tone at all.

"I'll keep her with me until she wants out."

A full ten seconds passed before he thought it over, then he nodded, went to the other side of his desk and pulled out a checkbook. When he finished writing he handed me a pretty green paper made out for five thousand dollars and watched while I folded it lengthwise.

"That's pretty big," I said.

"Big men don't come little. Nor do big things. I want Sue safe. I want Sue back. It's up to you now, Mr. Hammer. Where do you start?"

"By getting you to remember the name of the other guys who threatened to kill you."

"I doubt if those matters are of any importance."

"Suppose you let me do the deciding. A lot of trouble can come out of the past. A lot of dirt too. If you don't want me probing you can take your loot back. Then just for fun I might do it anyway."

"There's something personal about this with you, isn't there, Mr. Hammer? It isn't that you need the money or the practice. You needn't tell me, but there is something else."

We studied each other for the few ticks of time that it took for two pros in the same bit of business to realize that there wasn't much that could be hidden.

"You know me, Torrence."

"I know you, Mike. Doesn't everybody?"

I grinned and stuck the check in my pocket. "Not really," I said.

CHAPTER 3

You can always make a start with a dead man. It's an ultimate end and a perfect beginning. Death is too definite to be ambiguous and when you deal with it your toes are in the chocks and not looking for a place to grab hold.

But death can be trouble too. It had been a long time and in seven years people could forget or stop worrying or rather play the odds and get themselves a name in the dark shadows of the never land of the night people.

Kid Hand was dead. Somebody would be mad. Somebody would be worried. By now everybody would know what happened in that tenement room and would be waiting. There would be those who remembered seven years ago and would wonder what came next. Some would know. Some would have to find out.

Me, maybe.

Off Broadway on Forty-ninth there's a hotel sandwiched in between slices of other buildings and on the street it has a screwy bar with a funny name filled with screwier people and even funnier names. They were new people, mostly, but some were still there after seven years and when I spotted Jersey Toby I nodded and watched him almost drop his beer and went to the bar and ordered a Four Roses and ginger.

The bartender was a silent old dog who mixed the drink, took my buck, and said, "Hello, Mike."

I said, "Hello, Charlie."

"You ain't been around."

"Didn't have to be."

"Glad you dumped the slop chutes."

"You hear too much."

"Bartenders like to talk too."

"To who?"

"Whom," he said.

"So whom?"

"Like other bartenders."

"Anybody else?"

"Nobody else," he said gently.

"Business is business," I grinned.

"So be it, Mike."

"Sure, Charlie," I told him.

He walked away and set up a couple for the hookers working the tourist traffic at the other end, then sort of stayed in the middle with a small worried expression on his face. Outside it was hot and sticky and here it was cool and quiet with the dramatic music of Franck's Symphony in D Minor coming through the stereo speakers too softly to be as aggressive as it should. It could have been a logical place for anybody to drop in for a break from the wild city outside.

One of the hookers spotted my two twenties on the bar and broke away from her tourist friend long enough to hit the cigarette machine behind me. Without looking around she said, "Lonely?"

I didn't look around either. "Sometimes."

"Now?"

"Not now," I said.

She turned around, grinned, and popped a butt in her pretty mouth. "Crazy native," she said.

"A real aborigine."

She laughed down in her throat. "So back to the flatland foreigners."

Jersey Toby waited until she left, then did the cigarette-machine bit himself before taking his place beside me. He made it look nice and natural, even to getting into a set routine of being a sudden bar friend and buying a drink.

When the act was over he said, "Look, Mike . . ."

"Quit sweating, buddy."

"You come for me or just anybody?"

"Just anybody."

"I don't like it when you don't come on hard."

"A new technique, Toby."

"Knock it off, Mike. Hell, I know you from the old days. You think I don't know what happened already?"

"Like what?"

"Like what's with Levitt and Kid Hand. You got rocks in your head? You think you can come shooting into the city anymore? Man, things ain't like before. You been away and you should've stayed away. Now before you get me involved, let me tell you one big thing. Don't make me out a patsy. I ain't telling you nothing. Not one goddamn thing. Lay off me. I been doing a lot of small-time crap that don't get me no heat from either direction and that's the way I like it."

"Great."

"And no soft stuff too. Save that bull for the enlisted men."

"What are you pitching now?"

"I'm a pimp."

"You came down in the world."

"Yeah? Well maybe I did, but I got bucks going for me now and a couple of broads who like the bit. I do it square and not like some of the creeps and on top there's enough juice to pay off who needs paying off, like. Y'know?"

"I won't eat your bread, kiddo."

"Goddamn right."

He sat there glowering into his drink, satisfied that he had made his point, then I reached over and took his hand and held it against my side where the .45 was strung and said, "Remember?"

When he took his hand back he was shaking. "You're still nuts," he said. "You ain't nothing no more. One push with that rod and you've had it. I'm still paying juice."

This time I pulled the other cork. I took out the wallet and opened it like I was going to put my money back only I let him see the card in the window. He took a good look, his eyes going wide, then reached for his drink. "An ace, Toby," I said. "Now do we go to your place or my place?"

"I got a room upstairs," he told me.

"Where?"

"313."

"Ten minutes. You take off first."

It was a back-alley room that had the antiseptic appearance of all revamped hotel rooms, but still smelled of stale beer, old clothes, and tired air. Jersey Toby opened a beer for himself when I waved one off, then sat down with a resigned shrug and said, "Spill it, Mike."

"Kid Hand."

"He's dead."

"I know. I shot him. The top of his head came off and left a mess on the wall. He wasn't the first and he probably won't be the last."

Toby put the beer down slowly. *"You're nuts."*

"That's the best you can say?"

"No," he repeated. *"You're nuts.* I think you got a death wish."

"Toby . . ."

"I mean it, Mike. Like word goes around fast. You don't make a hit in this town without everybody knowing. You was crazy enough in those old days, but now you're real nuts. You think I don't know already? Hell, like everybody knows. I don't even want to be in the same room with you."

"You don't have a choice, Toby."

"Sure, so I'll pay later. So will you. Damn, Mike . . ."

"Kid Hand," I repeated.

"He took Tillson's job. Everybody knew about that."

"More."

"Like what, you nut! How the hell should I know about Kid? We ain't in the same game. I'm pimping. You know what he was? Like a big shot! Mr. Dickerson's right-hand boy. You think I'm going to . . .?"

"Who?"

"Knock it off . . . you know."

"Who, Toby?"

"Mr. Dickerson."

"Who's he, buddy?"

"Mike . . ."

"Don't screw around with me."

"Okay. So who knows from Dickerson? He's the new one in. He's the big one. He comes in with power and all the hard boys are flocking back. Hell, man, I can't tell you more. All I know is Mr. Dickerson and he's the gas."

"Political?"

"Not him, you nut. This one's power. Like firepower, man. You know what's happening in this town? They're coming in from the burgs, man. Bit shooters and they're gathering around waiting for orders. I feel the stream going by but I ain't fishing. Too long the mobs have been dead . . . now it's like Indians again. A chief is back and the crazy Soos is rejoicing. That's all I can say."

"Kid Hand?"

"Crazy, man. A shooter and he knew where his bread was. He was on the way up until he decided to get back in the ranks again. He should've stayed where he was."

"Why?"

"Why what?"

"He pulled on me. I don't take that crap."

"He knew it was you, maybe? He knew it was anybody?"

"Somebody said he might have been doing a personal favor."

Toby got up and faced the blank window. "Sure, why not? Favors are important. It makes you look big. It proves like you're not a punk. It proves . . ."

"It proves how fast you can get killed, too."

Slowly, he turned around. "Am I in the middle, Mike?"

"I don't see how."

"Ask it straight."

"Who is Dickerson?"

"Nobody knows. Just that he's big."

"Money?"

"I guess."

"Who takes Kid Hand's place?"

"Whoever can grab it. I'd say Del Penner. He's pretty tough. He had a fall ten years ago, but came back to grab off the jukes in Chi, then moved into the bolita and jai alai in Miami. He was pushing Kid pretty hard."

"Then maybe Kid's move in on me was part of a power grab."

"Favors don't hurt nobody."

"It killed Kid."

"So he didn't know it was you."

I looked at him a long time, then his face got tight and he turned away. When he gulped down his beer he looked at me, shrugged, and said, "Word goes it was a personal favor. You were a surprise. You just don't know what kind of a surprise. It wasn't with you. It was something else. That's all. I don't know . . . I don't want to know. Let me make my bucks my own way, only stay loose, man."

"Why?"

"You're hot now, man. Everybody knows. Everybody's looking."

"I've had heat before."

"Not like this." He looked into his beer, shrugged, and decided. "You ever hear of Marv Kania?"

"No."

"He's a contract man from St. Loo. Punk about twenty-eight, got a fall for murder second when he was a teenager, joined with Pax in K.C., then did the route with Arnold Philips on the coast and back to St. Loo. They figured he was a contract kill on Shulburger, Angelo, and Vince Pago and the big Carlysle hit in L.A. He's got plenty of cover and is as nuts as you are."

"What does that make me, Toby?"

"A target, man. He's in town with a slug in his gut and everybody knows how it happened. If he dies you're lucky. If he don't you're dead."

I got up and put on my hat. "My luck's been pretty good lately," I said.

He nodded gravely. "I hope it holds."

When I went to open the door he added, "Maybe I don't, too."

"Why?"

"I don't want to be around when it stops. You'll make an awful splash."

"It figures."

"Sure it does," he said.

Then I went back to her, the beautiful one whose hair hung dark and long, whose body was a quiet concert in curves and colors of white and shadow that rose softly under a single sheet into a woman's fulfillment of mounded breasts and soft clefts.

She didn't hear me come in until I said, "Velda . . ."

Then her eyes opened, slowly at first, then with the startled suddenness of a deer awakened and her hand moved and I knew what she had in it. When she knew it was me her fingers relaxed, came out from under the cover, and reached for mine.

"You can lose that way, kid," I said.

"Not when you're here."

"It wasn't always me."

"This is *now*, Mike," she said. It was almost me thinking again when I walked up the steps a couple of days ago.

I took her hand, then in one full sweep flipped the sheet off her body and looked at her.

What is it when you see a woman naked? *Woman.* Long. Lovely. Tousled. Skin that looks slippery in the small light. Pink things that are the summit. A wide, shadowy mass that is the crest. Desire that rests in the soft fold of flesh that can speak and taste and tell that it wants you with the sudden contractions and quickening intake of breath. A mouth that opens wetly and moves with soundless words of love.

I sat on the edge of the bed and let my fingers explore her. The invitation had always been there, but for the first time it was accepted. Now I could touch and feel and enjoy and know that this was mine. She gasped once, and said, "Your eyes are crazy, Mike."

"You can't see them."

"But I know. They're wild Irish brown green and they're crazy."

"I know."

"Then do what I want."

"Not me, kid. You're only a broad and I do what I want."

"Then do it."

"Are you ready?" I asked.

"I've always been ready."

"No you haven't."

"I am now."

Her face was turned toward mine, the high planes in her cheeks throwing dark shades toward her lips, her eyes bright with a strange wetness, and when I bent forward and kissed her it was like tasting the animal wildness of a tiger filled with an insensate hunger that wanted to swallow its victim whole and I knew what woman was like. Pure woman.

Across the room, muffled because of the alcove, came a peculiar distant tone that made the scales, rising and falling with an eerie quality that had a banshee touch, and Velda said, "She's awake."

I pulled the sheet up and tucked it around her shoulders. "She isn't."

"We can go somewhere."

"No. The biggest word."

"Mike . . ."

"First we get rid of the trouble. It won't be right until then."

I could feel her eyes. "With you there will always be trouble."

"Not this trouble."

"Haven't we had enough?"

I shook my head. "Some people it's always with. You know me now. It comes fast, it lasts awhile, then it ends fast."

"You never change, do you?"

"Kitten, I don't expect to. Things happen, but they never change."

"Will it be us?"

"It has to be. In the meantime there are things to do. You ready?"

She grinned at me, the implication clear. "I've always been ready. You just never asked before."

"I never ask. I take."

"Take."

"When I'm ready. Not now. Get up."

Velda was a woman. She slid out of bed and dressed, deliberately, so I could watch everything she did, then reached into the top drawer of the dresser and pulled out a clip holster and slid it inside her skirt, the slide going over the wide belt she wore. The flat-sided Browning didn't even make a bulge.

I said, "If anybody ever shot me with that I'd tear their arms off."

"Not if you got shot in the head," she told me.

I called Rickerby from downstairs and he had a man stand by while we were gone. Sue was asleep, I thought, but I couldn't be sure. At least she wasn't going anyplace until we got back. We walked to the parking lot where I picked up the rented Ford and cut over to the West Side Highway.

She waited until I was on the ramp to ask, "Where are we going?"

"There's a place called 'The Angus Bull.' It's a new one for the racket boys."

"Who told you?"

"Pat."

"And whom do I con?"

"A man named Del Penner. If he isn't there you'll pick up a lead if you work it right. He was pushing Kid Hand and will probably take his place in the group. What you want to know is this . . . who is Mr. Dickerson?"

She threw me a funny glance and I filled her in on the small details. I watched her out of the corner of my eyes while she picked it all apart and put it back together again. There was something new about her now that wasn't there seven years ago. Then she had been a secretary, a girl with her own P.I. ticket and the right to carry a gun. Then she had been a girl with a peculiar past I hadn't known about. Now she was a woman, still with a peculiar past and a gun, but with a strange new subtlety added that was nurtured during those years behind the Iron Curtain in the biggest chase scene civilization had ever known.

"Where do we clear?"

"Through Pat."

"Or your friend Rickerby?"

"Keep him as an alternate. It isn't his field yet, so we'll stay local."

"Where will you be?"

"Running down the immediate past of a guy called Basil Levitt. Pat came up with nothing. They're still on the job, but he had no office and no records. Whatever he carried he carried in his hat, but he sure was working for somebody. He was after you and the kid and was four days watching your joint. I don't know what we have going, but these are the only leads we have."

"There's Sue."

"She has nothing to say yet."

"Did you believe what she said about her father trying to kill her?"

"No."

"Why not?"

"Because it isn't logical. The kid's a neurotic type and until something proves out I'm not going along with childish notions."

"Two dead men aren't notions."

"There's more to it than that, baby. Let me do it my way, okay?"

"Sure. It's always your way, isn't it?"

"Sure."

"Is that why I love you?"

"Sure."

"And you love me because I think that way?"

"Why sure."

"I'm home, Mike."

I touched her knee and felt her leg harden. "You never were away, kid."

She was on her own when I dropped her downtown. She grinned at me, waved, and I let her go. There was something relaxing about the whole thing now. No more tight feeling in the gut. No more of that big empty hole that was her. She was there and bigger than ever, still with the gun on her belt and ready to follow.

Going through Levitt's place was only a matter of curiosity. It was a room, nothing more. The landlady said he had been there six months and never caused trouble, paid his rent, and she didn't want to talk to any more cops. The neighbors didn't know anything about him at all and didn't want to find out. The local tavern owner had never served him and couldn't care less. But up in his room the ashtrays had been full of butts and there were two empty cartons in the garbage and anyone who smokes that much had to pick up cigarettes somewhere.

Basil Levitt did it two blocks away. He got his papers there too.

The old lady who ran the place remembered him well and didn't mind talking about it.

"I know the one," she told me. "I wondered when the cops would get down here. I even woulda seen them only I wanted to see how fast they'd get here. Sure took you long enough. Where you from, son?"

"Uptown."

"You know what happened?"

"Not yet."

"So what do you want with me?"

"Just talk, Mom."

"So ask."

"Suppose you tell." I grinned at her. "Maybe you want the third degree, sweetie, just like in TV . . . okay?"

She waved her hand at me. "That stuff is dead. Who hits old ladies anymore except delinquents?"

"Me. I hit old ladies."

"You look like the type. So ask me."

"Okay . . . any friends?"

She shook her head. "No, but he makes phone calls. One of the hot boys . . . never shuts the door." She nodded toward the pay booth in back.

"You listened?"

"Why not? I'm too old to screw so I get a kick out of love talk."

"How about that?"

"Yeah, how?" She smiled crookedly and opened herself a Coke. "He never talked love talk, never. Just money and always mad."

"More, Mom."

"He'd talk pretty big loot. Five G's was the last . . . like he was a betting man. Was he, son?"

"He bet his skin and lost. Now more."

She made a gesture with her shoulders. "Last time he was real mad. Said something was taking too long and wanted more loot. I don't think he got it."

"Any names?"

"Nope. He didn't call somebody's house, either."

I waited and she grinned broadly.

"He only called at a certain time. He had to speak up like wherever the other party was, it was damn noisy. That's how come I heard him."

"You'd make a good cop, Mom."

"I been around long enough, son. You want to know something else?"

"That's what I'm here for."

"He carried a package once. It was all done up in brown paper and it wasn't light. It was a gun. Rifle all taken down, I'd say. You like that bit?"

"You're doing great. How'd you know?"

"Easy. It *clunked* when he set it down. Besides, I could smell the gun oil. My old man was a nut on those things before he kicked off. I smelled that stuff around the house for years."

Then I knew what bugged me right after Basil Levitt died. I said my thanks and turned to go. She said, "Hey . . ."

"What?"

"Would you really hit an old lady?"

I grinned at her. "Only when they need it," I said.

I stood in the room that had been Velda's and scanned the other side of the street. It didn't take long to sort out the only windows that were set right for an ambush. Ten bucks to a fat old man got me the key with no questions asked and when I opened the door to the first one that was it.

The gun was an expensive sporting rifle with a load in the chamber, blocked in on a tripod screwed to a tabletop and the telescopic sights were centered on the same window I had looked out of a few minutes before. There were two empty cigarette cartons beside the gun, a tomato-juice can full of butts and spent matches, and the remains of a dozen sandwiches scattered around.

Basil's vigil had been a four-day one. For that long a time he had waited. At any time he could have had Velda. He knew she was there. He told me so. He had watched her that long but couldn't move in.

The reason for his wait was plain now. It wasn't her he was after at all. It was the kid. He wanted her. He was on a contract to knock her off and had to wait for her to show.

Only she didn't. Velda had kept her upstairs out of sight. It was only when I came on the scene that he had to break his pattern. He didn't know why I was there but couldn't take any chances. I might be after the same target he was after but for a different reason: to get her out.

So now it was back to the little Lolita-type again.

It had been a long time since I had seen Joey Adams and his wife Cindy. Now, besides doing his major nightclub routines with time off for tent-circus Broadway musicals and worldwide junkets, he was president of AGVA. But he hadn't changed a bit. Neither had Cindy. She was still her same stunning self in the trademark colors of scarlet and midnight whamming out a column for *TV Guide*.

I told the girl not to announce me and when I went in Joey was perched on the edge of his desk trying to talk Cindy out of something new in minks. He wasn't getting anywhere. I said, "Hello, buddy."

He looked over his shoulder, grinned, and hopped off the desk with his hand out. "I'll be damned," he said, "you finally picked up the rain check. Where you been?"

"On the wrong street." I looked past him. "Hello, beautiful."

Cindy threw me a flashing smile. "I told Joey you'd show up. We've been following the obituaries. You leave a trail, Mike."

"I was following one."

"That's what Hy said. You big fink, why didn't you come visit when you needed help?"

"Hell, kid, I didn't need any help to stay drunk."

"That's not what I meant."

Joey waved at her impatiently. "Come on, come on, what's new? Look, suppose we . . ."

"I need help now, pal."

It caught him off balance a second. "Listen, I'm no AA, but . . ."

"Not that kind of help," I grinned.

"Oh?"

"You've been bugging me to play cop for how long, Joey?"

His eyes lit up like a marquee but Cindy got there first.

"Listen, old friend, you keep my boy away from the shooters. Like he's mine and I want to keep him in one piece. He's just a comedian and those gun routines are hard on the complexion."

"Cut it out, Cindy. If Mike wants . . ."

"Don't sweat it, friend. Just a simple favor."

He looked disappointed.

"But it's something you can get to where I can't," I added.

Joey laughed and faked a swing at my gut. "So name it, kid."

"How far back do your files go?"

"Well," he shrugged, "what do you want to know?"

I sat on the edge of the desk and lined things up in my mind. "There was a showgirl named Sally Devon who was in business over twenty years ago. Name mean anything?"

Joey squinted and shook his head. "Should it?"

"Not necessarily. I doubt if she was a headliner."

"Mike . . ." Cindy uncoiled from her chair and stood beside Joey. "Wasn't she Sim Torrence's wife at one time?"

I nodded.

"How'd you know?" Joey asked.

"I'm just clever."

"What do you know about her, honey?"

"Nothing at all, but I happened to be talking politics to one of Joey's friends and he dropped her name in the hat. He had worked with her at one time."

"Now she's in politics," Joey grunted. "So who were you talking to?"

"Bert Reese."

"What do you think, Joey? Do a rundown for me? Maybe Bert can steer you to somebody else that would know about her."

"Sure, but if it's politics you want, Cindy can . . ."

"It's not politics. Just get a line on her show-biz activities. She would've been in from twenty to thirty years back. Somebody at Equity might know her or the old chorus-line bunch. She was married to Sim Torrence while he was still a small-timer so the connection might bring somebody's memory back. Seem possible?"

"Sure, Mike, sure. The kids always keep in touch. They never forget. Hell, you know show business. I'll dig around."

"How long will it take?"

"I ought to have something by tomorrow. Where'll I get in touch?"

"My old office. I'm back in business, or reach me through the Blue Ribbon Restaurant."

He gave me that big grin again and winked. Now he was doing an act he liked. There are always frustrated cops and firemen. I shook hands with Joey, waved at Cindy, and left them to battle about the mink bit again.

Rickerby's man gave me a funny look and a curt nod when I showed, asked if there were anything else, and when I said no, made his phone call to clear and took off. Then I went upstairs.

I could hear her all the way, like a wild bird singing a crazy melody. She had an incredible range to her voice and just let it go, trilling some strange tune that had a familiar note, but was being interpreted out of its symphonic character.

The singing didn't come from the floor where I had left her, either. It was higher up and I made the last flight in a rush and stood at the end of the corridor with the .45 in my hand wondering what the hell was going on. She had everything wrapped up in that voice, fear, hate, anxiety, but no hope at all.

When I pushed the door open slowly her voice came flooding out from the peculiar echo chamber of the empty room. She stood facing the corner, both hands against the wall, her head down, her shoulders weaving gently with the rhythm of her voice, her silken blond hair a gold reflection from the small bulb overhead.

I said, "Sue . . ." and she turned slowly, never stopping, but, seeing me there, went into a quiet ballet step until she stopped and let her voice die out on a high lilting note. There was something gone in her eyes and it took a half minute for her to realize just who I was.

"What are you doing up here?"

"It's empty," she said finally.

"Why do you want it like that?"

222 • THE MIKE HAMMER COLLECTION

She let her hands drift behind her back. "Furniture looks at you. It means people and I don't want any people."

"Why, Sue?"

"They hurt you."

"Did somebody hurt you?"

"You know."

"I know that nobody has hurt you so far."

"So far. They killed my mother."

"You don't know that."

"Yes I do. A snake killed her."

"A what?"

"A snake."

"Your mother died of natural causes. She was . . . a sick woman."

This time Sue shook her head patiently. "I've been remembering. She was afraid of a snake. She told me so. She said it was the snake."

"You were too young to remember."

"No I wasn't."

I held out my hand to her and she took it. "Let's go downstairs, sugar. I want to talk to you."

"All right. Can I come back up here when I want to?"

"Sure. No trouble. Just don't go outside."

Those big brown eyes came up to mine with a sudden hunted look. "You know somebody wants to hurt me too, don't you?"

"Okay, kid, I won't try to con you. Maybe it will make you a little cautious. I think somebody is after you. Why, I don't know, but stick it out the way I tell you to, all right?"

"All right, Mike."

I waited until she had finished her coffee before I dropped the bomb on her. I said, "Sue . . ."

Then her eyes looked up and with a sudden intuition she knew what I was going to say.

"Would you mind going home?"

"I won't go," she said simply.

"You want to find out what really happened to your mother, don't you?"

She nodded.

"You can help if you do what I ask."

"How will that help?"

"You got big ears, kid. I'm an old soldier who knows his way around this business and you just don't fool me, baby. You can do anything you want to. Go back there and stay with it. Somebody wants you nailed, sugar, and if I can get you in a safe place I can scrounge without having you to worry about."

Sue smiled without meaning to and looked down at her hands. "*He* wants me dead."

"Okay, we'll play it your way. *If* he does there's nothing he can do about it now. There're too many eyes watching you."

"Are yours, Mike?"

I grinned. "Hell, I can't take 'em off you."

"Don't fool with me, Mike."

"All right, Sue. Now listen. Your old man paid me five grand to handle this mess. It isn't like he's caught in a trap and is trying to con me because he knows all about me. I'm no mouse. I've knocked over too many punks and broke too many big ones to play little-boy games with."

"Are you *really* convinced, Mike?"

"Honey, until it's all locked up, tight, I'm never convinced, but at this stage we have to work the angles. Now, will you go back?"

She waited a moment, then looked up again. "If you want me to."

"I want you to."

"Will I see you again?"

Those big brown eyes were a little too much. "Sure, but what's a guy like me going to do with a girl like you?"

A smile touched her mouth. "Plenty, I think," she said.

Sim Torrence was out, but Geraldine King made the arrangements for a limousine to pick up Sue. I waited for it to arrive, watched her leave, then went back to my office. I got out at the eighth floor, edged around the guy leaning up against the wall beside the buttons with his back to me, and if it didn't suddenly occur to me that his position was a little too awkward to be normal and that he might be sick I never would have turned around and I would have died face down on the marble floor.

I had that one split-second glance at a pain- and hate-contorted face before I threw myself back toward the wall scratching for the .45 when his gun blasted twice and both shots rocketed off the floor beside my face.

Then I had the .45 out and ready but it was too late. He had stepped back into the elevator I had just left and the doors were closing. There wasn't any sense chasing him. The exit stairs were down the far end of the corridor and the elevator was a quick one. I got up, dusted myself off, and looked up at the guy who stuck his head out of a neighboring door. He said, "What was that?"

"Be damned if I know. Sounded like it was in the elevator."

"Something's always happening to that thing," he said passively, then closed his door.

Both slugs were imbedded in the plaster at the end of the hall, flattened at the nose and scratched, but with enough rifling marks showing for the lab to make something out of it. I dropped them in my pocket and went to my office. I dialed Pat, told him what had happened, and heard him let out a short laugh. "You're still lucky, Mike. For how long?"

"Who knows?"

"You recognize him?"

"He's the guy Basil Levitt shot, buddy. I'd say his name was Marv Kania."

"Mike . . ."

"I know his history. You got something out on him?"

"For a month. He's wanted all over. You sure about this?"

"I'm sure."

"He must want you pretty badly."

"Pat, he's got a bullet in him. He's not going to last like he is and if he's staying alive it's to get me first. If we can nail him we can find out what this is all about. If he knows he's wanted he can't go to a doctor and if he knows he's dying he'll do anything to come at me again. Now damn it, a shot-up guy can't go prancing around the streets, you know that."

"He's doing it."

"So he'll fall. Somebody'll try to help him and he'll nail them too. He just can't follow me around, I move too fast."

"He'll wait you out, Mike."

"How?"

"You're not thinking straight. If he knows what this operation is about he'll know where you'll be looking sooner or later. All he has to do is wait there."

"What about in the meantime?"

"I'll get on it right away. If he left a trail we'll find it. There aren't too many places he can hole up."

"Okay."

"And, buddy . . ."

"What, Pat?"

"Hands off if you nail him, understand? I got enough people on my back right now. This new D.A. is trying to break your license."

"Can he?"

"It can be done."

"Well hell, tell him I'm cooperating all the way. If you look in the downstairs apartment in the building across the street from where Velda was staying you'll find a sniper's rifle that belonged to Basil Levitt. Maybe you can backtrack that."

"Now you tell me," he said softly.

"I just located it."

"What does it mean?"

I didn't tell him what I thought at all. "Got me. You figure it out."

"Maybe I will. Now you get those slugs down to me as fast as you can."

"By messenger service right now."

When I hung up I called Arrow, had a boy pick up the envelope with the two chunks of lead, got them off, then stretched out on the couch.

I slept for three hours, a hard, tight sleep that was almost dreamless, and when the phone went off it didn't awaken me until the fourth or fifth time. When I said hello, Velda's voice said, "Mike . . ."

"Here, kitten. What's up?"

"Can you meet me for some small talk, honey?"

My fingers tightened involuntarily around the receiver. *Small talk* was a simple code. *Trouble*, it meant, *be careful*.

In case somebody was on an extension I kept my voice light. "Sure, kid. Where are you?"

"A little place on Eighth Avenue near the Garden . . . Lew Green's Bar."

"I know where it is. Be right down."

"And, Mike . . . come alone."

"Okay."

On the way out I stopped by Nat Drutman's office and talked him out of a .32 automatic he kept in his desk, shoved it under my belt behind my back, and grabbed a cab for Lew Green's Bar. There was a dampness in the air and a slick was showing on the streets, reflecting the lights of the city back from all angles. It was one of those nights that had a bad smell to it.

Inside the bar a pair of chunkers were swapping stories in a half-drunken tone while a TV blared from the wall. A small archway led into the back room that was nestled in semi-darkness and when I went in a thin, reedy voice said from one side, "Walk easy, mister."

He had his hands in his side pockets and would have been easy to take, loaded or not, but I went along with him. He steered me past the booths to the side entrance where another one waited who grinned in an insolent way and said, "He carries a heavy piece. You look for it?"

"You do it," the thin guy said.

He knew right where to look. He dragged the .45 out, said, "Nice," grinned again, and stuck it in his pocket. "Now outside. We got transportation waiting. You're real V.I.P."

The place they took me to was in Long Island City, a section ready to be torn down to make way for a new factory building. The car stopped outside an abandoned store and when the smart one nodded I followed him around the back with the thin one six feet behind me and went on inside.

They sat at a table, three of them, with Velda in a chair at the end. A single Coleman lamp threw everything into sharp lights and shadows, making their faces look unreal.

I looked past them to Velda. "You okay, honey?"

She nodded, but there was a tight cast to her mouth.

The heavy-set guy in the homburg said, "So you're Mike Hammer."

I took a wild guess. "Del Penner."

His face hardened. "He clean?"

Both the guys at the door behind him nodded and the one took my .45 out and showed it. Del said, "You came too easy, Hammer."

"Who expected trouble?"

"In your business you should always expect it."

"I'll remember it. What's the action, Penner?"

"You sent her asking about me. Why?"

"Because I'm getting my toes stepped on. A guy named Kid Hand got shot and I hear you're taking his place. I don't like to get pushed. Now what?"

"You'll get more than pushed, Hammer. Word's around that you got yourself some top cover and knocking you off can make too much noise. Not that it can't be handled, but who needs noise? Okay, you're after something, so spill it."

"Sure. You are stepping up then?"

Penner shrugged elaborately. "Somebody takes over. What else?"

"Who's Dickerson?"

Everybody looked at everybody else before Del Penner decided to answer me. He finally made up his mind. "You know that much, then you can have this. *Nobody* knows who Mr. Dickerson is."

"Somebody knows."

"Maybe, but not you and not us. What else?"

"You pull this stunt on your own?"

"That you can bet your life on. When this broad started nosing around I wanted to know why. So I asked her and she told me. She said they were your orders. Now get this . . . I know about the whole schmear with you knocking off Kid Hand and getting Levitt bumped and leaving Marv Kania running around with a slug in his gut. I ain't got orders on you yet but like I said, when anybody noses around me I want to know why."

"Supposing I put it this way then, Penner . . . I'm the same way. Anybody tries to shoot me up is in for a hard time. You looked like a good place to start with and don't figure I'm the only one who'll think of it. You don't commit murder in this town and just walk away from it. If you're stepping into Kid Hand's job then you should know that too."

Penner smiled tightly. "The picture's clear, Hammer. I'm just stopping it before it gets started."

"Then this bit is supposed to be a warning?"

"Something like that."

"Or maybe you're doing a favor ahead of time."

"What's that mean?"

"Like Kid Hand was maybe doing a personal favor and stepped down off his pedestal to look like a big man."

The silence was tight. Del Penner just stared at me, not bothered at all by what I said. His hand reached up and touched his homburg and he sat back in his chair. "Warning then, Hammer. Don't make any more noise around me. I imagine you'd be about a fifteen-hundred-buck job. One thousand five hundred bucks can buy both of you dead and no mud on my hands. Clear?"

I put both hands on the table and leaned right into his face. "How much would you cost, Del?" I asked him. He glared at me, his eyes hard and bright. I said, "Come on, Velda. They're giving us a ride home."

We sat in the front next to the driver, the skinny guy in back. All the way into Manhattan he kept playing with my gun. When we got to my office the one behind the wheel said, "Out, Mac."

"Let's have the rod."

"Nah, it's too good a piece for a punk like you. I want a souvenir."

So I put the .32 up against his neck while Velda swung around in her seat and pointed the automatic at the skinny guy and his whine was a tinny nasal sound he had trouble making. He handed over the .45 real easy, licking his lips and trying to say something. The one beside me said, "Look, Mac . . ."

"I never come easy, buddy. You tell them all."

His eyes showed white all the way around and he knew. He knew all right. The car pulled away with a squeal of tires and I looked at Velda and laughed. "You play it that way by accident, honey?"

"I've had to read a lot of minds the past seven years. I knew how it would work. I just wanted you ready."

"I don't know whether to kiss you or smack your ass."

She grinned impishly. "You can *always* kiss me."

"Don't ask for it."

"Why not? It's the only way I'm going to get it, I think."

Teddy's place is a lush restaurant about as far downtown as it's pos-sible to get without falling in the river. It seemed an unlikely spot for good food and celebrities, but there you got both. Hy Gardner was having a late supper with Joey and Cindy Adams, and when he spotted us, waved us over to the table.

Before we could talk he ordered up scampi and a steak for both of us, then: "You come down for supper or information?"

"Both."

"You got Joey really researching. He comes to me, I go to somebody else, and little by little I'm beginning to get some mighty curious ideas. When are you going to recite for publication?"

"When I have it where it should be."

"So what's the pitch on Sally Devon?"

"All yours, Joey," I said.

He could hardly wait to get it out. "Boy, what a deal you handed me. You threw an old broad my way. There was more dust on her records than a Joe Miller joke. Then you know who comes up with the answers?"

"Sure, Cindy."

"How'd you know?"

"Who else?"

"Drop dead. Anyway, we contacted some of the kids who worked with her only like now they're ready for the old ladies' home. Sure, she was in show business, but with her it didn't last long and was more of a front. Her old friends wouldn't say too much, being old friends and all, but you knew what they were thinking. Sally Devon was a high-priced whore. She ran with some of the big ones for a while, then got busted and wound up with some of the racket boys."

Velda looked at me, puzzled. "If she was involved with the rackets, how'd she end up with Sim Torrence, who was supposed to be so clean? That doesn't make sense."

"Sure it does," Hy told her. "He got her off a hook when he was still an assistant D.A. Look, she was still a beautiful doll then and you know the power of a doll. So they became friends. Later he married her. I can name a couple other top politicos who are married to women who used to be in the business. It isn't as uncommon as you think."

He put his fork down and sipped at his drink. "What do you make of it now?" When I didn't answer he said, "Blackmail?"

"I don't know," I admitted.

"Well, what else do you want?"

For a moment I sat there thinking. "Torrence is a pretty big wheel now, isn't he?"

"As big as they get without being in office."

"Okay, he said repeated threats were made on him by guys he helped put away."

"Ah, they all get that."

"They all don't have a mess like this either."

"So what?"

"This, Hy . . . I'd like a rundown on his big cases, on everyone who ever laid a threat on him. You ought to have that much in your morgue."

Hy shrugged and grinned at me. "I suppose you want it tonight."

"Why not?"

"So we'll finish the party in my office. Come on."

Hy's file on Sim Torrence was a thick one composed of hundreds of clippings. We all took a handful and found desk space to look them over. A little after one we had everything classified and cross-indexed. Joey had four cases of threats on Sim's life, Cindy had six, Velda and I both had three, and Hy one. He put all the clips in a Thermofax machine, pulled copies, handed them over, and put the files back.

"Now can we go home?" he said.

Joey wanted to go on with it until Cindy gave him a poke in the ribs.

"So let's all go home," I told him.

We said so-long downstairs and Velda and I headed back toward the Stem. In the lower Forties I checked both of us into a hotel, kissed her at the door, and went down to my room. She didn't like it, but I still had work to do.

After a shower I sat on the bed and started through the clips. One by one I threw them all down until I had four left. All the rest who had threatened Sim Torrence were either dead or back in prison. Four were free, three on parole, and one having served a life sentence of thirty years.

Life.

Thirty years.

He was forty-two when he went in, seventy-two when he came out. His name was Sonny Motley and there was a picture of him in a shoe repair shop he ran on Amsterdam Avenue. I put the clips in the discard pile and looked at the others.

Sherman Buff, a two-time loser that Sim had put the screws to in court so that he caught a big fall. He threatened everybody including the judge, but Torrence in particular.

Arnold Goodwin who liked to be called Stud. Sex artist. Rapist. He put the full blame for his fall on Torrence, who not only prosecuted his case but processed it from the first complaint until his capture. No known address, but his parole officer could supply that.

Nicholas Beckhaus, burglar with a record who wound up cutting a cop during his capture. He and two others broke out of a police van during a routine transfer and it was Sim Torrence's office who ran him down until he was trapped in a rooming house. He shot a cop in that capture too. He promised to kill Torrence on sight when he got out. Address unknown, but he would have a parole officer too.

I folded the clips, put three in my pants pocket, and leaned back on the bed. Then there was a knock on the door.

I had the .45 in my hand, threw the bolt back, and moved to the side. Velda walked in grinning, closed the door, and stood there with her back against it. "Going to shoot me, Mike?"

"You crazy?"

"Uh-uh."

"What do you want?"

"You don't know?"

I reached out and pulled her in close, kissed her hair, then felt the fire of her mouth again. She leaned against me, her breasts firm and insistent against my naked chest, her body forming itself to mine.

"I'm going to treat you rough, my love . . . until you break down."

"You're going back to bed."

"To bed, yes, but not back." She smiled, pulled away, and walked to my sack. Little by little, slowly, every motion a time-honored motion, she took off her clothes. Then she stood there naked and smiling a moment before sliding into the bed where she lay there waiting.

"Let's see who's the roughest," I said, and lay down beside her. I punched out the light, got between the top sheet and the cover, turned on my side and closed my eyes.

"You big bastard," she said softly. "If I didn't love you I'd kill you."

CHAPTER 5

I was up and dressed before eight. The big, beautiful, tousled black-haired thing who had lain so comfortably against me all night stirred and looked at me through sleepy-lidded eyes, then stretched languidly and smiled.

"Frustrated?" I asked her.

"Determined." She stuck her tongue out at me. "You'll pay for last night."

"Get out of the sack. We have plenty to do."

"Watch."

I turned toward the mirror and put on my tie. "No, damn it."

But I couldn't help seeing her, either. It wasn't something you could take your eyes off very easily. She was too big, too lovely, her body a pattern of symmetry that was frightening. She posed deliberately, knowing I would watch her, then walked into the shower without bothering to close the door. And this time I saw something new. There was a fine, livid scar that ran diagonally across one hip and several parallel lines that traced themselves across the small of her back. I had seen those kind of marks before. Knives made them. Whips made them. My hands knotted up for a second and I yanked at my tie.

When she came out she had a towel wrapped sarong-fashion around her, smelling of soap and hot water, and this time I didn't watch her. Instead I pulled the clips out, made a pretense of reading them until she was dressed, gave them to her to keep in her hand-bag, and led her out the door.

At the elevator I punched the down button and put my hand through her arm. "Don't do that to me again, kitten."

Her teeth flashed through the smile. "Oh no, Mike. You've kept me waiting too long. I'll do anything to get you. You see . . . I'm not done with you yet. You can marry me right now or put up with some persecution."

"We haven't got time right now."

"Then get ready to suffer, gentleman." She gave my arm a squeeze and got on the elevator.

After breakfast I bypassed Pat's office to get a line on the parole officers handling Buff, Goodwin, and Beckhaus. Both Buff and Beckhaus were reporting to the same officer and he was glad to give me a rundown on their histories.

Sherman Buff was married, lived in Brooklyn, and operated a successful electronics shop that subcontracted jobs from larger companies. His address was good, his income sizable, and he had a woman he was crazy about and no desire to go back to the old life. The parole officer considered him a totally rehabilitated man.

Nicholas Beckhaus reported regularly, but he had to come in on the arm of his brother, a dentist, who supported him. At some time in prison he had been assaulted and his back permanently damaged so that he was a partial cripple. But more than that, there was brain damage too, so that his mental status was reduced to that of a ten-year-old.

The officer who handled Arnold Goodwin was more than anxious to talk about his charge. Goodwin had been trouble all the way and had stopped reporting in three months ago. Any information we could dig up on his whereabouts he'd appreciate. He was afraid of only one thing . . . that before Goodwin was found he'd kill somebody.

Arnold Goodwin looked like a good bet.

Velda said, "Did you want to see the other probable?"

"Sonny Motley?"

"It will only take a few minutes."

"He's in his seventies. Why?"

She moved her shoulders in thought. "He was a good story. The three-million-dollar killer."

"He wasn't in for murder. He was a three-time loser when they caught him in that robbery and he drew an automatic life sentence."

"That could make a man pretty mad," she reminded me.

"Sure, but guys in their seventies aren't going to hustle on a kill after thirty years in the pen. Be reasonable."

"Okay, but it wouldn't take long."

"Oh, hell," I said.

Sonny Motley's shoe repair shop had been open at seven as usual, the newsboy said, and pointed the place out to us. He was sitting in the window, a tired-looking old man bent over a metal foot a woman's shoe was fitted to, tapping on a heel. He nodded, peering up over his glasses at us like a shaven and partially bald Santa Claus.

Velda and I got up in the chairs and he put down his work to shuffle over to us, automatically beginning the routine of a shine. It wasn't a new place and the rack to one side of the machines was filled with completed and new jobs.

When he finished I gave him a buck and said, "Been here long?"

He rang the money up and smiled when I refused the change. "Year and a half." Then he pulled his glasses down a little more and looked at me closely. "Reporter?"

"Nope."

"Well, you look like a cop, but cops aren't interested in me anymore. Not city cops. So that makes you independent, doesn't it?"

When I didn't answer him he chuckled. "I've had lots of experience with cops, son. Don't let it discourage you. What do you want to know?"

"You own this place?"

"Yup. Thirty years of saving a few cents a day the state paid me and making belts and wallets for the civilian trade outside bought me this. Really didn't cost much and it was the only trade I learned in the pen. But that's not what you want to know."

I laughed and nodded. "Okay, Sonny, it's about a promise you made a long time ago to kill Sim Torrence."

"Yeah, I get asked that lots of times. Mostly by reporters though." He pulled his stool over and squatted on it. "Guess I was pretty mad back then." He smiled patiently and pushed his glasses up.

"Let's say that if he up and died I wouldn't shed any tears, but I'll tell you Mr. . . ."

"Hammer. Mike Hammer."

"Yes, Mr. Hammer . . . well, I'm just not about to go back inside walls again. Not that this is any different. Same work, same hours. But I'm on the outside. You understand?"

"Sure."

"Something else too. I'm old. I think different. I don't have those old feelings." He looked at Velda, then me. "Like with the women. Was a time when even thinking of one drove me nuts, knowing I couldn't have one. Oh, how I wanted to kill old Torrence then. But like I told you, once you get old the fire goes out and you don't care anymore. Same way I feel about Torrence. I just don't care. Haven't even thought about him until somebody like you or a reporter shows up. Then I think of him and it gets funny. Sound silly to you?"

"Not so silly, Sonny."

He giggled and coughed, then looked up. "Silly like my name. Sonny. I was a heller with the women in them days. Looked young as hell and they loved to mother me. Made a lot of scores like that." For a moment his eyes grew dreamy, then he came back to the present. "Sonny. Ah, yeah, they were the days, but the fire is out now."

"Well . . ." I took Velda's arm and he caught the motion.

Eagerly, a man looking for company, he said, "If you want I could show you the papers on what happened. I had somebody save 'em. You wait here a minute." He got up, shuffled off through a curtained door, and we could hear him rummaging through his things. When he came back he laid out a pitiful few front pages of the old *World* and there he was spread all over the columns.

According to the testimony, in 1932 the Sonny Motley mob, with Black Conley second in command, were approached secretly by an unknown expert on heisting through an unrevealed medium. The offer was a beautifully engineered armored-car stickup. Sonny accepted and was given the intimate details of the robbery including facets known only to insiders, which would make the thing come off.

Unfortunately, a young Assistant District Attorney named Sim Torrence got wind of the deal, checked it out, and with a squad of cops, broke up the robbery . . . but only after it had been accomplished. The transfer of three million dollars in cash had been made to a commandeered cab and in what looked like a spectacular double cross, or possibly an attempt to save his own skin, Black Conley had jumped in the cab when the shooting started and taken off, still firing back into the action with the rifle he had liked so well. One shot caught Sonny Motley and it was this that stopped his escape more than anything else. In an outburst of violence in the courtroom Sonny shouted that he had shot back at the bastard who double-crossed him and if he didn't hit him, then he'd get him and Torrence someday for sure. They never found the cab, the driver, the money, or Black Conley.

Sonny let me finish and when I handed the papers back said, "It would've gone if Blackie didn't pull out."

"Still sore?"

"Hell no."

"What do you think happened?"

"Tell you what, Mr. Hammer. I got me a guess. That was a double cross somehow, only a triple cross got thrown in. I think old Blackie wound up cab and all at the bottom of the river someplace."

"The money never showed."

"Nope. That went with Blackie too. Everybody lost. I just hope I did shoot the bastard before he died. I don't see how I coulda missed."

"You're still mad, Sonny."

"Naw, not really. Just annoyed about them thirty years he made me take. That Torrence really laid it on, but hell, he had it made. I was a three-timer by then anyway and would have taken life on any conviction. It sure made Torrence though." He pulled his glasses off, looked at the papers once with disgust, rolled them into a ball, and threw them away from him into a refuse carton. "Frig it. What's the sense thinking on them things?"

He looked older and more tired in that moment than when we came in. I said, "Sure, Sonny, sorry we bothered you."

"No trouble at all, Mr. Hammer. Come in for a shine any time."

On the street Velda said, "Pathetic, wasn't he?"

"Aren't they all?"

We waited there a few minutes trying to flag a cab, then walked two blocks before one cut over to our side and squealed to a stop. A blue panel truck almost caught him broadside, but the driver was used to those simple occupational hazards and didn't blink an eye.

I let Velda off at the office with instructions to get what she could from Pat concerning Basil Levitt and Kid Hand and to try to reestablish some old pipelines. If there were new faces showing in town like Jersey Toby said, there was a reason for it. There was a reason for two dead men and a murder attempt on me. There was a reason for an assassination layout with Sue Devon the target and somebody somewhere was going to know the answers.

When Velda got out I gave the cabbie Sim Torrence's Westchester address and sat back to try and think it out. Traffic was light on the ride north and didn't tighten up until we got to the upper end of Manhattan.

Then it was too thick. Just as the cab slowed for a light somebody outside let out a scream and I had time to turn my head, see the nose of a truck almost in the window, and throw myself across the seat as the cab took a tremendous jar that crushed in the side and sent glass and metal fragments ripping above my head. There was one awful moment as the cab tipped, rolled onto its side, and lay there in that almost total silence that follows the second after an accident.

Up front the cabbie moaned softly and I could smell the sharp odor of gasoline. Somebody already had the front door open and arms were reaching in for the driver. I helped lift him, crawled out the opening, and stood there in the crowd brushing myself off. A couple dozen people grouped around the driver, who seemed more shaken than hurt, and for a change a few were telling him they'd be willing to be witnesses. The driver of the truck had cut across and deliberately slammed into the cab like it was intentional or the driver was drunk.

But there wasn't any driver in the truck at all. Somebody said he had jumped out and gone down into a subway kiosk across the street and acted like he was hurt. He was holding his belly and stumbled as he ran. Then I noticed the truck. It was a blue panel job and almost identical to the one which almost nailed the cab when Velda and I first got in it.

Nobody noticed me leave at all. I took the number of the cab and would check back later, but right now there wasn't time enough to get caught up in a traffic accident. A block down I got another cab and gave him the same address. At the Torrence estate I told the driver to wait, went up, and pushed the bell chime.

Seeing Geraldine King again was as startling as it was the first time. She was in a sweater and skirt combination that set off the titian highlights in her hair, giving a velvet touch to the bright blue of her eyes. There was nothing businesslike about the way she was dressed. It was there only to enhance a lovely body and delight the viewer. I had seen too many strap marks not to know she was skin naked beneath the sweater.

She caught my eyes, let me look a moment longer, and smiled gently. "Stickler for convention?"

"Not me, honey."

"Women should be like pictures . . . nice to look at."

"Not if you haven't got the price to afford to take them home."

"Sometimes you don't have to buy. There are always free gifts."

"Thanks," I grunted. Then I laughed at her. "You sure must be one hell of a political advantage to have around."

"It helps." She held the door open. "Come on in. Mr. Torrence is in the study."

When I went in Sim pushed some papers aside, stood up, and shook hands. "Glad to see you again, Mike. What can I do for you?"

"Some gal you got there."

"What?" He frowned behind his glasses. "Oh . . . oh, yes, indeed. Now . . ."

"I've been checking out your enemies, Mr. Torrence. Those who wanted to kill you."

"Oh?"

"You said you knew of a dozen persons who threatened to kill you. Would Arnold Goodwin be one?"

"The sex offender?"

"Among other things."

"Yes . . . he made threats. Since he was so young I paid no attention to them. Why?"

"Because he's out and is in violation of his parole. He hasn't reported in for some time."

"He was quite an emotionally disturbed young man. Do you think . . .?"

I shrugged. "Those guys can do anything. They'd hurt anybody to get to the primary object of their hate. I haven't followed through on him, but I will."

"Well, the police should be informed immediately . . ."

"They will be. His parole officer has him listed already. The thing is, he can cut a wide path before they nail him. Meantime, any protection for Sue or yourself should be direct and personal. I'd suggest an armed guard."

"Mr. Hammer . . . we're coming into an election year. If this kind of thing gets out do you know what it means?"

"So take your chances then."

"I'll have to. Nevertheless, it may be sensible to keep somebody here in the house with me. I think Geraldine can arrange for someone."

"You want me to?"

"No, we'll take care of it."

"Okay then. Incidentally, I saw Sonny Motley."

"Sonny Motley?" He tugged at his glasses and pulled them off. "He was given a life sentence."

"Life ends at thirty years in the pen. He's out. You remember him then?"

"I certainly do! It was that case that made me a public figure. You don't think . . ."

"He's an old guy who runs a shoe shop uptown now. No, he's safe enough. You don't play tough when you're over seventy. Those brick walls took too much out of him. It was a pretty interesting case. Neither Blackie Conley or the loot ever showed up, did it?"

"Mike, we covered every avenue possible looking for that money. We alerted every state, every foreign government . . . but whatever happened to Conley or the money has never come to light."

"What do you think happened?" I asked him. Torrence made a vague gesture with his hands. "If he could have gotten out of the country, affected a successful new identity, and didn't try to make too much of a splash so as to attract attention he could have made it. Others have done it on a smaller scale. So might he. That job was well engineered. Whether or not Conley actually planned a double cross or took off when he saw how the fighting was going, we'll never know, but he got away."

"There was the cab."

"He could have killed the driver and dumped the cab somewhere. He was a ruthless man."

"Sonny seemed to think somebody else got to him."

Torrence shook his head, thinking. "I doubt it. There was still the cab and driver, still the money whose serial numbers were recorded. No, I think Conley made a successful escape. If he did, he's probably dead by now. He was eight years older than Sonny, if I remember right. That would put him in his eighties at the end of this time." He looked at me steadily. "Funny you should bring that up."

"Something's come out of the past, buddy. There's trouble. I'm in the middle of it."

"Yes," he nodded, "you are. Now, how can I be of further help?"

"Look back. No matter how slight it might seem, see who wants you badly enough to try to hurt Sue or yourself."

"I will, Mr. Hammer."

"One more thing."

"What's that?"

"Your former wife."

"Yes?"

"How much did you know about her?" I asked him.

Torrence flinched visibly, dropped his eyes to his hands, then brought them back to my face again. "I assume you went to the trouble of looking into her background."

"I heard a few things."

"Then let me say this . . . I was well aware of Sally's history before marrying her. In way of explanation I'll tell you that I loved her. In way of an excuse you might understand, say there's no accounting for taste. We met when she was in trouble. A business relationship developed into friendship that became love. Unfortunately, she maintained her alcoholism and died because of it. Why do you ask?"

"I was thinking of blackmail possibilities."

"Discard them. Everything is a matter of public record. I wouldn't tolerate blackmail."

"Maybe it hasn't been tried yet."

"What does that mean?"

"I don't know," I said. "There are just some interesting possibilities that have developed. You try to stay ahead of them." I got up and put on my hat. "Okay, if I need anything else I'll stop by."

"I'm always available, Mr. Hammer." With a gesture of dismissal he went back to his papers, so I eased out the door and looked for Geraldine King.

She was in a smaller room toward the front, one that had been converted into a small but efficiently equipped office. Behind a typewriter, with black-rimmed glasses perched on her nose, she looked like a calendar artist's idea of what a secretary should be. Through the knee well in the desk I could see her skirt hiked halfway up her thighs for comfort and the first thing she did when she saw me in the doorway was reach for the hem and tug it down.

I let out a half-silent wolf whistle and grinned. "Man," I said.

She pulled her glasses off and dropped them in front of her. "Distracting, aren't I?"

"Tell me, honey, how the hell does Torrence work with you around?"

Geraldine chuckled and shrugged. "With ease, that's how. I am a fixture, a political associate and nothing more. I can prance around this house in the buff and he'd never notice."

"Want to bet?"

"No, I mean it. Mr. Torrence is dedicated. His political life is all he knows and all he wants. He's been in public service so long that he thinks of nothing else. Any time he is seen with a woman having supper or at some social function is for a political advantage."

"The female votes?"

"Certainly. Women don't mind widowers who seem to still have a family instinct but they do seem to resent confirmed bachelors."

"That's what the men get for giving them the vote. Look, kid, Sim tells me you've been through a few of his political campaigns."

"That's right."

"He ever have any trouble before?"

"Like what?"

"Something from his past coming out to shake him. Any blackmail attempts or threats against his personal life. He says no, but sometimes these things go through the party rather than the individual."

She sat back, frowning, then shook her head. "I think I'd know of anything like that. The organization is well knit and knows the implications of these things and I would have been told, but as far as I know nothing can interfere with his career. He's exceptionally clean. That's why we were so concerned about Sue's running off. Even a thing like that can affect voting. A man who can't run his own house can hardly be expected to run a state."

"You know he's in a position to be hurt now."

"I realize that." She got up, pushed her chair back and walked toward me with a swaying stride, not conscious at all of the subtle undulations beneath the tight-fitting sweater and skirt. "Do you think Sue will be all right?"

"She's a big girl. She may not look it, but don't be fooled."

"This business . . . about Mr. Torrence killing her mother."

"That's an idea she'll have to get out of her mind."

Geraldine said, "She dreams it. Dreams can be pretty real sometimes. Her very early childhood couldn't have been very nice. I don't think she ever knew who her father was. If she makes open accusations it can damage Mr. Torrence."

"I'll speak to her. She around?"

"There's a summer house on the south side where she practices. She practically lives there."

She was standing in front of me now, concern deep inside those wild blue eyes. I said, "I'll see what I can do."

Geraldine smiled, reached up slowly, and put her arms around my neck. With the same deliberate slowness she pulled herself on her toes, wet her lips with her tongue, and brought my mouth down to hers. It was a soft teasing, tasting kiss, as if she were sampling the juice from a plum before buying the lot. Her mouth was a warm cavern filled with life and promise, then just as slowly she drew away, smiling.

"Thank you," she said.

I grinned at her. "Thank *you*."

"I could hate you easier than I could like you."

"Which is worse?"

"That you'll have to find out for yourself."

"Maybe I will, baby."

At first I didn't think she was there, then I heard the sounds of a cabinet opening and I knocked on the door. Her smile was like the sun breaking open a cloud and she reached for my hand. "Hello, Mike. Gee I'm glad to see you." She looked past me. "Isn't Velda with you?"

"Not this time. Can I come in?"

She made a face at me and stepped aside, then closed the door.

It was a funny little place, apparently done over to her specifications. One wall was all mirror with a dancer's practice bar against it. Opposite was a record player with a shelf of LP's, a shoe rack with all the implements of the trade, a standup microphone attached to a record player, a spinet piano covered with lead sheets of popular music and Broadway hits, with a few stuffed animals keeping them in place.

The rest of the room was a girl-style den with a studio couch, dresser, cabinets, and a small conference table. Cardboard boxes, books, and a few old-fashioned paper files covered the table and it was these she was going through when I found her.

"What're you up to, Sue?"

"Going through my mother's things."

"She's a long time dead. Face it."

"I know. Would you like to see what she looked like?"

"Sure."

There were a few clippings from the trade papers of the time and some framed nightclub shots taken by the usual club photographers and they all showed a well-built blonde with a slightly vacuous expression. Whether it was intended or built-in I couldn't tell, but she almost typified the beautiful but dumb showgirl. There were four photos, all taken in night spots long since gone. In two of them she was with a party of six. In the other two there were four people, and in those she was with the same man, a lanky dark-haired guy with deep-set eyes who almost seemed like a hell-fire preacher touring the sin spots for material for a sermon.

"She was pretty," I said.

"She was beautiful," Sue said softly. "I can still remember her face."

"These were taken before you were born." I pointed to the dates on the back of the photos.

"I know. But I can remember her. I remember her talking to me. I remember her talking about *him*."

"Come on, kid."

Her hair swirled as she made a small negative gesture. "I mean it. She hated him."

"Sue . . . they were married."

"I don't care."

I looked at her sharply. "Want me to be blunt?"

She shrugged and bit into her lip.

"Your mother was an alcoholic. Sim tried everything to dry her out. Alcoholics hate that. If she hated him it was because he wanted to help. Get it out of your mind that he killed her."

"She told me the snake killed her."

"Drunks see snakes and elephants and everything else. Don't go getting wrapped up in an obsession."

"She told me to look for a letter. Someday I'll find it."

"You were three years old. How could you remember those things?"

"I just do."

"Okay, you look for it then. Meanwhile, I want you to do something for me."

"What?"

"Don't cause trouble. You stay out of his hair until we clear this thing up. Promise me?"

"Maybe." She was smiling at me.

"What do you want?"

"Kiss me."

I grunted. "I just got done kissing Geraldine King."

"You're nasty, but I don't care." She sidled around the desk and stood there with her hands behind her back. "I'll take seconds," she said.

So I kissed her.

"Not like that."

"How?" The damn game was getting out of hand. The big broads I could handle, but how do you get the kids off your back?

Then she showed me how in a moment of sudden violence that was all soft and tender yet filled with some latent fury I couldn't understand. The contact was brief, but it shook me and left her trembling, her eyes darkly languid and her face flushed.

"I hope you like seconds best."

"By far, kid, only don't do it again." I faked a laugh and held her away. "Stay cool, okay?"

"Okay, Mike."

Then I got out of there and back into the taxi where I gave the driver Pat's address.

CHAPTER 6

The new Inspector was a transfer from another division, a hard apple I had seen around years ago. His name was Spencer Grebb and one of his passionate hatreds was personnel from other fields poking around in his domain, with first cut going to private investigators and police reporters. From the look he gave me, I seemed to have a special place in his book and was target one on his big S list.

Charles Force was a D.A. out for Charlie Force. He was young, talented, on the way up, and nothing was going to deter his ambition. He was a nice-looking guy, but you couldn't tell what was going on behind his face. He had made it the hard way, in the courtrooms, and was a pro at the game right down the line.

Now they both sat at one side of the room with Pat in the middle, looking at me like I was game they were going to let out of the box long enough to get a running start so that hunting me down would be a pleasure.

After the introductions I said, "You check those slugs out, Pat?"

"Both from the same gun that killed Basil Levitt. You mentioned Marv Kania. Could you identify the guy, the guy who pulled the trigger?"

"If he's Kania I could."

"Try this." Pat flipped a four-by-five photo across the desk and I picked it up.

I looked at it and tossed it back. "That's the one."

"Positive?"

"Positive. He's made two passes at me, once in the office building and today with a truck. It rammed a taxi I was in."

Inspector Grebb had a hard, low voice. "This you reported right away."

"Now I'm doing it. At the moment it could have been a simple traffic accident. I ducked out because I had something to do. Now I'm tying it all in."

His smile was a twisted thing. "You know, it wouldn't be too hard to find a charge to press there, would it, Mr. Force?"

Charlie Force smiled too, but pleasantly. A courtroom smile. "I don't think so, Inspector."

As insolently as I could make it, I perched on the edge of Pat's desk and faced them. "Let's get something straight. I know what you guys would like to see, but I'm not going to fall easily. The agency I represent is federal. It's obscure, but pulls a lot of weight, and if you want to see just how much weight is there, push me a little. I'm operating in an official capacity whether you like it or not, which gives me certain latitudes. I've been around long enough to know the score on both ends so play it straight, friends. I'm cooperating with all departments as Captain Chambers will tell you. Just don't push. You'd be surprised what kind of a stink I can raise if I want to."

I looked at Charlie Force deliberately. "Especially in the publicity circuit, buddy."

His eyebrows pulled together. "Are you threatening me, Mr. Hammer?"

I nodded and grinned at him. "That I am, buster. That's one edge I have on you. A bad schmear and you can go down a notch and never hit the big-time. So play ball."

They didn't like it, but they had to take it. In a way, I couldn't blame them a bit. An ex private jingle coming in with a big ticket isn't easy to take. Especially not one with a reputation like mine.

The D.A. seemed to relax. He was still stalling, but it wasn't for real. "We've been advised to cooperate."

Thanks, Rickerby, I thought. *You're still paying for The Dragon.*

Pat said, "We ran a pretty thorough check on Basil Levitt."

"Anything?"

"We located a girl he used to shack up with. She told us he was on a job but wouldn't say what it was. He said he was getting paid well for it but there would be more later and he was already making big plans. Outside of a few others who knew he had fresh money on him, nothing."

"What about the rifle?"

"Stolen from a sporting goods store upstate about a month ago. We had the numbers on file. He must have worn gloves in the room where he had the gun set up, but got careless when he loaded the clip. There was a single print that tied him in with it."

Before I could answer, Charlie Force said, "Now what we are interested in knowing is who he was shooting at."

I looked at my watch and then at his face. "Art Rickerby clued you in. You know what Velda was involved with."

"Yes," he agreed pleasantly. "We know. But I'm beginning to wonder about it all."

"Well, stop wondering."

"You were there too. Right in the middle."

"Fresh on the scene. Levitt had been there some time. Days."

"Waiting for you?"

Let them think it, I figured. I wasn't cutting him in on anything. "I'm trying to find that out too," I told him. "When I do you'll get the word."

Grebb and Force got up together and headed for the door. Their inspection trip was over. They were satisfied now that I'd make a good target. Grebb looked at me through those cold eyes, still smiling twistedly. "Be sure to do that," he said.

When they were gone Pat shook his head. "You don't make friends easily."

"Who needs them?"

"Someday you will."

"I'll wait until then. Look, buddy, you know what the action is in town?"

Pat just nodded.

"Dickerson?"

He spread his hands. "We're working on it."

"How can a wheel come in already operating and not be known?"

"It isn't hard. You want to know what we have?"

"Damn right."

"Hoods are showing up from all over the country. They're all clean, at least clean enough so we can't tumble them. We can roust them when we want to, but they have nothing we can pin on them."

"How many?"

"Not an army, but let a dozen wrong types hit town at once and it sets a pattern. Something's about to happen."

"They're not holding a convention."

"No, they're getting paid somehow. Either there's loot being laid out or they're operating under orders. There are Syndicate men in and sitting by nice and quietly waiting for the word. All we can do is wait too. In the meantime there's a shake-up in the rackets. Somebody's got the power to pull strings long enough to get action out of the Midwest and the coast. There's a power play going on and a big one. I wish I could figure it out."

He sat there drumming his fingertips on the desktop. "What do *you* think, Mike?"

I gave it to him straight, right down the line, laying the facts face up from the time I walked into the apartment until I reached his office. I watched his mind close around the details and put them into mental cubbyholes to hold there until he had time to assimilate them. But I gave him no opinions, nothing more than facts.

Finally he said, "There are some strange implications."

"Too many."

"I suppose you want something from me now."

"Yeah. Get a killer off my back."

His eyes touched mine and narrowed. "We'll do all we can. He can't get around too long with a bullet in him."

"Up to now he's been doing great."

I got up off the desk and put on my hat. "This Arnold Goodwin . . ."

"I'll get a team out on it. This is one of the implications I don't like. These are the real potential killers. Whether Torrence likes it or not, I'll see that somebody is staked out around his house. We'll keep it quiet, so what he doesn't know won't hurt him."

"Good deal. I'll see you later."

"By the way, Joey Adams called here for you. He wants to see you about something." He grinned at me. "Said he got stopped on a traffic violation and flashed his honorary badge with all the little diamonds and just found out from the arresting officer what it was good for."

"Old joke."

"Funny though."

I called Joey from downstairs and had him meet me in the Blue Ribbon. It was between the meal hours and nobody was there, so George and I sipped coffee until he got there.

After he ordered milk and cake I said, "What's the bit?"

"Look, you had me chasing down Sally Devon's old friends. Well, I'm up in the office when Pauline Coulter comes in to tell me what she forgot. About a week ago she ran into Annette Lee, who was with Sally when she died."

"Man, she was old then."

"She's older now, but still kicking. Annette Lee used to be a wardrobe mistress in a show Sally worked in and afterwards worked for Sally as sort of personal maid. Now how about that? You think I'll make a cop yet?"

"Not if you keep flashing that police badge." I grinned.

"Come on!"

"Okay, it was a joke." I laughed. "No kidding though . . . this Lee gal might clean up a few things. It's nice to have friends in important places."

"Anytime, Mike." He pulled out a card and scribbled down an address. "Here's where she is. It's a rooming house across town. She never goes anywhere so you can always find her home."

I stuck the card in my pocket. "How about now? You free?"

"Like a bird, man."

Annette Lee had a front room downstairs in one of the countless brownstones along the street. Her pension money kept her adequately, her cat kept her company, and whatever went on outside her window was enough to keep her busy. She was a small woman, shrunken with age, but in the straight-back rocker, with tiny feet pushing against the floor with tireless rhythm to keep her in motion, she had a funny pixyish quality that was reflected in her faded gray eyes.

There was no telling her accurate age, but it had crept up on her so that her talk wandered into peculiar directions and it was difficult to keep her on one track. But she remembered Sally Devon well. They had been good friends and it was Sally who had taken her in when she was sick and needed an operation, and Sally who cared for her and paid her expenses, so that when Sally needed her, she was glad to go.

She eyed us sharply when I questioned her about Sally's background, but until she was aware that I knew about her past, was reluctant to talk about it. It was Sally's earnings in the seamier side of life that paid her expenses and she was grateful. Little by little she gave it to us. Sally had left show business to take up with men, had gotten involved with the wrong ones and found herself in trouble.

Yes, she knew Sim Torrence, and although she didn't like him, thought he had done well by Sally. He had taken her in when she needed help, and if it hadn't been for Sally's drinking the marriage might have been successful. What she thought was that Sally's guilt complex for bringing a tarnished background into Sim Torrence's life drove her to alcoholism.

She remembered the night Sally died, too. Outside in the cold. Drunk. It was a shame. She couldn't revive her. I asked her directly if she thought Sim Torrence had anything to do with Sally's death.

Annette Lee gave me a shriveling glance. "Don't be silly," she said.

"Just clearing up a point," I told her.

"Then what's this all about, young man?"

"Sue thinks so."

"Sally's little baby?"

"That's right."

"Rubbish. She was only a mite."

"Maybe," I said. "But she's pretty insistent about it. One minute she has the idea Torrence was responsible, the next she says it was a snake."

Annette's face pulled into a tight expression and for a moment her eyes were less faded-looking. "Snake? Sally used to talk about that. When she was drunk. She kept mentioning the snake. Funny you should bring it up. Never thought it would make an impression on a child. Yes, she used to talk about the snake all right. But no snake killed her. She died right there in the front yard, right in my arms. Like to froze, the poor thing did, all drunk up and sick. Maybe it was for the best though."

She sat back in the rocker and closed her eyes. Too much talking was wearing her down. I motioned to Joey and we got up. "Well," I said, "thanks for the talk. Maybe I'll come back again sometime."

"Please do."

We walked to the door as the rhythm of her rocking slowed down. Just as I was about to leave it picked up again and she said, "Young man . . ."

"Ma'am?"

"They ever catch him?"

"Who's that?"

"The one who ran off with all that money. A whole lot of money. Sally's old boyfriend."

I called Joey back in and shut the door. "A lot of money?"

"Indeed. Three million dollars. Conley, I think his name was. Blackie Conley. He was a mean one. He was the meanest of them all. They ever catch him?"

"No, they never did."

With her eyes still closed she shook her head. "Never thought they would. He was a thinker. Even heard where he was going after they stole it."

"Where, Miss Lee?" I asked softly.

She didn't answer. She was asleep.

"*Damn,*" I said.

The picture was suddenly getting a sharp outline.

I dropped Joey at his AGVA office and went back to my own where Velda was waiting. She had compiled a report on Del Penner for me and from what it looked like he was in solidly now, a natural inheritor of Kid Hand's old territory. It was a step up and he was ready for it, taking advantage of an occupational hazard. Nothing was solidified yet, but he was there and holding on.

When I finished it I got Pat on the phone, asked him if he could pull a package on Blackie Conley from the file, then told Velda to run over and pick it up. When she left I sat back in my chair and swung around so I could stare out the window at the concrete escarpment that was New York.

It was getting dark out and a mist was closing in. Another hour and it would be raining again. The multicolor neons of the city were bursting against the gray overcast like summer heat lightning and someplace across town a siren wailed. Another followed it.

Trouble out there. Trouble all over, but trouble out there all the time. Someplace was a guy with a slug in him and a gun in his hand. Someplace was Marv Kania, hurting like hell, waiting for me to show up so he could put one in my gut too. It was Levitt who had done it, but me in his mind. I was the living one, so I did it. Screw him. Let him hurt.

Three million dollars. That could bring trouble to a city. That could bring a man back to power and buy muscle. That was big starter money and a prize for anybody.

Sim Torrence thought Blackie Conley could have made it. Okay, suppose he did. Suppose he sat on that three million all these years, afraid to spend it, not wanting to convert it because of the loss he'd take in the transaction. He just sat on it. It was power to him. Brother, he sure waited for the heat to cool, but it happens like that sometimes. Harmony Brothers sat on a million and a half for forty-one years and only told where it was on his deathbed. Frankie Boyle kept seventy thousand in his mattress for sixteen years, sleeping happily on it every night without ever touching it, then went out of his mind when the rooming house was burned down along with his unspent fortune.

So Blackie Conley got away and sat on three million for thirty years. In the last of his life he gets a power complex and wants to buy his way back in. He'd know how to do it all right. If he could stay undercover thirty years he could still do it.

Blackie Conley! Mr. Dickerson.

A big, fat possible.

Question: *Why try to knock off Sue Devon?*

Answer: A cute possible here too. If Blackie was in love with Sally, and IF Sally had a child by another man, there might be enough hatred to want the child destroyed.

There was only one thing wrong with the premise. Too many

people wanted Sue dead. Basil Levitt was trying for it when Kid Hand and Marv Kania came in.

But there was an answer to that one too, a money answer. Sue was a target with a price on her head and if it was big enough the shooters would fight each other for a crack at her. Kid Hand could use the dough and make himself a big one in somebody's eyes at the same time. That could explain why Levitt came in so fast after I got there. He thought I was after head money too.

Blackie Conley, Mr. Dickerson, three million bucks. And the vultures.

Velda came in then and laid the package on my desk. Inside the folder was a picture of Conley. I had seen one like it not too long before in Sue's room. Blackie Conley was the guy in the nightclubs with Sally Devon.

His arrest history went back to when he was a child and if he was alive today he'd be eighty-two years old. There were a lot older people still around and some of them right up there with the best. Age doesn't hit everybody the same way.

Pat had included some notes for me suggesting I go into a transcript of the trial if I wanted more information on Conley since it was the last that he was ever mentioned. He was tied in with the gang and his history brought out, but since the trial was a prolonged affair it would take a lot of reading to pick out the pieces.

I looked up at Velda and she stuck her tongue out at me. "I know, you want me to do it."

"You mind?"

"No, but what am I looking for?"

"Background on Conley."

"Why don't you ask Sonny Motley?"

"I intend to, kitten. We have to hit it from all sides."

I filled in the picture for her, watching her face put it together like I did. She nodded finally and said, "You could have it, Mike. It . . . seems right."

"But not quite?"

She ran the tip of her tongue between her teeth. "I just have a feeling."

"I know. Missing pieces. Suppose you meet Annette Lee and see if you can get any more out of her. It won't come easy, but try. She might give you someplace to start with Conley too."

"Okay, lover."

"And be careful, honey. That nut Kania is still loose. So is Arnold Goodwin. Those guys could be keys to this thing."

"Pat said he'd call you if anything came in on them."

"Good."

"And he said to tell you Charlie Force is protesting your association with the agency you work for."

"He knows what he can do."

"That Inspector Grebb is trouble. He's covering you like a blanket. Do you know you have a tail waiting downstairs?"

"I expected it. I know a way out too."

"You're asking for it, wise guy. I just don't want to see you get killed, that's all. I want to kill you myself. It'll take days and days."

"Knock it off." I swung off my chair and stood up. She grinned, kissed me lightly, and picked up her handbag.

"I arranged for an apartment for you. It's furnished and the key's in the desk. It's got a big double bed."

"It's polite to wait till you're asked."

Velda cocked her head and smiled. "There's a couch in the living room if you still want to be the gentleman."

"Can't you wait until we get married?"

"No." She pulled on her raincoat and belted it. "If I don't push you you'll never come."

"I suppose you have a key."

"Naturally."

"Change the damn lock."

She made a face and walked to the door. "So I'll do like you and shoot it off. *Adios*, doll."

Sonny Motley had closed his shop an hour ago, but the newsboy was still in his kiosk and told me the old guy had a beer or so every night in a joint two blocks down.

It was a sleazy little bar that had sort of just withered within the neighborhood, making enough to keep going, but nothing more. A half-dozen tables lined one wall and the air smelled of beer and greasy hamburgers. Two old broads were yakking it up at the bar, a couple of kids were at the other end watching the fights on TV while they pulled at their drinks, and Sonny Motley sat alone at the last table with a beer in front of him and a late-edition tabloid open in front of him. Beside his feet was a lunchbox and change of a dollar on the table.

I sat down opposite him and said, "Hello, Sonny."

He looked up, closed the paper, and gave me a half-toothless smile. "By damn, didn't expect you. Good you should come. I don't see many people socially."

"This isn't exactly social."

" 'Course not. When does a private cop and a con get social? But for me any talk is social. Sometimes I wish I didn't finish my time. At least then I'd get to see a parole officer for a chat once in a while. But who the hell has time for an old guy like me?"

"Ever see any of your old mob, Sonny?"

"Come on . . . what's your name? Hammer . . ." He ticked off his fingers, "Gleason, Tippy Wells, Harry the Fox, Guido Sunchi . . . all dead. Vinny Pauncho is in the nuthouse up by Beacon and that crazy Willie Fingers is doing his big stretch yet in Atlanta. I wrote to Willie once and never even heard back. Who's left?"

"Blackie Conley."

"Yeah, he's left dead."

"Sim Torrence thinks he might have made it."

"Baloney."

I told the bartender to bring me a beer and turned back to Sonny. "Suppose he did."

"So let him."

"Suppose he came back with the three million bucks you guys heisted?"

Sonny laughed abruptly and smacked his hands on the table. "That would be the funniest yet. What the hell could he do with it? All that stud wanted was broads and at his age it would be like shoving a wet noodle up a tiger's . . . no, Hammer, it wouldn't do him no good at all." He sat back and chuckled at the thought and waved for another beer.

"Let's consider it," I insisted.

"Sure, go ahead."

"So he's old. He wants one more crack at the big-time."

"Who the hell would listen to him?"

"You could pull a power play from behind the scenes. Three million bucks can do a lot of talking and if somebody is fronting for you who knows what you look like?"

Sonny stopped smiling then, his face wrapped in thought. Then he dragged on the beer and put half of it down at once. "No," he said, "Blackie ain't coming back, Hammer. He never ain't."

"Why not?"

His grin was tight-lipped, satisfied with what he was thinking. "Because I nailed old Blackie, I did. Man, with a rod I was good. I mean good, Hammer. You know he got me with that damn rifle. It put me down and stopped me, but I had one chance at him when he took off in that taxi and let one go while he still had the rifle poked out the window. I didn't miss with that shot. I think I got old Blackie and he crawled off and died or wound himself and the taxi both up in the drink."

"Maybe."

"Okay, so I'm wrong. Hope I am." He chuckled again and finished the beer. "Like to see old Blackie again. I'd like to find out if I really did get him or not."

"Ever hear of Mr. Dickerson?" I asked him.

"Nope. Should I?"

"Not especially."

"Who is he?"

"I don't know either."

"Like hell you don't."

"Why do you say that?" I asked him.

"Because I've lived with cons too damn long, Hammer. You get so you can tell things without them having to be said. Take now, f'instance. You ain't asked all you came here to ask yet, have you?"

It was my turn to buy and I yelled for another brew. "Okay, old-timer, I'll put it straight. You remember Sally Devon?"

Sonny frowned slightly and wiped his mouth with the back of his hand. "Sure. Used to be my broad."

"I thought she was Conley's."

"That bastard would go after anything in skirts no matter who she belonged to."

"Even yours?"

"Sure. I warned him off a few times. Had to knock him on his keister once. But hell, what difference does it make? In those days he was a sharp article. Older than we were and pretty smooth. Sally was always sweet on him. If I didn't bounce her around she woulda left me for him any day."

He stopped suddenly, his eyes going cold. "You're thinking maybe because of her Blackie dumped the heist and tried to take me?"

"Could be."

Then the coldness left his eyes and the age came back. He let out a muted cackle and shook his head at the joke. "Damn," he said, "that guy was always thinking."

"Where were you going with the money if that job paid off, Sonny?"

"What's the matter, don't you read?"

"You tell me."

He bobbed his head, relishing the moment. "I even see it done on some TV shows now, but it woulda worked. We had a truck with a tailgate ramped down. We was to drive the cab right in there and take off. So the cops found the truck and another one we was going to change to. It's all down. Instead that bastard Blackie crossed us."

"What were you going to do to the driver?"

"Toss him out, bump him. Who knows? We woulda figured somethin'."

"You had a hideout?"

"Yeah, a house in the Catskills we had rented ahead of time. The cops plastered that looking for Blackie. He made all the arrangements on that end and never got to use 'em. Coulda been the crime of the century."

"Maybe it was," I said.

Sonny was reaching for his glass and stopped short. "What're you thinking, boy?"

"Maybe while Blackie was making plans for you he was making other plans for himself. Suppose he arranged for an alternate hideout and made it after all. Suppose he bumped the driver, ditched the car, and holed up all these years and finally decided to come back again. Now he's here with three million bucks taking his last fling, buying himself an organization."

He listened, sat silent a moment, then shook his head and picked up his beer. "Not old Blackie. He couldn't live without the broads and now he's too old."

"Ever hear of a voyeur?"

"What's that?"

"They can't do it so they just watch. I know a few old jokers who get their kicks that way. They got millions too."

"I think you're nuts," he said, "but any time you want to talk about it come back and talk. You're the first company I had around in a long time."

"Sure." I wrote down my new address on a matchbook cover and passed it to him. "Reach me here or at the office if you get any ideas. You can earn some cash."

I put a buck on the table and left. Behind me Sonny was still chuckling. I'd like to be there if he ever got to meet Blackie face to face.

CHAPTER 7

I called Hy from a drugstore on the avenue and got Pete Ladero's address from him. I reached him at home and asked him if he could get the newspaper clips on the Motley-Conley job thirty years ago and bring them up to the office. He griped about leaving his favorite TV program, but his nose for news was too big and he said it would take an hour, but he'd be there.

At the Automat on Sixth between Forty-fourth and Forty-fifth I picked up a tray, loaded it with goodies, and went upstairs to think for a while. It wasn't accidental. I knew Jersey Toby would be there the same as he had been there at the same time every night the past ten years. I let him finish his meal, picked up my coffee, and joined him at his table. When he saw me he almost choked, gave a quick look around, and tightened up.

"Damn, can't you get off my neck? Whatta you want?"

"Talk, Toby, just talk."

"Well, I said all I'm gonna say. Scratch off, Mike. I don't want no part of you, buddy. You know I got asked questions already?"

"Who asked?"

"Some broad in the other joint. She knew you all right. I tried to lie out of it and said you was looking for a dame for that night but she wouldn't buy it. Said she knew you too well. You're hooked for somebody else. You're putting my tail in a sling."

"So I'll make it short."

"Like hell. You won't make nothing."

"Okay, Toby, then tomorrow a pickup goes out on you. You get rousted every time you step on the street. Lineup twice a week, complaints . . ."

Jersey Toby looked at me, his face white and drawn. "Come on, you wouldn't do that."

"Try me."

He finished his coffee, looked around nervously again until he was assured we were alone, and nodded. "You would at that. Okay, spill it."

"Let's go back to Dickerson again, Toby."

"We went through that once."

"You get the word."

"Sure . . . secondhand through the broads."

"Good enough. What's the word on the money angle? If out-of-town hoods are moving in, something's drawing them. Who's spreading the green around?"

Toby's tongue flicked at dry lips and he pulled on the butt. "Look . . . if I prime you, this is the last?"

I shrugged.

"Let's hear it, Mike."

"You bought it. I'll back off."

"Okay then, Marge . . . she's the redhead. She was with . . . a guy one night. No names, Mike. I ain't giving you names. I specialize in that end of the trade. Marge, she's a favorite with the hard boys. Does a lot of fancy tricks for them, see? Well, this guy . . . like he's representing somebody big. He's like muscle on lend. He comes in to do a favor. He's Chicago and ready. He ain't saying what's to do, but he stands ready. Now his boss man lends him out because a favor was asked, only his boss man don't *do* no favors. It's got to be bought or got to be forced. Somebody's got something on his boss man and is making a trade.

"Don't ask what it is. Who am I to know? I just put two and two together until it works out. Somebody is building an organization and although money is there it's the pressure that's bringing the boys in."

I tipped back in the chair watching him. "It plays if somebody is building an organization. Whatever the pressure is, it brings muscle in that can't be bought, then the muscle can be used to square the money."

"You play it," Toby said. "I don't even want to think on it no more."

"How many are in?"

"Enough. With a mob like's here I could damn near run the town single-handed."

"These boys all come from big sources?"

Toby's head bobbed once. "The biggest. The Syndicate's lending men. They come out of the individual operations, but the boss men are the Syndicate men. You're trouble, boy."

"Thanks, kiddo. You've been a help."

"For that I ain't happy. I hope they get you before they tie me into anything."

"Forget it," I said and got up from the table.

I left him there and walked out into the rain back toward my office. If Jersey Toby was right Mr. Dickerson was pulling off a cute trick. It figured right, too, because he'd be smart enough and would have had the time to work it out. Little by little he could have built the things he needed to pressure the big ones into line. He had the background, experience, and the desire. One thing led to another. Once the mob was in, an organization could be built that could utilize three million bucks properly.

If Mr. Dickerson was Blackie Conley it fitted just right.

Up in the office I had to wait only fifteen minutes before Pete Ladero came in with a folio under his arm. He laid the stuff on the table and opened it up. "Do I get an explanation first?"

"Research on Blackie Conley," I said.

"Aw, for crying out loud, he's been dead for years."

"Has he?"

"Well . . ." He paused and searched my face. "You on to something?"

"You familiar with this case?"

"I ran over it. The magazine writers rehashed it enough so I know the general background. Give."

"If Conley's alive he's got three million bucks in his kick. He might be old and fiesty enough to start trouble with it."

"Boy, bring-'em-back-alive Hammer." He reached for the paper. "You looking for anything special?"

"Conley's connection with the heist. Take half and we'll go through them."

So we sat down and read. Velda called and I told her to hop over, then went back to the papers again.

The prosecution had a cut-and-dried case. Sonny Motley pleaded guilty since he was nailed in the act and faced an automatic sentence anyway. He ranted and raved all the way through the trial, cursing everybody from the judge down, but Torrence and Conley in particular. Torrence because he wouldn't let him alone, but kept hammering for details, and Conley for the big double cross and a bullet in his shoulder.

The main item of interest was the missing three million dollars, but despite the speculation and the nationwide police search, not one thing was turning up. Sonny Motley didn't mind spilling his guts if it meant nailing Blackie Conley and the unseen face who engineered the deal. Right then he figured they pulled the double cross together, but Sim Torrence couldn't get any evidence whatsoever on the one behind the action.

There was another witness. Her name was Sally Devon and she was called because she was assumed to be a confederate of Sonny's. Her testimony was such that she turned out to be the beautiful but dumb type after all, knowing nothing of the mob's operation. Sonny and the others all admitted she was only a shack job as far as they were concerned and that seemed to end her part in the affair. Only one reporter mentioned a statement that had any significance. Just before she was discharged from the stand she said that *"she'd like to get the snake that was responsible."*

And that was what had bothered me. Sue had said the same thing, only there had been a minor discrepancy in her statements. First she said it was *a* snake that had killed her mother. Later she said *the* snake! Sue Devon remembered something, all right. Sally had raved in her drunkenness too . . . not about snakes . . . but about *the* snake. Old Mrs. Lee just hadn't understood right.

Now The Snake was emerging. It was the one who engineered the whole damn business. The one nobody knew about or saw. The one who could have engineered it into a massive double cross to start with.

Blackie Conley. He really played it cute. He stood by as a lieutenant to Sonny Motley, but it was his plan to start with. He worked it into a cross and took off with the profits. He was bigger than anybody gave him credit for being. He was big enough to hold on until he felt like it and make the most incredible comeback in the history of crime.

If it worked.

And it was working.

I had been looking over the paper too long. Pete said, "You found it, didn't you?"

"I think I have."

"Do I get it?"

"Why not?" I put the paper down and looked at him. "Can you hold it?"

"Better tell me about it first."

When I did he whistled softly and started writing. I said, "If it goes out now this guy might withdraw and we'll never get him. You can call the shots, buddy, but I'd advise you to wait. It could be bigger."

He put the pencil away, grinning. "This is bonus stuff, Mike. I'll sit on it. Make it mine though, will you?"

"Done."

"Want Hy in?"

"Damn right. The office can use the publicity. Give him the same poop."

"Sure, Mike." He folded the news clips together and headed for the door. "Call me when you need anything."

I waved when he left, then picked up the phone and dialed Pat. He was home for a change, and sore about being dragged out of bed. I said, "How'd you make out, Pat?"

"Got something new for you."

"Oh?"

"Write off Arnold Goodwin. He's dead."

"What happened?"

"He was killed a couple of months ago in an automobile accident near Saratoga. His body's been lying in a morgue up there unclaimed. The report just came in with his prints."

"Positive?"

"Look, it was a stiff with good prints. He was on file. He checked out. The dead man was Goodwin. The accident involved a local car and was just that . . . an accident."

"Then it narrows things down. You still working on Basil Levitt?"

"All the way. We've gone over his record in detail and are trying to backtrack him up to the minute he died. It won't be easy. That guy knew how to cover a trail. Two of my men are working from a point they picked up three months ago and might be able to run it through. Incidentally, I have an interesting item in his history."

"What's that?"

"After he lost his P.I. license he had an arrest record of nineteen. Only two convictions, but some of the charges were pretty serious. He was lucky enough each time to have a good lawyer. The eleventh time he was picked up for assault and it was Sim Torrence who defended him and got him off."

"I don't like it, Pat."

"Don't worry about it. Sim was in civil practice at the time and it was one of hundreds he handled. Levitt never used the same lawyer twice, but the ones he used were good ones. Torrence had a damn good record and the chances are the tie-in was accidental. We got on this thing this morning and I called Torrence personally. He sent Geraldine King up here with the complete file on the case. It meant an hour in court to him, that's all, and the fee was five hundred bucks."

"Who made the complaint?"

"Some monkey who owned a gin mill but who had a record himself. It boils down to a street fight, but Torrence was able to prove that Levitt was merely defending himself. Here's another cute kick. Our present D.A., Charlie Force, defended Levitt on charge seventeen. Same complaint and he got him off too."

"Just funny that those two ever met."

"Mike, in the crime business they get to meet criminals. He does, I do, and you do. Now there's one other thing. The team I have out are circulating pictures of Levitt. Tonight I get a call from somebody who evidently saw the photo and wanted to know what it was all about. He wouldn't give him name and there wasn't time to get a tracer on the call. I didn't tell him anything but said that if he had any pertinent information on Levitt to bring it to us. I was stalling, trying for a tracer. I think he got wise. He said sure, then hung up. As far as we got was that the call came from Flatbush."

"Hell, Pat, that's where Levitt comes from."

"So do a couple million other people. We'll wait it out. All I knew was that it was an open phone, not a booth unless the door was left open, and probably in a bar. I could hear general background talk and a juke going."

"We'll wait that one out then. He has something on his mind."

"They usually call again," Pat said. "You have anything special?"

"Some ideas."

"When do I hear them?"

"Maybe tomorrow."

"I'll stand by."

When I hung up I stared at the phone, then leaned my face into my hands trying to make the ends meet in my mind. Screwy, that's all I could think of. Screwy, but it was making sense.

The phone rang once, jarring me out of my thought. I picked it up, said hello, and the voice that answered was tense. "Geraldine King, Mike. Can you come out here right away?"

"What's up, Geraldine?"

She was too agitated to try to talk. She simply said, "Please, Mike, come right away. *Now.* It's very important." Then she gave me no choice. She hung up.

I wrote a note to Velda telling where I was going and that I'd head right back for the apartment when I was done, then left it in the middle of her desk.

Downstairs I cut around back of the cop assigned to watch me, took the side way out without being seen, and picked up a cruising cab at the street corner. The rain was heavier now, a steady, straight-down New York rain that always seemed to come in with the trouble. Heading north on the West Side Highway I leaned back into the cushions and tried to grab a nap. Sleep was out of the question, even for a little while, so I just sat there and remembered back to those last seven years when forgetting was such a simple thing to do.

All you needed was a bottle.

The cop on the beat outside Torrence's house checked my identity before letting me go through. Two reporters were already there talking to a plainclothesman and a fire captain, but not seeming to be getting much out of either one of them.

Geraldine King met me at the door, her face tight and worried. I said, "What happened?"

"Sue's place . . . it burned."

"What about the kid?"

"She's all right. I have her upstairs in bed. Come on inside."

"No, let's see that building first."

She pulled a sweater on and closed the door behind us. Flood-lights on the grounds illuminated the area, the rain slanting through it obliquely.

There wasn't much left, just charred ruins and the concrete foundation. Fire hoses and the rain had squelched every trace of smoldering except for one tendril of smoke that drifted out of one corner, and I could see the remains of the record player and the lone finger that was her microphone stand. Scattered across the floor were tiny bits of light bouncing back from the shattered mirror that had lined the one wall. But there was nothing else. Whatever had been there was gone now.

I said, "We can go back now."

When we were inside Geraldine made us both a drink and stood in the den looking out the window. I let her wait until she was ready to talk, finishing half my drink on the way. Finally she said, "This morning Sue came inside. I . . . don't know what started it, but she came out openly and accused Mr. Torrence of having killed her mother. She kept saying her mother told her."

"How could she say her mother told her she was murdered when she was alive to tell her?" I interrupted.

"I know, I know, but she insisted her mother wrote something and she was going to find it. You know she kept all her mother's old personal things out there."

"Yes, I saw some of them."

"Mr. Torrence is in the middle of an important campaign. He was quite angry and wanted this thing settled once and for all, so while Sue was in here he went out and went through her things, trying to prove that there was nothing.

"Sue must have seen him from upstairs. She came down crying, ran outside, and told him to leave. Neither one of us could quiet her down. She locked herself inside and wouldn't come out and as long as she was there we didn't worry about it. This . . . wasn't exactly the first time this has happened. We were both used to her outbursts.

"Late this afternoon Mr. Torrence got a call and had to leave for his office on some campaign matter. It was about two hours later that I happened to look out and saw the smoke. The building was burning from the inside and Sue was still there. The record player was going and when I looked in the window she was doing some crazy kind of dance with one of those big stuffed toys that used to belong to her mother.

"She wouldn't come out, wouldn't answer me . . . nothing. I . . . guess I started screaming. There was a policeman outside the fence, fortunately. He just happened to be there."

I shook my head. "No, he wasn't. This department was cooperating with the requests of the city police. He was there purposely. Go on."

"He came in and broke down the door. By that time Sue was almost unconscious, lying there on the floor with the flames shooting up the walls. We dragged her out, got her in the house, and I put her to bed. One of the neighbors saw the flames and called the fire department. They came, but there was nothing to do. The damage was not really important . . . except now we'll never know what Sue had of her mother's that she was always searching for."

"Where was Torrence at this time?"

Slowly, she turned around, fingering the drink in her hand. "I know what you're thinking, but perhaps twenty minutes before that I spoke to him on the phone. He was in the city."

"How can you be sure?"

"Because I spoke to two others in his office on some party matters."

"Where is he now?"

"On the way to Albany with some of his constituents. If you want I'll see that he's notified and we'll get him right back."

"I don't think it's necessary. Can I see Sue?

"She'll be asleep. She was totally worn out. She started the fire, you know."

"I don't."

"But I do."

"How?"

"She told me. She'll tell you too when she's awake."

"Then we'll awaken her."

"All right."

Sue's bedroom was a composite of little girl and grown-up. There were framed still pictures of Sally Devon on her dresser and vanity along with some of herself in leotards and ballet costumes. There was another record player here and an almost identical stack of classical L.P.'s. Scattered here and there were toys from another year, mostly fuzzy animals and dolls in dancing clothes.

She lay in bed like a child, her yellow hair spilling around her face, one arm snuggling an oversized animal whose fur had been partially burned off, the face charred so that it was almost unrecognizable for whatever it was. She smiled dreamily, held the toy close to her, and buried her face against it. Some of the straw was sticking out on one side and she pushed it out of the way.

I touched her arm. "Sue . . ."

She didn't awaken immediately. I spoke her name twice again before she opened her eyes.

She said, "Hello, Mike."

"Sue . . . did you set the fire?"

"Yes, I was . . . burning Mother's old papers. I didn't want him to see anything of hers."

"What happened?"

She smiled again. "I . . . don't know. Everything . . . seemed to start burning. I sort of felt happy then. I didn't care. I sang and danced while it was burning and felt good. That's all I remember."

"Okay, go back to sleep."

"Mike . . ."

"What?"

"I'm sorry."

"That's all right."

"He'll . . . put me away or something now, won't he?"

"I don't think so. It *was* an accident."

"Not really it wasn't. I meant it."

I sat on the edge of the bed and took her hand. She was still in a state of semi-shock and sometimes that's the time when they can say the right thing. I said, "Sue . . . you remember telling me your mother was killed by the snake?"

Her eyes drifted away momentarily, then came back to mine. "The snake did it. She said so. The snake would kill her because he had to."

"Who is the snake, honey?"

"She said the snake would kill her," she repeated. "I remember." Her eyes started to widen and under my hand her arm grew taut. "She said . . ."

But I wouldn't let her talk any more. She was too near the breaking point, so I leaned over and kissed her and the fear left her face as suddenly as it appeared and she smiled.

"Go back to sleep, honey. I'll see you in the morning."

"Don't leave, Mike."

"I'll be around."

"Please, Mike."

I winked and stood up. "Sleep, baby, for me."

"All right, Mike."

I left a night-light on and the door partly open and went back downstairs with Geraldine. I sat back on the couch and took the drink she made me, sipping it slowly.

Outside the rain slapped at the windows, massaging them with streaky, wet fingers. She turned on the record player, drew the heavy draperies across the windows, and turned out all the lights except one. Then she sat down beside me.

Only then did she say, "What shall we do, Mike?"

"Nothing yet."

"There were reporters out there."

"What did you tell them?"

"That it was accidental. It really wasn't too important . . . just a small outbuilding. If it weren't Mr. Torrence's place it would never draw a mention, but . . . well, you understand."

"They won't make much out of it."

"But if Sue keeps making these accusations . . . it's an election year, Mike. The campaign for governor of a state is of maximum importance. You know how both parties look at it. This is a key state. From here a governor can go into the White House or at least have a major effect on national policy. If anything . . . anything at all comes up that can be detrimental to a selected candidate it can be disastrous. This . . . this business with Sue is getting out of hand."

"Your bunch knows about it then?"

She nodded, then took a swallow of her drink. "Yes . . . in a way it's why I'm here. I've been with Sim Torrence on his other campaigns as much as a guardian for Sue as an assistant to Mr. Torrence. She doesn't realize all this and I've made it a point to keep it almost businesslike, but I do manage to find things for Sue to do and distract this antagonistic attitude she has. All her life she's been trying to emulate her mother . . . trying to be a showgirl. She's been coached in singing, dancing, the arts . . . given the very best Mr. Torrence can give her. She's taken advantage of those opportunities, not just to help her into show business but it gets her away from him. Sad, but true."

"You speculating now?"

She looked at me over her glass. "No, she's told me that. You can ask her."

"I believe it."

"What can we do? It's critical now."

"I'll think of something."

"Will you, Mike? We need help badly."

"You sure love this political crap, don't you?"

"My life, Mike. I gave my life to it."

"Hell, you're too young to die. Maybe you should have been born a man."

"There's a place for women in politics."

"Bull."

"You just like them to be women, don't you?"

"That's what they are."

"All right. For you I'll be a woman."

She put her drink down on the coffee table, took mine from my hand and put it next to hers, both unfinished. There was a sudden hunger in her eyes and a warmth to her face that made her mouth seem to blossom into a new fullness. Her fingers went to her throat and one by one she unbuttoned her blouse until it lay open, then with the slightest shrug of her shoulders it slid away so that her fingers could work more magic with the soft fabric of the bra. She whisked it away and it floated to the floor where it lay unnoticed.

I looked at her, not touching her, taking in the lovely slope of her breasts that were swelled with emotion and tipped with the firm pinkness of passion. I could smell the fragrant heat of her only inches away, and as I watched, her stomach undulated and moved spasmodically against the waistband of her skirt.

"How am I . . . as a woman, Mike?"

"Lovely," I told her. I reached for her, turned her around, then lay her as she was, half naked, across my lap, my fingers caught in her hair, touching her gently at first, then with firm insistence that made her shudder.

She raised herself against me, twisting her head, searching for my mouth until she found it, then with a small whimper she was part of me, her lips a ripe, succulent fruit, her tongue an alive, vital organ that was a soul seeking another soul. I let her fall away from me reluctantly, her mouth still working as though it were kissing mine yet, her eyes closed, her breath coming heavily.

Someplace in the house a clock chimed and a dull rumble of thunder outside echoed it. I let my hand run down the naked expanse of her stomach until the tips of my fingers traced a path across her waist under the skirt. She moaned softly and sucked in her breath so there would be a looseness at her belt. I felt her briefly, kneaded the pliant flesh, then took my hand away.

Her eyes opened, she smiled once and closed them again. Then she was asleep. It had been a hard day for her too. I held her until I was sure she wouldn't awaken, then raised her, propped a cushion beneath her shoulders, and let her down onto it. I covered her with her blouse and a plaid car blanket that was folded over the back of a chair.

In the morning she'd feel better. She'd hate me maybe, but then again, maybe not. I went upstairs and checked Sue. She had turned on her side and the oversized stuffed toy was almost crushed beneath her.

I called a cab in from town, let myself out, and waited by the gate. The cop on the beat asked me if everything was all right and I told him the women were both asleep and to stay on his toes. He still couldn't read me but with the card I carried he wasn't taking any chances. He saluted cordially and walked off into the darkness.

Inspector Grebb should have seen that, I thought. He'd flip. He'd sooner I got a boot in the tail.

When the cab came he didn't want to take me clean into the city so I changed cabs at the George Washington Bridge and gave that driver the address of my new apartment. I started to grin, thinking of what Velda would do if she knew where I was an hour ago. Hell, she never would believe me if I told her the truth anyway, so why say a word? But you can't go through two of those deals in one night and stand up to it. If Velda was there I hoped she was sacked out tight. Right then I needed sleep more than anything I could think of.

I paid the cab off and went inside. The place was freshly renovated and smelled of paint. I took the automatic elevator to the third floor, found my new apartment at the very end of the hall, and stuck the key in the lock. There was a soft glow from a table lamp at the end of the couch in the living room and a radio was playing softly. From where I stood I could see her stretched out comfortably and laughed to myself. Velda had determination, but sleep had won out. She got the couch and I got the bed this time. Tomorrow she'd sizzle, but she'd still be waiting.

I went in on the balls of my feet, walking quietly so as not to wake her, but I couldn't help looking at her as I passed. And when I saw her I turned ice cold inside because she wasn't just asleep at all. Somebody had brought something down across her temple turning it into a livid welt that oozed dark blood under her ear into her hairline.

I grabbed her, said *"Velda!"* once, then she let out a little meowing sound and her eyes flicked open. She tried to talk but couldn't and it was her eyes that got the message across. I looked up to the side where he stood with one hand holding his belly and the other a gun and he had it pointed right at my head.

Marv Kania had finally found me.

His eyes had death in them, his and mine. His belly was bloated and I could smell the stench of a festering wound, the sickening odor of old blood impregnated into cloth. There was a wildness in his face and his mouth was a tight slash that showed all his teeth. Marv Kania was young, but right there he was as old as death itself.

"I was waiting for you, mister."

Slowly, I got up. I was going to have to pull against a drawn gun and there wasn't a chance I could make it. He was dying, but the gun in his hand was there with the deft skill of the professional and it never wavered an inch. He let the muzzle drift down from my head until it pointed at my stomach.

"Right where I got it, man, and there's no coming back after that. Everything inside goes. You'll live a little while and you'll hurt like I hurt. You try to move away from it and I put one more in your head."

I was thinking fast, wondering how fast I could move away from the shot. He knew what I was going to do and grinned through the pain he felt. Just to let me know it was no good he made two quick wrist motions to show he still had it and I had it, then he thumbed the hammer back.

"The girl. What about her?"

"What do you care? You'll be dead."

"What about her?"

His face was a mask of pain and hate. "I'll tell you what I'm going to do. With her she gets one shot. Same as you. Then I go outside and die. Out in the rain, just so long as I don't die in no crummy room. In the park, that's where I die. I always wanted to die there." His eyes half shut momentarily as a spasm of pain took him, then he snapped them open and grinned, his teeth bare against his gums.

Velda turned on the couch, whispering my name softly. She must have come in when he was there. He held a gun on her, belted her out, and kept on waiting. Now he was going to kill her along with me.

"You ready, you bastard?"

I didn't move. I just stood there hoping Velda could do something while my own body half shielded her from him, hoping she could move fast enough to get the hell out. He saw that too and started to laugh. It was so funny to him with all the hate bottled up inside he laughed even harder as he aimed the rod with every ounce of professional technique he ever had.

And it was the laugh that did it. The laugh that broke the last thing inside. The laugh that burst the lifeline. He felt it go and his eyes went so wide the whites of them showed the horror he felt because he was still a loser and before he could put that final fraction of pressure on the trigger the gun dropped from his hand and he pitched facedown on the floor with a sickening squashing sound as some ghastly, putrescent fluid burst from his belly.

I picked Velda up, carried her into the bedroom, and washed the blood from her temple. Then I loosened her clothes and pulled the blanket over her before flopping down on the bed beside her.

Outside I had another dead man at my feet, but he was going to have to wait until morning.

CHAPTER 8

Pat was there at nine in the morning. So was Inspector Grebb and Charles Force. Pat's face told me he had no choice so I threw him a brief nod so he knew I got the picture.

The police photographers got all the shots they wanted, the body was carried out, Velda had a doctor in with her, and Grebb pointed at a chair for me and sat down himself.

"You've been a thorn in our side, Hammer," he said pleasantly.

"Tough."

"But I think we have you nailed now."

"For failing to report a body?"

"It's enough. You don't step that far outside and still get a gun-carrying privilege. It will break you with that fancy agency because they like closed mouths about their operations. They lift your ticket and you're back in the ranks again."

Charlie Force was standing there with that same old courtroom smile, like his bait had caught the fish. I said, "I warned you, Charlie."

"Mr. Force, if you don't mind?"

This time I let him see the kind of grin I had, the one with teeth in it. I said, "Okay, buddy, I'll come to your party, only I'm bringing my friends. I'm bringing in pressures you never heard of. Get something in your goddamn heads . . . you're two public servants and all you're looking for is another step up. If you got the idea you'll get it over me you're wrong. Don't think that agency is going to back down a bit. I gave them too much and they're still paying off for it. I'll keep giving them more and more until they can't afford to lose me. The agency is bigger than both you guys and now you're going to find it out the hard way.

"As for you, Force, before you were playing in courtrooms I was pushing a legal gun around this town and there are guys I know and friends I made who'd like nothing better than to wipe your nose in a mess. Believe me, buddy, if you ever did one lousy thing in your life . . . and you can bet your ass you did because everybody does, I'll nail it down and you'll go with it. It won't even be a hard job. But I'll do even better than that to you, kid. I'll pull the stool right out from under you. This little bugger I'm on now is a hot little bugger and it's mine. You get no slice of it at all. I'll make the action and get the yaks."

I spun around and looked at Pat. "Tell them, friend."

"You did a pretty good job. I'm still a Captain."

"Well, maybe we'll get you raised one after this, okay, Inspector?"

He didn't say anything. He sat there glowering at me, not knowing what to think. But he was an old hand and knew when the wind was blowing bad. It showed in his eyes, only he didn't want me to to see it. Finally he looked at his watch, then up to me. "We'll wait some more," he said. "It's bound to happen sometime."

"Don't hold your breath waiting," I said.

"You take care of things here, Captain," he said to Pat. "I'll want to see the report later."

"I'll have it on your desk, Inspector."

They left then, two quiet men with one idea in their minds nobody was ever going to shake loose. When they were out I said to Pat, "Why the heat?"

"Because the city is on edge, Mike. They haven't got the answers and neither have I. Somehow you always get thrown in the middle of things so that you're the one to pull the switch."

"You got everything I know."

Pat nodded sagely. "Great. Facts are one thing, but there's still that crazy mind of yours. You make the same facts come out with different answers somehow." He held up his hand to shut me up. "Oh, I agree, you're cooperative and all that jazz. You lay it on the line like you're requested to do and still make it look like your own idea. But all the time you're following a strange line of reasoning nobody who looks at the facts would take. I always said you should have been a straight cop in the first place."

"I tried it a long time ago and it didn't work."

"You would have made a perfect crook. Sometimes I wonder just what the hell you really are inside. You live in a half world of your own, never in, never out, always on the edge."

"Nuts to you, Pat. It works."

"The hard way."

Pat walked to the window, stared down into the courtyard a moment, then came back. "Kania say anything to you before he died?"

"Only how he was going to enjoy killing me."

"You didn't ask him any questions?"

"With a gun on me and him ready to shoot? There wasn't anything to ask."

"There wasn't any chance you could have taken him?"

"Not a one."

"So I'll buy it. Now, how'd he find you?"

"I'm not that hard to find. He did it twice before. He probably picked up Velda at my office and followed her here."

"She talk yet?"

"No," I told him, "but maybe she will now. Let's ask her."

The doctor had finished with Velda, assuring us both that it was only a minor concussion that should leave no aftereffects, gave me a prescription for a sedative, and left us alone with her.

She smiled up at me crookedly, her face hurting with the effort.

"Think you can talk, kitten?"

"I'm all right."

"How'd that punk get in here?"

She shook her head and winced. "I don't know. I left the door unlocked thinking you'd be in shortly, then I went to the bathroom. When I went back into the living room he stepped out of the bedroom. He held the gun on me . . . then made me lie on the couch. I knew he was afraid I'd scream or something so he just swung the gun at me. I remember . . . coming awake once, then he hit me again. That's all I remember until you spoke to me."

I glanced at Pat. "That's how he did it then. He waited at the office."

"Did you know Grebb kept a man staked out there?"

"Didn't everybody? I told you to stay off my neck."

"It wasn't my idea."

"Kania must have spotted him the same as I did. He simply waited outside or across the street until Velda came out. When she came alone he figured she could lead him to me and stayed with her. She made the job easy by leaving the door open."

"I'm sorry, Mike."

"No sweat, baby," I said. "It won't happen again."

"Mike . . ."

"What?"

"Mrs. Lee. She'd like to see you again."

She was bypassing Pat, but he caught it and grinned. "I haven't heard about her."

"An old lady. Sally Devon's old wardrobe mistress. She was with her when she died. She'll talk to anybody for company's sake but she might come up with something."

"Still going back thirty years?"

"Does money get old?" I asked him.

There was a jack next to the bed so I got the phone from the living room and plugged it in and laid it on the nightstand where Velda could reach it. "You stay put all day, honey. I'll check in with you every now and then and if you want anything, just call down for it. I'll leave your key with the super and he can check on anybody who comes in."

"Mike . . . I'll be fine. You don't have to . . ."

I cut her off. "Look, if I want you for anything, I'll call. There's a lot you can do without getting out of bed. Relax until I need you. Shall I get somebody to stay with you?"

"No."

"I'll be moving fast. I don't know where I'll be. But I'll check in every couple of hours. Maybe Pat here can give you a buzz too."

"Be glad to," he said. There was restraint in his voice and I knew how he was hurting. It isn't easy for a guy who loves a woman to see her going down the road with somebody else. War, love . . . somebody's got to be the loser.

So I covered her up and went outside with Pat. About twenty minutes later two men from his division came in, got a rundown on Kania, and started backtracking him. A contract killer wasn't notorious for leaving a trail, but Marv Kania had a record, he was known. He might have been tight-lipped about his operation, but somewhere somebody was going to know something.

One thing. That's all we needed. You could start with dead men, all right, but it won't do you any good if they only lead to other dead men. Mr. Dickerson had played some smart cards. He had picked his people well. The ones here were clean. The ones who weren't were dead. The hoods in town could be taken in and questioned, but if they knew nothing because the orders hadn't been issued yet, they couldn't say anything. It was still a free country and you couldn't make them leave the state as long as they stayed clean. The men behind them were power who could still turn on the heat through odd but important channels so you couldn't roust them too far.

I told Pat I'd see him sometime after lunch, walked him downstairs, left a key with the super, and gave him a fin for his trouble. Pat went on downtown and I hopped a cab across town to Annette Lee's place, got the landlady to let me in, and stepped into her living room.

The old gal was still in her rocker, still going through that same perpetual rhythm, stopping only when her chair had inched against another piece of furniture. Her curtains were drawn back, letting in the early light, and she smiled a big hello when she saw me.

"How nice of you to come back, young man," she said. She held out her hand without getting up and I took it. "Sit down, please."

I tossed my hat on a table and pulled up another straight-back chair and perched on the end of it.

"Your young lady was here yesterday. We had a lovely visit. It isn't often I get company, you know."

I said, "She mentioned you wanted to see me."

"Yes." Annette Lee nodded, then leaned her head back against the chair with her eyes half shut. "We were talking. I . . ." She waved her hand vaguely in front of her face. "Sometimes I forget things. I'm going on ninety now. I think I've lived too long already."

"You never live too long."

"Perhaps so. I can still enjoy things. I can dream. Do you dream, Mr. . . . ?"

"Hammer."

"Mr. Hammer. Do you dream?"

"Sometimes."

"You're not old enough to dream back like I do. It's something like being reborn. I like to dream. They were good days then. I dream about them because they're all I have to dream about. Yes, they were fine days."

"What was it you wanted to tell me, Miss Lee?" I asked her gently.

"Oh?" She thought a moment, then: "There was something. Your young lady and I talked about Sally and Sue. Yes, that was it. Dear Sally, she was so lovely. It was a pity she died."

"Miss Lee . . ."

"Yes?"

"The night she died . . . do you remember it well?"

"Oh yes. Oh yes indeed." Her rocking slowed momentarily so she could shift positions, then started again.

"Was she drunk, really drunk?"

"Dear me, yes. Sally drank all the time. From very early in the morning. There was nothing I could do so I tried to keep her company and talk to her. She didn't want to talk too much, you know. When she did it was drunk talk I couldn't always understand. Do you know what I mean?"

"I've heard it."

"There was that thing with the snakes you mentioned. It was rather an obsession with her."

"She was frightened of the snake?"

Annette Lee lifted her head and peered at me. "No, that was the strange thing. She wasn't afraid. It was . . . well, she hated it."

"Was the snake a person?"

"Excuse me?"

"Could she have been referring to a person as The Snake? Not snakes or a snake. *The Snake*."

The rocking stopped completely. She looked at me curiously in the semi-darkened room, her fingertip touching her lips. "So that was what she meant."

"Go on."

"No wonder I didn't understand. My goodness, never understood in all this time. Yes, she said *the* snake. It was always *the* snake.

She hated *the* snake, that was why she wanted to live so far away from the city. She never wanted to go back."

"Annette . . . who was Sue's father?"

The old girl made a face at me and raised the thin line of her eyebrows. "Does it matter?"

"It might."

"But I'm afraid I couldn't tell you."

"Why not?"

"Simply because I don't know. Sue has Sally's maiden name, you know. She never got her father's name because she doesn't know who he is. I'm afraid Sally was . . . a bit promiscuous. She had many men and among them would be Sue's father. I doubt if Sally ever really knew either. A pity. Sue was such a lovely baby."

"Could it have been Blackie Conley?"

For the first time Annette Lee giggled. "Dear no. Not him. Never Blackie."

"Why?"

"Simply because he wasn't capable. I think that was one of the reasons Blackie was so . . . so frustrated. He *did* like the ladies, you know. He slept with one after the other. He even married two of them but it never worked out. He always wanted an heir but he wasn't capable. Why . . . the boys used to kid him about it."

Her feet pushed harder until she had to edge the chair away from the wall so that she faced me more directly. "Do you ever remember Bud Packer?"

"Just the name."

"Bud was . . . joshing him one day about his . . . impotence and Blackie shot him. You know where. I think Blackie did time for that but I don't rightly remember. No, Blackie was not Sue's father by any means. Besides, you're forgetting one big thing."

I let her say it.

"Blackie's been gone . . . for years. Long before Sue was born. Blackie is dead somewhere."

She put her head back and closed her eyes. I said, "Tired?"

"No, just thinking. Daydreaming."

"How about this angle . . . could Sim Torrence have been the father?"

Her giggle broke into a soft cackle only the old can make. "Sim Torrence? I'm afraid not. Sue was born before they were married."

"He could still be the father."

"You don't understand, Mr. . . ."

"Hammer."

"Mr. Hammer. You see, I was with Sally always before. I knew the many faces she was with. I know who she slept with and none of them were Sim Torrence. It wasn't until after the baby was born that they were married when he took her in and provided for them." The flat laugh came out again. "Those two could never have a baby of their own though."

"Why not?"

"Because she and Sim never slept together. After the baby was born Sally never let a man near her. She underwent a change. All she thought of was the baby, making plans for her, hoping for her to grow up and be somebody. You know, I hate to give away women-secrets, but Sally deliberately cultivated Sim Torrence. They knew each other for some time earlier. Some court case. She managed to meet him somehow and I remember them going out for a couple of weeks before she brought him to our apartment and told me they were going to get married."

"Did Torrence take it well?"

"How does any man take it who is going to lose his bachelor-hood?" She smiled knowingly. "He was rather shaken. Almost embarrassed. But he did provide well for Sally and Sue. They had a simple ceremony and moved into his town house."

"Were you with them?"

"Oh yes. Sally wouldn't leave me. Why, I was the only one who could take care of her and the baby. She wasn't very domestic, you know. She wasn't supposed to be. Yes, those were different women then. Showgirls. They had to be pampered."

"Why wouldn't she let Torrence near her in bed?"

"Does it sound strange that a woman who was a . . . a whore would be afraid of sex?"

I shook my head. "Most of them are frigid anyway," I said bluntly.

"So true, so true. Well, that was Sally. Frigid. Having the baby scared her. Even having a man scared her."

"Was she scared of Torrence?"

"Of every man, Mr. . . ." and this time she remembered my name and smiled, ". . . Hammer. Yes, Sim Torrence scared her but I think he understood. He let her stay at that place in the country. He came up on occasions and it was very strained but he was very understanding about it too. Of course, like all men, he could bury himself in his work. That was his real wife, his work."

"Miss Lee . . . the last time I was here we talked about Blackie Conley, remember?"

"I remember."

"You said you knew about the plans he made for that robbery he and Sonny Motley were involved in. What were they?"

She stopped rocking, her face curious again. "Are you looking for the money?"

"I'm a cop, Miss Lee. I'm looking for a killer, for the money . . . for anything that will help keep trouble from Sue."

"Sue? But that was before she was born."

"It can come back to hurt her. Now what did you hear?"

She nodded, pressing her lips together, her hands grasping the arms of the rocker. "Do you really think . . . ?"

"It might help."

"I see." She paused, thought a moment, then said, "You know that Sonny really didn't plan the robbery. It was his gang, but he didn't plan it. They were . . . acting for someone."

"I know about that."

"Blackie had instructions to find a place where they were going to hide out. He was told where to go and how to do it. I remember because I listened to the call." She chuckled at the thought. "I never did like Blackie. He was at Sally's place when he took the call. In fact, that was where they did all their planning, at Sally's apartment. Sonny was going with her then when she wasn't sneaking off with Blackie."

"I see."

"Really," she told me, "I wasn't supposed to know about these things. I was always in the other room out of sight, but I was worried about Sally and tried to find out what was going on. I listened in and they didn't know it."

"None of this came out at the trial," I reminded her.

"Nor was it about to, young man. I didn't want to involve Sally any more than she was. She *did* appear in court, you know."

"Briefly. She wasn't implicated. She was treated as an innocent victim."

Those watery old eyes found mine and laughed in their depths. "No, Sally wasn't so innocent. She knew everything that went on. Sally's pose was very deliberate. Very deliberate. She was a better actress than anyone imagined."

Annette Lee leaned forward like some old conspirator. "Now that it can't hurt her, let me tell you something. It was through dear Sally that this robbery came about. All arrangements, all contacts were made through her. Sonny was quite a man in those days and ran a sizable operation. But it was through Sally Devon that another party interested Sonny in that robbery. No, Sally was hardly the innocent victim."

I didn't let her see me take it in. I passed it off quickly to get her back on the track again, but now the angles were starting to show. I said, "When Blackie Conley got this call . . . what happened?"

Jerked suddenly from one train of thought, she sat back frowning. "Oh . . . Blackie . . . well, I heard this voice . . ."

"A man?"

"Yes. He told Blackie to see a man in a certain real estate agency, one that could be trusted. He gave him the phone number."

I added, "And Blackie arranged to rent a house in the Catskills?"

"That's right. He made the call right then and said he'd be in the next day." She opened her eyes again, now her fingers tapping a silent tune on the chair. "But then he made another call to Howie Green."

"Who?"

"Howie Green. He was a bootlegger, dearie, but he owned properties here in the city. He invested his money wisely, Howie did, and always had something to show for it. Howie was as crooked as they come, but smarter than most of them. One of Howie's enterprises was a real estate agency that used to be someplace on Broadway. Oh yes, Howie was a big man, but he owed Blackie Conley a favor. Blackie killed a man for Howie and held it over his head. He told Howie he wanted a place to hole up in somewhere away from the city and to pick it out."

"Where was it, Annette?"

"I don't know, young man. Howie merely said he'd do it for him. That was all. I suppose Blackie took care of it later. However, it's all over now. Howie Green's dead too. He died in an accident not long afterward."

"Before the robbery?"

"I really don't remember that."

I reached for my hat and stood up. "You've been a great help, Annette."

"Have I really?"

I nodded.

"Will Sue be . . . all right?"

"I'm sure she will."

"Someday," she asked me, "will you bring her to me? I would like to see her again."

"We'll make a point of it."

"Good-bye then. It was nice of you to come over,"

"My pleasure, Miss Lee."

At two o'clock I contacted Pat and made a date to meet him at his office. He didn't like the idea because he knew Grebb would want to sit in on the conversation but thought he could arrange it so we could be alone.

I took a cab downtown, found Pat alone at his desk buried in the usual paperwork, waited for him to finish, then said, "What officers were in on the Motley holdup? Any still around?"

"This your day for surprises?"

"Hit me."

"Inspector Grebb was one. He was a beat cop who was alerted for the action."

"Oh hell."

"Why?"

"Think he'd remember the details?"

"I don't remember Grebb ever forgetting anything."

"Then let's call him in."

"You sure about this?" Pat asked me.

"It's the easy way. So we give him a bite after all."

Pat nodded, lifted the phone, and made a call. When he hung up he said, "The Inspector will be happy to see you."

"I bet."

It didn't take him long to get up there. He didn't have Charlie Force with him either. He came in with the patient attitude of the professional cop, always ready to wait, always ready to act when the time came. He might have been a tough, sour old apple, but he made it the hard way and you couldn't take it away from him.

Inwardly I laughed at myself because if I wasn't careful I could almost like him.

"Whose party is it this time?" he asked.

Pat said, "He's throwing it."

"I never thought you'd ask, Hammer." He dragged a chair out with his foot, sat in it heavily and sighed, but it was all an act. He was no more tired or bored than I was. "Shoot," he said.

"Pat tells me you were in on the Motley thing thirty years ago."

"My second day on the beat, Hammer. That shows you how close to retirement I am. My present job is a gratuity. One last fling for the old dog in a department he always wanted to run."

"Better luck in your next one."

"We aren't talking about that. What's with the Motley job?"

"How did the cops get wise?"

"Why don't you read the transcript of the trial? It was mentioned."

"This is easier. Besides, I wanted to be sure."

Grebb pulled a cigar from his pocket, snapped off the end, and fired it up. "Like a lot of big ones that went bust," he said, "somebody pulled the cork. The department got a call. It went through the D.A.'s office."

"Torrence?"

"No, one of the others got it and passed it to him. Torrence handled it personally though."

"Where were you?"

"Staked out where the truck was hidden in case they got through somehow. They never made it. We got the truck and the driver. Second day on the beat too, I'll never forget it. Fresh out of school, still hardly shaving, and I get a hot one right off. Made me decide to stay in the department."

"How long did you have to get ready?"

"About an hour, if I remember right. It was plenty of time. We could have done it in fifteen minutes."

"They ever find out who made the call?"

"Nope."

"They look very hard?"

Grebb just shrugged noncommittally. Then he said, "Let's face it, we'd sooner have stoolies on the outside where they can call these things in than a live guy testifying in court who winds up a dead squealer a day later. We didn't break our backs running down anybody. Whoever it was played it the way we liked it. The job was a bust and we nailed the crew."

"It wasn't a bust, Inspector."

He stared at me until his face hurt.

"Nobody ever located the money."

"That's happened before. One of those things."

"Blackie Conley simply disappeared."

The cigar bobbed in his mouth. "And if he lived very long afterward he's a better man than I am. By now he'd be dead anyway." He took the cigar away from his mouth and flipped the ash off with his pinky. "But let's get back to the money . . . that's the interesting part."

"I have an idea it might show up."

"Maybe we better listen to your idea."

"Uh-uh. Facts I'll give you, ideas stay in my pocket until I can prove them out."

"Facts then."

"None you don't already have if you want to check the transcript like you suggested. I just make something different out of them, that's all."

Grebb put the cigar back between his teeth and pushed himself out of his chair. When he was on his feet he glanced at Pat meaningfully, said, "Don't let me wait too long, Captain," then went out.

"I wish you'd quit pushing him," Pat told me. "Now what's with this bit?"

I sat in the chair Grebb had vacated and propped my feet on Pat's desk. "I think Blackie Conley's alive."

"How'd he do it?"

"He was the planner behind the operation. He set it up, then phoned in a double cross. Trouble was, he should have cut it shorter. He almost lost it himself. He laid out one escape plan, but took an alternate. He got away in that cab with the three million bucks and sat on it someplace."

Pat tapped a pencil on the desk as I gave him the information Annette Lee gave me. Every once in a while he'd make a note on a pad, study it, then make another.

"We'll have to locate whatever records are left of Howie Green's business. If he was dealing in real estate it will be a matter of public record."

"You don't think Blackie would use his own name, do you?"

"We can narrow it down. Look, check your file on Green."

Pat put in another call and for the twenty minutes it took to get the papers up we went over the angles of the case. I still wouldn't lay it out the way I saw it, but he had enough to reach the same conclusion if he thought the same way.

The uniformed officer handed Pat a yellowed folder and Pat opened it on his desk. Howie Green, deceased. Known bootlegger, six arrests, two minor convictions. Suspected of duplicity in a murder of one Francis Gorman, another bootlegger who moved into his territory. Charge dropped. Known to have large holdings that were legally acquired as far as the law could prove. His annual income made him a rich man for the times. He was killed by a hit-and-run driver not far from his own house and the date given was three days before the robbery of the three million bucks.

"Pretty angle, Pat."

"Spell it out."

"If Conley did get hideout property from Green, paid for it, made the transaction, and accepted the papers in a phony name and took possession, then killed him before Green knew what he wanted it for, who could say where he was? Chances were that nobody but Conley and Green ever saw each other and Green wasn't around to talk anymore."

Pat closed the folder and shoved it in his desk. "We could check all the transactions Green made in the few weeks prior to his death."

"Time, buddy. We haven't got the time."

"But I have one thing you don't have."

I knew what he was going to say.

"Men. We can put enough troops on it to shorten the time."

"It'll still be a long job."

"You know a better way?"

The phone rang before I could answer and although I could hear the hurried chatter at the other end I couldn't make it out. When he cradled the phone Pat said, "One of my squad in Brooklyn on that Levitt rundown."

"Oh?"

"He was eating with one of the men from the precinct over there when a call came in about a body. He went along with his friend and apparently the dead guy is one of the ones he showed Basil Levitt's picture to."

"A starter," I said.

"Could be. Want to take a run over?"

"Why not?"

Pat got his car from the lot and we hopped in, cutting over the bridge into the Brooklyn section. The address was in the heart of Flatbush, one block off the Avenue, a neighborhood bar and grill that was squeezed in between a grocery and a dry-cleaning place.

A squad car was at the curb and a uniformed patrolman stood by the door. Two more, obviously detectives from the local precinct, were in the doorway talking. Pat knew the Lieutenant in charge, shook hands with him, introduced him to me as Joe Cavello, then went inside.

Squatting nervously on a stool, the bartender watched us, trying to be casual about the whole thing. Lieutenant Cavello nodded toward him and said, "He found the body."

"When?"

"About an hour ago. He had to go down to hook into some fresh beer kegs and found the guy on the floor. He'd been shot once in the head with a small-caliber gun . . . I'd say about a .32."

"The M.E. set the time of death?" I asked him.

"About twelve to fifteen hours. He'll be more specific after an autopsy."

"Who was he?" Pat said.

"The owner of the place."

"You know him?"

"Somewhat," Cavello said. "We've had him down to the precinct a few times. Twice on wife beating and another when he was picked up in a raid on a card game. This is kind of a chintzy joint. Local bums hang out here because the drinks are cheap. But that's all they sell anyway, cheap booze. We've had a few complaints about some fights in here but nothing ever happened. You know, the usual garbage that goes with these slop chutes."

Pat said, "I had Nelson and Kiley over here doing a rundown on Basil Levitt. You hear about it?"

"Yeah, Lew Nelson checked in with me right after it happened. He saw the body. It was the guy he spoke to all right. I asked around but nobody here seemed to know Levitt."

"How about the bartender?" I said.

Cavello shook his head. "Nothing there. He does the day work and nothing more. When the boss came on, he went off. He doesn't know the night crowd at all."

"He live around here?"

"Red Hook. Not his neighborhood here and he couldn't care less."

While Pat went over the details of what the police picked up I wandered back to the end of the bar. There was a back room used as a storeroom and a place for the food locker with a doorway to one side that opened into the cellar. The lights were on downstairs and I went down to the spot behind the stairs where the chalk marks outlined the position of the body. They were half on the floor and half on the wall, so the guy was found in a sitting position.

Back upstairs Cavello had taken Pat to the end of the bar and I got back in on the conversation. Cavello said, "Near as we could figure it out, this guy Thomas Kline closed the bar earlier than usual, making the few customers he had leave. It was something he had never done before apparently. He'd stick it out if there was a dime in the joint left to be spent. This time he bitched about a headache, closed up, and shut off the lights. That was it. We spoke to the ones who were here then, but they all went off to another place and closed it down much later, then went home. Clean alibis. All working men for a change. No records.

"We think he met somebody here for some purpose. Come here." He led the way to a table in one corner and pointed to the floor. A small stain showed against the oiled wood. "Blood. It matched the victim's. Here's where he was shot. The killer took the body downstairs, dumped it behind the staircase where it couldn't be seen very easily, then left. The door locks by simply closing it so it was simple enough to do. One block down he's in traffic, and anyplace along the Avenue he could have picked up a cab if he didn't have his own car. We're checking all the cabbies' sheets now."

But I had stopped listening to him about then. I was looking at the back corner of the wall. I tapped Pat on the arm and pointed. "You remember the call you got from someone inquiring about Levitt?"

"Yeah," he said.

There was an open pay phone on the wall about four feet away from a jukebox.

Pat walked over to it, looked at the records on the juke, but who could tell rock and roll from the titles? He said to Cavello, "Many places got these open phones?"

"Sure," Cavello told him, "most of the spots that haven't got room for a booth. Mean anything?"

"I don't know. It could."

"Anything I could help with?"

Pat explained the situation and Cavello said he'd try to find anyone who saw Kline making a phone call about that time. He didn't expect much luck though. People in that neighborhood didn't talk too freely to the police. It was more likely that they wouldn't remember anything rather than get themselves involved.

Another plainclothes officer came in then, said hello to Pat, and he introduced me to Lew Nelson. He didn't have anything to add to the story and so far that day hadn't found anybody who knew much about Levitt at all.

I tapped his shoulder and said, "How did Kline react when you showed him Levitt's photo?"

"Well, he jumped a little. He said he couldn't be sure and I figured he was lying. I got the same reaction from others besides him. That Levitt was a mean son and I don't think anybody wanted to mess around with him. He wanted to know what he was wanted for and I wouldn't say anything except that he was dead and he seemed pretty satisfied at that.

"Tell you one thing. That guy was thinking of something. He studied that photo until he was sure he knew him and then told me he never saw him before. Maybe he thought he had an angle somewhere."

There wasn't much left there for us. Pat left a few instructions, sent Nelson back on the streets again, and started outside. He stopped for a final word to Cavello so I went on alone and stood on the side-walk beside the cop on guard there. It wasn't until he went to an-swer the radio in the squad car that I saw the thing his position had obscured.

In the window of the bar was a campaign poster and on it a full-face picture of a smiling Torrence, who was running in the primaries for governor, and under it was the slogan, *WIN WITH SIM*.

CHAPTER 9

I made the call from the drugstore on the corner. I dialed the Torrence estate and waited while the phone rang a half-dozen times, each time feeling the cold go through me deeper and deeper.

Damn, it couldn't be too late!

Then a sleepy voice said, "Yes?" and there was no worry in it at all.

"Geraldine?"

"Mike, you thing you."

"Look . . ."

"Why did you leave me? How could you leave me?"

"I'll tell you later. Has Torrence come home yet?"

My voice startled her into wakefulness. "But . . . no, he's due here in an hour though. He called this morning from Albany to tell me when he'd be home."

"Good, now listen. Is Sue all right?"

"Yes . . . she's still in bed. I gave her another sedative."

"Well, get her out of it. Both of you hop in a car and get out of there. Now . . . not later, now."

"But, Mike . . ."

"Damn it, shut up and do what I say. There's going to be trouble I can't explain."

"Where can we go? Mike, I don't . . ."

I gave her my new address and added, "Go right there and stay there. The super has the key and will let you in. Don't open that door for anybody until you're sure it's me, understand? I can't tell you any more except that your neck and Sue's neck are out a mile.

We have another dead man on our hands and we don't need any more. You got that?"

She knew I wasn't kidding. There was too much stark urgency in my voice. She said she'd leave in a few minutes and when she did I could sense the fear that touched her.

I tapped the receiver cradle down, broke the connection, dropped in a dime, and dialed my own number. Velda came on after the first ring with a guarded hello.

I said, "It's breaking, baby. How do you feel?"

"Not too bad. I can get around."

"Swell. You go downstairs and tell the super that a Geraldine King and Sue Devon are to be admitted to my apartment. Nobody else. Let him keep the key. Then you get down to Sim Torrence's headquarters and check up on his movements all day yesterday. I want every minute of the day spelled out and make it as specific as you can. He got a phone call yesterday. See if it originated from there. I don't care if he took ten minutes out to go to the can . . . you find out about it. I'm chiefly interested in any time he took off last night."

"Got it, Mike. Where can I reach you?"

"At the apartment. When I get through I'll go right there. Shake it up."

"Chop chop. Love me?"

"What a time to ask."

"Well?"

"Certainly, you nut."

She laughed that deep, throaty laugh and hung up on me and I had a quick picture of her sliding out of bed, those beautiful long legs rippling into a body . . . oh hell.

I put the phone back and went back to Pat.

"Where'd you go?" he said.

"We got a killer, buddy."

He froze for a second. "You didn't find anything?"

"No? Then make sense out of this." I pointed to the picture of Sim Torrence in the window.

"Go ahead."

"Sim's on the way up. He's getting where he always wanted to be. He's got just one bug in his life and that's the kid, Sue Devon.

All her life she's been on his back about something in their past and there was always that chance she might find it.

"One time he defended a hard case and when he needed one he called on the guy. Basil Levitt. He wanted Sue knocked off. Some instinct told Sue what he intended to do and she ran for it and wound up at Velda's. She didn't know it, but it was already too late. Levitt was on her tail all the while, followed her, set up in a place opposite the house, and waited for her to show.

"The trouble was, Velda was in hiding too. She respected the kid's fears and kept her undercover until she was out of trouble herself, then she would have left the place with her. Hell, Pat, Levitt didn't come in there for Velda . . . he was after the kid. When he saw me he must have figured Torrence sent somebody else because he was taking too long and he wasn't about to lose his contract money. That's why Levitt bust in like that.

"Anyway, when Torrence made the deal he must have met Levitt in this joint here thinking he'd never be recognized. But he forgot that his picture is plastered all over on posters throughout the city. Maybe Kline never gave it a thought if he recognized him then. Maybe Kline only got the full picture when he saw Levitt's photo. But he put the thing together. First he called your department for information and grew suspicious when nobody gave him anything concrete.

"Right here he saw Torrence over a barrel so yesterday he called him and told him to meet him. Sim must have jumped out of his skin. He dummied an excuse and probably even led into a trip to Albany for further cover . . . this we'll know about when I see Velda. But he got here all right. He saw Kline and that was the last Kline saw of anything."

"You think too much, Mike."

"The last guy that said that is dead." I grinned.

"We'd better get up there then."

New York, when the traffic is thick, is a maddening place. From high above the streets the cars look like a winding line of ants, but when you are in the convoy it becomes a raucous noise, a composite of horns and engines and voices cursing at other voices. It's a heavy smell of exhaust fumes and unburned hydrocarbons and in the desire to compress time and space the distance between cars is infinitesimal.

The running lights designed to keep traffic moving at a steady pace seem to break down then. They all become red. Always, there is a bus or truck ahead, or an out-of-town driver searching for street signs. There are pedestrians who take their time, sometimes deliberately blocking the lights in the never-ceasing battle against the enemy, those who are mounted.

In the city the average speed of a fire truck breaks down to eighteen miles an hour with all its warning devices going, so imagine what happens to time and distance when the end-of-day rush is on. Add to that the rain that fogged the windshields and made every sudden stop hazardous.

Ordinarily from Brooklyn the Torrence place would have been an hour away. But not this night. No, this was a special night of delay and frustration, and if Pat hadn't been able to swing around two barriers with his badge held out the window it would have been an hour longer still.

It was a quarter to eight when we turned in the street Sim Torrence lived on. Behind the wall and the shrubbery I could see lights on in the house and outside that there was no activity at all. From the end of the street, walking toward us, was the patrolman assigned to the beat on special duty, and when we stopped his pace quickened so that he was there when we got out.

Pat held his badge out again, but the cop recognized me. Pat said, "Everything all right here?"

"Yes, sir. Miss King and the girl left some time ago and Torrence arrived, but there has been no trouble. Anything I can help with?"

"No, just routine. We have to see Torrence."

"Sure. He left the gate open."

We left the car on the street and walked in, staying on the grass. I had the .45 in my hand and Pat had his Police Positive out and ready. Sim Torrence's Cadillac was parked in front of the door and when I felt it the hood was still warm.

Both of us knew what to do. We checked the windows and the back, met again around the front, then I went up to the door while Pat stood by in the shadows.

I touched the buzzer and heard the chime from inside.

Nobody answered so I did it again.

I didn't bother for a third try. I reached out, leaned against the door latch, and it swung in quietly. I went in first, Pat right behind me covering the blind spots. First I motioned him to be quiet, then to follow me since I knew the layout.

There was a deathly stillness about the house that didn't belong there. With all the lights that were going there should have been some sort of sound. But there was nothing.

We checked through the downstairs room, opening closets and probing behind the furniture. Pat looked across the room at me, shook his head, and I pointed toward the stairs.

The master bedroom was the first door on the right. The door was partly open and there was a light on there too. We took that one first.

And that was where we found Sim Torrence. He wasn't winning anymore.

He lay facedown on the floor with a bullet through his head and a puddle of blood running away from him like juice from a stepped-on tomato. We didn't stop there. We went into every room in the house looking for a killer before we finally came back to Sim.

Pat wrapped the phone in a handkerchief, called the local department, and reported in. When he hung up he said, "You know we're in a sling, don't you?"

"Why?"

"We should have called in from Brooklyn and let them cover it from this end."

"My foot, buddy. Getting in a jam won't help anything. As far as anyone is concerned we came up here on a social call. I was here last night helping out during an emergency and I came back to check, that's all."

"And what about the women?"

"We'll get to them before anybody else will."

"You'd better be right."

"Quit worrying."

While we waited we checked the area around the body for anything that might tie in with the murder. There were no spent cartridges so we both assumed the killer used a revolver. I prowled around the house looking for a sign of entry, since Geraldine would have locked the door going out and Sim behind him, coming in. The killer must have already been here and made his own entry the easy way through the front door.

The sirens were screaming up the street outside when I found out where he got in. The window in Sue's room had been neatly jimmied from the trellis outside and was a perfect, quiet entry into the house. Anybody could have come over the walls without being seen by the lone cop on the beat. From there up that solid trellis was as easy as taking the steps.

Sue's bed was still rumpled. Geraldine must have literally dragged her out of it because the burned stuffed toy was still there crammed under the covers, almost like a body itself.

Then I could see that something new had been added. There was a bullet hole and powder burns on the sheet and when I flipped it back I saw the hole drilled into the huge toy.

Somebody had mistaken that charred ruin for Sue under the covers and tried to put a bullet through her!

Back to Lolita again. Damn, where would it end?

What kind of a person were we dealing with?

I went to put the covers back in their original position before calling Pat in when I saw the stuffed bear up close for the first time. It had been her mother's and the fire had burned it stiff. The straw sticking out was hard and crisp with age, the ends black from the heat. During the night Sue must have lain on it and her weight split open a seam.

An edge of a letter stuck out of it.

I tugged it loose, didn't bother to look at it then because they were coming in downstairs now, racing up the stairs. I stuck the letter in my pocket and called for Pat.

He got the import of it right away but didn't say anything. From all appearances this was a break-in and anybody could have done it. The implications were too big to let the thing out now and he wasn't going to do much explaining until we had time to go over it.

The reporters had already gathered and were yelling for admittance. Tomorrow this kill would make every headline in the country and the one in Brooklyn would be lucky if it got a squib in any sheet at all. There was going to be some high-level talk before this one broke straight and Pat knew it too.

It was an hour before we got out of there and back in the car. Some of the bigwigs of the political party had arrived and were being pressed by the reporters, but they had nothing to say. They got in on VIP status and were immediately sent into the den to be quizzed by the officers in charge and as long as there was plenty to do we could ride for a while.

Pat didn't speak until we were halfway back to the city, then all he said was, "One of your theories went out the window today."

"Which one?"

"If Sim planned to kill Sue, how would he excuse it?"

"I fell into that one with no trouble, Pat," I said. "You know how many times he has been threatened?"

"I know."

"So somebody was trying to get even. Revenge motive. They hit the kid."

"But Sue is still alive."

"Somebody thought he got her tonight. I'll tell you this . . . I bet the first shot fired was into that bed. The killer turned on the light to make sure and saw what happened. He didn't dare let it stand like that so he waited around. Then in came Sim. Now it could be passed off as a burglary attempt while the real motive gets lost in the rush."

I tapped his arm. "There's one other thing too. The night of the first try there were two groups. Levitt and Kid Hand. They weren't working together and they were both after the same thing . . . the kid."

"All right, sharpie, what's the answer?"

"I think it's going to be three million bucks," I said.

"You have more than that to sell."

"There's Blackie Conley."

"And you think he's got the money?"

"Want to bet?"

"Name it."

"A night on the town. A foursome. We'll find you a broad. Loser picks up all the tabs."

Pat nodded. "You got it, but forget finding me a broad. I'll get my own."

"You'll probably bring a policewoman."

"With you around it wouldn't be a bad idea," he said.

He let me out in front of my apartment and I promised to call him as soon as I heard from Velda. He was going to run the Torrence thing through higher channels and let them handle this hotcake.

I went upstairs, called through the door, and let Geraldine open it. Velda still hadn't gotten back. Sue was inside on the couch, awake, but still drowsy from the sedatives she had taken. I made Geraldine sit down next to her, then broke the news.

At first Sue didn't react. Finally she said, "He's really dead?"

"Really, sugar."

Somehow a few years seemed to drape themselves around her. She looked at the floor, made a wry face, and shrugged. "I'm sorry, Mike. I don't feel anything. Just free. I feel free."

Geraldine looked like she was about to break, but she came through it. There was a stricken expression in her eyes and her mouth hung slackly. She kept repeating, "Oh, no!" over and over again and that was all. When she finally accepted it she asked, "Who, Mike, who did it?"

"We don't know."

"This is terrible. The whole political . . ."

"It's more terrible than that, kid. Politicians can always be replaced. I suggest you contact your office when you feel up to it. There's going to be hell to pay and if your outfit gets into power this time it'll be by a miracle . . . and those days, believe me, are over."

She started asking me something else, but the phone rang and I jumped to answer it. Velda said, "Mike . . . I just heard. Is it true?"

"He's had it. What did you come up with?"

"About the time you mentioned . . . nobody could account for Torrence's whereabouts for almost two hours. Nobody really looked for him and they all supposed he was with somebody else, but nobody could clear him for that time."

"That does it then. Come on back."

"Twenty minutes."

"Shake it."

In a little while I was going to be tied in with this mess and would be getting plenty of visitors and I didn't want either Geraldine or Sue around. Their time would come, but not right now. I called a hotel, made reservations for them both, dialed for a cab, and told them to get ready. Neither wanted to leave until I told them there was no choice. I wanted them completely out of sight and told Geraldine to stay put again, having her meals sent up until I called for her.

Events had moved too quickly and she couldn't think for herself any longer. She agreed dumbly, the girls got into their coats, and I walked them out to the cab.

Upstairs I sat at the desk and took the letter out of my pocket. Like the straw, it was crisp with age, but still sealed, and after all these years smelled faintly of some feminine perfume. I slid my finger under the flap and opened it.

The handwriting was the scrawl of a drunk trying hard for sobriety. The lines were uneven and ran to the edge of the page, but it was legible enough.

It read:

Darling Sue:

> *My husband Sim is the one we called The Snake. Hate him, darling, because he wants us dead. Be careful of him. Someday he will try to kill us both. Sim Torrence could prove I helped deliver narcotics at one time. He could have sent me to prison. We made a deal that I was to be the go-between for him and Sonny Motley and he was going to arrange the robbery. He could do it because he knew every detail of the money exchange. What he really wanted was for Sonny and the rest to be caught so he could boost his career. That happened, didn't it, darling? He never should have left me out in the cold. After I had you I wanted security for you and knew how to get it. I didn't love Sim Torrence. He hated me like he hates anybody in his way. I made him do it for you, dearest. I will hide this letter where he won't find it but you will someday. He searches every-*

*thing I have to be sure this can't happen. Be careful my
darling. He is The Snake and he will try to kill you if he
can. Be careful of accidents. He will have to make it look
like one.*

All My Love,
Mother

The Snake . . . the one thing they all feared . . . and now he was
dead. Dedicated old Win with Sim, an engineer of robberies, hirer
of murderers, a killer himself . . . what a candidate for governor.
The people would never know how lucky they were.

The Snake. A good name for him. I was right . . . it worked the
way I figured it. The votes weren't all counted yet, but the deck was
stacked against Sim Torrence. In death he was going to take a fall
bigger than the one he would have taken in life.

Torrence never got the three million. He never gave a damn
about it in the first place. All breaking up that robbery did was earn
him prestige and some political titles. It was his first step into the
big-time and he made it himself. He put everybody's life on the
block including his own and swung it. I wondered what plans he had
made for Sally if she hadn't nipped into him first. In fact, marrying
her was even a good deal for him. It gave him a chance to keep her
under wraps and lay the groundwork for a murder.

Hell, if I could check back that far with accuracy I knew what
I would find. Sim paid the house upstate a visit, found Annette Lee
asleep and Sally in a dead drunk. He simply dragged her out into
the winter night and the weather did the rest. He couldn't have
done anything with the kid right then without starting an investigation. Sally would have been a tragic accident; the kid too meant
trouble.

So he waited. Like a good father, which added to his political
image, he adopted her into his house. When it was not expedient
for him to have her around any longer he arranged for her execution
through Levitt. He sure was a lousy planner there. Levitt talked too
much. Enough to die before he could do the job.

In one way Sue forced her own near-death with her crazy behavior. Whatever she couldn't get out of her mind were the things her mother told her repeatedly in her drunken moods. It had an effect all right. She made it clear to Sim that he was going to have to kill her if he didn't want her shooting her mouth off.

Sim would have known who The Snake was. Sally had referred to him by that often enough. No wonder he ducked it at the trial. No wonder it seared him silly when Sue kept insisting her mother left something for her to read. No wonder he searched her things. That last time in Sue's little house was one of desperation. He knew that sooner or later something would come to light and if it happened he was politically dead, which to him was death *in toto*.

But somebody made a mistake. There was a bigger snake loose than Torrence ever was. There was a snake with three million bucks buried in its hole and that could be the worst kind of snake of all. Hell, Sim wasn't a snake at all. He was a goddamn worm.

I folded the letter and put it back in my pocket when the bell rang. When I opened the door Velda folded into my arms like a big cat, kicked it shut with her heel, and buried her face against my neck.

"You big slob," she said.

While she made coffee I told her about it, taking her right through from the beginning. She read the letter twice, getting the full implication of it all.

"Does Pat know all this?"

"Not yet. He'd better take first things first."

"What are you going to do?"

"Call Art Rickerby."

I picked the unlisted number out of memory and got Art on the phone. It took a full thirty minutes to rehash the entire situation, but he listened patiently, letting me get it across. It was the political side of it he was more concerned with at the moment, realizing what propaganda ammunition the other side could use against us.

One thing about truth . . . let it shine and you were all right. It was the lies that could hurt you. But there were ways of letting the truth come out so as to nullify the awkward side of it and this was what the striped-pants boys were for.

Art said he'd get into it right away, but only because of my standing as a representative of the agency he was part of.

I said, "Where do I go from here, Art?"

"Now who's going to tell you, big man?"

"It isn't over yet."

"It's never over, Mike. When this is over there will be something else."

"There will be some big heat coming my way. I'd hate to lose my pretty little ticket. It's all I have."

He was silent for a moment, then he said, "I'll let you in on a confidence. There are people here who like you. We can't all operate the same way. Put a football player on the diamond and he'd never get around the bases. A baseball player in the middle of a pileup would never get up. You've never been a total unknown and now that you're back, stay back. When we need you, we'll yell. Meanwhile nobody's going to pick up your ticket as long as you stay clean enough. I didn't say legal . . . I said clean. One day we'll talk some more about this, but not now. You do what you have to do. Just remember that everybody's watching so make it good."

"Great, all I have to do is stay alive."

"Well, if you do get knocked off, let me repeat a favorite old saying of yours, 'Kismet, buddy.'"

He hung up and left me staring at the phone. I grinned, then put it down and started to laugh. Velda said, "What's so funny?"

"I don't know," I told her. "It's just funny. Grebb and Charlie Force are going to come at me like tigers when this is over to get my official status changed and if I can make it work they don't have a chance."

That big, beautiful thing walked over next to me and slid her arms around my waist and said, "They never did have a chance. You're the tiger, man."

I turned around slowly and ran my hands under her sweater, up the warm flesh of her back. She pulled herself closer to me so that every curve of hers matched my own and her breasts became rigid against my chest.

There was a tenderness to her mouth that was only at the beginning, then her lips parted with a gentle searching motion and her tongue flicked at mine with the wordless gestures of love. Somehow the couch was behind us and we sank down on it together. There was no restraint at all, simply the knowledge that it was going to happen here and now at our own time and choosing.

No fumbling motions. Each move was deliberate, inviting, provoking the thing we both wanted so badly. Very slowly there was a release from the clothes that covered us, each in his own way doing what he wanted to do. I kissed her neck, uncovered her shoulders, and ran my mouth along them. When my hands cradled her breasts and caressed them they quivered at my touch, nuzzling my palms for more like a hungry animal.

Her stomach swelled gently against my fingers as I explored her, making her breath come in short, hard gasps. But even then there was no passiveness in her. She was as alive as I was, as demanding and as anxious. Her eyes told me of all the love she had for so long and the dreams she had had of its fulfillment.

The fiery contact of living flesh against living flesh was almost too much to stand and we had gone too far to refuse the demand any longer. She was mine and I was hers and we had to belong to each other.

But it didn't happen that way.

The doorbell rang like some damn screaming banshee and the suddenness of it wiped the *big now* right out of existence. I swore under my breath, then grinned at Velda, who swore back the same words and grinned too.

"When will it be, Mike?"

"Someday, kitten."

Before I could leave she grabbed my hand. "Make it happen."

"I will. Go get your clothes on."

The bell rang again, longer this time, and I heard Pat's voice calling out in the hall.

I yelled, "All right, damn it, hold on a minute."

He didn't take his finger off the bell until I had opened the door.

"I was on the phone," I explained. "Come on in."

There were four others with him, all men I had seen around the precinct. Two I knew from the old days and nodded to them. The others went through a handshake.

"Velda here?"

"Inside, why?"

"She was down asking questions around the party headquarters. They want an explanation. Charlie Force is pushing everybody around on this."

"So sit down and I'll explain."

Velda came out as they were pulling up chairs, met the officers and perched on the arm of the couch next to me. I laid it out for Pat to save him the time of digging himself, supplied him with Velda's notes and the names of the persons she spoke to, and wrapped it up with Art's little speech to me.

When Pat put his book away he said, "That's one reason why I'm here. We're going to see what we can get on Howie Green. These officers have been working on it already and have come up with something that might get us started."

"Like what?"

"The real estate agency Howie Green operated went into the hands of his partner after his death. The guy's name was Quincy Malek. About a year later he contracted T.B. and died in six months. Now from a nephew we gather that Malek was damn near broke when he kicked off. He had sold out everything and his family picked over what was left. The original records left over from his partnership with Green went into storage somewhere, either private or commercial.

"Right now I have one bunch checking all the warehouses to see what they can dig up. The nephew does remember Malek asking that the records be kept so it's likely that they were. It wouldn't take up much room and a few hundred bucks would cover a storage bill on a small package for a long, long time.

"Now that's a supposition, the commercial angle. Malek and Green had a few other properties still in existence and we'll go through them too. Until everything is checked out you can't tell what we'll find. Meanwhile, we're taking another angle. We're checking all property transactions carried out by Green within a certain time of his death. If you're right something will show up. We'll check every damn one of them if we have to."

"You know how long it will take, Pat?"

"That's what I want to know. You got a better idea in that screwy mind of yours?"

"I don't know," I told him. "I'll have to think about it."

"Oh no, not you, boy. If you got anything you have it now. You just aren't the prolonged-thinking type. You got something going this minute and I want to know what it is."

"Stow it."

"Like that?"

"Like that. If it proves out I'll get it to you right away. The only reason I'm slamming it to you like this is because you're in deep enough as it is. Let me try my way. If there's trouble I'll take it alone."

"Mike . . . I don't like it. We have a killer running loose."

"Then let me be the target."

His eyes drifted to Velda beside me.

I said, "She'll stay safe. I went through that once before."

"Watch her," Pat said softly, and I knew he was never going to change about the way he felt for her.

"How many men you going to put through the files?"

"As many as I can spare."

"Suppose you get to it first?" I queried.

He smiled crookedly. "Well, with your official status I imagine I can pass on a tip to you. Just make sure it works both ways."

"Deal. How will we make contact?"

"Keep in touch with my office. If anything looks promising I'll leave word."

He got up to go and I reached for my coat. I picked the letter out and handed it to him. "It was in Sue's teddy bear. It puts a lock on Sim all the way. I don't advise showing it to the kid though."

Pat read it through once, shook his head, and put it in his inside coat pocket. "You're a card, man, a real card. What kind of luck have you got?"

"The best kind."

"Don't pull that kind of stunt on Grebb, buddy."

"You know me."

"Sure I know you."

I let them out and went back and stretched out on the couch. Velda made me some coffee and had one with me. I drank mine staring at the ceiling while I tried to visualize the picture from front to back. It was all there except the face. Blackie Conley's face. I knew I was going to see it soon. It was a feeling I had.

"Mike . . . where are we going?"

"You're thinking ahead of me, kiddo."

"Sometimes I have to."

"You're not going anyway."

"Don't cut me out, Mike." Her hand touched the side of my jaw, then traced a tingling line down my chin.

"Okay, doll."

"Want to tell me what you have in your mind?"

"A thought. The only thing that's wrong with the picture."

"Oh? What?"

"Why Blackie Conley would want to kill Sim."

"Mike . . ." She was looking past me, deep in thought. "Since it was Torrence who engineered that robbery and not Conley as you first thought, perhaps Conley suspected what was going to come off. Supposing he outguessed Torrence. In that case, he would have had the whole bundle to himself. He would have made his own getaway plans and broken out at the right time. Don't forget, Conley was older than Sonny and he was no patsy. There was no love between the pair either. In fact, Conley might even have guessed who the brain was behind the whole thing and had reasons for revenge."

"You might have something there, kitten."

"The first try was for Sue," she went on. "That really was an indirect blow at Sim. The next try was for them both."

"There's a possible flaw in your picture too, but I can supply an answer."

She waited. I said, "It's hard to picture a guy in his eighties going up that trellis. He'd have to hire it done . . . but that's why the hoods are in town."

"I don't know, Mike. Remember Bernarr Macfadden making his first parachute jump into the river when he was about the same age?"

"Uh-huh. It could be done."

"Then the answer is still to find Blackie Conley."

"That's right."

"How?"

"If we can restore another old man's memory we might get the answer."

"Sonny Motley?"

"Yup."

"Tonight?"

"Right now, sugar."

CHAPTER 10

Finding Sonny Motley's apartment wasn't easy. Nobody in the gin mills knew where he lived; the cop on the beat around his store knew him but not his address. I checked the few newsstands that were open and they gave me a negative. It was at the last one that a hackie standing by heard me mention the name and said, "You mean that old con?"

"Yeah, the one who has the shoe shop."

"What's the matter?"

"Nothing. We need some information about a missing person and he might be able to help us."

"Ha, I'd like to see those old cons talk. They won't give nobody the right time."

"You know where he lives?"

"Sure. Took him home plenty of times. Hop in."

We climbed in the cab, went angling up to a shoddy section that bordered on the edge of Harlem, and the cabbie pointed out the place. "He's downstairs there on this side. Probably in bed by now."

"I'll get him up." I gave him a buck tip for his trouble and led the way down the sandstone steps to the iron gate at the bottom. I pushed the bell four or five times before a light came on inside.

A voice said, "Yeah, whatta ya want?"

"Sonny?"

"Who're you?"

"Mike Hammer."

"Oh, fer . . ." He came to the door, opened it, and reached for the grilled gate that held us out. He had a faded old robe wrapped around his body and a scowl on his face as black as night. Then he saw Velda and the sky lightened. "Hey . . . how about that."

"This is Velda, my secretary. Sonny Motley."

"Hello, Sonny."

"Well, don't just stand there. Come on in. Hot damn, I ain't had a broad in my joint since before I went to stir. Hot damn, this is great!" He slammed the gate, locked the door, and led the way down the hall. He pushed his door open and said, "Don't mind the place, huh? So it's a crummy place and who comes here? I'm a crummy old man anyway. Sure feels good to have a broad in the joint. Want a drink?"

"I'll pass," I said.

"Not me." He grinned. "A sexy broad comes in like her and I'm gonna have me a drink."

"I thought you were all over the sex angle, Sonny."

"Maybe inside I am, but my eyes don't know it. No, sir. You sit down and let me get dressed. Be right back."

Sit down? We had a choice of box seats. Egg boxes or apple boxes. There was one old sofa that didn't look safe and a chair to match that had no cushion in it. The best bet was the arms of the chair so Velda took one side and I took the other.

A choice between living here or a nice comfortable prison would be easy to make. But like the man said, at least he was free. Sonny was back in a minute, hitching suspenders over bony shoulders, a bottle of cheap booze in his hand.

"You sure you don't want nothing?"

"No, thanks."

"No need to break out glasses then." He took a long pull from the bottle, ambled over to the couch, and sat down facing us. "Hot damn," he said, "those are the prettiest legs I ever saw."

Velda shifted uncomfortably, but I said, "That's what I keep telling her."

"You keep telling her, boy. They love to hear that kind of talk. Right, lady?"

She laughed at the impish look on his face. "I guess we can stand it."

"Damn right you can. Used to be a real killer with the ladies myself. All gone now though." He pulled at the bottle again. "'Cept for looking. Guess a man never tires of looking." He set the bottle down on the floor between his feet and leaned back, his eyes glowing. "Now, what can I do for you?"

"I'm still asking questions, Sonny."

He waved his hands expansively. "Go ahead. If I can answer 'em it's all free."

"I can't get rid of the idea your old partner's still alive."

His shoulders jerked with a silent laugh. "Can't, eh? Well, you better, because that no-good is gone. Dead. I don't know where or how, but he's dead."

"Let's make like he isn't."

"I got lots of time."

"And I got news for you."

"How's that?"

"Sim Torrence is dead."

Briefly, his eyes widened. "True?"

"True."

Then he started to cackle again. "Good. Had it coming, the bugger. He put the screws on enough guys. I hope it wasn't easy."

"He was shot."

"Good. Bring the guy in and I'll fix his shoes free every time. I mean that. Free shine too."

"I thought you didn't care anymore."

"Hell, I said I didn't hate him, not that I didn't care. So he's dead. I'm glad. Tomorrow I'll forget he was even alive. So what else is new?"

"Sim Torrence was the big brain who engineered your last job."

He was reaching for the bottle and stopped bent over. He looked up, not believing me. "Who says?"

"You'll read about it in the papers."

He straightened, the bottle entirely forgotten. "You mean . . ."

"Not only that, he engineered it right into a deliberate frame-up. That case made him the D.A. After that coup he was a landslide candidate."

"This is square, what you're telling me?"

"On the level, Sonny."

"The dirty son of a bitch. Sorry, lady."

"Here's an added note I want you to think about. If Blackie

Conley got wise in time he could have worked the double cross to his own advantage, taking the loot and dumping you guys."

Sonny sounded almost out of breath. "I'll be damned," he said. Some of the old fire was in his voice. "A real switcheroo. How do you like that? Sure, now I get what the score is. Blackie laid out the getaway route. Hell, he never followed through with the plan. He had something else schemed up and got away." Abruptly he dropped his head and laughed at the floor. "Boy, he was smarter than I figured. How do you like that?" he repeated.

"Sonny . . ."

He looked up, a silly grin on his face. Egg. He couldn't get over it. I said, "Blackie rented the property you were supposed to hole up in from Howie Green."

"That's right."

"He must have bought another place at the same time for his own purpose using another name."

"Just like that bastard Green to fall in with him. He'd do anything for a buck. I'm glad Blackie knocked him off!"

"He did?"

"Sure he did. Before the heist. You think we wanted somebody knowing where we was headed?"

I looked at him, puzzled.

He caught the look and said, "Yeah, I know. There ain't no statute of limitations on murder. So they could still take me for being in it. Hell, you think I really care? Look around here. What do I have? Nothing. That's what. I already served life. What could they do that's worse? Maybe at the best I can live ten years, but what can I do with ten years? Live in a crummy rat hole? Beat on shoes all day? No friends? Man, it was better doin' time. You just don't know."

I waved him down. "Look, I don't care about Green. He asked for it, so he got it. I want Blackie Conley."

"How you gonna find him?"

"Did you know Green?"

"You kiddin'? Him and me grew up together on the same block. I took more raps for that punk when I was a kid . . . aw, forget it."

"Okay, now Green was a stickler for detail. He kept records

somewhere. He passed on his business to his partner, Quincy Malek."

"I knew him too."

"Now Quincy kept the records. Wherever they are, they'll have a notation of the transactions carried out by the business. It will show the property locations and we can run them down one by one until we get the place Blackie bought from him."

"You think Blackie'll still be there?"

"He hasn't showed up any place else, has he?"

"That just ain't like Blackie." He rubbed his hands together and stared at them. "Maybe I didn't know Blackie so good after all. Now what?"

"Did you know Quincy Malek?"

"Sure. From kids yet. Him too. He was another punk."

"Where would he put something for safekeeping?"

"Quincy? Man, who knows?" He chuckled and leaned back against the cushions. "He had places all over. You know he operated a couple of houses without paying off? The boys closed him on that one."

"The records, Sonny. Right now we're checking up on all of Quincy's former properties and every commercial warehouse in the city, but if you remember anything about what he had you can cut the time right down."

"Mister, you're dragging me back thirty years."

"What did you have to think about all the time you were in prison, Sonny? Whatever it was belonged back there too because in prison there was nothing to think about."

"Broads," he grinned. "Until I was sixty all I thought about was broads. Not the used ones I had before, but ones that didn't even exist. Maybe after sixty I went back, but it took some time."

"Now you got something to think about."

Sonny sat there a long moment, then his mouth twisted into a sour grimace. "Tell me, mister. What would it get me? You it would get something. Me? Nothing. Trouble, that's all it would bring. Right now I ain't got nothin' but I ain't got trouble either. Nope. Don't think I can help you. I've had my belly full of trouble and now it's over. I don't want no more."

"There won't be trouble, Sonny."

"No? You think with all the papers down my throat I'd get any peace? You think I'd keep the lease on the shoe shop? It's bad enough I'm a con and a few people know it, but let everybody know it and I get booted right out of the neighborhood. No business, nothin'. Sorry, mister."

"There might be a reward in it."

"No dice. I'd have everybody in the racket chiseling it outa me. I'd wind up a drunk or dead. Somebody'd try to take me for the poke and I'd be out. Not me, Mister Hammer. I'm too old to even worry about it."

Damn, he was tying me up tight and he was right. There had to be a way. I said, "If I wanted to I could put the heat on you for the Howie Green kill. The way things stand I wouldn't be a bit surprised if we got some quick and total cooperation from the police."

Sonny stared a second, then grunted. "What a guest *you* are. You sure want me to fall bad."

"Not that bad. If you want to push it I'd probably lay back. I'm just trying you, Sonny."

Once again his eyes caught Velda's legs. She had swung them out deliberately and the dress had pulled up over her knee. It was enough to make Sonny giggle again. "Oh, hell, why not? So maybe I can feed you something. What's it they call it? Public duty or some kind of crap like that."

"Quincy Malek, Sonny."

He sat back and squinted his eyes shut. "Now let's see. What would that punk do? He up and died but he never expected to, I bet. He was the kind who'd keep everything for himself if he could. Even if he left something to his family I bet they'd have to dig for it.

"Quincy owned property around town. Tenements, stuff like that. He'd buy cheap and hold. Got plenty in rentals and he seemed to know what was coming down and what was going up. Always had a hot iron in the fire."

"Would he keep any records there?"

"Nope, don't think so. Something might happen to 'em. My guess is he'd leave 'em with somebody."

"Who?"

"Something about old Quincy nobody knew. He kept a pair of

sisters in an apartment building he owned. Tricky pair that. Real queer for anything different. I got the word once that he had a double deal with them. They owned the apartment with some papers signed so that he could take it back any time he wanted. He couldn't get screwed that way. Me, I'd look for those sisters. That building would be the only income they had and they couldn't dump it so they were stuck with it, but since it was a good deal all around, why not, eh?"

"Who were they, Sonny?"

"Now you got me, mister. I think if you poke around you'll find out who. I remember the deal, but not the dames. That any help?"

"It's a lead."

"Maybe I'll think of it later. You want me to call if I do?"

I picked a scrap of paper off the table, wrote down the office and home numbers, and gave them to him. "Keep calling these numbers until you get me or Velda here."

"Sure." He tucked the paper in his pants pocket. Then he got an idea. "Hey," he said, "if you find that crumb Blackie, you let me know. Hell, I'd even like a feel of that money. Just a feel. I think I'm entitled. It cost me thirty years."

"Okay, a feel," I said kiddingly.

Then Velda swung her leg out again and he grinned. "You know what I'd really like to feel, don't you?"

With a laugh Velda said, "You're a dirty old man."

"You bet, lady. But I'd sure like to see you with your clothes off just once."

"If you did you'd drop dead," I told him.

"What a way to go," he said.

Pat wasn't bothering to get any sleep either. I reached him at the office and gave him the dope Sonny passed on to me. He thought it had merit enough to start working on and was going to put two men on it right away. Nothing else had paid off yet, although they had come up with a few former properties Malek had owned. They had made a search of the premises, but nothing showed. A team of experts were on a twenty-four-hour detail in the records section digging up old titles, checking possibles, and having no luck at all so far.

Offhand I asked for Quincy's old address and Pat gave me the location of his home and the building the real estate agency was housed in. He had checked them both personally and they were clean.

I hung up the phone and asked Velda if she wanted something to eat. The Automat was right down the street so she settled for a cup of coffee and a sandwich. We waited for the light, cut over, and ducked inside.

Right at the front table Jersey Toby was having coffee and when he saw me he simply got up and left with his coffee practically untouched.

We fed nickels into the slots, got what we wanted, and picked a table.

Outside the damn rain had started again.

Velda said, "What's on your mind?"

"How can you tell?"

"Your poker face slipped. You're trying to think of something."

I slammed the coffee cup down. "One lousy thing. I can feel it. One simple goddamn thing I can't put my finger on and it's right there in front of me. I keep forgetting things."

"It'll come back."

"Now is when I need it."

"Will talking about it help?"

"No."

"You're close, aren't you?"

"We're sitting right on top of it, baby. We're riding three million bucks into the ground and have a killer right in front of us someplace. The damn guy is laughing all the way too."

"Suppose the money isn't there?"

"Honey . . . you don't just *lose* that kind of capital. You don't misplace it. You put it someplace for a purpose. Somebody is ready to move in this town and that money is going to buy that person a big piece of action. If that one is as smart as all this, the action is going to be rough and expensive."

"Why don't you call Pat again? They might have something."

"I don't want to bug him to death."

"He won't mind."

We pushed away from the table and found a phone booth. Pat was still at his desk and it was three a.m. He hadn't found anything yet. He did have one piece of news for me and I asked what it was.

"We picked up one of the out-of-town boys who came in from Detroit. He was getting ready to mainline one when he got grabbed and lost his fix. He sweated plenty before he talked; now he's flipping because he's in trouble. The people who sent him here won't have anything to do with a junkie and if they know he's on H he's dead. Now he's yelling for protection."

"Something hot?"

"We know the prime factor behind the move into town. Somebody has spent a lot of time collecting choice items about key men in the Syndicate operation. He's holding it over their heads and won't let go. The payoff is for them to send in the best enforcers who are to be the nucleus of something new and for this they're paying and keeping still about it. None of them wants to be caught in a bind by the Syndicate itself so they go with the demand."

"Funny he'd know that angle."

"Not so funny. Their security isn't that good. Word travels fast in those circles. I bet we'll get the same story if we can put enough pressure on any of the others."

"You said they were clean."

"Maybe we can dirty them up a little. In the interest of justice, that is."

"Sometimes it's the only way. But tell me this, Pat . . . who could pull a play like that? You'd need to know the in of the whole operation. That takes some big smarts. You'd have to pinpoint your sucker and concentrate on him. This isn't a keyhole game."

"It's been done."

"Blackie Conley could have done it," I suggested. "He could have used a bite of the loot for expenses and he would have had the time and the know-how."

"That's what I think too."

"Anything on Malek's women?"

"Hold it a minute." I heard him put the phone down, speak to somebody, then he picked it up again. "Got a note here from a retired officer who was contacted. He remembers the girls Malek used to run with but can't recall the building. His second wife put in a complaint to have it raided for being a disorderly house at one time and he was on the call. Turned out to be a nuisance complaint and nothing more. He can't place the building anymore though."

"Hell," I said.

"We'll keep trying. Where will you be?"

"Home. I've had it."

"See you tomorrow," Pat said.

I hung up and looked at Velda. "Malek," I said. "Nobody can find where he spent his time."

"Why don't you try the Yellow Pages?" Velda kidded.

I paused and nodded. "You just might be right at that, kid."

"It was a joke, Mike."

I shook my head. "Pat just told me he had a second wife. That meant he had a first. Let's look it up."

There were sixteen Maleks in the directory and I got sixteen dimes to make the calls. Thirteen of them told me everything from drop dead to come on up for a party, but it was the squeaky old voice of the fourteenth that said yes, she was Mrs. Malek who used to be married to Quincy Malek. No, she never used the Quincy or the initial because she never cared for the name. She didn't think it was the proper time to call, but yes, if it was as important as I said it was, I could come right over.

"We hit something, baby," I said.

"Pat?"

"Not yet. Let's check this one out ourselves first."

The cab let us out on the corner of Eighth and Forty-ninth. Somewhere along the line over one of the storefronts was the home of Mrs. Quincy Malek the first. Velda spotted the number over the darkened hallway and we went in, found the right button, and pushed it. Seconds later a buzzer clicked and I opened the door.

It was only one flight up. The stairs creaked and the place reeked of fish, but the end could be up there.

She was waiting at the top of the landing, a garishly rouged old lady in a feathered wrapper that smelled of the twenties and looked it. Her hair was twisted into cloth curlers with a scarf hurriedly thrown over it and she had that querulous look of all little old ladies suddenly yanked out of bed at a strange hour.

She forced a smile, asked us in after we introduced ourselves, and had us sit at the kitchen table while she made tea. Neither Velda nor I wanted it, but if she was going to put up with us we'd have to go along with her.

Only when the tea was served properly did she ask us what we wanted.

I said, "Mrs. Malek . . . it's about your husband."

"Oh, he died a long time ago."

"I know. We're looking for something he left behind."

"He left very little, very little. What he left me ran out years ago. I'm on my pension now."

"We're looking for some records he might have kept."

"My goodness, isn't that funny?"

"What is?"

"That you should want them too."

"Who else wanted them, Mrs. Malek?"

She poured another cup of tea for me and put the pot down daintily. "Dear me, I don't know. I had a call . . . oh, some months ago. They wanted to know if Quincy left any of his business records with me. Seems that they needed something to clear up a title."

"Did he, Mrs. Malek?"

"Certainly, sir. I was the only one he could ever trust. He left a large box with me years ago and I kept it for him as I said I would in case it was ever needed."

"This party who called . . ."

"I told him what I'm telling you."

"Him?"

"Well . . . I really couldn't say. It was neither a man's nor a woman's voice. They offered me one hundred dollars if they could inspect the box and another hundred if I was instrumental in proving their claim."

"You take it?"

Her pale blue eyes studied me intently. "Mr. Hammer, I am no longer a woman able to fend for herself. At my age two hundred dollars could be quite an asset. And since those records had been sitting there for years untouched, I saw no reason why I shouldn't let them have them."

It was like having a tub of ice water dumped over you. Velda sat there, the knuckles of her hand white around the teacup.

"Who did you give it to, Mrs. Malek?"

"A delivery boy. He left me an envelope with one hundred dollars in it."

"You know the boy?"

"Oh dear no. He was just . . . a boy. Spanish, I think. His English was very bad."

"Damn," I said.

"Another cup of tea, Mr. Hammer?"

"No, thanks." Another cup of tea would just make me sick. I looked at Velda and shook my head.

"The box was returned, of course," she said suddenly.

"What!"

"With another hundred dollars. Another boy brought it to me."

"Look, Mrs. Malek . . . if we can take a look at that box and find what we're looking for, I'll make a cash grant of five hundred bucks. How does that sound to you?"

"Lovely. More tea?"

I took another cup of tea. This one didn't make me sick. But she almost did. She sat there until I finished the cup, then excused herself and disappeared a few minutes. When she came back she was carrying a large cardboard carton with the top folded down and wrapped in coarse twine.

"Here you are, Mr. Hammer."

Velda and I opened the carton carefully, flipped open the top, and looked down at the stacked sheafs of notations that filled the entire thing. Each one was an independent sales record that listed prices, names, and descriptions and there were hundreds of them. I checked the dates and they were spread through the months I wanted.

"Are you satisfied, sir?"

I reached for my wallet and took out five bills. There were three singles left. I laid them on the table but she didn't touch them.

She said, "One of those pieces of paper is missing, I must tell you."

All of a sudden I had that sick feeling again. I looked at the five hundred bucks lying on the table and so did Mrs. Malek.

"How do you know?" I asked her.

"Because I counted them. Gracious, when Quincy trusted me with them I wanted to be sure they were always there. Twice a year I used to go through them to make sure the tally was identical with the original one. Then when I got them back I counted them again and one was missing." She looked at me and nodded firmly. "I'm positive. I counted twice."

"That was the one we wanted, Mrs. Malek."

"I may still be of help." She was smiling at some private secret. "Some years back I was sick. Quite sick. I was here in bed for some months and for lack of something to do I decided to make my own record of Quincy's papers. I listed each and every piece much as he did."

She reached into the folds of her wrapper and brought out a thick, cheap note pad and laid it down on the table. "You'll have to go through them all one by one and find the piece that's missing, but it's here, Mr. Hammer."

I picked up the pad, hefted it, and stuck it in my pocket. "One question, Mrs. Malek. Why are you going so far with us?"

"Because I don't like to be stolen from. That other party deliberately stole something of value from me. That person was dishonest. Therefore I assume you are honest. Am I wrong?"

"You aren't wrong, Mrs. Malek. You may get more out of this than you think."

"This is sufficient for my needs, sir."

I picked up the box and put on my hat. "You'll get them all back this time. The police may want to hold them for a while, but eventually they'll be returned."

"I'm sure they will. And I thank you, sir."

I grinned at her. "I could kiss you."

"That would be a pleasure." She glanced at Velda. "Do you mind?"

"Be my guest," Velda said.

So I kissed her.

Damn if the blush didn't make the rouge spots fade right out.

———

The last three bucks bought a cab ride back to the apartment and two hamburgers apiece. We dumped the contents of the box on the floor, spread them out into piles, opened the notebook, and started to go through them.

At dawn I called Pat without telling him what I had. So far he had nothing. Then we went back to the scoreboard. It could have taken a few days but we got lucky. At three in the afternoon Velda instituted a quick system of cross-checking and we found the missing item.

It was a deed made out to one Carl Sullivan for a piece of property in Ulster County, New York, and the location was accurately described. Beneath it, apparently copied from the original notation, were the initials, B.C. *Blackie Conley!*

CHAPTER 11

I had to borrow fifty bucks from George over at the Blue Ribbon to get on my way, but he came up with the dough and no questions. Down the street I rented a Ford and Velda got in it for the drive upstate. Instead of taking the Thruway I got on old Route 17 and stopped at Central Valley to see a real estate dealer I knew. It wasn't easy to keep the glad-handing and old-times talk to a minimum, but we managed. I gave him my property location and he pulled down a wall map and started locating it on the grid.

He found it quickly enough. Then he looked at me strangely and said, "You own this?"

"No, but I'm interested in it."

"Well, if you're thinking of buying it, forget it. This is in the area they located those gas wells on and several big companies have been going nuts trying to find the owner. It's practically jungle up there and they want to take exploration teams in and can't do it without permission. The taxes have been paid in advance so there's no squawk from the state and nobody can move an inch until the owner shows up."

"Tough."

His face got a little bit hungry. "Mike . . . do you know the owner?"

"I know him."

"Think we can swing a deal?"

"I doubt it."

His face fell at the thought of the money he was losing. "Well, if he wants to sell, put in a word for me, okay?"

"I'll mention it to him."

That seemed to satisfy him. We shook hands back at the car and took off. An hour and ten minutes later we were at the turnoff that led to the property. The first road was a shale and dirt one that we took for a mile, looking for a stream. We found that too, and the barely visible indentation that showed where another road had been a long time back.

I drove down the road and backed the Ford into the bushes, hiding it from casual observation, then came back to Velda and looked at the jungle we were going into.

The trees were thick and high, pines intermingled with oaks and maples, almost hopelessly tangled at their bases with heavy brush and thorny creepers. Towering overhead was the uneven roll of the mountain range.

It was getting late and we wouldn't have too much sun left.

"It's someplace in there," I said. "I don't know how he did it, but it was done. He's in there."

Animals had made their way in ahead of us. The trail was barely visible and some of the brush was fuzzed with the hair of deer, the earth, where it was soft in spots, showing the print of their hoofs. We made it crawling sometimes, fighting the undergrowth constantly. But little by little we got inside.

The ground slope ranged upward, leveled off, then slanted down again. We saw the remains of a shack and headed toward it, but that was all it was, a vermin-infested building that had long ago fallen into ruin. At one side there was a carton of rusted tins that had spilled over and rotted out, and another wooden crate of cooking utensils, still nested inside each other. The remains of a mattress had been scattered over the floor making permanent nests for thousands of mice.

It didn't make sense.

We started down the slope and burst through the brush into a clearing that was shaped like a bowl. Nature had somehow started something growing there, a peculiar soft grass that refused to allow anything else to intrude on its domain.

Velda said, "Mike . . ."

I stopped and looked back.

"I'm tired, Mike. Can't we rest a minute?"

"Sure, honey. This is a good place."

She sank to the ground with a long sigh and stretched out languidly looking at the sky. The clouds were tinged with a deep red and the shadows were beginning to creep down the mountainside. "This is lovely, Mike."

"Not much like the city, is it?"

She laughed, said, "No," and lifted her legs to strip off the ruins of her nylons. She stopped with one leg pointed toward the mountain. "You do it."

What a broad.

I held her foot against my stomach, unhooked the snaps that held the stockings, and peeled one down, then the other. She said, "Ummm," and patted the ground beside her. I crossed my legs and sat down, but she grabbed for me, tipped me over toward her, and held my face in her hands. "It's going to be dark soon, Mike. We can't go back through that again. Not until morning." Her smile was impish.

"Any time, any place. You're crazy."

"I want you, Mike. Now."

"It's going to get cold."

"Then we'll suffer."

I kissed her then, her mouth slippery against mine.

"It's awfully warm now," she murmured. She raised her legs and the dress slid down her thighs.

"Stop that."

Her hand took mine and held it against the roundness of one thigh, keeping it there until she could take hers away and knew mine would stay. Ever so slowly my hand began a movement of its own, sensing the way to love, unable to stop the motion. With an age-old feminine motion she made it easier for me, her entire being trying to bring me into its vortex and I tried to fill the void. There was something I was fighting against, but it wasn't a fight I knew I could win. There was a bulk between us and Velda's hand reached inside my coat and pulled out the .45 and laid it on the ground in back of her.

The sun was low now, the rays angling into the trees. One of them picked up a strange color in the brush at the foot of the hill, an odd color that never should have been there. I stared at it, trying to make out what it was.

Then I knew.

The fingers of my hand squeezed involuntarily and Velda let out a little cry, the pain of it shocking her. I said, "Stay here," and snapped to my feet.

"Mike . . ."

I didn't take the time to answer her. I ran down the hill toward the color and with each step it took shape and form until it was what I knew it had to be.

A thirty-year-old taxi cab. A yellow and black taxi that had been stolen off the streets back in the thirties.

The tires were rotted shreds now, but the rest of it was intact. Only a few spots of rust showed through the heavy layers of paint that the cab had been coated with to protect it against the destruction of the wind-driven grit in the city.

I looked it over carefully and almost wanted to say that they sure didn't make them like this anymore. The windows were still rolled shut hard against their rubber cushions so that the stuff fused them right into the body of the car with age. The car had been new when it was stolen, and they made that model to last for years. It was an airtight vault now, a bright yellow, wheeled mausoleum for two people.

At least they had been two people.

Now they were two mummies. The one in the front was slumped across the wheel, hat perched jauntily on a skeletal head covered with drawn, leathery flesh. There wasn't much to the back of the head. That had been blown away.

The guy who did it was the other mummy in the backseat. He leaned against the other side of the car, his mouth gaping open so that every tooth showed, his clothes hanging from withered limbs. Where his eyes were I could see two little dried bits of things that still had the appearance of watching me.

He still held the rifle across his lap aimed at the door in front of me, fingers clutched around its stock and his right forefinger still on the trigger. There was a black stain of blood on the shirt that could still give it a startlingly white background.

Between his feet were three canvas sacks.

A million dollars in each.

I had finally found Blackie Conley.

She came up on bare feet and I didn't hear her until her breath hissed with the horror of what she saw. She pressed the back of her hand against her mouth to stop the scream that started to come, her eyes wide open for long moments.

"Mike . . . who . . .?"

"Our killer, Velda. The Target. The one we were after. That's Blackie Conley in the backseat there. He almost made it. How close can a guy come?"

"Pretty close, Mr. Hammer. Some of us come all the way."

I didn't hear him either! He had come up the side of the hill on sneak-ered feet and stood there with a gun on us and I felt like the biggest fool in the world! My .45 was back there in the love nest and now we were about to be as dead as the others. It was like being right back at the beginning again.

I said, "Hello, Sonny."

The Snake. The real snake, as deadly as they come. The only one that had real fangs and knew how to use them. His face had lost the tired look and his eyes were bright with the desirous things he saw in his future. There was nothing stooped about him now, nothing of the old man there. Old, yes, but he wasn't the type who grew old easily. It had all been a pose, a cute game, and he was the winner.

"You scared me, Mr. Hammer. When you got as far as Malek you really scared me. I was taking my time about coming here because I wasn't ready yet and then I knew it was time to move. You damn near ruined everything." What I used to call a cackle was a pose too. He did have a laugh. He thought it was funny.

Velda reached for my arm and I knew she was scared. It was too much too fast all over again and she could only take so much.

"Smart," he said to me. "You're a clever bastard. If all I had was the cops to worry about it would have been no trouble, but I had to draw you." His mouth pulled into a semblance of a grin. "Those nice talks we had. You kept me right up to date. Tell me, did you think I had a nice face?"

"I thought you had more sense, Sonny."

He dropped the grin then. "Get off it, guy. More sense? For what? You think I was going to spend all my life in the cooler without getting some satisfaction? Mister, that's where you made your mistake. You should have gone a little further into my case history. I always was a mean one because it paid off. If I had to play pretty-face to make it pay off I could do that too."

"You won't make it, Sonny."

"No? Well, just lose that idea. For thirty years I worked this one out. I had all the time in the world to do it too. With the contacts I had in the can I got enough on the big boys to make them jump my way when I was ready. I put together a mob and now I'll have to move to get it rolling. You think I won't live big for what little time I have left? Well, you're making a mistake when you think that. A lot of planning went into this dodge, kid."

"You still hate, don't you?"

Sonny Motley nodded slowly, a smile of pure pleasure forming. "You're goddamn right. I hated that bastard Torrence and tried to get at him through his kid. Mistake there . . . I thought he loved the kid. I would've been doin' him a favor to rub her out, right?"

"He was trying for her too."

"I got the picture fast enough. When I knocked him off in his house I thought I'd get the kid just for the fun of it. She fooled me. Where was she, mister?"

I shrugged.

"Hell, it don't matter none now." He lifted the gun so I could see down the barrel. "I thought sure you'd get on to me sooner. I pulled a boner, you know that, don't you?"

I knew it now, all right. When Marv Kania tried to nail me with the cab it was because Sonny had called him from the back room when he faked getting me old clippings of his crime and told him where I was going. When Marv almost got me in my apartment it was because Sonny told him my new address and that I'd be there. I made it easy because I told Sonny both times.

I said, "Marv Kania was holed up in your place, wasn't he?"

"That's right, dying every minute, and all he wanted was to get that last crack at you. It was the one thing that kept him alive."

"It was the thing that killed him too, Sonny."

"Nobody'll miss him but me. The kid had guts. He knew nobody could help him, but he stuck the job out."

"You got the guts too, Sonny?"

"I got the guts, Hammer." He laughed again. "You gave old

Blackie credit for having my guts though. That was pretty funny. You were so sure it was him. Never me. Blackie the slob. You know, I figured out that cross when I was in stir. It came through to me and when I put the pieces together bit by bit I knew what I was going to do. I even figured out how Blackie got wise at the last minute and what he'd do to plan a getaway. He wasn't such a hard guy to second-guess. After all, I had thirty years to do it in. Now it's the big loot I waited all that time to spend."

"You won't do it, Sonny."

"How you figure to stop me? You got no gun and you're under one. I can pump a fast one into you both and nobody will hear a sound. Blackie picked this place pretty well. You're gonna die, you know. I can't let you two run around."

Velda's fingers bit into my arm harder. "See the money in the car, Hammer? It still there? It wasn't in the shack so it's gotta be there or around here somewhere."

"Look for yourself."

"Step back."

We moved slowly, two steps, then stood there while Sonny grinned and looked into the window of the cab.

It was hard to tell what was happening to his face. For one second I thought I'd have a chance to jump him but he caught himself in time and swung the gun back on us. His eyes were dancing with the joy of the moment and the laugh in his throat was real.

Sonny Motley was doing what he had wanted to do for so long, meeting Blackie Conley face to face.

"Look at him. It's him back there! Look at that dirty double-crosser sitting there just like I shot him. Goddamn, I didn't miss with that shot. I killed the son of a bitch thirty years ago! See that, Hammer . . . see the guy I killed thirty years ago? Damn, if that isn't a pretty sight."

He paused, sucking in his breath, his chest heaving. "Just like he was, still got that rifle he loved. See where I got him, Hammer . . . right in the chest. Right through the open window before he could get his second shot off.

"Hello, Blackie, you dirty bastard!" he shrieked. "How'd you like that shot? How'd it feel to die, Blackie? This is worth waiting all the thirty years for!"

Sonny turned and grimaced at me, his eyes burning. "Always figured to make it, Blackie did. Had the driver pull him into his hidey-hole and shot him in the head. But he never lived through my shot. No chance of that. Man, this is my *big* day . . . the biggest damn day in my life! Now I got everything!"

He drew himself erect at the thought, a funny expression changing his face. He said, "Only one thing I ain't got anymore," and this time he was looking at Velda.

"Take those clothes off, lady."

Her fingers that were so tight on my arm seemed to relax and I knew she was thinking the same thing as I was. It could be a diversion. If she could step aside and do it so we were split up I might get the chance to jump him.

I didn't watch her. I couldn't. I had to watch him. But I could tell from his eyes just what she was doing. I knew when she took the skirt off, then the bra. I watched his eyes follow her hands as she slid the skirt down over her ankles and I knew by the quick intake of his breath and the sudden brightness of his eyes when she had stepped out of the last thing she wore.

She made the slightest motion to one side then, but he was with it. He said, "Just stay there, lady. Stay there close where I can get to you both."

Not much time was left now. The fire in his eyes was still burning, but it wouldn't last.

"Real nice, lady," he said. "I like brunettes. Always have. Now you can die like that, right together."

No time at all now.

"Too bad you didn't get the money, Sonny."

He shook his head at me, surprised that I'd make such a bad attempt. "It's right on the floor there."

"You'd better be sure, Sonny. We got here ahead of you."

If he had trouble opening the door I might be able to make the move. All he had to do was falter once and if I could get past the first shot I could take him even if he caught me with it. Velda would hit the ground the second he pulled the trigger and together we'd have him.

"No good, Hammer. It's right there and Old Blackie is still guarding it with his rifle. You saw it."

"You didn't."

"Okay, so you get one last look." He reached for the door handle and gave it a tentative tug. It didn't budge. He laughed again, knowing what I was waiting for but not playing it my way at all. The gun never wavered and I knew I'd never get the chance. From where he stood he could kill us both with ease and we all knew it.

The next time he gave the door a sharp jerk and it swung open, the hinges groaning as the rust ground into them. He was watching us with the damndest grin I ever saw and never bothered to see what was happening in the cab. The pull on the door was enough to rock the car and ever so steadily the corpse of Blackie Conley seemed to come to life, sitting up in the seat momentarily. I could see the eyes and the mouth open in a soundless scream with the teeth bared in a grimace of wild hatred.

Sonny knew something was happening and barely turned his head to look . . . just enough to see the man he had killed collapse into dust fragments, and as it did the bony finger touched the trigger that had been filed to react to the smallest of pressures and the rifle squirted a blossom of roaring flame that took Sonny Motley square in the chest and dropped him lifeless four feet away.

While the echo still rumbled across the mountainside, the leather-covered skull of Blackie Conley bounced out of the cab and rolled to a stop face to face with Sonny and lay there grinning at him idiotically.

You can only sustain emotion so long. You can only stay scared so long. It stops and suddenly it's like nothing happened at all. You don't shake, you don't break up. You're just glad it's over. You're a little surprised that your hands aren't trembling and wonder why it is you feel almost perfectly normal.

Velda said quietly, "It's finished now, isn't it?"

Her clothes were in a heap beside her and in the dying rays of the sun she looked like a statuesque wood nymph, a lovely naked wood nymph with beautiful black hair as dark as a raven against a sheen of molded flesh that rose and dipped in curves that were unbelievable.

Up there on the hill the grass was soft where we had lain in the nest. It smelled flowery and green and the night was going to be a warm night. I looked at her, then toward the spot on the hill. Tomorrow it would be something else, but this was now.

I said, "You ready?"

She smiled at me, savoring what was to come. "I'm ready."

I took her hand, stepped over the bodies, new and old, on the ground, and we started up the slope.

"Then let's go," I said.

THE
TWISTED
THING

To Sid Graedon, who saw the charred edges

CHAPTER 1

The little guy's face was a bloody mess. Between the puffballs of blue-black flesh that used to be eyelids, the dull gleam of shock-deadened pupils watched Dilwick uncomprehendingly. His lips were swollen things of lacerated skin, with slow trickles of blood making crooked paths from the corners of his mouth through the stubble of a beard to his chin, dripping onto a stained shirt.

Dilwick stood just outside the glare of the lamp, dangling like the Sword of Damocles over the guy's head. He was sweating too. His shirt clung to the meaty expanse of his back, the collar wilted into wrinkles around his huge neck. He pushed his beefy hand further into the leather glove and swung. The solid smack of his open hand on the little guy's jaw was nasty. His chair went over backward and his head cracked against the concrete floor of the room like a ripe melon. Dilwick put his hands on his hips and glared down at the caricature that once was human.

"Take him out and clean 'im up. Then get 'im back here." Two other cops came out of the darkness and righted the chair. One yanked the guy to his feet and dragged him to the door.

Lord, how I hated their guts. Grown men, they were supposed to be. Four of them in there taking turns pounding a confession from a guy who had nothing to say. And I had to watch it.

It was supposed to be a warning to me. Be careful, it said, when you try to withhold information from Dilwick you're looking for a broken skull. Take a look at this guy for example, then spill what you know and stick around so I, the Great Dilwick, can get at you when I want you.

I worked up a husky mouthful of saliva and spat it as close to his feet as I could. The fat cop spun on his heel and let his lips fold back over his teeth in a sneer. "You gettin' snotty, Hammer?"

I stayed slouched in my seat. "Any way you call it, Dilwick," I said insolently. "Just sitting here thinking."

Big stuff gave me a dirty grimace. "Thinking . . . you?"

"Yeah. Thinking what you'd look like the next day if you tried that stuff on me."

The two cops dragging the little guy out stopped dead still. The other one washing the bloodstains from the seat quit swishing the brush over the wicker and held his breath. Nobody ever spoke that way to Dilwick. Nobody from the biggest politician in the state to the hardest apple that ever stepped out of a pen. Nobody ever did because Dilwick would cut them up into fine pieces with his bare hands and enjoy it. That was Dilwick, the dirtiest, roughest cop who ever walked a beat or swung a nightstick over a skull. Crude, he was. Crude, hard and dirty and afraid of nothing. He'd sooner draw blood from a face than eat and everybody knew it. That's why nobody ever spoke to him that way. That is, nobody except me.

Because I'm the same way myself.

Dilwick let out his breath with a rush. The next second he was reaching down for me, but I never gave him the chance to hook his hairy paws in my shirt. I stood up in front of him and sneered in his face. Dilwick was too damn big to be used to meeting guys eye to eye. He liked to look down at them. Not this time.

"What do you think you'll do?" he snarled.

"Try me and see," I said.

I saw his shoulder go back and didn't wait. My knee came up and landed in his groin with a sickening smash. When he doubled over my fist caught him in the mouth and I felt his teeth pop. His face was starting to turn blue by the time he hit the floor. One cop dropped the little guy and went for his gun.

"Cut it, stupid," I said, "before I blow your goddamn head off. I still got my rod." He let his hand fall back to his side. I turned and walked out of the room. None of them tried to stop me.

Upstairs I passed the desk sergeant still bent over his paper. He looked up in time to see me and let his hand snake under the desk.

Right then I had my own hand six inches from my armpit practically inviting him to call me. Maybe he had a family at home. He brought his hand up on top of the desk where I could see it. I've seen eyes like his peering out of a rat hole when there was a cat in the room. He still had enough I AM THE LAW in him to bluster it out.

"Did Dilwick release you?" he demanded.

I snatched the paper from his hand and threw it to the floor, trying to hold my temper. "Dilwick didn't release me," I told him. "He's downstairs vomiting his guts out the same way you'll be doing if you pull a deal like that again. Dilwick doesn't want *me*. He just wanted me to sit in on a cellar séance in legal torture to show me how tough he is. I wasn't impressed. But get this, I came to Sidon to legally represent a client who used his one phone call on arrest to contact me, not to be intimidated by a fat louse that was kicked off the New York force and bought his way into the cops in this hick town just to use his position for a rake-off."

The sergeant started to interrupt, licking his loose lips nervously, but I cut him short. "Furthermore, I'm going to give you just one hour to get Billy Parks out of here and back to his house. If you don't," and I said it slowly, "I'm going to call the State's Attorney and drop this affair in his lap. After that I'll come back here and mash your damn face to a pulp. Understand now? No habeas corpus, no nothing. Just get him out of here."

For a cop he stunk. His lower lip was trembling with fear. I pushed my hat on the back of my head and stamped out of the station house. My heap was parked across the street and I got in and turned it over. Damn, I was mad.

Billy Parks, just a nice little ex-con trying to go straight, but do you think the law would help him out? Hell no. Let one thing off-color pop up and they drag him in to get his brains kicked out because he had a record. Sure, he put in three semesters in the college on the Hudson, and he wasn't too anxious to do anything that would put him in his senior year where it took a lifetime to matriculate. Ever since he wrangled that chauffeur's job from Rudolph York I hadn't heard from him . . . until now, after York's little genius of a son had been snatched.

Rain started to spatter against the windshield when I turned into the drive. The headlights picked out the roadway and I followed it up to the house. Every light in the place was on as if the occupants were afraid a dark corner might conceal some unseen terror.

It was a big place, a product of wealth and good engineering, but in spite of its stately appearance and wrought-iron gates, somebody had managed to sneak in, grab the kid and beat it. Hell, the kid was perfect snatch bait. He was more than a son to his father, he was the result of a fourteen-year experiment. Then, that's what he got for bringing the kid up to be a genius. I bet he'd shell out plenty of his millions to see him safe and sound.

The front door was answered by one of those tailored flunkies who must always count up to fifty before they open up. He gave me a curt nod and allowed me to come in out of the rain anyway.

"I'm Mike Hammer," I said, handing him a card. "I'd like to see your boss. And right away," I added.

The flunky barely glanced at the pasteboard. "I'm awfully sorry, sir, but Mr. York is temporarily indisposed."

When I shoved a cigarette in my mouth and lit it I said, "You tell him it's about his kid. He'll un-indispose himself in a hurry."

I guess I might as well have told him I wanted a ransom payment right then the way he looked at me. I've been taken for a lot of things in my life, but this was the first for a snatch artist. He started to stutter, swallowed, then waved his hand in the general direction of the living room. I followed him in.

Have you ever seen a pack of alley cats all set for a midnight brawl when something interrupts them? They spin on a dime with the hair still up their backs and watch the intruder through hostile eye slits as though they were ready to tear him so they could continue their own fight. An intense, watchful stare of mutual hate and fear.

That's what I ran into, only instead of cats it was people. Their expressions were the same. A few had been sitting, others stopped their quiet pacing and stood poised, ready. A tableau of hate. I looked at them only long enough to make a mental count of a round dozen and tab them as a group of ghouls whose morals had been eaten into by dry rot a long time.

Rudolph York was slumped in a chair gazing blankly into an empty fireplace. The photos in the rags always showed him to be a big man, but he was small and tired-looking this night. He kept muttering to himself, but I couldn't hear him. The butler handed him my card. He took it, not bothering to look at it.

"A Mr. Hammer, sir."

No answer.

"It . . . It's about Master Ruston, sir."

Rudolph York came to life. His head jerked around and he looked at me with eyes that spat fire. Very slowly he came to his feet, his hands trembling. "Have you got him?"

Two boys who might have been good-looking if it weren't for the nightclub pallor and the squeegy skin came out of a settee together. One had his fists balled up, the other plunked his highball glass on a coffee table. They came at me together. Saps. All I had to do was look over my shoulder and let them see what was on my face and they called it quits outside of swinging distance.

I turned my attention back to Rudolph York. "No."

"Then what do you want?"

"Look at my card."

He read, "Michael Hammer, Private Investigator," very slowly, then crushed the card in his hand. The contortions in his face were weird. He breathed silent, unspeakable words through tight lips, afraid to let himself be heard. One look at the butler and the flunky withdrew quietly, then he turned back to me. "How did you find out about this?" he charged.

I didn't like this guy. As brilliant a scientist as he might be, as wealthy and important, I still didn't like him. I blew a cloud of smoke in his direction. "Not hard," I answered, "not hard at all. I got a telephone call."

He kept beating his fist into an open palm. "I don't want the police involved, do you hear! This is a private matter."

"Cool off, Doc. I'm not the police. However, if you try to keep me out of this I'll buzz one of the papers, then your privacy will really be shot to hell."

"Whom do you represent?" he asked coldly.

"Your chauffeur, Billy Parks."

"So?"

"So I'd like to know why you put the finger on him when you found out your kid was missing. I'd like to know why you let them

346 • THE MIKE HAMMER COLLECTION

346 • THE MIKE HAMMER COLLECTION

Sure, they'd be quiet, who wouldn't? Do you think they'd split the kind of reward money you'd be offering if they could help it?"

I felt like rapping him in the teeth. "Throwing Billy to the wolves was stupid. Suppose he was an ex-con. With three convictions to his credit he wasn't likely to stick his neck out for that offence. He'd be the first suspect as it was. Damn, I'd angle for Dilwick before I would Billy. He's more the type."

York was sweating freely. He buried his face in his hands and swayed from side to side, moaning to himself. He stopped finally, then looked up at me. "What will I do, Mr. Hammer? What *can* be done?"

I shook my head.

"But something must be done! I must find Ruston. After all these years . . . I can't call the police. He's such a sensitive boy . . . I—I'm afraid."

"I merely represent Billy Parks, Mr. York. He called me because he was in a jam and I'm his friend. What I want from you is to give him back his job. Either that or I call the papers."

"All right. It really doesn't matter." His head dropped again. I put on my hat and stood up, then, "But you? Mr. Hammer, you aren't the police as you say. Perhaps you could help me, too."

I threw him a straw. "Perhaps."

He grabbed at it. "Would you? I need somebody . . . who will keep this matter silent."

"It'll cost you."

"Very well, how much?"

"How much did you offer Dilwick?"

"Ten thousand dollars."

I let out a whistle, then told him, "Okay, ten G's plus expenses."

Relief flooded his face like sunlight. The price was plenty steep but he didn't bat an eye. He had been holding this inside himself too long and was glad to hand it to someone else.

But he still had something to say. "You drive a hard bargain, Mr. Hammer, and in my position I am forced, more or less, to accept. However, for my own satisfaction I would like to know one thing. How good a detective are you?"

He said it in a brittle tone and I answered him the same way. An answer that made him pull back away from me as though I had a contagious disease. I said, "York, I've killed a lot of men. I shot the guts out of two of them in Times Square. Once I let six hundred people in a nightclub see what some crook had for dinner when he tried to gun me. He got it with a steak knife. I remember because I don't want to remember. They were too nasty. I hate the bastards that make society a thing to be laughed at and preyed upon. I hate them so much I can kill without the slightest compunction. The papers call me dirty names and the kind of rats I monkey with are scared stiff of me, but I don't give a damn. When I kill I make it legal. The courts accuse me of being too quick on the trigger but they can't revoke my license because I do it right. I think fast, I shoot fast, I've been shot at plenty. And I'm still alive. That's how good a detective I am."

For a full ten seconds he stood speechless, staring at me with an undisguised horror. There wasn't a sound from the room. It isn't often that I make a speech like that, but when I do it must be convincing. If thoughts could be heard that house would be a babble of fearful confusion. The two punks I biffed looked like they had just missed being bitten by a snake. York was the first one to compose himself. "I suppose you'd like to see the boy's room?"

"Uh-uh."

"Why not? I thought . . ."

"The kid's gone, that's enough. Seeing the room won't do any good. I don't have the equipment to fool around with clues, York. Fingerprints and stuff are for technical men. I deal with motives and people."

"But the motive . . ."

I shrugged. "Money, probably. That's what it usually is. Let's start at the beginning first." I indicated the chair and York settled back. I drew up closer to him. "When did you discover him to be missing?"

"Yesterday morning. At eight o'clock, his regular rising hour, Miss Malcom, his governess, went into his room. He was not in bed. She looked for him throughout the house, then told me he could not be found. With the aid of the gardener and Parks we searched the grounds. He was not there."

"I see. What about the gatekeeper?"

"Henry saw nothing, heard nothing."

"Then you called the police, I suppose?" He nodded. "Why did you think he was kidnapped?"

York gave an involuntary start. "But what other reason could account for his disappearance?"

I leaned forward in my seat. "According to all I've ever read about your son, Mr. York, he is the most brilliant thing this side of heaven. Wouldn't a young genius be inclined to be highly strung?"

He gripped the arms of the chair until the veins stood out on the back of his hands. The fire was in his eyes again. "If you are referring to his mental health, you are mistaken. Ruston was in excellent spirits as he has been all his life. Besides being his father and a scientist, I am also a doctor."

It was easy to see that he didn't want any doubts cast upon the mind of one he had conditioned so carefully so long. I let it go for the time being.

"Okay, describe him to me. Everything. I have to start somewhere."

"Yes. He is fourteen. In appearance he is quite like other boys. By appearance I mean expressions, manners and attitudes. He is five feet one inch tall, light brown hair, ruddy complexion. He weighs one hundred twelve pounds stripped. Eyes, brown, slight scar high on the left side of his forehead as the result of a fall when he was younger."

"Got a picture of him?" The scientist nodded, reached inside his jacket pocket and came out with a snapshot. I took it. The boy was evidently standing in the yard, hands behind his back in a typically shy-youth manner. He was a good-looking kid at that. A slight smile played around his mouth and he seemed to be pretty self-conscious. He had on shorts and a dark sweater. Romping in the background was a spotted spaniel.

"Mind if I keep it?" I asked.

York waved his hand. "Not at all. If you want them, there are others."

When I pocketed the snap I lit another cigarette. "Who else is in the house? Give me all the servants, where they sleep, anyone who has been here recently. Friends, enemies, people you work with."

"Of course." He cleared his throat and listed the household. "Besides myself, there is Miss Malcom, Parks, Henry, two cooks, two maids and Harvey. Miss Grange works for me as a laboratory assistant, but lives at home in town. As for friends, I have few left that I ever see since I stopped teaching at the university. No enemies I can think of. I believe the only ones who have been inside the gate the past few weeks were tradesmen from town. That is," he indicated the gang in the room with a thumb, "outside these, my closest relatives. They are here and gone constantly."

"You are quite wealthy?" The question was unnecessary, but I made my point.

York cast a quick look about him, then a grimace that was half disgust passed over him. "Yes, but my health is still good."

I let the ghouls hear it. "Too bad for them."

"The servants all sleep in the north wing. Miss Malcom has a room adjoining Ruston's and connected to it. I occupy a combination study and bedroom at the front of the house.

"I work with no one and for no one. The nature of my work you must be familiar with; it is that of giving my son a mind capable of greater thought and intelligence than is normally found. He may be a genius to you and others, but to me he is merely one who makes full use of his mind. Naturally, my methods are closely guarded secrets. Miss Grange shares them with me, but I trust her completely. She is as devoted to my son as I am. Since the death of my wife when the child was born, she has aided me in every way. I think that is all?"

"Yeah, I guess that'll do."

"May I ask how you will proceed?"

"Sure. Until we get a sign from whoever kidnapped your son I'm going to sit tight. The ones that grabbed the kid must think they know what they're doing, otherwise they wouldn't pick someone like your boy who is always in the public eye. If you wanted to you could have every cop in the state beating the bushes. I take it there was no note . . ."

"None at all."

". . . so they're playing it close to see what you'll do. Call the cops and they're liable to take a powder. Hold off a bit and they will contact you. Then I'll go to work . . . that is if it's really a snatch."

He bit into his lip and gave me another of those fierce looks. "You say that as though you don't think he was kidnapped."

"I say that because I don't *know* he was kidnapped. It could be anything. I'll tell you better when I see a ransom note."

York didn't get a chance to answer, for at that moment the butler reappeared, and between him and the luscious redhead they supported a bloody, limp figure. "It's Parks, sir. Miss Malcom and I found him outside the door!"

We ran to him together. York gasped when he saw Parks' face then sent the butler scurrying off for some hot water and bandages. Most of the gore had been wiped off, but the swellings were as large as ever. The desk sergeant had done as I told him, the hour wasn't up yet, but somebody was still going to pay for this. I carried Billy to a chair and sat him down gently.

I stepped back and let York go to work when the butler returned with a first-aid kit. It was the first good chance I had to give Miss Malcom the once-over all the way from a beautiful set of legs through a lot of natural curves to an extraordinarily pretty face. Miss Malcom they called her.

I call her Roxy Coulter. She used to be a strip artist in the flesh circuit of New York and Miami.

But Roxy had missed her profession. Hollywood should have had her. Maybe she didn't remember Atlantic City or that New Year's Eve party in Charlie Drew's apartment. If she did she held a dandy deadpan and all I got in return for my stare was one of those go ahead, peek, but don't touch looks.

A peek was all I got, because Billy came around with a groan and made an effort to sit up. York put his hand against his chest and forced him down again. "You'll have to be quiet," he cautioned him in a professional tone.

"My face," his eyes rolled in his head, "jeez, what happened to my face?"

I knelt beside him and turned over the cold compress on his forehead. His eyes gleamed when he recognized me. "Hello, Mike. What happened?"

"Hi, Billy. They beat up on you. Feel any better?"

"I feel awful. Oh, that bastard. If only I was bigger, Mike . . . damn, why couldn't I be big like you? That dirty . . ."

"Forget about him, kid." I patted his shoulder. "I handed him a little of the same dish. His map'll never be the same."

"Cripes! I bet you did! I thought something funny happened down there. Thanks, Mike, thanks a lot."

"Sure."

Then his face froze in a frightened grimace. "Suppose . . . suppose they come back again? Mike . . . I—I can't stand that stuff. I'll talk, I'll say anything. I can't take it, Mike!"

"Ease off. I'm not going anywhere. I'll be around."

Billy tried to smile and he gripped my arm. "You will?"

"Yup. I'm working for your boss now."

"Mr. Hammer." York was making motions from the side of the room. I walked over to him. "It would be better if he didn't get too excited. I gave him a sedative and he should sleep. Do you think you can manage to carry him to his room? Miss Malcom will show you the way."

"Certainly," I nodded. "And if you don't mind, I'd like to do a little prowling afterward. Maybe question the servants."

"Of course. The house is at your disposal."

Billy's eyes had closed and his head had fallen on his chin when I picked him up. He'd had a rough time of it all right. Without a word Miss Malcom indicated that I was to follow her and led me through an arch at the end of the room. After passing through a library, a study and a trophy room that looked like something out of a museum, we wound up in a kitchen. Billy's room was off an alcove behind the pantry. As gently as I could I laid him under the covers. He was sound asleep.

Then I stood up. "Okay, Roxy, now we can say hello."

"Hello, Mike."

"Now why the disguise and the new handle? Hiding out?"

"Not at all. The handle as you call it is my real name. Roxy was something I used on the stage."

"Really? Don't tell me you gave up the stage to be a diaper changer. What are you doing here?"

"I don't like your tone, Mike. You change it or go to hell."

This was something. The Roxy I knew never had enough self-respect to throw her pride in my face. Might as well play it her way.

"Okay, baby, don't get teed off on me. I have a right to be just a little bit curious, haven't I? It isn't very often that you catch somebody jumping as far out of character as you have. Does the old man know about the old life?"

"Don't be silly. He'd can me if he did."

"I guessed as much. How did you tie up in this place?"

"Easy. When I finally got wise to the fact that I was getting my brains knocked out in the big city I went to an agency and signed up as a registered nurse. I was one before I got talked into tossing my torso around for two hundred a week. Three days later Mr. York accepted me to take care of his child. That was two years ago. Anything else you want to know?"

I grinned at her. "Nope. It was just funny meeting you, that's all."

"Then may I leave?"

I let my grin fade and eased her out through the door. "Look, Roxy, is there somewhere we can go talk?"

"I don't play those games anymore, Mike."

"Get off my back, will you? I mean talk."

She arched her eyebrows and watched me steadily a second, then seeing that I meant it, said, "My room. We can be alone there. But only talk, remember?"

"Roger, bunny, let's go."

This time we went into the outer foyer and up a stairway that seemed to have been carved out of a solid piece of mahogany. We turned left on the landing and Roxy opened the door for me.

"In here," she said.

While I picked out a comfortable chair she turned on a table lamp then offered me a smoke from a gold box. I took one and lit it. "Nice place you got here."

"Thank you. It's quite comfortable. Mr. York sees that I have every convenience. Now shall we talk?"

She was making sure I got the point in a hurry. "The kid. What is he like?"

Roxy smiled a little bit, and the last traces of hardness left her face. She looked almost maternal. "He's wonderful. A charming boy."

"You seem to like him."

"I do. You'd like him too." She paused, then, "Mike . . . do you really think he was kidnapped?"

"I don't know, that's why I want to talk about him. Downstairs I suggested that he might have become temporarily unbalanced and the old man nearly chewed my head off. Hell, it isn't unreasonable to figure that. He's supposed to be a genius and that automatically puts him out of the normal class. What do you think?"

She tossed her hair back and rubbed her forehead with one hand. "I can't understand it. His room is next door, and I heard nothing although I'm usually a light sleeper. Ruston was perfectly all right up to then. He wouldn't simply walk out."

"No? And why not?"

"Because he is an intelligent boy. He likes everyone, is satisfied with his environment and has been very happy all the time I've known him."

"Uh-huh. What about his training? How did he get to be a genius?"

"That you'll have to find out from Mr. York. Both he and Miss Grange take care of that department."

I squashed the butt into the ashtray. "Nuts, it doesn't seem likely that a genius can be made. They have to be born. You've been around him a lot. Tell me, just how much of a genius is he? I know only what the papers print."

"Then you know all I know. It isn't what he knows that makes him a genius, it's what he is capable of learning. In one week he mastered every phase of the violin. The next week it was the piano. Oh, I realize that it seems impossible, but it's quite true. Even the music critics accept him as a master of several instruments. It doesn't stop there, either. Once he showed an interest in astronomy. A few days later he exhausted every book on the subject. His father and I took him to the observatory where he proceeded to amaze the experts with his uncanny knowledge. He's a mathematical wizard besides. It doesn't take him a second to give you the cube root of a six-figure number to three decimal points. What more can I say? There is no field that he doesn't excel in. He grasps fundamentals at the snap of the fingers and learns in five minutes what would take you or me years of study. That, Mike, is the genius in a nutshell, but that's omitting the true boy part of him. In all respects he is exactly like other boys."

"The old man said that too."

"He's quite right. Ruston loves games, toys and books. He has a pony, a bicycle, skates and a sled. We go for long walks around the estate every once in a while and do nothing but talk. If he wanted to he could expound on nuclear physics in ten-syllable words, but that isn't his nature. He'd sooner talk football."

I picked another cigarette out of the box and flicked a match with my thumbnail. "That about covers it, I guess. Maybe he didn't go off his nut at that. Let's take a look at his room."

Roxy nodded and stood up. She walked to the end of the room

and opened a door. "This is it." When she clicked on the light switch I walked in. I don't know what I expected, but this wasn't it. There were pennants on the walls and pictures tucked into the corners of the dresser mirror. Clothes were scattered in typical boyish confusion over the backs of chairs and the desk.

In one corner was the bed. The covers had been thrown to the foot and the pillow still bore the head print of its occupant. If the kid had really been snatched I felt for him. It was no night to be out in your pajamas, especially when you left the top of them hanging on the bedpost.

I tried the window. It gave easily enough, though it was evident from the dust on the outside of the sill that it hadn't been opened recently.

"Keep the kid's door locked at night?" I asked Roxy.

She shook her head. "No. There's no reason to."

"Notice any tracks around here, outside the door or window?"

Another negative. "If there were any," she added, "they would have been wiped out in the excitement."

I dragged slowly on the cigarette, letting all the facts sink in. It seemed simple enough, but was it? "Who are all the twerps downstairs, bunny?"

"Relatives, mostly."

"Know 'em?"

Roxy nodded. "Mr. York's sister and her husband, their son and daughter, and a cousin are his only blood relations. The rest are his wife's folks. They've been hanging around here as long as I've been here, just waiting for something to happen to York."

"Does he know it?"

"I imagine so, but he doesn't seem bothered by them. They try to outdo each other to get in the old boy's favor. I suppose there's a will involved. There usually is."

"Yeah, but they're going to have a long wait. York told me his health was perfect."

Roxy looked at me curiously, then dropped her eyes. She fidgeted with her fingernails a moment and I let her stew a bit before I spoke.

"Say it, kid."

"Say what?"

"What you have on your mind and almost said."

She bit her lip, hesitating, then, "This is between you and me, Mike. If Mr. York knew I told you this I'd be out of a job. You won't mention it, will you?"

"I promise."

"About the second week I was here I happened to overhear Mr. York and his doctor after an examination. Apparently Mr. York knew what had happened, but called in another doctor to verify it. For some time he had been working with special apparatus in his laboratory and in some way became overexposed to radiation. It was enough to cause some internal complications and shorten his life span. Of course, he isn't in any immediate danger of dying, but you never can tell. He wasn't burned seriously, yet considering his age, and the fact that his injury has had a chance to work on him for two years, there's a possibility that any emotional or physical excitement could be fatal."

"Now isn't that nice," I said. "Do you get what that means, Roxy?" She shook her head. "It might mean that somebody else knows that too and tried to stir the old boy up by kidnapping the one closest to him in the hope that he kicks off during the fun. Great . . . that's a nice subtle sort of murder."

"But that's throwing it right on the doorstep of the beneficiary of his estate."

"Is it? I bet even a minor beneficiary would get enough of the long green to make murder worthwhile. York has plenty."

"There are other angles too, Mike."

"Been giving it some thought, haven't you?" I grinned at her. "For instance, one of the family might locate the kid and thus become number-one boy to the old man. Or perhaps the kid was the chief beneficiary and one of them wanted to eliminate him to push himself further up the list. Yeah, kid, there's a lot of angles, and I don't like any of 'em."

"It still might be a plain kidnapping."

"Roger. That it might. It's just that there're a lot more possibilities to it that could make it interesting. We'll know soon enough." I opened the door and hesitated, looking over my shoulder. "'Night, Roxy."

"Good night."

York was back by the fireplace again, still brooding. I would have felt better if he had been pacing the floor. I walked over and threw myself in a big chair. "Where'll I spend the night?" I asked him.

He turned very slowly. "The guest room. I'll ring for Harvey."

"Never mind. I'll get him myself when I'm ready."

We sat in silence a few minutes then York began a nervous tapping of his fingers. Finally, "When do you think we'll have word?"

"Two, three days maybe. Never can tell."

"But he's been gone a day already."

"Tomorrow, then. I don't know."

"Perhaps I should call the police again."

"Go ahead, but you'll probably be burying the boy after they find him. Those punks aren't cops, they're political appointees. You ought to know these small towns. They couldn't find their way out of a paper bag."

For the first time he showed a little parental anxiety. His fist came down on the arm of the chair. "Damn it, man, I can't simply sit here! What do you think it's like for me? Waiting. Waiting. He may be dead now for all we know."

"Perhaps, but I don't think so. Kidnapping's one thing, murder's another. How about introducing me to those people?"

He nodded. "Very well." Every eye in the room was on me as we made the rounds. I didn't suppose there would be anyone too anxious to meet me after the demonstration a little while ago.

The two gladiators were first. They were sitting on the love seat trying not to look shaky. Both of them still had red welts across their cheeks. The introduction was simple enough. York merely pointed in obvious disdain. "My nephews, Arthur and William Graham."

We moved on. "My niece, Alice Nichols." A pair of deep brown eyes kissed mine so hard I nearly lost my balance. She swept them up and down the full length of me. It couldn't have been any better if she did it with a wet paintbrush. She was tall and she had seen thirty, but she saw it with a face and body that were as fresh as a new daisy. Her clothes made no attempt at concealment; they barely covered. On some people skin is skin, but on her it was an invitation to dine. She told me things with a smile that most girls since Eve have been trying to put into words without being obvious or seeming too eager and I gave her my answer the same way. I can run the ball a little myself.

York's sister and her husband were next. She was a middle-aged woman with "Matron" written all over her. The type that wants to entertain visiting dignitaries and look down at "peepul" through a lorgnette. Her husband was the type you'd find paired off with such a specimen. He was short and bulgy in the middle. His single-breasted gray suit didn't quite manage to cross the equator without putting a strain on the button. He might have had hair, but you'd never know it now. One point of his collar had jumped the tab and stuck out like an accusing finger.

York said, "My sister, Martha Ghent, her husband, Richard." Richard went to stick out his hand but the old biddie shot him a hasty frown and he drew back, then she tried to freeze me out. Failing in this she turned to York. "Really, Rudolph, I hardly think we should meet this . . . this person."

York turned an appealing look my way, in apology. "I'm sorry, Martha, but Mr. Hammer considers it necessary."

"Nevertheless, I don't see why the police can't handle this."

I sneered at her in my finest manner. "I can't see why you don't keep your mouth shut, Mrs. Ghent."

The way her husband tried to keep the smile back, I thought he'd split a gut. Martha stammered, turned blue and stalked off. York looked at me critically, though approvingly.

A young kid in his early twenties came walking up as though the carpet was made of eggs. He had Ghent in his features, but strictly on his mother's side. A pipe stuck out of his pocket and he sported a set of thick-lensed glasses. The girl at his side didn't resemble anyone, but seeing the way she put her arm around Richard I took it that she was the daughter.

She was. Her name was Rhoda, she was friendly and smiled. The boy was Richard, Junior. He raised his eyebrows until they drew his eyes over the rims of his glasses and peered at me disapprovingly. He perched his hands on his hips and "Humphed" at me. One push and he would be over the line that divides a man and a pansy.

The introductions over, I cornered York out of earshot of the others. "Under the circumstances, it might be best if you kept this gang here until things settle down a bit. Think you can put them up?"

"I imagine so. I've been doing it at one time or another for the last ten years. I'll see Harvey and have the rooms made up."

"When you get them placed, have Harvey bring me a diagram showing where their rooms are. And tell him to keep it under his hat. I want to be able to reach anyone anytime. Now, is there anyone closely connected with the household we've missed?"

He thought a moment. "Oh, Miss Grange. She went home this afternoon."

"Where was she during the kidnapping?"

"Why . . . at home, I suppose. She leaves here between five and six every evening. She is a very reserved woman. Apparently has very little social activity. Generally she furthers her studies in the library rather than go out anywhere."

"Okay, I'll get to her. How about the others? Have they alibis?"

"Alibis?"

"Just checking, York. Do you know where they were the night before last?"

"Well . . . I can't speak for all of them, but Arthur and William were here. Alice Nichols came in about nine o'clock then left about an hour later."

This part I jotted down on a pad. "How did you collect the family . . . or did they all just drift in?"

"No, I called them. They helped me search, although it did no good. Mr. Hammer, what are we going to do? Please . . ."

Very slowly, York was starting to go to pieces. He'd stood up under this too calmly too long. His face was pale and withered-looking, drawn into a mask of tragedy.

"First of all, you're going to bed. It won't do any good for you to be knocking yourself out. That's what I'm here for." I reached over his shoulder and pulled a velvet cord. The flunky came in immediately and hurried over to us. "Take him upstairs," I said.

York gave the butler instructions about putting the family up and Harvey seemed a little surprised and pleased that he'd be allowed in on the conspiracy of the room diagram.

I walked to the middle of the floor and let the funeral buzz down before speaking. I wasn't nice about it. "You're all staying here tonight. If it interferes with other plans you've made it's too bad. Anyone that tries to duck out will answer to me. Harvey will give you your rooms and be sure you stay in them. That's all."

Lady sex appeal waited until I finished then edged up to me with a grin. "See if you can grab the end bedroom in the north wing," she said, "and I'll get the one connected to it."

I said in mock surprise, "Alice, you can get hurt doing things like that."

She laughed. "Oh, I bruise easily, but I heal fast as hell."

Swell girl. I hadn't been seduced in a long time.

I wormed out through a cross fire of nasty looks to the foyer and winked at Richard Ghent on the way. He winked back; his wife wasn't looking.

I slung on my coat and hat and went out to the car. When I rolled it through the gate I turned toward town and stepped on the gas. When I picked up to seventy I held it there until I hit the main drag. Just before the city line I pulled up to a gas station and swung in front of a pump. An attendant in his early twenties came out of the miniature Swiss Alpine cottage that served as a service station and automatically began unscrewing the gas cap. "Put in five," I told him.

He snaked out the hose and shoved the nose in the tank, watching the gauge. "Open all night?" I quizzed.

"Yeah."

"On duty yourself?"

"Yup. 'Cept on Sundays."

"Don't suppose you get much to do at night around here."

"Not very much."

This guy was as talkative as a pea pod. "Say, was much traffic along here night before last?"

He shut off the pump, put the cap back on and looked at me coldly. "Mister, I don't know from nothing," he said.

It didn't take me long to catch on to that remark. I handed him a ten-spot and followed him inside while he changed it. I let go a flyer. "So the cops kind of hinted that somebody would be nosing around, huh?"

No answer. He rang the cash register and began counting out bills. "Er . . . did you happen to notice Dilwick's puss? Or was it one of the others?"

He glanced at me sharply, curiously. "It was Dilwick. I saw his face."

Instead of replying I held out my right hand. He peered at it and saw where the skin had been peeled back off half the knuckles. This time I got a great big grin.

"Did you do that?"

"Uh-huh."

"Okay, pal, for that we're buddies. What do you want to know?"

"About traffic along here night before last."

"Sure, I remember it. Between nine o'clock and dawn the next morning about a dozen cars went past. See, I know most of 'em. A couple was from out of town. All but two belonged to the up-country farmers making milk runs to the separator at the other end of town."

"What about the other two?"

"One was a Caddy. I seen it around a few times. Remember it because it had one side dented in. The other was that Grange dame's two-door sedan. Guess she was out wolfing." He laughed at that.

"Grange?"

"Yeah, the old bag that works out at York's place. She's a stiff one."

"Thanks for the info, kid." I slipped him a buck and he grinned. "By the way, did you pass that on to the cops too?"

"Not me. I wouldn't give them the right time."

"Why?"

"Lousy bunch of bastards." He explained it in a nutshell without going into detail.

I hopped in and started up, but before I drove off I stuck my head out the window. "Where's this Grange babe live?"

"At the Glenwood Apartments. You can't miss it. It's the only apartment house in this burg."

Well, it wouldn't hurt to drop up and see her anyway. Maybe she had been on her way home from work. I gunned the engine and got back on the main drag, driving slowly past the shaded fronts of the stores. Just outside the business section a large green canopy extended from the curb to the marquee of a modern three-story building. Across the side in small, neat letters was GLEN-WOOD APARTMENTS. I crawled in behind a black Ford sedan and hopped out.

Grange, Myra, was the second name down. I pushed the bell and waited for the buzzer to unlatch the door. When it didn't come I pushed it again. This time there was a series of clicks and I shoved the door open. One flight of stairs put me in front of her apartment. Before I could ring, the metal peephole was pulled back and a pair of dark eyes threw insults at me.

"Miss Grange?"

"Yes."

"I'd like to speak to you if you can spare a few moments."

"Very well, go ahead." Her voice sounded as if it came out of a tree trunk. This made the third person I didn't like in Sidon.

"I work for York," I explained patiently. "I'd like to speak to you about the boy."

"There's nothing I care to discuss."

Why is it that some dames can work me up into a lather so fast with so little is beyond me, but this one did. I quit playing around. I pulled out the .45 and let her get a good look at it. "You open that door or I'll shoot the lock off," I said.

She opened it. The insults in her eyes turned to terror until I put the rod back under cover. Then I looked at her. If she was an old bag I was Queen of the May. Almost as tall as I was, nice brown hair cut short enough to be nearly mannish and a figure that seemed to be well molded, except that I couldn't tell too well because she was wearing slacks and a house jacket. Maybe she was thirty, maybe forty. Her face had a built-in lack of expression like an old painting. Wearing no makeup didn't help it any, but it didn't hurt, either.

I tossed my hat on a side table and went inside without being invited. Myra Grange followed me closely, letting her wooden-soled sandals drag along the carpet. It was a nice dump, but small. There was something to it that didn't sit right, as though the choice of furniture didn't fit her personality. Hell, maybe she just sublet.

The living room was ultramodern. The chairs and the couch were surrealist dreams of squares and angles. Even the coffee table was balanced precariously on little pyramids that served as legs. Two framed wood nymphs seemed cold in their nudity against the background of the chilled blue walls. I wouldn't live in a room like this for anything.

Myra held her position in the middle of the floor, legs spread, hands shoved in her side pockets. I picked a leather-covered ottoman and sat down.

She watched every move I made with eyes that scarcely concealed her rage. "Now that you've forced your way in here," she said between tight lips, "perhaps you'll explain why, or do I call the police?"

"I don't think the police would bother me much, kiddo." I pulled my badge from my pocket and let her see it. "I'm a private dick myself."

"Go on." She was a cool tomato.

"My name is Hammer. Mike Hammer. York wants me to find the kid. What do you think happened?"

"I believe he was kidnapped, Mr. Hammer. Surely that is evident."

"Nothing's evident. You were seen on the road fairly late the night the boy disappeared. Why?"

Instead of answering me she said, "I didn't think the time of his disappearance was established."

"As far as I'm concerned it is. It happened that night. Where were you?"

She began to raise herself up and down on her toes like a British major. "I was right here. If anyone said he saw me that night he was mistaken."

"I don't think he was." I watched her intently. "He's got sharp eyes."

"He was mistaken," she repeated.

"All right, we'll let it drop there. What time did you leave York's house?"

"Six o'clock, as usual. I came straight home." She began to kick at the rug impatiently, then pulled a cigarette from a pocket and stuck it in her mouth. Damn it, every time she moved she did something that was familiar to me but I couldn't place it. When she lit the cigarette she sat down on the couch and watched me some more.

"Let's quit the cat and mouse, Miss Grange. York said you were like a mother to the kid and I should suppose you'd like to see him safe. I'm only trying to do what I can to locate him."

"Then don't classify me as a suspect, Mr. Hammer."

"It's strictly temporary. You're a suspect until you alibi yourself satisfactorily then I won't have to waste my time and yours fooling around."

"Am I alibied?"

"Sure," I lied. "Now can you answer some questions civilly?"

"Ask them."

"Number one. Suspicious characters loitering about the house anytime preceding the disappearance."

She thought a moment, furrowing her eyebrows. "None that I can recall. Then again, I am inside all day working in the lab. I wouldn't see anyone."

"York's enemies. Do you know them?"

"Rudolph . . . Mr. York has no enemies I know of. Certain persons working in the same field have expressed what you might call professional jealousy, but that is all."

"To what extent?"

She leaned back against the cushions and blew a smoke ring at the ceiling. "Oh, the usual bantering at the clubs. Making light of his work. You know."

I didn't know anything of the kind, but I nodded. "Anything serious?"

"Nothing that would incite a kidnapping. There were heated discussions, yes, but few and far between. Mr. York was loath to discuss his work. Besides, a scientist is not a person who would resort to violence."

"That's on the outside. Let's hear a little bit about his family. You've been connected with York long enough to pick up a little something on his relatives."

"I'd rather not discuss them, Mr. Hammer. They are none of my affair."

"Don't be cute. We're talking about a kidnapping."

"I still don't see where they could possibly enter into it."

"Damn it," I exploded, "you're not supposed to. I want information and everybody wants to play repartee. Before long I'm going to start choking it out of people like you."

"Please, Mr. Hammer, that isn't necessary."

"So I've been told. Then give."

"I've met the family very often. I know nothing about them although they all try to press me for details of our work. I've told them nothing. Needless to say, I like none of them. Perhaps that is a biased opinion but it is my only one."

"Do they feel the same toward you?"

"I imagine they are very jealous of anyone so closely connected with Mr. York as I am," she answered with a caustic grimace. "You might surmise that of any rich man's relatives. However, for your information and unknown to them, I enjoy a personal income outside the salary Mr. York pays me and I am quite unconcerned with the disposition of his fortune in the event that anything should happen to him. The only possession he has that I am interested in is the boy. I have been with him all his life, and as you say, he is like a son to me. Is there anything else?"

"Just what is York's work . . . and yours?"

"If he hasn't told you, I'm not at liberty to. Naturally, you realize that it centered around the child."

"Naturally." I stood up and looked at my watch. It was nine fifteen. "I think that covers it, Miss Grange. Sorry to set you on your ear to get in, but maybe I can make it up sometime. What do you do nights around here?"

Her eyebrows went up and she smiled for the first time. It was more of a stifled laugh than a smile and I had the silly feeling that the joke was on me. "Nothing you'd care to do with me," she said.

I got sore again and didn't know why. I fought a battle with the look, stuck my hat on and got out of there. Behind me I heard a muffled chuckle.

The first thing I did was make a quick trip back to the filling station. I waited until a car pulled out then drove up to the door. The kid recognized me and waved. "Any luck?" he grinned.

"Yeah, I saw her. Thought she was an old bag?"

"Well, she's a stuffy thing. Hardly ever speaks."

"Listen," I said, "are you sure you saw her the other night?"

"Natch, why?"

"She said no. Think hard now. Did you see her or the car?"

"Well, it was her car. I know that. She's the only one that ever drives it."

"How would you know it?"

"The aerial. It's got a bend in it so it can only be telescoped down halfway. Been like that ever since she got the heap."

"Then you can't be certain she was in it. You wouldn't swear to it?"

"Well . . . no. Guess not when you put it that way. But it was her car," he insisted.

"Thanks a lot." I shoved another buck at him. "Forget I was around, will you?"

"Never saw you in my life," he grinned. Nice kid.

This time I took off rather aimlessly. It was only to pacify York that I left the house in the first place. The rain had let up and I shut off the windshield wipers while I turned onto the highway and cruised north toward the estate. If the snatch ran true to form there would be a letter or a call sometime soon. All I could do would be to advise York to follow through to get the kid back again then go after the ones that had him.

If it weren't for York's damn craving for secrecy I could buzz the state police and have a seven-state alarm sent out, but that meant the house would crawl with cops. Let a spotter get a load of that and they'd dump the kid and that'd be the end of it until some campers came across his remains sometime. As long as the local police had a sizable reward to shoot for they wouldn't let it slip. Not after York told them not to.

I wasn't underestimating Dilwick any. I'd bet my bottom dollar he'd had York's lines tapped already, ready to go to town the moment a call came through. Unless I got that call at the same time I was liable to get scratched. Not me, brother. Ten G's was a lot of mazuma in any language.

The lights were still on en masse when I breezed by the estate. It was still too early to go back, and as long as I could keep the old boy happy by doing a little snooping I figured I was earning my keep, at least. About ten miles down the highway the town of Bayview squatted along the water's edge waiting for summer to liven things up.

A kidnap car could have gone in either direction, although this route was unlikely. Outside Bayview the highway petered off into a tar road that completely disappeared under drifting winter sands. Anything was worth trying, though. I dodged an old flivver that was standing in the middle of the road and swerved into the gravel parking place of a two-bit honky-tonk. The place was badly run-down at the heels and sadly in need of a paint job. A good deodorant would have helped, too. I no sooner got my foot on the rail when a frowsy blonde sidled up to me and I got a quick once-over. "You're new around here, ain't you?"

"Just passing through."

"Through to where? That road outside winds up in the drink."

"Maybe that's where I'm going."

"Aw now, Buster, that ain't no way to feel. We all got our troubles but you don't wanna do nothing like that. Lemme buy you a drink, it'll make you feel better."

She whistled through her teeth and when that got no response, cupped her hands and yelled to the bartender who was busy shooting trap on the bar. "Hey, Andy, get your tail over here and serve your customers."

Andy took his time. "What'll you have, pal?"

"Beer."

"Me too."

"You too nothing. Beat it, Janie, you had too much already."

"Say, see here, I can pay my own way."

"Not in my joint."

I grinned at the two of them and chimed in. "Give her a beer why don't you?"

"Listen, pal, you don't know her. She's half tanked already. One more and she'll be making like a Copa cutie. Not that I don't like the Copa, but the dames there are one thing and she's another, just like night and day. Instead of watching, my customers all get the dry heaves and trot down to Charlie's on the waterfront."

"Well, I like that!" Janie hit an indignant pose and waved her finger in Andy's face. "You give me my beer right now or I'll make better'n the Copa. I'll make like . . . like . . ."

"Okay, okay, Janie, one more and that's all."

The bartender drew two beers, took my dough instead of Janie's and rang it up. I put mine away in one gulp. Janie never reached completely around her glass. Before Andy could pick out the change Janie had spilled hers halfway down the bar.

Andy said something under his breath, took the glass away then fished around under the counter for a rag. He started to mop up the mess.

I watched. In my head the little bells were going off, slowly at first like chimes on a cold night. They got louder and louder, playing another scrambled, soundless symphony. A muscle in my neck twitched. I could almost feel that ten grand in my pocket already. Very deliberately I reached out across the bar and gathered a handful of Andy's stained apron in my fist. With my other hand I yanked out the .45 and held it an inch away from his eye. He was staring death in the face and knew it.

I had trouble keeping my voice down. "Where did you get that bar rag, Andy?"

His eyes shifted to the blue-striped pajama bottoms that he held in his hand, beer soaked now, but recognizable. The other half to them were in Ruston York's bedroom hanging on the foot of the bed.

Janie's mouth was open to scream. I pointed the gun at her and said, "Shut up." The scream died before it was born. She held the edge of the bar with both hands, shaking like a leaf. Ours was a play offstage; no one saw it, no one cared. "Where, Andy?"

". . . Don't know, mister. Honest . . ."

I thumbed the hammer back. He saw me do it. "Only one more chance, Andy. Think hard."

His breath came in little jerks, fright thickened his tongue. "Some . . . guy. He brought it in. Wanted to know . . . if they were mine. It . . . was supposed to be a joke. Honest, I just use it for a bar rag, that's all."

"When?"

". . . 's afternoon."

"Who, Andy?"

"Bill. Bill Cuddy. He's a clam digger. Lives in a shack on the bay."

I put the safety back on, but I still held his apron. "Andy," I told him, "if you're leveling with me it's okay, but if you're not, I'm going to shoot your head off. You know that, don't you?"

His eyes rolled in his head then came back to meet mine. "Yeah, mister. I know. I'm not kidding. Honest, I got two kids . . ."

"And Janie here. I think maybe you better keep her with you for a while. I wouldn't want anyone to hear about this, understand?"

Andy understood, all right. He didn't miss a word. I let him go and he had to hang on to his bar to keep from crumbling. I slid the rod back under my coat, wrung out the pajamas and folded them into a square.

When I straightened my hat and tie I said, "Where is Cuddy's place?"

Andy's voice was so weak I could hardly hear it. "Straight . . . down the road to the water. Turn left. It's the deck . . . deckhouse of an old boat pulled up on the . . . beach."

I left them standing there like Hansel and Gretel in the woods, scared right down to their toes. Poor Andy. He didn't have anymore to do with it than I did, but in this game it's best not to take any chances.

As Janie had said, the road led right to the drink. I parked the car beside a boarded-up house and waded through the wet sand on foot. Ten feet from the water I turned left and faced a line of broken-down shacks that were rudely constructed from the junk that comes in on the tide. Some of them had tin roofs, with the advertisements for soft drinks and hot dogs still showing through.

Every once in a while the moon would shine through a rift in the clouds, and I took advantage of it to get a better look at the homemade village.

Cuddy's place was easier to find than I expected. It was the only dump that ever had seen paint, and on the south side hung a ship's nameplate with CARMINE spelled out in large block letters. It was a deckhouse, all right, probably washed off during a storm. I edged up to a window and looked in. All I could see were a few vague outlines. I tried the door. It opened outward noiselessly. From one corner of the room came the raspy snore of a back-sleeper with a load under his belt.

A match lit the place up. Cuddy never moved, even when I put the match to the ship's lantern swinging from the center of the ceiling. It was a one-room affair with a few chairs, a table and a double-decker bed along the side. He had rigged up a kerosene stove with the pipe shooting through the roof and used two wooden crates for a larder. Beside the stove was a barrel of clams.

Lots of stuff, but no kid.

Bill Cuddy was a hard man to awaken. He twitched a few times, pawed the covers and grunted. When I shook him some more his eye-lids flickered, went up. No pupils. They came down ten seconds later. A pair of bleary, bloodshot eyes moved separately until they came to an accidental focus on me.

Bill sat up. "Who're you?"

I gave him a few seconds to study me, then palmed my badge in front of his face. "Cop. Get up."

His legs swung to the floor, he grabbed my arm. "What's the matter, officer? I ain't been poachin'. All I got is clams, go look." He pointed to the barrel. "See?"

"I'm no game warden," I told him.

"Then whatcha want of me?"

"I want you for kidnapping. Murder maybe."

"Oh . . . No!" His voice was a hoarse croak. "But . . . I ain't killed nobody atall. I wouldn't do that."

He didn't have to tell me that. There are types that kill and he wasn't one of them. I didn't let him know I thought so.

"You brought a set of pajamas into Andy's place this afternoon. Where did you get them?"

He wrinkled his nose, trying to understand what I was talking about. "Pajamas?"

"You heard me."

He remembered then. His face relaxed into a relieved grin. "Oh, that. Sure, I found 'em lying on Shore Road. Thought I'd kid Andy with 'em."

"You almost kidded him to death. Put on your pants. I want you to show me the spot."

He stuck his feet into a pair of dungarees and pulled the suspenders over his bony shoulders, then dragged a pair of boots out from under the bed. A faded denim shirt and a battered hat and he was dressed. He kept shooting me sidewise glances, trying to figure it out but wasn't getting anyplace.

"You won't throw me in the jug, will you?"

"Not if you tell the truth."

"But I did."

"We'll see. Come on." I let him lead the way. The sand had drifted too deep along the road to take the car so we plodded along slowly, keeping away from the other shacks. Shore Road was a road in name only. It was a strip of wet Sahara that separated the tree line from the water. A hundred yards up and the shacks had more room between them. Bill Cuddy pointed ahead.

"Up there is the cove where I bring the boat in. I was coming down there and where the old cistern is I see the pants lying right in the middle of the road."

I nodded. A few minutes later we had reached the cistern, a huge, barrel-shaped thing lying on its side. It was big enough to make a two-car garage. Evidently it, like everything else around here, had been picked up during a storm and deposited along the shore. Bill indicated a spot on the ground with a gnarled forefinger.

"Right here's the spot, officer, they was lying right here."

"Fine. See anyone?"

"Naw. Who would be out here? They was washed up, I guess."

I looked at him, then the water. Although the tide was high the water was a good forty yards from the spot. He saw what I meant and he shifted uneasily.

"Maybe they blew up."

"Bill?"

"Huh?"

"Did you ever see wet clothes blow along the ground? Dry clothes, maybe, but wet?"

He paused. "Nope."

"Then they didn't blow up or wash up. Somebody dropped them there."

He got jittery then, his face was worried. "But I didn't do it. No kidding, I just found them there. They was new-looking so I brung 'em to Andy's. You won't jug me, will you? I . . ."

"Forget it, Bill. I believe you. If you want to keep your nose clean turn around and trot home. Remember this, though. Keep your mouth shut, you hear?"

"Gee, yeah. Thanks . . . thanks, officer. I won't say nothing to nobody." Bill broke into a fast shuffle and disappeared into the night.

Alone like that you can see that what you mistook for silence was really a jungle of undertones, subdued, foreign, but distinct. The wind whispering over the sand, the waves keeping time with a steady lap, lap. Tree sounds, for which there is no word to describe bark rubbing against bark, and the things that lived in the trees. The watch on my wrist made an audible tick.

Somewhere oars dipped into the water and scraped in the oar-locks. There was no telling how far away it was. Sounds over water carry far on the wind.

I tried to see into the night, wondering how the pajamas got there. A road that came from the cove and went nowhere. The trees and the bay. A couple of shacks and a cistern.

The open end faced away from me, making it necessary to push through yards of saw grass to reach it. Two rats ran out making ugly squeaking noises. When I lit a match I seemed to be in a hall of green slime. Droplets of water ran down the curved sides of the cistern and collected in a stinking pool of scum in the middle. Some papers had blown in, but that was all. The only things that left their footprints in the muck had tails. When I couldn't hold my breath any longer I backed out and followed the path I had made to the road.

Right back where I started. Twenty-five yards away was the remains of a shack. The roof had fallen in, the sides bulged out like it had been squeezed by a giant hand. Further down was another. I took the first one. The closer I came to it the worse it looked. Holes in the side passed for windows, the door hung open on one hinge and was wedged that way by a pile of sand that had blown around the corner. No tracks, no nothing. It was as empty as the cistern.

Or so I thought.

Just then someone whimpered inside. The .45 leaped into my hand. I took a few wooden matches, lit them all together and threw them inside and went in after them.

I didn't need my gun. Ruston York was all alone, trussed up like a Christmas turkey over in the corner, his naked body covered with bruises.

In a moment I was on my knees beside him, working the knots loose. I took it easy on the adhesive tape that covered his mouth so I wouldn't tear the skin off. His body shook with sobs. Tears of fright and relief filled his large, expressive eyes, and when he had his arms free he threw them around my neck. "Go ahead and cry, kid," I said.

He did, then. Hard, body-racking gasps that must have hurt. I wiggled out of my jacket and put it around him, talking quickly and low to comfort him. The poor kid was a mess.

It came with jarring suddenness, that sound. I shoved the kid on his back and pivoted on my heels. I was shooting before I completed the turn. Someone let out a short scream. A heavy body crashed into my chest and slammed my back against the wall. I kicked out with both feet and we spilled to the floor. Before I could get my gun up a heavy boot ripped it out of my hand.

They were all over me. I gave it everything I had, feet, fingernails and teeth, there wasn't enough room to swing. Somehow I managed to hook my first two fingers in a mouth and yank, and I felt a cheek rip clear to the ear.

There was no more for me. Something smashed down on my skull and I stopped fighting. It was a peaceful feeling, as if I were completely adrift from my body. Feet thudded into my ribs and pounded my back raw, but there was no pain, merely vague impressions. Then even the impressions began to fade.

CHAPTER 3

I came back together like a squadron of flak-eaten bombers re-forming. I heard the din of their motors, a deafening, pulsating roar that grew louder and louder. Pieces of their skin, fragments of their armor drifted to earth and imbedded themselves in my flesh until I thought I was on fire.

Bombs thudded into the earth and threw great flashes of flame into my face and rocked my body back and forth, back and forth. I opened my eyes with an effort.

It was the kid shaking me. "Mister. Can you get up? They all ran away looking for me. If you don't get up they'll be back and find us. Hurry, please hurry."

I tried to stand up, but I didn't do too good a job. Ruston York got his arms around me and boosted. Between the two of us I got my feet in position where I could shove with my legs and raise myself. He still had on my coat, but that was all.

I patted his shoulder. "Thanks, kid. Thanks a lot."

It was enough talk for a while. He steered me outside and up into the bushes along the trees where we melted into the darkness. The sand muffled our footsteps well. For once I was grateful for the steady drip of rain from the trees; it covered any other noises we made.

"I found your gun on the floor. Here, do you want it?" He held the .45 out gingerly by the handle. I took it in a shaking hand and stowed it in the holster. "I think you shot somebody. There's an awful lot of blood by the door."

"Maybe it's mine," I grunted.

"No, I don't think so. It's on the wall, too, and there's a big hole in the wall where it looks like a bullet went through."

I prayed that he was right. Right now I half hoped they'd show again so I could have a chance to really place a few where they'd hurt.

I don't know how long it took to reach the car, but it seemed like hours. Every once in a while I thought I could discern shouts and guarded words of caution. By the time Ruston helped slide me under the wheel I felt as though I had been on the Death March.

We sat there in silence a few moments while I fumbled for a cigarette. The first drag was worth a million dollars. "There's a robe in the back," I told the kid. He knelt on the seat, got it and draped it over his legs.

"What happened?"

"Gosh, mister, I hardly know. When you pushed me away I ran out the door. The man I think you shot nearly grabbed me, but he didn't. I hid behind the door for a while. They must have thought I ran off because when they followed me out one man told the others to scatter and search the beach, then he went away too. That's when I came in and got you."

I turned the key and reached for the starter. It hurt. "Before that. What happened then?"

"You mean the other night?"

"Yeah."

"Well, I woke up when the door opened. I thought maybe it was Miss Malcom. She always looks in before she goes to bed, but it wasn't her. It was a man. I wanted to ask him who he was when he hit me. Right here." Ruston rubbed the top of his head and winced.

"Which door did he come in?"

"The one off the hall, I think. I was pretty sleepy."

Cute. Someone sneaks past the guard at the gate, through a houseful of people and puts the slug on the kid and walks off with him.

"Go on." While he spoke I let in the clutch and swung around, then headed the car toward the estate.

"I woke up in a boat. They had me in a little room and the door was locked. I could hear the men talking in the stern and one called the man who was steering Mallory. That's the only time I heard a name at all."

The name didn't strike any responsive chord as far as I was concerned, so I let him continue.

"Then I picked the lock and . . ."

"Wait a second, son." I looked at him hard. "Say that again."

"I picked the lock. Why?"

"Just like that you picked the lock. No trouble to it or anything?"

"Uh-uh." He flashed a boyish grin at me, shyly. "I learned all about locks when I was little. This one was just a plain lock."

He *must* be a genius. It takes me an hour with respectable burglar tools to open a closet door.

". . . and as soon as I got out I opened a little hatch and crawled up on the deck. I saw the lights from shore and jumped overboard. Boy, was that water cold. They never even heard me at all. I nearly made it at that. After I jumped the boat kept right on going and disappeared, but I guess they found the door open down below. I should have locked it again but I was sort of scared and forgot. Just when I got up on the shore some man came running at me and they had me again. He said he'd figured I'd head for the lights, then he slapped me. He was waiting for the others to come and he made me go into the shack with him. Seems like they tied up in the cove and had to wait awhile before they could take me back to the boat.

"He had a bottle and started drinking from it, and pretty soon he was almost asleep. I waited until he was sort of dopey then threw my pajama pants out the window with a rock in them hoping someone would find them. He never noticed what I did. But he did know he was getting drunk, and he didn't have any more in the bottle. He hit me a few times and I tried to get away. Then he really gave it to me. When he got done he took some rope and tied me up and went down the beach after the others. That was when you came in."

"And I went out," I added.

"Gee, mister, I hope you didn't get hurt too badly." His face was anxious, truly anxious. It's been a long time since someone worried about me getting hurt. I ran my fingers through his hair and shook his head gently.

"It isn't too bad, kid," I said. He grinned again, pulled the robe tighter and moved closer to me. Every few seconds he'd throw me a searching glance, half curious, half serious.

"What's your name?"

"Mike Hammer."

"Why do you carry a gun?"

"I'm a detective, Ruston. A private detective."

A sigh of relief escaped him. He probably figured me for one of the mob who didn't like the game, I guess.

"How did you happen to find me?"

"I was looking for you."

"I'm . . . I'm glad it was you, Mr. Hammer, and not somebody else. I don't think anyone would have been brave enough to do what you did."

I laughed at that. He was a good kid. If any bravery was involved he had it all. Coming back in after me took plenty of nerve. I told him so, but he chuckled and blushed. Damn, you couldn't help but like him. In spite of a face full of bruises and all the hell he had been through he could still smile. He sat there beside me completely at ease, watching me out of the corner of his eye as though I was a tin god or something.

For a change some of the lights were off in the house. Henry, the gatekeeper, poked a flashlight in the car and his mouth fell open. All he got out was, "M . . . Master Ruston!"

"Yeah, it's him. Open the gates." He pulled a bar at the side and the iron grillwork rolled back. I pushed the buggy through, but by the time I reached the house Henry's call had the whole family waiting on the porch.

York didn't even wait until I stopped. He yanked the door open and reached for his son. Ruston's arms went around his neck and he kept repeating, "Dad . . . Dad."

I wormed out of the car and limped around to the other side. The family was shooting questions at the kid a mile a minute and completely ignored me, not that it mattered. I shoved them aside and took York by the arm. "Get the kid in the house and away from this mob. He's had enough excitement for a while."

The scientist nodded. Ruston said, "I can walk, Dad." He held the robe around himself and we went in together.

Before the others could follow, York turned. "If you don't mind, please go to your rooms. You will hear what happened in the morning."

There was no disputing who was master in that house. They looked at one another then slouched off in a huff. I drew a few nasty looks myself.

I slammed the door on the whole pack of them and started for the living room, but Harvey interrupted me en route. Having once disrupted his composure, events weren't likely to do it a second time. When he handed me the tray with the diagram of the bedroom layout neatly worked up he was the perfect flunky.

"The guest plan, sir," he said. "I trust it is satisfactory?"

I took it without looking at it and thanked him, then stuck it in my pocket.

York was in an anteroom with his son. The kid was stretched out on a table while his father went over each bruise carefully, searching for abrasions. Those he daubed with antiseptic and applied small bandages. This done he began a thorough examination in the most professional manner.

When he finished I asked, "How is he?"

"All right, apparently," he answered, "but it will be difficult to tell for a few days. I'm going to put him to bed now. His physical condition has always been wonderful, thank goodness."

He wrapped Ruston in a robe and rang for Harvey. I picked up the wreckage that was my coat and slipped into it. The butler came in and at York's direction, picked the kid up and they left the room. On the way out Ruston smiled a good-night at me over the butler's shoulder.

York was back in five minutes. Without a word he pointed at the table and I climbed on. By the time he finished with me I felt like I had been in a battle all over again. The open cuts on my face and back stung from iodine, and with a few layers of six-inch tape around my ribs I could hardly breathe. He told me to get up in a voice shaky from suppressed emotion, swallowed a tablet from a bottle in his kit and sat down in a cold sweat.

When I finished getting dressed I said, "Don't you think you ought to climb into the sack yourself? It's nearly daybreak."

He shook his head. "No. I want to hear about it. Everything. Please, if you don't mind . . . the living room."

We went in and sat down together. While I ran over the story he poured me a stiff shot of brandy and I put it away neat.

"I don't understand it. Mr. Hammer . . . it is beyond me."

"I know. It doesn't seem civilized, does it?"

"Hardly." He got up and walked over to a Sheraton secretary, opened it and took out a book. He wrote briefly and returned waving ten thousand dollars in my face. "Your fee, Mr. Hammer. I scarcely need say how grateful I am."

I tried not to look too eager when I took that check, but ten G's is ten G's. As unconcernedly as I could, I shoved it in my wallet. "Of course, I suppose you want me to put a report in to the state police," I remarked. "They ought to be able to tie into that crew, especially with the boat. A thing like that can't be hidden very easily."

"Yes, yes, they will have to be apprehended. I can't imagine why they chose to abduct Ruston. It's incredible."

"You are rich, Mr. York. That is the primary reason."

"Yes. Wealth does bring disadvantages sometimes, though I have tried to guard against it."

I stood up. "I'll call them then. We have one lead that might mean something. One of the kidnappers was called Mallory. Your boy brought that up."

"What did you say?"

I repeated it.

His voice was barely audible. "Mallory . . . No!"

As if in a trance he hurried to the side of the fireplace. A pressure on some concealed spring-activated hidden mechanism and the side swung outward. He thrust his hand into the opening. Even at this distance I could see him pale. He withdrew his hand empty. A muscular spasm racked his body. He pressed his hands against his chest and sagged forward. I ran over and eased him into a chair.

"Vest . . . pocket."

I poked my fingers under his coat and brought out a small envelope of capsules. York picked one out with trembling fingers and put it on his tongue. He swallowed it, stared blankly at the wall. Very slowly a line of muscles along his jaw hardened into knots, his lips curled back in an animal-like snarl. "The bitch," he said, "the dirty man-hating bitch has sold me out."

"Who, Mr. York? Who was it?"

He suddenly became aware of me standing there. The snarl

faded. A hunted-quarry look replaced it. "I said nothing, you understand? Nothing."

I dropped my hand from his shoulder. I was starting to get a dirty taste in my mouth again. "Go to hell," I said, "I'm going to report it."

"You wouldn't dare!"

"Wouldn't I? York, old boy, that son of yours pulled me out of a nasty mess. I like him. You hear that? I like him more than I do a lot of people. If you want to expose him to more danger that's your affair, but I'm not going to have it."

"No . . . that's not it. This can't be made public."

"Listen, York, why don't you stow that publicity stuff and think of your kid for a change? Keep this under your hat and you'll invite another snatch and maybe you won't be so lucky. Especially," I added, "since somebody in your household has sold you out."

York shuddered from head to foot.

"Who was it, York? Who's got the bull on you?"

"I . . . have nothing to say."

"No? Who else knows you're counting your hours because of those radiation burns? What's going to happen to the kid when you kick off?"

That did it. He turned a sick color. "How did you find out about that?"

"It doesn't matter. If I know it others probably do. You still didn't tell me who's putting the squeeze on you."

"Sit down, Mr. Hammer. Please."

I pulled up a chair and parked.

"Could I," he began, "retain you as sort of a guardian instead of reporting this incident? It would be much simpler for me. You see, there are certain scientific aspects of my son's training that you, as a layman, would not understand, but if brought to light under the merciless scrutiny of the newspapers and a police investigation might completely ruin the chances of a successful result.

"I'm not asking you to understand, I'm merely asking that you cooperate. You will be well paid, I assure you. I realize that my son is in danger, but it will be better if we can repel any danger rather than prevent it at its source. Will you do this for me?"

Very deliberately I leaned back in my chair and thought it over. Something stunk. It smelled like Rudolph York. But I still owed the kid a debt.

"I'll take it, York, but if there's going to be trouble I'd like to know where it will come from. Who's the man-hating turnip that has you in a brace?"

His lips tightened. "I'm afraid I cannot reveal that, either. You need not do any investigating. Simply protect my interests, and my son."

"Okay," I said as I rose. "Have it your own way. I'll play dummy. But right now I'm going to beat the sheet. It's been a tough day. You'd better hit it yourself."

"I'll call Harvey."

"Never mind, I'll find it." I walked out. In the foyer I pulled the diagram out of my pocket and checked it. The directions were clear enough. I went upstairs, turned left at the landing and followed the hand-carved balustrade to the other side. My room was next to last and my name was on white cardboard, neatly typed, and framed in a small brass holder on the door. I turned the knob, reached for the light and flicked it on.

"You took long enough getting here."

I grinned. I wondered what Alice Nichols had used as a bribe to get Harvey to put me in next to her. "Hello, kitten."

Alice smiled through a cloud of smoke. "You were better-looking the last time I saw you."

"So? Do I need a shave?"

"You need a new face. But I'll take you like you are." She shrugged her shoulders and the spiderweb of a negligee fell down to her waist. What she had on under it wasn't worth mentioning. It looked like spun moonbeams with a weave as big as chicken wire. "Let's go to bed."

"Scram, kitten. Get back in your own hive."

"That's a corny line, Mike, don't play hard to get."

I started to climb out of my clothes. "It's not a line, kitten, I'm beat."

"Not that much."

I draped my shirt and pants over the back of the chair and

flopped in the sack. Alice stood up slowly. No, that's not the word. It was more like a low-pressure spring unwinding. The negligee was all the way off now. She was a concert of savage beauty.

"Still tired?"

"Turn off the light when you go out, honey." Before I rolled over she gave me a malicious grin. It told me that there were other nights. The lights went out. Before I corked off one thought hit me. It couldn't have been Alice Nichols he had meant when he called some babe a man-hating bitch.

Going to sleep with a thought like that is a funny thing. It sticks with you. I could see Alice over and over again, getting up out of that chair and walking across the room, only this time she didn't even wear moonbeams. Her body was lithe, seductive. She did a little dance. Then someone else came into my dream, too. Another dame. This one was familiar, but I couldn't place her. She did a dance too, but a different kind. There was none of that animal grace, no fluid motion. She took off her clothes and moved about stiffly, ill at ease. The two of them started dancing together, stark naked, and this new one was leading. They came closer, the mist about their faces parted and I got a fleeting glimpse of the one I couldn't see before.

I sat bolt upright in bed. No wonder Miss Grange did things that bothered me. It wasn't the woman I recognized in her apartment, it was her motions. Even to striking a match toward her the way a man would. Sure, she'd be a man-hater, why not? She was a lesbian.

"Damn!"

I hopped out of bed and climbed into my pants. I picked out York's room from the diagram and tiptoed to the other side of the house. His door was partly opened. I tapped gently. No answer.

I went in and felt for the switch. Light flooded the room, but it didn't do me any good. York's bed had never been slept in. One drawer of his desk was half open and the contents pushed aside. I looked at the oil blot on the bottom of the drawer. I didn't need a second look at the hastily opened box of .32 cartridges to tell me what had been in there. York was out to do murder.

Time, time, there wasn't enough of it. I finished dressing on the way out. If anyone heard the door slam after me or the motor start up they didn't care much. No lights came on at all. I slowed up by the gates, but they were gaping open. From inside the house I could hear a steady snore. Henry was a fine gatekeeper.

I didn't know how much of a lead he had. Sometime hours ago my watch had stopped and I didn't reset it. It could have been too long ago. The night was fast fading away. I don't think I had been in bed a full hour.

On that race to town I didn't pass a car. The lights of the kid's filling station showed briefly and swept by. The unlit headlamps of parked cars glared in the reflection of my own brights and went back to sleep.

I pulled in behind a line of cars outside the Glenwood Apartments, switched off the engine and climbed out. There wasn't a sign of life anywhere. When this town went to bed it did a good job.

It was one time I couldn't ring doorbells to get in. If Ruston had been with me it wouldn't have taken so long; the set of skeleton keys I had didn't come up with the right answer until I tried two dozen of them.

The .45 was in my fist. I flicked the safety off as I ran up the stairs. Miss Grange's door was closed, but it wasn't locked; it gave when I turned the knob.

No light flared out the door when I kicked it open. No sound broke the funeral quiet of the hall. I stepped in and eased the door shut behind me.

Very slowly I bent down and unlaced my shoes, then put them beside the wall. There was no sense sending in an invitation. With my hand I felt along the wall until I came to the end of the hall. A switch was to the right. Cautiously, I reached around and threw it up, ready for anything.

I needn't have been so quiet. Nobody would have yelled. I found York, all right. He sat there grinning at me like a blooming idiot with the top of his head holding up a meat cleaver.

CHAPTER 4

Now it was murder. First it was kidnapping, then murder. There seems to be no end to crime. It starts off as a little thing, then gets bigger and bigger like an overinflated tire until it busts all to hell and gone.

I looked at him, the blood running red on his face, seeping out under the clots, dripping from the back of his head to the floor. It was only a guess, but I figured I had been about ten minutes too late.

The room was a mess, a topsy-turvy cell of ripped-up furniture and emptied drawers. The carpet was littered with trash and stuffing from the pillows. York still clutched a handful of papers, sitting there on the floor where he had fallen, staring blankly at the wall. If he had found what he was searching for it wasn't here now. The papers in his hand were only old receipted electric bills made out to Myra Grange.

First I went back and got my shoes, then I picked up the phone. "Give me the state police," I told the operator.

A Sergeant Price answered. I gave it to him briefly. "This is Mike Hammer, Sergeant," I said. "There's been a murder at the Glenwood Apartments and as far as I can tell it's only a few minutes old. You'd better check the highways. Look for a Ford two-door sedan with a bent radio antenna. Belongs to a woman named Myra Grange. Guy that's been bumped is Rudolph York. She works for him. Around thirty, I'd say, five-six or -seven, short hair, well built. Not a bad-looking tomato. No, I don't know what she was wearing. Yeah . . . yeah, I'll stay here. You want me to inform the city cops?"

The sergeant said some nasty things about the city boys and told me to go ahead.

I did. The news must have jarred the guy on the desk awake because he started yelling his fool head off all over the place. When he asked for more information I told him to come look for himself, grinned into the mouthpiece and hung up.

I had to figure this thing out. Maybe I could have let it go right then, but I didn't think that way. My client was dead, true, but he had overpaid me in the first place. I could still render him a little service gratis.

I checked the other rooms, but they were as scrambled as the first one. Nothing was in place anywhere. I had to step over piles of clothes in the bedroom that had been carefully, though hurriedly, turned inside out.

The kitchen was the only room not torn apart. The reason for that was easy to see. Dishes and pans crashing against the floor would bring someone running. Here York had felt around, moved articles, but not swept them clear of the shelves. A dumbwaiter door was built into the wall. It was closed and locked. I left it that way. The killer couldn't have left by that exit and still locked it behind him, not with a hook-and-eye clasp. I opened the drawers and peered inside. The fourth one turned up something I hadn't expected to see. A meat cleaver.

That's one piece of cutlery that is rarely duplicated in a small apartment. In fact, it's more or less outdated. Now there were two of them.

The question was: Who did York surprise in this room? No, it wasn't logical. Rather, who surprised York? It had to be that way. If York had burst in here on Grange there would have been a scene, but at least she would have been here too. It was hard picturing her stepping out to let York smash up the joint.

When York came in the place was empty. He came to kill, but finding his intended victim gone, forgot his primary purpose and began his search. Kill. Kill. That was it. I looked at the body again. What I looked for wasn't there anymore.

Somebody had swiped the dead man's gun.

Why? Damn these murderers anyway, why must they mess things up so? Why the hell can't they just kill and be done with it?

York sat there grinning for all he was worth, defying me to find the answer. I said, "Cut it out, pal. I'm on your side."

Two cleavers and a grinning dead man. Two cleavers, one in the kitchen and one in his head. What kind of a killer would use a cleaver? It's too big to put in a pocket, too heavy to swing properly unless you had a fairly decent wrist. It would have to be a man, no dame likes to kill when there's a chance of getting spattered with blood.

But Myra Grange . . . the almost woman. She was more half man. Perhaps her sensibilities wouldn't object to crunching a skull or getting smeared with gore. But where the hell did the cleaver come from?

York grinned. I grinned back. It was falling into place now. Not the motive, but the action of the crime, and something akin to motive. The killer knew York was on his way here and knew Grange was out. The killer carried the cleaver for several reasons. It might have just been handy. Having aimed and swung it was certain to do the job. It was a weapon to which no definite personality could be attached.

Above all things, it was far from being an accidental murder. I hate premeditation. I hate those little thoughts of evil that are suppressed in the mind and are being constantly superimposed upon by other thoughts of even greater evil until they squeeze out over the top and drive a person to the depths of infamy.

And this murder was premeditated. Perhaps that cleaver was supposed to have come from the kitchen, but no one could have gone past York to the kitchen without his seeing him, and York had a gun. The killer had chosen his weapon, followed York here and caught him in the act of rifling the place. He didn't even have to be silent about it. In the confusion of tearing the place apart York would never have noticed little sounds . . . until it was too late.

The old man half stooping over the desk, the upraised meat-ax, one stroke and it was over. Not even a hard stroke. With all that potential energy in a three-pound piece of razor-sharp steel, not much force was needed to deliver a killing blow. Instantaneous death, the body twisting as it fell to face the door and grin at the killer.

I got no further. There was a stamping in the hall, the door was pushed open and Dilwick came in like a summer storm. He didn't waste any time. He walked up to me and stood three inches away, breathing hard. He wasn't pretty to look at.

"I ought to kill you, Hammer," he grated.

We stood there in that tableau a moment. "Why don't you?"

"Maybe I will. The slightest excuse, any excuse. Nobody's going to pull that on me and get away with it. Not you or anybody."

I sneered at him. "Whenever you're ready, Dilwick, here or in the mayor's office, I don't care."

Dilwick would have liked to have said more, but a young giant in the gray and brown leather of the state police strode over to me with his hand out. "You Mike Hammer?" I nodded.

"Sergeant Price," he smiled. "I'm one of your fans. I had occasion to work with Captain Chambers in New York one time and he spent most of the time talking you up."

The lad gave me a bone-crushing handshake that was good to feel.

I indicated the body. "Here's your case, Sergeant."

Dilwick wasn't to be ignored like that. "Since when do the state police have jurisdiction over us?"

Price was nice about it. "Ever since you proved yourselves to be inadequately supplied with material . . . and men." Dilwick flushed with rage. Price continued, addressing his remarks to me. "Nearly a year ago the people of Sidon petitioned the state to assist in all police matters when the town in general and the county in particular was being used as a rendezvous and sporting place by a lot of out-of-state gamblers and crooks."

The state cop stripped off his leather gloves and took out a pad. He noted a general description of the place, time, then asked me for a statement. Dilwick focused his glare on me, letting every word sink in.

"Mr. York seemed extremely disturbed after his son had been returned to him. He . . ."

"One moment, Mr. Hammer. Where was his son?"

"He had been kidnapped."

"So?" Price's reply was querulous. "It was never reported to us."

"It was reported to the city police." I jerked my thumb at Dilwick. "He can tell you that."

Price didn't doubt me, he was looking for Dilwick's reaction. "Is this true?"

"Yes."

"Why didn't we hear about it?"

Dilwick almost blew his top. "Because we didn't feel like telling you, that's why." He took a step nearer Price, his fists clenched, but the state trooper never budged. "York wanted it kept quiet and that's the way we handled it, so what?"

It came back to me again. "Who found the boy?"

"I did." Dilwick was closer to apoplexy than ever. I guess he wanted that ten grand as badly as I did. "Earlier this evening I found the boy in an abandoned shack near the waterfront. I brought him home. Mr. York decided to keep me handy in case another attempt was made to abduct the kid."

Dilwick butted in. "How did you know York was here?"

"I didn't." I hated to answer him, but he was still the police. "I just thought he might be. The boy had been kicked around and I figured that he wanted Miss Grange in the house."

The fat cop sneered. "Isn't York big enough to go out alone anymore?"

"Not in his condition. He had an attack of some sort earlier in the evening."

Price said, "How did you find out he was gone, Mr. Hammer?"

"Before I went to sleep I decided to look in to see how he was. He hadn't gone to bed. I knew he'd mentioned Miss Grange and, as I said, figured he had come here."

Price nodded. "The door . . . ?"

"It was open. I came in and found . . . this." I swept my hand around. "I called you, then the city police. That's all."

Dilwick made a face and bared what was left of his front teeth. "It stinks."

So it did, but I was the only one who was sure of it.

"Couldn't it have been like this, Mr. Hammer." Dilwick emphasized the *mister* sarcastically. "You find the kid, York doesn't like to pay out ten thousand for hardly any work, he blows after you threaten him, only you followed him and make good the threat."

"Sure, it could," I said, "except that it wasn't." I poked a butt in my mouth and held a match to it. "When I kill people I don't have to use a meat hatchet. If they got a gun, I use a gun. If they don't I use my mitts." I shifted my eyes to the body. "I could kill him with my fingers. On bigger guys . . . I'd use both hands. But no cleaver."

"How did York get here, Mr. Hammer?"

"Drove, I imagine. You better detail a couple of boys to lock up his car. A blue '64 Caddy sedan."

Price called a man in plainclothes over with his forefinger and repeated the instructions. The guy nodded and left.

The coroner decided that it was time to get there with the photo guys and the wicker basket. For ten minutes they went around dusting the place and snapping flashes of the remains from all positions until they ran out of bulbs. I showed Price where I'd touched the wall and the switch so there wouldn't be a confusion of the prints. For the record he asked me if I'd give him a set of impressions. It was all right with me. He took out a cardboard over which had been spread a light paraffin of some sort and I laid both hands on it and pressed. Price wrote my name on the bottom, took the number off my license and stowed it back in his pocket.

Dilwick was busy going through the papers York had scattered about, but finding nothing of importance returned his attention to the body. The coroner had spread the contents of the pockets out on an end table and Price rifled through them. I watched over his shoulder. Just the usual junk: a key ring, some small change, a wallet with two twenties and four ones and membership cards for several organizations. Under the wallet was the envelope with the capsules.

"Anything missing?" Price asked.

I shook my head. "Not that I know of, but then, I never went through his pockets."

The body was stuffed into a wicker basket, the cleaver wrapped in a towel and the coroner left with his boys. More troopers came in with a few city guys tagging along and I had to repeat my story all over again. Standing outside the crowd was a lone newspaperman, writing like fury in a note pad. If this was New York they'd have to bar the doors to hold back the press. Just wait until the story reached the wires. This town wouldn't be able to hold them all.

Price called me over to him. "You'll be where I'll be able to reach you?"

"Yeah, at York's estate."

"Good enough. I'll be out sometime this morning."

"I'll be with him," Dilwick cut in. "You keep your nose out of things, too, understand?"

"Blow it," I said. "I know my legal rights."

I shoved my hat on and stamped my butt out in an ashtray. There was nothing for me here. I walked to the door, but before I could leave Price hurried after me. "Mr. Hammer."

"Yeah, Sergeant?"

"Will I be able to expect some cooperation from you?"

I broke out a smile. "You mean, if I uncover anything will I let you in on it, don't you?"

"That covers it pretty well." He was quite serious.

"Okay," I agreed, "but on one condition."

"Name it."

"If I come across something that demands immediate action, I'm going to go ahead on it. You can have it too as soon as I can get it to you, but I won't sacrifice a chance to follow a lead to put it in your hands."

He thought a moment, then, "That sounds fair enough. You realize, of course, that this isn't a permit to do as you choose. The reason I'm willing to let you help out is because of your reputation. You've been in this racket longer than I have, you've had the benefit of wide experience and are familiar with New York police methods. I know your history, otherwise you'd be shut out of this case entirely. Shorthanded as we are, I'm personally glad to have you help out."

"Thanks, Sergeant. If I can help, I will. But you'd better not let Dilwick get wise. He'd do anything to stymie you if he heard about this."

"That pig," Price grunted. "Tell me, what are you going to do?"

"The same thing you are. See what became of the Grange dame. She seems to be the key figure right now. You putting out a dragnet?"

"When you called, a roadblock was thrown across the highways. A seven-state alarm is on the Teletype this minute. She won't get far. Do you know anything of her personally?"

"Only that she's supposed to be the quiet type. York told me that she frequents the library a lot, but I doubt if you'll find her there. I'll see what I can pick up at the house. If I latch on to anything about her I'll buzz you."

I said so long and went downstairs. Right now the most important thing in my life was getting some sleep. I felt like I hadn't seen a pillow in months. A pair of young troopers leaned against the fender of a blue Caddy sedan parked down further from my heap. They were comparing notes and talking back and forth. I'd better remind Billy to come get it.

The sun was thumbing its nose at the night when I reached the estate. Early-morning trucks that the gas station attendant had spoken of were on the road to town, whizzing by at a good clip. I honked my horn at the gate until Henry came out, still chewing on his breakfast.

He waved. "So it was you. I wondered who opened the gates. Why didn't you get me up?"

I drove alongside him and waited until he swallowed. "Henry, did you hear me go out last night?"

"Me? Naw, I slept like a log. Ever since the kid was gone I couldn't sleep thinking that it was all my fault because I sleep so sound, but last night I felt pretty good."

"You must have. Two cars went out, the first one was your boss."

"York? Where'd he go?"

"To town."

He shifted uneasily from one foot to the other. "Do . . . do you think he'll be sore because I didn't hear him?"

I shook my head. "I don't think so. In fact, I don't think he wanted to be heard."

"When's he coming back?"

"He won't. He's dead." I left him standing there with his mouth open. The next time he'd be more careful of those gates.

I raced the engine outside the house and cut it. If that didn't wake everyone in the house the way I slammed the door did. Upstairs I heard a few indignant voices sounding off behind closed doors. I ran up the stairs and met Roxy at the top, holding a quilted robe together at her middle.

She shushed me with her hand. "Be quiet, please. The boy is still asleep." It was going to be hard on him when he woke up.

"Just get up, Roxy?"

"A moment ago when you made all the noise out front. What are you doing up?"

"Never mind. Everybody still around?"

"How should I know? Why, what's the matter?"

"York's been murdered."

Her hand flew to her mouth. For a long second her breath caught in her throat. "W . . . who did it?" she stammered.

"That's what I'd like to know, Roxy."

She bit her lip. "It . . . it was like we were talking about, wasn't it?"

"Seems to be. The finger's on Myra Grange now. It happened in her apartment and she took a powder."

"Well, what will we do?"

"You get the gang up. Don't tell them anything, just that I want to see them downstairs in the living room. Go ahead."

Roxy was glad to be doing something. She half ran to the far end of the hall and threw herself into the first room. I walked around to Ruston's door and tried it. Locked. Roxy's door was open and I went in that way, closing it behind me, then stepped softly to the door of the adjoining room and went in.

Ruston was fast asleep, a slight smile on his face as he played in his dreams. The covers were pulled up under his chin making him look younger than his fourteen years. I blew a wisp of hair away that had drifted across his brow and shook him lightly. "Ruston."

I rocked him again. "Ruston."

His eyes came open slowly. When he saw me he smiled. "Hello, Mr. Hammer."

"Call me Mike, kid, we're pals, aren't we?"

"You bet . . . Mike." He freed one arm and stretched. "Is it time to get up?"

"No, Ruston, not yet. There's something I have to tell you." I wondered how to put it. It wasn't easy to tell a kid that the father he loved had just been butchered by a blood-crazy killer.

"What is it? You look awfully worried, Mike, is something wrong?"

"Something is very wrong, kid, are you pretty tough?"

Another shy smile. "I'm not tough, not really. I wish I were, like people in stories."

I decided to give it to him the hard way and get it over with. "Your dad's dead, son."

He didn't grasp the meaning of it at first. He looked at me, puzzled, as though he had misinterpreted what I had said.

"Dead?"

I nodded. Realization came like a flood. The tears started in the corners. One rolled down his cheek. "No . . . he can't be dead. He can't be!" I put my arms around him for a second time. He hung on to me and sobbed.

"Oh . . . Dad. What happened to him, Mike? What happened?"

Softly, I stroked his head, trying to remember what my own father did with me when I hurt myself. I couldn't give him the details. "He's . . . just dead, Ruston."

"Something happened, I know." He tried to fight the tears, but it was no use. He drew away and rubbed his eyes. "What happened, Mike, please tell me?"

I handed him my handkerchief. He'd find out later, and it was better he heard it from me than one of the ghouls. "Someone killed him. Here, blow your nose." He blew, never taking his eyes from mine. I've seen puppies look at me that way when they've been kicked and didn't understand why.

"Killed? No . . . nobody would kill Dad . . . not my dad." I didn't say a word after that. I let it sink in and watched his face contort with the pain of the thought until I began to hurt in the chest myself.

For maybe ten minutes we sat like that, quietly, before the kid dried his eyes. He seemed older now. A thing like that will age anyone. His hand went to my arm. I patted his shoulder.

"Mike?"

"Yes, Ruston?"

"Do you think you can find the one who did it?"

"I'm going to try, kid."

His lips tightened fiercely. "I want you to. I wish I were big enough to. I'd shoot him, that's what I'd do!" He broke into tears again after that outburst. "Oh . . . Mike."

"You lay there, kid. Get a little rest, then when you feel better get dressed and come downstairs and we'll have a little talk. Think of something, only don't think of . . . that. It takes time to get over these things, but you will. Right now it hurts worse than anything in the world, but time will fix it up. You're tough, Ruston. After last night I'd say that you were the toughest kid that ever lived. Be tough now and don't cry anymore. Okay?"

"I'll try, Mike, honest, I'll try."

He rolled over in the bed and buried his face in the pillow. I unlocked his door to the hall and went out. I had to stick around now whether I wanted to or not. I promised the kid. And it was a promise I meant to keep.

Once before I made a promise, and I kept it. It killed my soul, but I kept it. I thought of all the blood that had run in the war, all that I had seen and had dripped on me, but none was redder or more repulsive than that blood I had seen when I kept my last promise.

CHAPTER 5

Their faces were those that stare at you from the walls of a museum: severe, hostile, expectant. They stood in various attitudes waiting to see what apology I had to offer for dragging them from their beds at this early hour.

Arthur Graham awkwardly sipped a glass of orange juice between swollen lips. His brother puffed nervously at a cigarette. The Ghents sat as one family in the far corner, Martha trying to be aloof as was Junior. Rhoda and her father felt conspicuous in their hurried dressing and fidgeted on the edge of their chairs.

Alice Nichols was . . . Alice. When I came into the living room she threw an eyeful of passion at me and said under her breath, "'Lo, lover." It was too early for that stuff. I let the bags under my eyes tell her so. Roxy, sporting a worried frown, stopped me to say that there would be coffee ready in a few minutes. Good. They were going to need it.

I threw the ball from the scrimmage line before the opposition could break through with any bright remarks. "Rudolph York is dead. Somebody parted his hair with a cleaver up in Miss Grange's apartment."

I waited.

Martha gasped. Her husband's eyes nearly popped out. Junior and Rhoda looked at each other. Arthur choked on his orange juice and William dropped his cigarette. Behind me Alice said, "Tsk, tsk."

The silence was like an explosion, but before the echo died away Martha Ghent recovered enough to say coldly, "And where was Miss Grange?"

I shrugged. "Your guess is as good as mine." I laid it on the table then. "It's quite possible that she had nothing to do with it. Could be that someone here did the slaughtering. Before long the police are going to pay us a little visit. It's kind of late to start fixing up an alibi, but if you haven't any, you'd better think of one, fast."

While they swallowed that I turned on my heel and went out to the kitchen. Roxy had the coffee on a tray and I lifted a cup and carried it into Billy's room. He woke up as soon as I turned the knob.

"Hi, Mike." He looked at the clock. "What're you doing up?"

"I haven't been to bed yet. York's dead."

"What!"

"Last night. Got it with a cleaver."

"Good night! What happens now?"

"The usual routine for a while, I guess. Listen, were you in the sack all this time?"

"Hell, yes. Wait a minute, Mike, you . . ."

"Can you prove it? I mean did anyone see you there?"

"No. I've been alone. You don't think . . ."

"Quit worrying, Billy. Dilwick will be on this case and he's liable to have it in for you. That skunk will get back at you if he can't at me. He's got what little law there is in this town on his side now. What I want to do is establish some way you can prove you were here. Think of any?"

He put his finger to his mouth. "Yeah, I might at that. Twice last night I thought I heard a car go out."

"That'd be York then me."

"Right after the first car, someone came downstairs. I heard 'em inside, then there was some funny sound like somebody coughing real softly, then it died out. I couldn't figure out what it was."

"That might do it if we can find out who came down. Just forget all about it until you're asked, understand?"

"Sure, Mike. Geez, why did this have to happen? I'll be out on my ear now." His head dropped into his hands. "What'll I do?"

"We'll think of something. If you feel okay you'd better get dressed. York's car is still downtown, and when the cops get done with it you'll have to drive it back."

I handed him the coffee and he drank it gratefully. When he

finished I took it away and went into the kitchen. Harvey was there drying his eyes on a handkerchief. He saw me and sniffed, "It's terrible, sir. Miss Malcom just told me. Who could have done such a thing?"

"I don't know, Harvey. Whoever it was will pay for it. Look, I'm going to climb into bed. When the police come, get me up, will you?"

"Of course, sir. Will you eat first?"

"No thanks, later."

I skirted the living room and pushed myself up the stairs. The old legs were tired out. The bedclothes were where I had thrown them, in a heap at the foot of the bed. I didn't even bother to take off my shoes. When I put my head down I didn't care if the house burned to the ground as long as nobody awakened me.

The police came and went. Their voices came to me through the veil of sleep, only partially coherent. Voices of insistence, voices of protest and indignation. A woman's voice raised in anger and a meeker man's voice supporting it. Nobody seemed to care whether I was there or not, so I let the veil swirl into a gray shroud that shut off all sounds and thoughts.

It was the music that woke me. A terrible storm of music that reverberated through the house like a hurricane, shrieking in a wonderful agony. There had never been music like that before. I listened to the composition, wondering. For a space of seconds it was a song of rage, then it dwindled to a dirge of sorrow. No bar or theme was repeated.

I slipped out of the bed and opened the door, letting the full force of it hit me. It was impossible to conceive that a piano could tell such a story as this one was telling.

He sat there at the keyboard, a pitiful little figure clad in a Prussian blue bathrobe. His head was thrown back, the eyes shut tightly as if in pain, his fingers beating notes of anguish from the keys.

He was torturing himself with it. I sat beside him. "Ruston, don't."

Abruptly, he ceased in the middle of the concert and let his head fall to his chest. The critics were right when they acclaimed him a genius. If only they could have heard his latest recital.

"You have to take it easy, kid. Remember what I told you."

"I know, Mike, I'll try to be better. I just keep thinking of Dad all the time."

"He meant a lot to you, didn't he?"

"Everything. He taught me so many things, music, art . . . things that it takes people so long to get to know. He was wonderful, the best dad ever."

Without speaking I walked him over to the big chair beside the fireplace and sat down on the arm of the chair beside him. "Ruston," I started, "your father isn't here anymore, but he wouldn't want you to grieve about it. I think he'd rather you went on with all those things he was teaching you, and be what he wanted you to be."

"I will be, Mike," he said. His voice lacked color, but it rang earnestly. "Dad wanted me to excel in everything. He often told me that a man never lived long enough to accomplish nearly anything he was capable of because it took too long to learn the fundamentals. That's why he wanted me to know all these things while I was young. Then when I was a doctor or a scientist maybe I would be ahead of myself, sort of."

He was better as long as he could talk. Let him get it out of his system, I thought. It's the only way. "You've done fine, kid. I bet he was proud of you."

"Oh, he was. I only wish he could have been able to make his report."

"What report?"

"To the College of Scientists. They meet every five years to turn in reports, then one is selected as being the best one and the winner is elected President of the College for a term. He wanted that awfully badly. His report was going to be on me."

"I see," I said. "Maybe Miss Grange will do it for him."

I shouldn't have said that. He looked up at me woefully. "I don't think she will, not after the police find her."

It hit me right between the eyes. "Who's been telling you things, kid?"

"The policemen were here this morning. The big one made us all tell where we were last night and everything. Then he told us about Miss Grange."

"What about her?"

"They found her car down by the creek. They think she drowned herself."

I could have tossed a brick through a window right then. "Harvey!" I yelled. "Hey, Harvey."

The butler came in on the double. "I thought I asked you to wake me up when the police got here. What the hell happened?"

"Yes, sir. I meant to, but Officer Dilwick suggested that I let you sleep. I'm sorry, sir, it was more an order than a request."

So that was how things stood. I'd get even with that fat slob. "Where is everybody?"

"After the police took their statements he directed the family to return to their own homes. Miss Malcom and Parks are bringing Mr. York's car home. Sergeant Price wished me to tell you that he will be at the headquarters on the highway this evening and he would like to see you."

"I'm glad someone would like to see me," I remarked. I turned to Ruston. "I'm going to leave, son. How about you go to your room until Roxy . . . I mean Miss Malcom gets here? Okay?"

"All right, Mike. Why did you call her Roxy?"

"I have pet names for everybody."

"Do you have one for me?" he asked, little lights dancing in his eyes.

"You bet."

"What?"

"Sir Lancelot. He was the bravest of the brave."

As I walked out of the room I heard him repeat it softly. "Sir Lancelot, the bravest of the brave."

I reached the low fieldstone building set back from the road at a little after eight. The sky was threatening again, the air chilly and humid. Little beads of sweat were running down the windshield on the side. A sign across the drive read, STATE POLICE HEAD-QUARTERS, and I parked beside it.

Sergeant Price was waiting for me. He nodded when I came in and laid down the sheaf of papers he was examining. I threw my hat on an empty desk and helped myself to a chair. "Harvey gave me your message," I said. "What's the story?"

He leaned back in the swivel seat and tapped the desk with a pencil. "We found Grange's car."

"So I heard. Find her yet?"

"No. The door was open and her body may have washed out. If it did we won't find it so easily. The tide was running out and would have taken the body with it. The river runs directly into the bay, you know."

"That's all supposition. She may not have been in the car."

He put the pencil between his teeth. "Every indication points to the fact that she was. There are clear tire marks showing where the car was deliberately wrenched off the road before the guardrails to the bridge. The car was going fast, besides. It landed thirty feet out in the water."

"That's not what you wanted to see me about?" I put in.

"You're on the ball, Mr. Hammer."

"Mike. I hate titles."

"Okay, Mike. What I want is this kidnapping deal."

"Figuring a connection?"

"There may be one if Grange was murdered."

I grinned. "You're on the ball yourself." Once again I went over the whole story, starting with Billy's call when he was arrested. He listened intently without saying a word until I was finished.

"What do you think?" he asked.

"Somebody's going to a lot of trouble."

"Do you smell a correlation between the two?"

I squinted at him. "I don't know . . . yet. That kidnapping came at the wrong time. A kidnapper wants money. This one never got away with his victim. Generally speaking, it isn't likely that a second try would be made on the same person, but York wanted the whole affair hushed up ostensibly for fear of the publicity it would bring. That would leave the kid open again. It is possible that the kidnapper, enraged at having his deal busted open, would hang around waiting to get even with York and saw his chance when he took off at that hour of the morning to see Grange."

Price shook out a cig from his pack and offered me one. "If that was the case, money would not have been the primary motive. A kidnapper who has muffed his snatch wants to get far away fast."

402 • THE MIKE HAMMER COLLECTION

I lit up and blew a cloud of smoke at the ceiling. "Sounds screwed up, doesn't it?" He agreed. "Did you find out that York didn't have long to live anyway?"

He seemed startled at the change of subject. "No. Why?"

"Let's do it this way," I said. "York was on the list. He had only a few years at best to live. At the bottom of every crime there's a motive no matter how remote, and nine times out of ten that motive is cold, hard cash. He's got a bunch of relations that have been hanging around waiting for him to kick the bucket for a long time. One of them might have known that his condition was so bad that any excitement might knock him off. That one arranges a kidnapping, then when it fails takes direct action by knocking off York, making it look like Grange did it, then kills Grange to further the case by making it appear that she was a suicide in a fit of remorse."

Price smiled gently. "Are you testing me? I could shoot holes in that with a popgun. Arranging for a kidnapping means that you invite blackmail and lose everything you tried to get. York comes into it somewhere along the line because he was searching for something in that apartment. Try me again."

I laughed. "No good. You got all the answers."

He shoved the papers across the desk to me. "There are the statements of everybody in the house. They seem to support each other pretty well. Nobody left the house according to them so nobody had a chance to knock off York. That puts it outside the house again."

I looked them over. Not much there. Each sheet was an individual statement and it barely covered a quarter of the page. Besides a brief personal history was the report that once in bed, each person had remained there until I called them into the living room that morning.

I handed them back. "Somebody's lying. Is this all you got?"

"We didn't press for information although Dilwick wanted to. Who lied?"

"Somebody. Billy Parks told me he heard someone come downstairs during the night."

"Could it have been you?"

"No, it was before I followed York."

"He made no mention of it to me."

"Probably because he's afraid somebody will refute it if he does just to blacken him. I half promised him I'd check on it first."

"I see. Did York take you into his confidence at any time?"

"Nope. I didn't know him that long. After the snatch he hired me to stick around until he was certain his son was safe."

Price threw the pencil on the desk. "We're climbing a tree," he said tersely. "York was killed for a reason. Myra Grange was killed for the same reason. I think that for the time being we'll concentrate our efforts on locating Grange's body. When we're sure of her death we can have something definite to work on. Meanwhile I'm taking it for granted that she is dead."

I stood up to leave. "I'm not taking anything for granted, Sergeant. If she's dead she's out of it; if not the finger is still on her. I'm going to play around a little bit and see what happens. What's Dilwick doing?"

"Like you. He won't believe she's dead until he sees her either."

"Don't underestimate that hulk," I told him. "He's had a lot of police work and he's shrewd. Too shrewd, in fact, that's why he was booted off the New York force. He'll be looking out for himself when the time comes. If anything develops I'll let you know."

"Do that. See you later."

That ended the visit. I went out to the car and sat behind the wheel a while, thinking. Kidnapping, murder, a disappearance. A house full of black sheep. One nice kid, an ex-stripper for a nurse and a chauffeur with a record. The butler, maybe the butler did it. Someday a butler would do it for a change. A distraught father who stuck his hand in a hole in the fireplace and found something gone. He sets out to kill and gets killed instead. The one he wanted to kill is gone, perhaps dead too. Mallory. That was the name that started the ball of murder rolling. But Mallory figured in the kidnapping.

Okay, first things first. The kidnapping was first and I'd take it that way. It was a hell of a mess. The only thing that could make it any worse was to have Grange show up with an airtight alibi. I hated to hold out on Price about Mallory, but if he had it Dilwick would have to get it too, and that would put the kibosh on me. Like hell. I promised the kid.

I shoved the car in gear and spun out on the highway. Initial clue, the cops call it, the hand that puts the hound on the trail, that's what I had to have. York thought it was in Grange's apartment. Find what he was searching for and you had the answer. Swell, let's find it.

This time I parked around the block. The rain had started again, a light mist that you breathed into your lungs and that dampened matches in your pocket. From the back of the car I pulled a slicker and climbed into it, turning the collar up high. I walked back to Main Street, crossed over to the side of the street opposite the apartment and joined the few late workers in their dash toward home.

I saw what I was looking for, a black, unmarked sedan occupied by a pair of cigar-smoking gentlemen who were trying their best to remain unnoticed. They did a lousy job. I circled the block until I was behind the apartment. A row of modest one-family houses faced me, their windows lighted with gaiety and cheer. Each house was flanked by a driveway.

Without waiting I picked the right one and turned down the cinder drive, staying to the side in the shadow of a hedgerow where the grass partially muffled my feet. Somehow I slipped between the garage and the hedges to the back fence without making too much of a racket. For ten minutes I stood that way, motionless. It wasn't a new experience for me. I remembered other pits of blackness where little brown men waited and threw jeers into our faces to draw us out. That was a real test of patience. This guy was easier. When another ten minutes passed the match lit his face briefly, then subsided into the ill-concealed glow of a cigarette tip.

Dilwick wasn't taking any chances on Myra Grange slipping back to her apartment. Or anyone else for that matter.

Once I had him spotted I kept my eyes a few feet to the side of him so I wouldn't lose him. Look directly at an object in the dark and you draw a blank spot. I went over the fence easily enough, then flanked the lookout by staying in the shadows again. By the time I reached the apartment building I had him silhouetted against the lights of another house. The janitor had very conveniently left a row of ash barrels stacked by the cellar entrance. I got up that close, at least. Six feet away on the other side of the gaping cavern of the entrance the law stood on flat feet, breathing heavily, cursing the rain under his breath.

My fingers snaked over the lip of a barrel, came away with a piece of ash the size of a marble. I balanced it on my thumb, then flipped it. I heard nothing, but he heard it and turned his head, that was all. I tried again with the same results. The next time I used a bigger piece. I got better results, too. He dropped the butt, ground it under his heel and walked away from the spot.

As soon as he moved I ducked around the barrels and down the stairs, then waited again, flattened against the wall. Finding nothing, the cop resumed his post. I went on tiptoes down the corridor, my hand out in front like a sleepwalker.

This part was going to take clever thinking. If they had both exits covered it was a sure bet that the apartment door was covered, too. I came to a bend in the tunnel and found myself in the furnace room. Overhead a dim bulb struggled against dust and cobwebs to send out a feeble glow. On the other side of the room a flight of metal steps led to the floor above. Sweet, but not practical. If I could make the roof I might be able to come down the fire escape, but that meant a racket or being seen by the occupants.

Right then I was grateful to the inventor of the dumbwaiter. The empty box yawned at me with a sleepy invitation. The smell was bad, but it was worth it. I climbed aboard and gave the rope a tentative pull to see if the pulleys squealed. They were well oiled. *Danke schön*, janitor. You get an *A*.

When I passed the first floor I was beginning to doubt whether I could make it all the way. Crouching there like that I had no leverage to bear on the ropes. It was all wrist motion. I took a hitch in the rope around the catch on the sliding door and rested a second, then began hauling away again. Somewhere above me voices passed back and forth. Someone yelled, "Put it on the dumbwaiter."

I held my breath. Let them catch me here and I was sunk. Dilwick would like nothing better than to get me on attempted burglary and work me over with a few of his boys.

A moment went by, two, then, "Later, honey, it's only half full."

Thanks, pal. Remind me to scratch your back. I got another grip on the rope and pulled away. By the time I reached Myra's door I was exhausted. Fortunately, one of the cops had forgotten to lock it after taking a peek down the well, not that it mattered. I didn't care whether anyone was inside or not. I shoved the two-bit door open and tumbled to the floor. I was lucky. The house was quiet as a tomb. If I ever see that trick pulled in a movie and the hero steps out looking fresh as a daisy I'll throw rocks at the screen. I lay there until I got my wind back.

The flash I used had the lens taped, so the only light it shed was a round disk the size of a quarter. I poked around the kitchen a bit taking it all in. Nobody had cleaned up since the murder as far as I could see. I went into the living room, avoiding the litter on the floor. The place was even worse than it was before. The police had finished what York had started, pulling drawers open further, tearing the pictures from the walls and scuffling up the rug.

But they hadn't found it. If they had I wouldn't've had to use the dumbwaiter to get in. Dilwick was better than shrewd. He was waiting for Grange to come back and find it for him.

Which meant that he was pretty certain Grange was alive. Dilwick knew something that Price and I didn't know, in that case.

In the first half hour I went through every piece of junk that had been dragged out without coming across anything worthwhile. I kicked at the pile and tried the drawers in the desk again. My luck stunk; Grange didn't go in for false bottoms or double walls. I thought of every place a dame hides things, but the cops had thought of them too. Every corner had been poked into, every closet emptied out. Women think of cute places like the hollows of bedposts and the inside of lamps, but the bedposts turned out to be solid and the lamps of modern transparent glass.

Hell, she had to have important things around. College degrees, insurance policies and that sort of stuff. I finally realized what was wrong. My psychology. Or hers. She only resembled a woman. She looked like one and dressed like one, physically, she was one, but Myra Grange had one of those twisted complexes. If she thought it was like a man. That was better. Being partially a woman she would want to secrete things; being part man she would hide them in a place not easily accessible, where it would take force, and not deduction, to locate the cache.

I started grinning then. I pulled the cabinets away from the walls and tried the sills of the doors. When I found a hollow behind the radiator I felt better. It was dust-filled and hadn't been used for some time, mainly because a hand reaching in there could be burned if the heat was on, but I knew I was on the right track.

It took time, but I found it when I was on my hands and knees, shooting light along the baseboards under the bed. It wasn't even a good job of concealment. I saw where a claw hammer had probably knocked a hole in the plaster behind it.

A package of envelopes held together by a large rubber band was the treasure. It was four inches thick, at least, with corners of stock certificates showing in the middle. A nice little pile.

I didn't waste time going through them then. I stuck the package inside my coat and buttoned the slicker over it. I had one end of the baseboard in place when I thought what a fine joke it would be to pull on slobbermouth to leave a calling card. With a wrench I pulled it loose, laid it on the floor where it couldn't be missed and got out to the kitchen. Let my fat friend figure that one out. He'd have the jokers at the doors shaking in their shoes by the time he was done with them.

The trip down was better. All I had to do was hang on and let the rope slide through my hands. Between the first floor and the basement I tightened up on the hemp and cut down the descent. It was a good landing, just a slight jar and I walked away from there. Getting out was easier than coming in. I poked my head out the cellar window on the side where the walk led around to the back and the concrete stared me in the face, gave a short whistle and called, "Hey, Mac."

It was enough. Heavy feet came pounding around the side and I made a dash up the corridor, out the door and dived into the bushes before the puzzled cop got back to his post scratching his head in bewilderment. The fence, the driveway, and I was in my car pulling up the street behind a trailer truck.

The package was burning a hole in my pocket. I turned down a side street where the neon of an open diner provided a stopping-off place, parked and went in and occupied a corner booth. When a skinny waiter in an oversized apron took my order I extracted the bundle. I rifled through the deck, ignoring the bonds and policies. I found what I was after.

It was York's will, made out two years ago, leaving every cent of his dough to Grange. If that female was still alive this put her on the spot for sure. Here was motive, pure, raw motive. A several-million-dollar motive, but it might as well be a can tied to her tail. She was a lucky one indeed if she lived to enjoy it.

Sloppy Joe came back with my hamburgers and coffee. I shelved the package while he dished out the slop, then forced it down my gullet, with the coffee as a lubricant. I was nearly through when I noticed my hands. They were dusty as hell. I noticed something else, too. The rubber band that had been around the package lay beside my coffee cup, stiff and rotted, and in two pieces.

Then I didn't get it after all, at least not what York was searching for. This package hadn't been opened for a hell of a long time, and it was a good bet that whatever had been in the fireplace had been there until the other night. The will had been placed in the package years ago.

Damn. Say it again, Mike, you outsmarted yourself that time. Damn.

CHAPTER 6

I set my watch by the clock on the corner while I waited for the light to change. Nine fifteen, and all was far from well. Just what the hell was it that threw York into a spasm? I knew damn well now that whatever it was, either Grange had it with her or she never had it at all. I was right back where I started from. Which left two things to be done. Find Mallory, or see who came downstairs the night of the murder and why that movement was denied in the statements. All right, let it be Mallory. Maybe Roxy could supply some answers. I pulled the will from the package and slipped it inside my jacket, then tossed the rest of the things in the back of the glove compartment.

Henry had the gates open as soon as I turned off the road. When he shut them behind me I called him over. "Anyone been here while I was gone?"

"Yes, sir. The undertaker came, but that was all."

I thanked him and drove up the drive. Harvey nodded solemnly when he opened the door and took my hat. "Have there been any developments, sir?"

"Not a thing. Where's Miss Malcom?"

"Upstairs, I believe. She took Master Ruston to his room a little while ago. Shall I call her for you?"

"Never mind, I'll go up myself."

I rapped lightly and opened the door at the same time. Roxy took a quick breath, grabbed the negligee off the bed and held it in front of her. That split second of visioning nudity that was classic beauty made the blood pound in my ears. I shut my eyes against it.

"Easy, Roxy," I said, "I can't see so don't scream and don't throw things. I didn't mean it."

She laughed lightly. "Oh, for heaven's sake, open them up. You've seen me like this before." I looked just as she tied the wrapper around her. That kind of stuff could drive a guy bats.

"Don't tempt me. I thought you'd changed?"

"Mike . . . don't say it that way. Maybe I have gone modest, but I like it better. In your rough way you respected it too, but I can't very well heave things at you for seeing again what you saw so many times before."

"The kid asleep?"

"I think so." The door was open a few inches, the other room dark. I closed it softly, then went back and sat on the edge of the bed. Roxy dragged the chair from in front of her vanity and set it down before me.

"Do I get sworn in first?" she asked with a fake pout.

"This is serious."

"Shoot."

"I'm going to mention a name to you. Don't answer me right away. Let it sink in, think about it, think of any time since you've been here that you might have heard it, no matter when. Roll it around on your tongue a few times until it becomes familiar, then if you recognize it tell me where or when you heard it and who said it . . . if you can."

"I see. Who is it?"

I handed her a cigarette and plucked one myself. "Mallory," I said as I lit it for her. I hooked my hands around my knee and waited. Roxy blew smoke at the floor. She looked up at me a couple of times, her eyes vacant with thought, mouthing the name to herself. I watched her chew on her lip and suck in a lungful of smoke.

Finally she rubbed her hand across her forehead and grimaced. "I can't remember ever having heard it," she told me. "Is it very important?"

"I think it might be. I don't know."

"I'm sorry, Mike." She leaned forward and patted my knee.

"Hell, don't take it to heart. He's just a name to me. Do you think any of the characters might know anything?"

"That I couldn't say. York was a quiet one, you know."

"I didn't know. Did he seem to favor any of them?"

She stood up and stretched on her toes. Under the sheer fabric little muscles played in her body. "As far as I could see, he had an evident distaste for the lot of them. When I first came here he apparently liked his niece, Rhoda. He remembered her with gifts upon the slightest provocation. Expensive ones, too. I know, I bought them for him."

I snubbed my butt. "Uh-huh. Did he turn to someone else?"

"Why, yes." She looked at me in faint surprise. "The other niece, Alice Nichols."

"I would have looked at her first to begin with."

"Yes, you would," she grinned. "Shall I go on?"

"Please."

"For quite a while she got all the attention, which threw the Ghents into an uproar. I imagine they saw Rhoda being his heir and didn't like the switch. Mr. York's partiality to Alice continued for several months then fell off somewhat. He paid little attention to her after that, but never forgot her on birthdays or holidays. His gifts were as great as ever. And that," she concluded, "is the only unusual situation that ever existed as far as I know."

"Alice and York, huh? How far did the relationship go?"

"Not that far. His feelings were paternal, I think."

"Are you sure?"

"Pretty sure. Mr. York was long past his prime. If sex meant anything to him it was no more than a biological difference between the species."

"It might mean something to Alice."

"Of that I'm sure. She likes anything with muscles, but with Mr. York she didn't need it. She did all right without it. I noticed that she cast a hook in your direction."

"She didn't use the right bait," I stated briefly. "She showed up in my room with nothing on but a prayer and wanted to play. I like to be teased a little. Besides, I was tired. Did York know she acted that way?"

Roxy plugged in a tiny radio set and fiddled with the dial. "If he did he didn't care."

"Kitten, did York ever mention a will?"

An old Benny Goodman tune came on. She brought it in clearer and turned around with a dance step. "Yes, he had one. He kept the family on the verge of a nervous breakdown every time he alluded to it, but he never came right out and said where his money would go."

She began to spin with the music. "Hold still a second, will you? Didn't he hand out any hints at all?"

The hem of her negligee brushed past my face, higher than any hem had a right to be. "None at all, except that it would go where it was most deserving."

Her legs flashed in the light. My heart began beating faster again. They were lovely legs, long, firm. "Did Grange ever hear that statement?"

She stopped, poised dramatically and threw her belt at me. "Yes." She began to dance again. The music was a rhumba now and her body swayed to it, jerking rhythmically. "Once during a heated discussion Mr. York told them all that Miss Grange was the only one he could trust and she would be the one to handle his estate."

There was no answer to that. How the devil could she handle it if she got it all? I never got a chance to think about it. The robe came off and she used it like a fan, almost disclosing everything, showing nothing. Her skin was fair, cream-colored, her body graceful. She circled in front of me, letting her hair fall to her shoulders. At the height of that furious dance I stood up.

Roxy flew into my arms. "Kiss me . . . you thing."

I didn't need any urging.

Her mouth melted into mine like butter. I felt her nails digging into my arms. Roughly, I pushed her away, held her there at arm's length. "What was that for?"

She gave me a delightfully evil grin. "That is because I could love you if I wanted to, Mike. I did once, you know."

"I know. What made you stop?"

"You're Broadway, Mike. You're the bright lights and big money . . . sometimes. You're bullets when there should be kisses. That's why I stopped. I wanted someone with a normal life expectancy."

"Then why this?"

"I missed you. Funny as it sounds, someplace inside me I have a spot that's always reserved for you. I didn't want you to ever know it, but there it is."

I kissed her again, longer and closer this time. Her body was talking to me, screaming to me. There would have been more if Ruston hadn't called out.

Roxy slipped into the robe again, the cold static making it snap. "Let me go," I said. She nodded.

I opened the door and hit the light switch. "Hello, Sir Lancelot." The kid had been crying in his sleep, but he smiled at me.

"Hello, Mike. When did you come?"

"A little while ago. Want something?"

"Can I have some water, please? My throat's awfully dry."

A pitcher half full of ice was on the desk. I poured it into a glass and handed it to him and he drank deeply. "Have enough?"

He gave the glass back to me. "Yes, thank you."

I gave his chin a little twist. "Then back to bed with you. Get a good sleep."

Ruston squirmed back under the covers. "I will. Good night, Mike."

"'Night, pal." I closed the door behind me. Roxy had changed into a deep maroon quilted job and sat in the chair smoking a cigarette. The moment had passed. I could see that she was sorry, too. She handed me my deck of butts and I pocketed them, then waved a good-night. Neither of us felt like saying anything.

Evidently Harvey had retired for the night. The staircase was lit only by tiny night-lights shaped to resemble candle flames, while the foyer below was a dim challenge to the eyesight. I picked my way through the rooms and found Billy's without upsetting anything. He was in bed, but awake. "It's Mike, Billy," I said.

He snapped on the bed lamp. "Come on in."

I shut the door and slumped in a chair next to him. "More questions. I know it's late, but I hope you don't mind."

"Not at all, Mike. What's new?"

"Oh, you know how these things are. Haven't found Miss Grange yet and things are settling around her. Dilwick's got his men covering her place like a blanket."

"Yeah? What for? Ain't she supposed to be drowned?"

"Somebody wants it to look that way, I think. Listen, Billy, you told me before that you heard someone come downstairs between York and me the night of the murder. It wasn't important before except to establish an alibi for you if it was needed, but now what you heard may have a bearing on the case. Go over it again, will you? Do it in as much detail as you can."

"Let's see. I didn't really hear York leave, I just remember a car crunching the gravel. It woke me up. I had a headache and a bad taste in my mouth from something York gave me. Pills, I think."

"It was supposed to keep you asleep. He gave you a sedative."

"Whatever it was I puked up in bed, that's why it didn't do me any good. Anyway, I lay here half awake when I heard somebody come down the last two stairs. They squeak, they do. This room is set funny, see. Any noise outside the room travels right in here. They got a name for it."

"Acoustics."

"Yeah, that's it. That's why nobody ever used this room but me. They couldn't stand the noise all the time. Not only loud noises, any kind of noises. This was like whoever it was didn't want to make a sound, but it didn't do any good because I heard it. Only I thought it was one of the family trying to be quiet so they wouldn't wake anyone up and I didn't pay any attention to it. About two or three minutes after that comes this noise like someone coughing with their head under a coat and it died out real slow and that's all. I was just getting back to sleep when there was another car tearing out the drive. That was you, I guess."

"That all?"

"Yeah, that's all, Mike. I went back to sleep after that."

This was the ace. It had its face down so I couldn't tell whether it was red or black, but it was the ace. The bells were going off in my head again, those little tinkles that promised to become the pealing of chimes. The cart was before the horse, but if I could find the right buckle to unloosen I could put them right back.

"Billy, say nothing to nobody about this, understand? If the local police question you, say nothing. If Sergeant Price wants to know things, have him see me. If you value your head, keep your mouth shut and your door locked."

His eyes popped wide open. "Geez, Mike, is it that important?"

I nodded. "I have a funny feeling, Billy, that the noises you heard were made by the murderer."

"Good Golly!" It left him breathless. Then, "You . . . you think the killer . . ."—he swallowed—". . . might make a try for me?"

"No, Billy, not the killer. You aren't that important to him. Someone else might, though. I think we have a lot more on our hands than just plain murder."

"What?" It was a hoarse whisper.

"Kidnapping, for one thing. That comes in somewhere. You sit tight until you hear from me." Before I left I turned with my hand on the knob and looked into his scared face again. "Who's Mallory, Billy?"

"Mallory who?"

"Just Mallory."

"Gosh, I don't know."

"Okay, kid, thanks."

Mallory. He might as well be Smith or Jones. So far he was just a word. I navigated the gloom again half consciously, thinking of him. Mallory of the kidnapping; Mallory whose very name turned York white and added a link to the chain of crime. Somewhere Mallory was sitting on his fanny getting a large charge out of the whole filthy mess. York knew who he was, but York was dead. Could that be the reason for his murder? Likely. York, by indirect implication and his peculiar action, intimated that Myra Grange knew of him too, but she was dead or missing. Was that Mallory's doing? Likely. Hell, I couldn't put my finger on anything more definite than a vague possibility. Something had to blow up, somebody would have to try to take the corners out of one of the angles. I gathered all the facts together, but they didn't make sense. A name spoken, the speaker unseen; someone who came downstairs at night, unseen too, and denying it; a search for a stolen something-or-other, whose theft was laid at the feet of the vanished woman. I muttered a string of curses under my breath and kicked aimlessly at empty air. Where was there to start? Dilwick would have his feelers out for Grange and so would Price. With that many men they could get around much too fast for me. Besides, I had the feeling that she was only part of it all, not the key figure that would unlock the mystery, but more like one whose testimony would cut down a lot of time and work. I still couldn't see her putting the cleaver into York then doing the Dutch afterward. If she was associated with him professionally she would have to be brilliant, and great minds either turn at murder or attempt to conceive of a flawless plot. York's death was brutal. It was something you might find committed in a dark alley in a slum section for a few paltry dollars, or in a hotel room when a husband returns to find his woman in the arms of her lover. A passion kill, a revenge kill, a crude murder for small money, yes, but did any of these motives fit here? For whom did York hold passion . . . or vice versa? Roxy hit it when she said he was too old. Small money? None was gone from his wallet apparently. That kind of kill would take place outside on a lonely road or on a deserted street anyway. Revenge . . . revenge. Grange said he had no enemies. That was now. Could anything have happened in the past? You could almost rule that out too, on the basis of precedent. Revenge murders usually happen soon after the event that caused the desire for revenge. If the would-be murderer has time to think he realizes the penalty for murder and it doesn't happen. Unless, of course, the victim, realizing what might happen, keeps on the move. That accentuates the importance of the event to the killer and spurs him on. Negative. York was a public figure for years. He had lived in the same house almost twenty years. Big money, a motive for anything. Was that it? Grange came into that. Why did she have the will? Those things are kept in a safe-deposit box or lawyer's files. The chief beneficiary rarely ever got to see the document much less have it hidden among her personal effects for so long a time. Damn, Grange had told me she had a large income aside from what York gave her. She didn't care what he did with his money. What a very pretty attitude to take, especially when you know where it's going. She could afford to be snotty with me. I remembered her face when she said it, aloof, the hell-with-it attitude. Why the act if it wasn't important then? What was she trying to put across?

Myra Grange. I didn't want it to, but it came back to her every time. Missing the night of the kidnapping; seen on the road, but she said no. Why? I started to grin a little. An unmarried person goes out at night for what reason? Natch . . . a date. Grange had a date, and her kind of dates had to be kept behind closed doors, that's why she was rarely seen about. York wouldn't want it to get around either for fear of criticism, that's why he was nice about it. Grange would deny it for a lot of reasons. It would hurt her professionally, or worse, she might lose a perfectly good girlfriend. It was all supposition, but I bet I was close.

The night air hit me in the face. I hadn't realized I was standing outside the door until a chilly mist ran up the steps and hugged me. I stuck my hands in my pockets and walked down the drive. Behind me the house watched with staring eyes. I wished it could talk. The gravel path encircled the gloomy old place with gray arms and I followed it aimlessly, trying to straighten out my thoughts. When I came to the fork I stood motionless a moment then followed the turn off to the right.

Fifty yards later the colorless bulk of the laboratory grew out of the darkness like a crypt. It was a drab cinder-block building, the only incongruous thing on the estate. No windows broke the contours of the walls on either of the two sides visible, no place where prying eyes might observe what occurred within. At the far end a thirty-foot chimney poked a skinny finger skyward, stretching to clear the treetops. Upon closer inspection a ventilation system showed just under the eaves, screened air intakes and outlets above eye level.

I went around the building once, a hundred-by-fifty-foot structure, but the only opening was the single steel door in the front, a door built to withstand weather or siege. But it was not built to withstand curiosity. The first master key I used turned the lock. It was a laugh. The double tongue had prongs as thick as my thumb, but the tumbler arrangement was as uncomplicated as a glass of milk.

Fortunately, the light pulls had tiny phosphorescent tips that cast a greenish glow. I reached up and yanked one. Overhead a hundred-watt bulb flared into daylight brilliance. I checked the door and shut it, then looked about me. Architecturally, the building was a study in simplicity. One long corridor ran the length of it. Off each side were rooms, perhaps sixteen in all. No dirt marred the shining marble floor, no streaks on the enameled white walls. Each door was shut, the brass of the knobs gleaming, the woodwork smiling in varnished austerity. For all its rough exterior, the inside was spotless.

The first room on the one side was an office, fitted with a desk, several filing cabinets, a big chair and a water cooler. The room opposite was its mate. So far so good. I could tell by the pipe rack which had been York's.

Next came some sort of supply room. In racks along the walls were hundreds of labeled bottles, chemicals unknown to me. I opened the bins below. Electrical fittings, tubes, meaningless coils of copper tubing lay neatly placed on shelves alongside instruments and parts of unusual design. This time the room opposite was no mate. Crouched in one corner was a generator, snuggling up to a transformer. Wrist-thick power lines came in through the door, passed through the two units and into the walls. I had seen affairs like this on portable electric chairs in some of our more rural states. I couldn't figure this one out. If the education of Ruston was York's sole work, why all the gadgets? Or was that merely a shield for something bigger?

The following room turned everything into a cockeyed mess. Here was a lounge that was sheer luxury. Overstuffed chairs, a seven-foot couch, a chair shaped like a French curve that went down your back, up under your knees and ended in a cushioned foot rest. Handy to everything were magazine racks of popular titles and some of more obscure titles. Books in foreign languages rested between costly jade bookends. A combination radio-phonograph sat in the corner, flanked by cabinets of symphonic and pop records. Opposite it at the other end of the room was a grand piano with operatic scores concealed in the seat. Cleverly contrived furniture turned into art boards and reading tables. A miniature refrigerator housed a bottle of ice water and several frosted glasses. Along the wall several Petri dishes held agar-agar with yellow bacteria cultures mottling the tops. Next to them was a double-lensed microscope of the best manufacture.

What a playpen. Here anyone could relax in comfort with his favorite hobby. Was this where Ruston spent his idle hours? There was nothing here for a boy, but his mind would appreciate it.

It was getting late. I shut the door and moved on, taking quick peeks into each room. A full-scale lab, test tubes, retorts, a room of books, nothing but books, then more electrical equipment. I crossed the corridor and stuck my head in. I had to take a second look to be sure I was right. If that wasn't the hot seat standing in the middle of the floor it was a good imitation.

I didn't get a chance to go over it. Very faintly I heard metal scratching against metal. I pulled the door shut and ran down the corridor, pulling at the light cords as I went. I wasn't the only one that was curious this night.

Just as I closed the door of Grange's office behind me the outside door swung inward. Someone was standing there in the dark waiting. I heard his breath coming hard with an attempt to control it. The door shut, and a sliver of light ran along the floor, shining through the crack onto my shoes. The intruder wasn't bothering with the overheads, he was using a flash.

A hand touched the knob. In two shakes I was palming my rod, holding it above my head ready to bring it down the second he stepped in the door. It never opened. He moved to the other side and went into York's office instead.

As slowly as I could I eased the knob around, then brought it toward my stomach. An inch, two, then there was room enough to squeeze out. I kept the dark paneling of the door at my back, stood there in the darkness, letting my breath in and out silently while I watched Junior Ghent rifle York's room.

He had the flashlight propped on the top of the desk, working in its beam. He didn't seem to be in a hurry. He pulled out every drawer of the files, scattering their contents on the floor in individual piles. When he finished with one row he moved to another until the empty cabinet gaped like a toothless old man.

For a second I thought he was leaving and faded to one side, but all he did was turn the flash to focus on the other side of the room. Again, he repeated the procedure. I watched.

At the end of twenty minutes his patience began to give out. He yanked things viciously from place and kicked at the chair, then obviously holding himself in check tried to be calm about it. In another fifteen minutes he had circled the room, making it look like a bomb had gone off in there. He hadn't found what he was after.

That came by accident.

The chair got in his way again. He pushed it so hard it skidded along the marble, hit an empty drawer and toppled over. I even noticed it before he did.

The chair had a false bottom.

Very clever. Search a room for hours and you'll push furniture all over the place, but how often will you turn up a chair and inspect it? Junior let out a surprised gasp and went down on his knees, his fingers running over the paneling. When his fingernails didn't work he took a screwdriver from his pocket and forced it into the wood. There was a sharp snap and the bottom was off.

A thick envelope was fastened to a wire clasp. He smacked his lips and wrenched it free. With his forefinger he lifted the flap and drew out a sheaf of papers. These he scanned quickly, let out a sarcastic snort, and discarded them on the floor. He dug into the envelope and brought out something else. He studied it closely, rubbing his hand over his stomach. Twice he adjusted his glasses and held them closer to the light. I saw his face flush. As though he knew he was being watched he threw a furtive glance toward the door, then shoved the stuff back in the envelope and put it in his side pocket.

I ducked back in the corridor while he went out the door, waited until it closed then snapped the light on and stepped over the junk. One quick look at the papers he had found in the envelope told me what it was. This will was made out only a few months ago, and it left three-quarters of his estate to Ruston and one-quarter to Alice. York had cut the rest out with a single buck.

Junior Ghent had something more important, though. I folded the will into my pocket and ran to the door. I didn't want my little pal to get away.

He didn't. Fifty yards up the drive he was getting the life beat out of him.

I heard his muffled screams, and other voices, too. I got the .45 in my hand and thumbed the safety off and made a dash for them.

Maybe I should have stayed on the grass, but I didn't have that much time. Two figures detached themselves from the one on the ground and broke for the trees. I let one go over their heads that echoed over the grounds like the roiling of thunder, but neither stopped. They went across a clearing and I put on speed to get free of the brush line so I could take aim. Junior stopped that. I tripped over his sprawled figure and went flat on my kisser. The pair scrambled over the wall before I was up. From the ground I tried a snap shot that went wild. On the other side of the wall a car roared into life and shot down the road.

A woman's quick, sharp scream split the air like a knife and caught me flat-footed. Everything happened at once. Briars ripped at my clothes when I went through the brush and whipped at my face. Lights went on in the house and Harvey's voice rang out for help. By the time I reached the porch Billy was standing beside the door in his pajamas.

"Upstairs, Mike, it's Miss Malcom. Somebody shot her!"

Harvey was waving frantically, pointing to her room. I raced inside. Roxy was lying on the floor with blood making a bright red picture on the shoulder of her nightgown. Harvey stood over me, shaking with fear as I ripped the cloth away. I breathed with relief. The bullet had only passed through the flesh under her arm.

I carried her to bed and called to the butler over my shoulder. "Get some hot water and bandages. Get a doctor up here."

Harvey said, "Yes, sir," and scurried away.

Billy came in. "Can I do anything, Mike? I . . . I don't want to be alone."

"Okay, stay with her. I want to see the kid."

I opened the door to Ruston's room and turned on the light. He was sitting up, holding himself erect with his hands, his eyes were fixed on the wall in a blank stare, his mouth open. He never saw me. I shook him, he was stiff as a board, every muscle in his body as rigid as a piece of steel. He jerked convulsively once or twice, never taking his eyes from the wall. It took a lot of force to pull his arms up and straighten him out.

"Harvey, did you call that doctor?"

Billy sang out, "He's doing it now, Mike."

"Damn it, tell him to hurry. The kid's having a fit or something."

He hollered down the stairs to Harvey; I could hear the excited stuttering over the telephone, but it would be awhile before a medic would reach the house. Ruston began to tremble, his eyes rolled back in his head. Leaning over I slapped him sharply across the cheek.

"Ruston, snap out of it." I slapped him again. "Ruston."

This time his eyelids flickered, he came back to normal with a sob. His mouth twitched and he covered his face with his hands. Suddenly he sat up in bed and shouted, "Mike!"

"I'm right here, kid," I said, "take it easy." His face found mine and he reached for my hand. He was trembling from head to foot, his body bathed in cold sweat.

"Miss Malcom . . . ?"

"Is all right," I answered. "She just got a good scare, that's all." I didn't want to frighten him any more than he was. "Did someone come in here?"

He squeezed my hand. "No . . . there was a noise, and Miss Malcom screamed. Mike, I'm not very brave at all. I'm scared."

The kid had a right to be. "It was nothing. Cover up and be still. I'll be in the next room. Want me to leave the door open?"

"Please, Mike."

I left the light on and put a rubber wedge under the door to keep it open. Billy was standing by the bed holding a handkerchief to Roxy's shoulder. I took it away and looked at it. Not much of a wound, the bullet was of small caliber and had gone in and come out clean. Billy poked me and pointed to the window. The pane had spiderwebbed into a thousand cracks with a neat hole at the bottom a few inches above the sill. Tiny glass fragments winked up from the floor. The shot had come in from below, traveling upward. Behind me in the wall was the bullet hole, a small puncture head high. I dug out the slug from the plaster and rolled it over in my hand. A neat piece of lead whose shape had hardly been deformed by the wall, caliber .32. York's gun had found its way home.

I tucked it in my watch pocket. "Stay here, Billy, I'll be right back."

"Where are you going?" He didn't like me to leave.

"I got a friend downstairs."

Junior was struggling to his feet when I reached him. I helped him with a fist in his collar. This little twerp had a lot of explaining to do. He was a sorry-looking sight. Pieces of gravel were imbedded in the flesh of his face and blood matted the hair of his scalp. One lens of his specs was smashed. I watched him while he detached his lower lip from his teeth, swearing incoherently. The belting he took had left him half dazed, and he didn't try to resist at all when I walked him toward the house.

When I sat him in a chair he shook his head, touching the cut on his temple. He kept repeating a four-letter word over and over until realization of what had happened hit him. His head came up and I thought he was going to spit at me.

"You got it!" he said accusingly on the verge of tears now.

"Got what?" I leaned forward to get every word. His eyes narrowed.

Junior said sullenly, "Nothing."

Very deliberately I took his tie in my hand and pulled it. He tried to draw back, but I held him close. "Little chum," I said, "you are in a bad spot, very bad. You've been caught breaking and entering. You stole something from York's private hideaway and Miss Malcom has been shot. If you know what's good for you, you'll talk."

"Shot . . . killed?"

There was no sense letting him know the truth. "She's not dead yet. If she dies you're liable to face a murder charge."

"No. No. I didn't do it. I admit I was in the laboratory, but I didn't shoot her. I . . . I didn't get a chance to. Those men jumped on me. I fought for my life."

"Did you? Were you really unconscious? Maybe. I went after them until I heard Miss Malcom scream. Did she scream because you shot her, then faked being knocked out all the while?"

He turned white. A little vein in his forehead throbbed, his hands tightened until his nails drew blood from the palms. "You can't pin it on me," he said. "I didn't do it, I swear."

"No? What did you take from the room back there?"

A pause, then, "Nothing."

I reached for his pockets, daring him to move. Each one I turned inside out, dumping their contents around the bottom of the chair. A wallet, theater stubs, two old letters, some keys and fifty-five cents in change. That was all.

"So somebody else wanted what you found, didn't they?" He didn't answer. "They got it, too."

"I didn't have anything," he repeated.

He was lying through his teeth. "Then why did they wait for you and beat your brains out? Answer that one." He was quiet. I took the will out and waved it at him. "It went with this. It was more important than this, though. But what would be more important to you than a will? You're stupid, Junior. You aren't in this at all, are you? If you had sense enough to burn it you might have come into big dough when the estate was split up, especially with the kid under age. But no, you didn't care whether the will was found and probated or not, because the other thing was more important. It meant more money. How, Junior, how?"

For my little speech I had a sneer thrown at me. "All right," I told him, "I'll tell you what I'm going to do. Right now you look like hell, but you're beautiful compared to what you'll look like in ten minutes. I'm going to slap the crap out of you until you talk. Yell all you want to, it won't do any good."

I pulled back my hand. Junior didn't wait, he started speaking. "Don't. It was nothing. I . . . I stole some money from my uncle once. He caught me and made me sign a statement. I didn't want it to be found or I'd never get a cent. That was it."

"Yes? What made it so important that someone else would want it?"

"I don't know. There was something else attached to the statement that I didn't look at. Maybe they wanted that."

It could have been a lie, but I wasn't sure. What he said made sense. "Did you shoot Miss Malcom?"

"That's silly." I tightened up on the tie again. "Please, you're choking me. I didn't shoot anyone. I never saw her. You can tell, the police have a test haven't they?"

"Yes, a paraffin test. Would you submit to it?"

Relief flooded his face and he nodded. I let him go. If he had pulled the trigger he wouldn't be so damn anxious. Besides, I knew for sure that he hadn't been wearing gloves.

A car pulled up outside and Harvey admitted a short, stout man carrying the bag of his profession. They disappeared upstairs. I turned to Junior. "Get out of here, but stay where you can be reached. If you take a powder I'll squeeze your skinny neck until you turn blue. Remember one thing, if Miss Malcom dies you're it, see, so you better start praying."

He shot out of the chair and half ran for the door. I heard his feet pounding down the drive. I went upstairs.

"How is she?" The doctor applied the last of the tape over the compress and turned.

"Nothing serious. Fainted from shock." He put his instruments back in his bag and took out a notebook. Roxy stirred and woke up.

"Of course you know I'll have to report this. The police must have a record of all gunshot wounds. Her name, please."

Roxy watched me from the bed. I passed it to her. She murmured, "Helen Malcom."

"Address?"

"Here." She gave her age and the doctor noted a general description then asked me if I had found the bullet.

"Yeah, it was in the wall. A .32 lead-nose job. I'll give it to the police." He snapped the book shut and stuck it in his bag. "I'd like you to see the boy, too, Doctor," I mentioned. "He was in a bad way."

Briefly, I went over what had happened the past few days. The doctor picked his bag up and followed me inside. "I know the boy," he said. "Too much excitement is bad for any youngster, particularly one as finely trained as he is."

"You've seen him before? I thought his father was his doctor."

"Not the boy. However I had occasion to speak to his father several times in town and he spoke rather proudly of his son."

"I should imagine. Here he is."

The doctor took his pulse and I winked over his shoulder. Ruston grinned back. While the doctor examined him I sat at the desk and looked at nine-by-twelve photos of popular cowboy actors Ruston had in a folder. He was a genius, but the boy kept coming out around the seams. A few of the books in the lower shelves were current Western novels and some books on American geography in the 1800s. Beside the desk was a used ten-gallon hat and lariat with the crown of the skimmer autographed by Hollywood's foremost heroic cattle hand. I don't know why York didn't let his kid alone to enjoy himself the way boys should. Ruston would rather be a cowboy than a child prodigy any day, I'd bet. He saw me going over his stuff and smiled.

"Were you ever out West, Mike?" he asked.

"I took some training in the desert when I was with Uncle Whiskers."

"Did you ever see a real cowboy?"

"Nope, but I bunked with one for six months. He used to wear high-heeled boots until the sergeant cracked down on him. Some card. Wanted to wear his hat in the shower. First thing he'd do when he'd get up in the morning was to put on his hat. He couldn't get used to one without a six-inch brim and was forever wanting to tip his hat to the Lieutenant instead of saluting."

Ruston chuckled. "Did he carry a six-shooter?"

"Naw, but he was a dead shot. He could pick the eyes out of a beetle at thirty yards."

The doctor broke up our chitchat by handing the kid some pills. He filled a box with them, printed the time to take them on the side and dashed off a prescription. He handed it to me. "Have this filled. One teaspoonful every two hours for twenty-four hours. There's nothing wrong with him except a slight nervous condition. I'll come back tomorrow to see Miss Malcom again. If her wound starts bleeding call me at once. I gave them both a sedative so they should sleep well until morning."

"Okay, Doctor, thanks." I gave him over to Harvey, who ushered him to the door.

Roxy forced a smile. "Did you get them, Mike?"

"Forget about it," I said. "How did you get in the way?"

"I heard a gun go off and turned on the light. I guess I shouldn't have done that. I ran to the window but with the light on I couldn't see a thing. The next thing I knew something hit me in the shoulder. I didn't realize it was a bullet until I saw the hole in the window. That's when I screamed," she added sheepishly.

"I don't blame you, I'd scream too. Did you see the flash of the gun?"

Her head shook on the pillow. "I heard it I think, but it sounded sort of far off. I never dreamed . . ."

"You weren't hurt badly, that's one thing."

"Ruston, how . . ."

"Okay. You scared the hell out of him when you yelled. He's had too much already. That set him off. He was stiff as a fence post when I went in to him."

The sedative was beginning to take effect. Roxy's eyes closed sleepily. I whispered to Billy, "Get me a broom handle or something long and straight, will you?"

He went out and down the corridor. While I waited I looked at the hole the bullet had made, and in my mind pictured where Roxy had stood when she was shot. Billy came in with a long brass tube.

"Couldn't find a broom, but would this curtain rod do?"

"Fine," I said softly. Roxy was asleep now. "Stand over here by the window."

"What are you going to do?"

"Figure out where that shot came from."

I had him hold the rod under his armpit and I sighted along the length of it, lining the tube up with the hole in the wall and the one in the window. This done I told him to keep it that way then threw the window up. More pieces of glass tinkled to the floor. I moved around behind him and peered down the rod.

I was looking at the base of the wall about where the two assailants had climbed the top. That put Junior out of it by a hundred feet. The picture was changing again, nothing balanced. It was like trying to make a mural with a kaleidoscope. Hell's bells. Neither of those two had shot at me, yet that was where the bullet came from. A silencer maybe? A wild shot at someone or a shot carefully aimed. With a .32 it would take an expert to hit the window from that range much less Roxy behind it. Or was the shot actually aimed at her?

"Thanks, Billy, that's all."

He lowered the rod and I shut the window. I called him to one side, away from the bed. "What is it, Mike?"

"Look, I want to think. How about you staying up here in the kid's room tonight? We'll fix some chair cushions up on the floor."

"Okay, if you say so."

"I think it will be best. Somebody will have to keep an eye on them in case they wake up, and Ruston has to take his medicine," I looked at the box, "every three hours. I'll give Harvey the prescription to be filled. Do you mind?"

"No, I think I'll like it here better'n the room downstairs."

"Keep the doors locked."

"And how. I'll push a chair up against them too."

I laughed. "I don't think there will be any more trouble for a while."

His face grew serious. "You can laugh, you got a rod under your arm."

"I'll leave it here for you if you want."

"Not me, Mike. One more strike and I'm out. If I get caught within ten feet of a heater they'll toss me in the clink. I'd sooner take my chances."

He began pulling the cushions from the chairs and I went out. Behind me the lock clicked and a chair went under the knob. Billy wasn't kidding. Nobody was going to get in there tonight.

CHAPTER 7

Downstairs I dialed the operator and asked for the highway patrol. She connected me with headquarters and a sharp voice crackled at me. "Sergeant Price, please."

"He's not here right now, is there a message?"

"Yeah, this is Mike Hammer. Tell him that Miss Malcom, the York kid's nurse, was shot through the shoulder by a .32 caliber bullet. Her condition isn't serious and she'll be able to answer questions in the morning. The shot was fired from somewhere on the grounds but the one who fired it escaped."

"I got it. Anything else?"

"Yes, but I'll give it to him in person. Have they found any trace of Grange yet?"

"They picked up her hat along the shore of the inlet. Sergeant Price told me to tell you if you called."

"Thanks. They still looking for her?"

"A boat's grappling the mouth of the channel right now."

"Okay, if I get time I'll call back later." The cop thanked me and hung up. Harvey waited to see whether I was going out or not, and when I headed for the door got my hat.

"Will you be back tonight, sir?"

"I don't know. Lock the door anyway."

"Yes, sir."

I tooled my car up the drive and honked for Henry to come out and open the gates. Although there was a light on in his cottage, Henry didn't appear. I climbed out again and walked in the place.

The gatekeeper was sound asleep in his chair, a paper folded across his lap.

After I shook him and swore a little his eyes opened, but not the way a waking person's do. They were heavy and dull, he was barely able to raise his head. The shock of seeing me there did more to put some life in him than the shaking. He blinked a few times and ran his hand over his forehead.

"I'm . . . sorry, sir. Can't understand myself . . . lately. These awful headaches, and going to sleep like that."

"What's the matter with you, Henry?"

"It's . . . nothing, sir. Perhaps it's the aspirin." He pointed to a bottle of common aspirin tablets on the table. I picked it up and looked at the label. A well-known brand. I looked again, then shook some out on my palm. There were no manufacturer's initials on the tablets at all. There were supposed to be, I used enough of them myself.

"Where did you get these, Henry?"

"Mr. York gave them to me last week. I had several fierce head-aches. The aspirin relieved me."

"Did you take these the night of the kidnapping?"

His eyes drifted to mine, held. "Why, yes. Yes, I did."

"Better lay off them. They aren't good for you. Did you hear anything tonight?"

"No, I don't believe I did. Why?"

"Oh, no reason. Mind if I take some of these with me?" He shook his head and I pocketed a few tablets. "Stay here," I said, "I'll open the gates."

Henry nodded and was asleep before I left the room. That was why the kidnapper got in so easily. That was why York left and the killer left and I left without being heard at the gate.

It was a good bet that someone substituted sleeping tablets for the aspirins. Oh, brother, the killer was getting cuter all the time.

But the pieces were coming together one by one. They didn't fit the slots, but they were there, ready to be assembled as soon as someone said the wrong word, or made a wrong move. The puzzle was closer to the house now, but it was outside, too. Who wanted Henry to be asleep while Ruston was snatched? Who wanted it so bad that his habits were studied and sleeping pills slipped into his aspirin bottle? If someone was that thorough they could have given him something to cause the headaches to start with. And who was in league with that person on the outside?

A wrong move or a wrong word. Someone would slip sometime. Maybe they just needed a little push. I had Junior where the hair was short now, that meant I had the old lady, too. Jump the fence to the other side now. Alice. She said *tsk, tsk* when I told them York was dead. Sweet thing.

I had to make another phone call to trooper headquarters to collect the list of addresses from the statements. Price still hadn't come in, but evidently he had passed the word to give me any help I needed, for there was no hesitation about handing me the information.

Alice lived west of town in a suburb called Wooster. It was little less than a crossroad off the main highway, but from the size of the mansions that dotted the estates it was a refuge of the wealthy. The town itself boasted a block of storefronts whose windows showed nothing but the best. Above each store was an apartment. The bricks were white, the metalwork bright and new. There was an aura of dignity and pomp in the way they nestled there. Alice lived above the fur shop, two stores from the end.

I parked between a new Ford and a Caddy convertible. There were no lights on in Alice's apartment, but I didn't doubt that she'd want to see me. I slid out and went into the tiny foyer and looked at the bell. It was hers. For a good five seconds I held my finger on it, then opened the door and went up the steps. Before I reached the top, Alice, in the last stages of closing her robe, opened the door, sending a shaft of light in my face.

"Well, I'll be damned," she exclaimed. "You certainly pick an awful time to visit your friends."

"Aren't you glad to see me?" I grinned.

"Silly, come on in. Of course I'm glad to see you."

"I hate to get you up like this."

"You didn't. I was lying in bed reading, that's all." She paused just inside the door. "This isn't a professional visit, is it?"

"Hardly. I finally got sick and tired of the whole damn setup and decided to give my mind a rest."

She shut the door. "Kiss me."

I pecked her on the nose. "Can't I even take my hat off?"

"Oooo," she gasped, "the way you said that!"

I dropped my slicker and hat on a rack by the door and trailed her to the living room. "Have a drink?" she asked me.

I made with three fingers together. "So much, and ginger."

When she went for the ice I took the place in with a sweep of my head. Swell, strictly swell. It was better than the best Park Avenue apartment I'd ever been in, even if it was above a store. The furniture cost money and the oils on the wall even more. There were books and books, first editions and costly manuscripts. York had done very well by his niece.

Alice came back with two highballs in her hand. "Take one," she offered. I picked the big one. We toasted silently, she with the devil in her eyes, and drank.

"Good?"

I bobbed my head. "Old stuff, isn't it?"

"Over twenty years. Uncle Rudy gave it to me." She put her drink down and turned off the overhead lights, switching on a shaded table lamp instead. From a cabinet she selected an assortment of records and put them in the player. "Atmosphere," she explained impishly.

I didn't see why we needed it. When she had the lamp at her back the robe became transparent enough to create its own atmosphere. She was all woman, this one, bigger than I thought. Her carriage was seduction itself and she knew it. The needle came down and soft Oriental music filled the room. I closed my eyes and visualized women in scarlet veils dancing for the sultan. The sultan was me. Alice said something I didn't catch and left.

When she came back she was wearing the cobwebs. Nothing else.

"You aren't too tired tonight?"

"Not tonight," I said.

She sat down beside me. "I think you were faking the last time, and after all my trouble."

Her skin was soft and velvety-looking under the cobwebs, a vein in her throat pulsed steadily. I let my eyes follow the contours of her shoulders and down her body. Impertinent breasts that mocked my former hesitance, a flat stomach waiting for the touch to set off the fuse, thighs that wanted no part of shielding cloth.

I had difficulty getting it out. "I *had* to be tired."

She crossed her legs, the cobwebs parted. "Or crazy," she added.

I finished the drink off in a hurry and held out the glass for another. I needed something to steady my nerves.

Ice clinked, glass rang against glass. She measured the whiskey and poured it in. This time she pulled the coffee table over so she wouldn't have to get up again. The record changed and the gentle strains of a violin ran through the *Hungarian Rhapsody*. Alice moved closer to me. I could feel the warmth of her body through my clothes. The drinks went down. When the record changed again she had her head on my shoulder.

"Have you been working hard, Mike?"

"No, just legwork."

Her hair brushed my face; soft, lovely hair that smelled of jasmine. "Do you think they'll find her?"

I stroked her neck, letting my fingers bite in just a little. "I think so. Sidon is too small a town to try to hide in. Did you know her well?"

"Ummm. What? Oh, no. She was very distant to all of us."

More jasmine. She buried her face in my shoulder. "You're a thing yourself," I grinned. "Shouldn't you be wearing black?"

"No. It doesn't become me."

I blew in her ear. "No respect for the dead."

"Uncle never liked all those post-funeral displays anyway."

"Well, you should do something since you were his favorite niece. He left you a nice lump of cash."

She ran her fingers through my hair, bending my head close to hers. "Did he?" Lightly, her tongue ran over her lips, a pink, darting temptation.

"Uh-huh." We rubbed noses, getting closer all the time. "I saw his will. He must have liked you."

"Just you like me, Mike, that's all I want." Her mouth opened slightly. I couldn't take any more. I grabbed her in my arms and crushed her lips against mine. She was a living heartbeat, an endless fire that burned hot and deep. Her arms went about me, holding tightly. Once, out of sheer passion, she bit me like a cat would bite.

She tore her mouth away and pressed it against my neck, then rubbed her shoulders from side to side against my chest until the cobwebs slipped down her arms and pinioned them there. I touched her flesh, bruised her until she moaned in painful ecstasy, demanding more. Her fingers fumbled with the buttons of my coat. Somehow I got it off and draped it over a chair, then she started on my tie. "So many clothes, Mike, you have so many clothes." She kissed me again.

"Carry me inside." I scooped her off the couch, cradling her in my arms, the cobwebs trailing beneath her. She pointed with her finger, her eyes almost closed. "In there."

No lights. The comforter was cool and fluffy. She told me to stay there and kissed my eyes shut. I felt her leave the bed and go into the living room. The record changed and a louder piece sent notes of triumph cascading into the room. Agonizing minutes passed waiting until she returned, bearing two half-full glasses on a tray like a gorgeous slave girl. Gone now were even the cobwebs.

"To us, Mike, and this night." We drank. She came to me with arms outstretched. The music came and went, piece after piece, but we heard nothing nor cared. Then there was no sound at all except the breathing.

It was well into morning before we stirred. Alice said no, but I had to leave. She coaxed, but now the sight of her meant less and I could refuse. I found my shoes, laced them, and tucked the covers under her chin.

"Kiss me." She held her mouth up.

"No."

"Just one?"

"All right, just one." She wasn't making it any too easy. I pushed her back against the pillows and said good night.

"You're so ugly, Mike. So ugly you're beautiful."

"Thanks, so are you." I waved and left her. In the living room I picked my coat up from the floor and dusted it off. My aim was getting worse, I thought I had it on the chair.

On the way out I dropped the night latch and shut the door softly. Alice, lovely, lovely Alice. She had a body out of this world. I ran down the stairs pulling on my slicker. Outside the sheen of the rain glimmered from the streets. I gave the brim of my hat a final tug and stepped out.

There were no flashes of light, no final moments of distortion. Simply that one sickening, hollow-sounding smash on the back of the head and the sidewalk came up and hit me in the face.

I was sick. It ran down my chin and wet my shirt. The smell of it made me sicker. My head was a huge balloon that kept getting bigger and bigger until it was taut and ready to burst into a thousand fragments. Something cold and metallic jarred my face repeatedly. I was cramped, horribly cramped. Even when I tried to move I stayed cramped. Ropes bit into my wrists leaving hempen splinters imbedded under the skin, burning like darts. Whenever the car hit a bump the jack on the floor would slam into my nose.

No one else was with me back there. The empty shoulder holster bit into my side. Nice going, I thought, you walked into that with your mouth open and your eyes shut. I tried to see over the back of the seat, but I couldn't raise myself that far. We turned off the smooth concrete of the highway and the roadway became sloshy and irregular. The jack bounced around more often. First I tried to hold it down with my forehead, but it didn't work, then I drew back from it. That was worse. The muscles in my back ached with the torture of the rack.

I got mad as hell. Sucker. That's what I was. Sucker. Someone was taking me for a damn newcomer at this racket. Working me over with a billy then tossing me in the back of a car. Just like the prohibition days, going for a ride. What the hell did I look like? I had been tied up before and I had been in the back of a car before, but I didn't stay there long. After the first time I learned my lesson. Boy Scout stuff, be prepared. Some son of a bitch was going to get his brains kicked out.

The car skidded to a stop. The driver got out and opened the door. His hands went under my armpits and I was thrown into the mud. Feet straddled me, feet that merged into a dark overcoat and a masked face, and a hand holding my own gun so that I was looking down the muzzle.

"Where is it?" the guy said. His voice carried an obvious attempt at disguise.

"What are you talking about?"

"Damn you anyway, what did you do with it? Don't try to stall me, what did you do with it? You hid it somewhere, you bastard, it wasn't in your pocket. Start talking or I'll shoot your head off!"

The guy was working himself up into a kill-crazy mood. "How do I know where it is if you won't tell me what you want?" I snarled.

"All right, you bastard, get smart. You stuck your neck out once too often. I'll show you." He stuck the gun in his pocket and bent over, his hands fastening in my coat collar and under my arm. I didn't help him any. I gave him damn near two hundred pounds of dead weight to drag into the trees.

Twice the guy snagged himself in the brush and half fell. He took it out on me with a slap in the head and a nasty boot in the ribs. Every once in a while he'd curse and get a better grip on my coat, muttering under his breath what was going to happen to me. Fifty yards into the woods was enough. He dropped me in a heap and dragged the rod out again, fighting for his breath. The guy knew guns. The safety was off and the rod was ready to spit.

"Say it. Say it now, damn you, or you'll never say it. What did you do with them . . . or should I work you over first?"

"Go to hell, you pig."

His hand went up quickly. The gun described a chopping arc toward my jaw. That was what I was waiting for. I grabbed the gun with both hands and yanked, twisting at the same time. He screamed when his shoulder jumped out of the socket, screamed again when I clubbed the edge of my palm against his neck.

Feet jabbed out and ripped into my side, he scrambled to get up. In the middle of it I lost the gun. I held on with one arm and sank my fist into him, but the power of the blow was lost in that awkward position.

But it was enough. He wrenched away, regained his feet and went scrambling through the underbrush. By the time I found the gun he was gone. Time again. If I had had only a minute more I could have chased him, but I hadn't had time to cut my feet loose. Yeah, I'd been on the floor of a car before with my hands tied behind my back. After that first time I have always carried a safety razor blade slipped through the open seam into the double layer of cloth under my belt. It works nice, very handy. Someday I'd get tied up with my hands in front and I'd be stuck.

The knots were soft. A few minutes with them and I was on my feet. I tried to follow his tracks a few yards, but gave it up as a bad job. He had fallen into a couple of soft spots and left hunks of his clothes hanging on some tree limbs. He didn't know where he was going and didn't care. All he knew was that if he stopped and I caught him he'd die in that swamp as sure as he was born. It was almost funny. I turned around and waded back through the tangled underbrush, dodging snaky low-hanging branches that tried to whip my eyes out.

At least I had the car. My erstwhile friend was going to have to hoof it back to camp. I walked around the job, a late Chevy sedan. The glove compartment was empty, the interior in need of a cleaning. Wrapped around the steering post was the ownership card with the owner's name: Mrs. Margaret Murphy, age fifty-two, address in Wooster, occupation, cook. A hell of a note, lifting some poor servant's buggy. I started it up. It would be back in town before it was missed.

When I turned around I plowed through the ruts of a country road for five minutes before reaching the main highway. My lights hit a sign pointing north to Wooster. I must have been out some time, it was over fifteen miles to the city. Once on the concrete I stepped on the gas. More pieces of the puzzle. I had something. I felt in my pocket; the later will was still there. Then what the hell was it? What was so almighty important that I'd been taken for a ride and threatened to make me talk?

Ordinarily I'm not stupid, on the contrary, my mind can pick up threads and weave them into whole cloth, but now I felt like putting on the dunce cap and sitting in the corner.

Nuts.

Twenty minutes to nine I was on the outskirts of Wooster. I turned down the first side street I came to, parked and got out of the car after wiping off any prints I might have made. I didn't know just how the local police operated, but I wasn't in the mood to do any explaining. I picked up the main road again and strode uphill toward Alice's. If she was up there was no indication of it. I recovered my hat from the foyer, cast one look up to the shuttered window and got in my own car. Things were breaking all around my head and I couldn't make any sense out of anything. It was like taking an exam with the answer sheet in front of you and failing because you forgot your glasses.

Going back to Sidon I had time to think. No traffic, just the steady hum of the engine and the sharp whirr of the tires. I was supposed to have something. I didn't have it. Yet certain parties were so sure I did have it they put the buzz on me. *It, it,* for Pete's sake, why don't they name the name? I had two wills and some ideas. They didn't want the wills and they didn't know about the ideas. Something else I might have picked up . . . or didn't pick up.

Of course. Of all the potted, tin-headed fools, I took the cake. Junior Ghent got more than the one will. That was all he had left after the two boys got done with him. They took something else, but whatever it was Junior didn't want me messing in his plans by telling me about it. They took it all right, but somewhere between me and the wall they dropped that important something, and figuring me to be smarter than I should have been, thought I must have found it.

I grinned at myself in the rearview mirror. I'm thick sometimes, but hit me often enough and I get the idea. I didn't even have to worry about Junior beating me to it. He *knew* they had it . . . he wouldn't plan on them dropping it. My curiosity was getting tired of thinking in terms of *its*. This had better be good or I was going to be pretty teed off.

Nice, sweet little case. Two hostile camps. Both fighting each other, both fighting me. In between a lot of people getting shot at and Ruston kidnapped to boot. Instead of a logical starting place it traveled in circles. I kicked the gas pedal a little harder.

Harvey was waiting with the door open when I turned up the drive. I waved him inside and followed the gravel drive to the spot where Junior had taken his shellacking. After a few false starts, I picked out the trail the two had taken across the yard and began tracking. Here and there a footprint was still visible in the soft sod, a twig broken off, flower stalks bent, a stone kicked aside. I let my eyes read over every inch of the path and six feet to the sides, too.

If I knew what I was looking for it wouldn't have been so bad. As it was, it took me a good twenty minutes to reach the wall.

That was where it was. Lying face up in full view of anybody who cared to look. A glaring white patch against the shrubbery, a slightly crinkled, but still sealed envelope.

The IT.

Under my fingers I felt a handful of what felt like postcards. With a shrug I shoved the envelope unopened into my pocket. Item one. I poked around in the grass and held the shrubs aside with my feet. Nothing. I got down on the ground and looked across the grass at a low angle, hoping to catch the sunlight glinting off metal. The rough calculations I took from Roxy's room showed this to be the point of origin of the bullet, but nowhere could I see an empty shell. Hell, it could have been a revolver, then there would be no ejected shell. Or it could have been another gun instead of York's. Nuts there. A .32 is a defensive weapon. Anybody who wants to kill uses a .38 or better, especially at that range. I checked the distance to Roxy's window again. Just to hit the house would mean an elevation of thirty degrees. The lad who made the window was good. Better than that, he was perfect. Only he must have fired from a hole in the ground, because there was no place he could have hidden in this area. That is, if it wasn't one of the two who went over the wall.

I gave up and went back to the car and drove around to the front of the house.

Dutiful Harvey stared at the dirt on my clothes and said, "There's been an accident, sir?"

"You might call it that," I agreed pleasantly. "How is Miss Malcom?"

"Fine, sir. The doctor was here this morning and said she was not in any danger at all."

"The boy?"

"Still quite agitated after his experience. The doctor gave him another sedative. Parks has remained with them all this while. He hasn't set foot out of the room since you left."

"Good. Has anyone been here at all?"

"No, sir. Sergeant Price called several times and wants you to call him back."

"Okay, Harvey, thanks. Think you can find me something to eat? I'm starved."

"Certainly, sir."

I trotted upstairs and knocked on the door. Billy's voice cautiously inquired who it was, and when I answered he pulled a chair away from the door and unlocked it.

"Hi, Billy."

"Hello, Mike . . . what the hell happened?"

"Somebody took me for a ride."

"Cripes, don't be so calm about it."

"Why not? The other guy has to walk back."

"Who?"

"I don't know yet."

Roxy was grinning at me from the bed. "Come over and kiss me, Mike." I gave her a playful tap on the jaw.

"You heal fast."

"I'll do better if you kiss me." I did. Her mouth was a field of burning poppies.

"Okay?"

"I want more."

"When you get better." I squeezed her hand. Before I went into Ruston's room I dusted myself off in front of the mirror. He had heard me come in and was all smiles.

"Hello, Mike. Can you stay here awhile this time?"

"Oh, maybe. Feeling good?"

"I feel all right, but I've been in bed too long. My back is tired."

"I think you'll be able to get up today. I'll have Billy take you for a stroll around the house. I'd do it myself only I have some work to clean up."

"Mike . . . how is everything coming? I mean . . ."

"Don't think about it, Ruston."

"That's all I can do when I lie here awake. I keep thinking of that night, and Dad and Miss Grange. If only there was something I could do I'd feel better."

"The best you can do is stay right here until everything's settled."

"I read in books . . . they were books of no account . . . but sometimes in cases like this the police used the victim as bait. That is, they exposed a person to the advantage of the criminal to see if the criminal would make another attempt. Do you think . . ."

"I think you have a lot of spunk to suggest a thing like that, but the answer is no. You aren't being the target for another snatch, not if I can help it. There're too many other ways. Now how about you hopping into your clothes and getting that airing." I peeled the covers back and helped him out of bed. For a few seconds he was a bit unsteady, but he settled down with a grin and went to the closet. I called Billy in and told him what to do. Billy wasn't too crazy about the idea, but it being daylight, and since I said that I'd stick around, he agreed.

I left the two of them there, winked at Roxy and went downstairs in time to lift a pair of sandwiches and a cup of coffee from Harvey's tray. Grunting my thanks through a mouthful of food I went into the living room and parked in the big chair. For the first time since I had been there a fire blazed away in the fireplace. Good old Harvey. I wolfed down the first sandwich and drowned it in coffee. Only then did I take the envelope out of my pocket. The flap was pasted on crooked, so it had to be the morning dew that had held it shut. I remembered that look on Junior's face when he had seen what was in it. I wondered if *it* was so good mine would look the same way.

I ran my finger under the flap and drew out six pictures.

Now I saw why Junior got so excited. Of the two women in the photos, the only clothes in evidence were shoes. And Myra Grange only had one on at that. Mostly, she wore a leer. A big juicy leer. Alice Nichols looked expectant. The pictures were pornography of the worst sort. Six of them, every one different, both parties fully recognizable, yet the views were of a candid sort, not deliberately posed. No, that wasn't quite it, they were posed, yet unposed . . . at least Myra Grange wasn't posing.

I had to study the shots a good ten minutes before I got the connection. What I had taken to be a border around the pictures done in the printing was really part of the shot. These pics were taken with a hidden camera, one concealed behind a dresser, with the supposed border being some books that did the concealing. A hidden camera and a time arrangement to trip it every so often.

No, Myra Grange wasn't posing, but Alice Nichols was. She had deliberately maneuvered for position each time so Grange was sure to be in perfect focus.

How nice, Alice. How very nicely you and York framed Grange. A frame to neutralize another frame. So?

I fired up a butt and shoved the pics back in my pocket. The outer rim of the puzzle was falling into the grooves in my mind now. Grange had an old will. Why? Would York have settled his entire estate on her voluntarily? Or could he have been forced into it? If Grange had something on her boss . . . something big . . . it had to be big . . . then she could call the squeeze play, and be reasonably sure of making a touchdown, especially when York didn't have long to go anyway. But sometime later York had found out about Grange and her habits and saw a way out. Damn, it was making sense now. He played up to Rhoda Ghent, plied her with gifts, then asked her to proposition Grange. She refused and he dropped her like a hot potato then started on Alice. York should have talked to her first. Alice had no inhibitions anyway, and a cut of York's will meant plenty of action to her. She makes eyes at Grange, Grange makes eyes at Alice and the show is on with the lights properly fed and the camera in position. Alice hands York the negatives, York has a showdown with Grange, threatening to make the pictures public and Grange folds up, yet holds on to the old will in the hope something would happen to make York change his mind. Something like a meat cleaver perhaps? It tied in with what Roxy told me. It could even explain the big play after the pictures. Junior had found out about them somehow, possibly from his sister. If he could get the shots in a law court he could prove how Alice came by her share and get her kicked right out of the show. At least then the family might have some chance to split the quarter of the estate. One hostile camp taken care of. Alice had to be the other. She had to have the pictures before Junior could get them . . . or anybody else for that matter. What could be better than promising a future split of her quarter if they agreed to get the pictures for her? That fit, too. Except that they came too late and saw Junior, knew that he had beaten them to it, so they waylay him, take the stuff and blow. Only I happened in at the wrong time and in the excitement the package gets lost.

I dragged heavily on the cigarette and ran over it again, checking every detail. It stayed the same way. I liked it. Billy and Ruston yelled to me on their way out, but I only waved to them. I was trying to reason out what it was that Grange had on York in the beginning to start a snowball as big as this one rolling downhill.

Flames were licking the top of their sooty cavern. Dante's own inferno, hot, roasting, destroying. It would have been so nice if I could only have known what York had hidden in the pillar of the fireplace. York's secret hiding place, that and the chair bottom. Why two places unless he didn't want to have all his eggs in one basket? Or was it another ease of first things first? He could have put something in the fireplace years ago and not cared to change it.

With a show of impatience I flipped the remains of the butt into the flames, then stretched my legs out toward the fireplace. Secrets, secrets, so damn many secrets. I moved my head to one side so I could see the brick posts on the end of the smoke-blackened pit. It was well concealed, that cache. Curiosity again. I got up and looked it over more closely. Not a brick out of line, not a seam visible. Unless you saw it open you would never guess it to be there.

I went over every inch of it, rapping the bricks with my bare knuckles, but unlike wood, they gave off no sound. There had to be a trip for it somewhere. I looked again where the stone joined the wall. One place shoulder-high was smudged. I pressed.

The tiny door clicked and swung open.

Nice. It was faced with whole brick that joined with a fit in a recess of the concrete that the eye couldn't discern. To get my hand in I had to hold the door open against the force of a spring. I fished around, but felt nothing except cold masonry until I went to take my hand out. A piece of paper caught in the hinge mechanism brushed my fingers. I worked it out slowly, because at the first attempt to dislodge it, part of the paper crumbled to dust. When I let the door go it snapped shut, and I was holding a piece of an ancient newspaper.

It was brown with age, ready to fall apart at the slightest pressure. The print was faded, but legible. It bore the dateline of a New York edition, one that was on the stands October 9, fourteen years ago. What happened fourteen years ago? The rest of the paper had been stolen, this was a piece torn off when it was lifted from the well in the fireplace. A dateline, nothing but a fourteen-year-old dateline.

I'm getting old, I thought. These things ought to make an impression sooner. Fourteen years ago Ruston had been born.

CHAPTER 8

Somehow, the library had an unused look. An ageless caretaker shuffled up the aisle carrying a broom and a dustpan, looking for something to sweep. The librarian, untrue to type, was busy painting her mouth an unholy red, and never looked up until I rapped on the desk. That got me a quick smile, a fast once-over, then an even bigger smile.

"Good morning. Can I help you?"

"Maybe. Do you keep back copies of New York papers?"

She stood up and smoothed out her dress around her hips where it didn't need smoothing at all. "This way, please."

I followed her at a six-foot interval, enough so I could watch her legs that so obviously wanted watching. They were pretty nice legs. I couldn't blame her a bit for wanting to show them off. We angled around behind ceiling-high bookcases until we came to a stairwell. Legs threw a light switch and took me downstairs. A musty odor of old leather and paper hit me on the last step. Little trickles of moisture beaded the metal bins and left dark stains on the concrete walls. A hell of a place for books.

"Here they are." She pointed to a tier of shelves, stacked with newspapers, separated by layers of cardboard. Together we located the old *Globe* editions then began peeling off the layers. In ten minutes we both looked like we had been playing in coal. Legs threw me a pout. "I certainly hope that whatever you're after is worth all this trouble."

"It is, honey," I told her, "it is. Keep your eyes open for October 9."

Another five minutes, then, "This it?"

I would have kissed her if she didn't have such a dirty face. "That's the one. Thanks."

She handed it over. I glanced at the dateline, then at the one in my hand. They matched. We laid the paper out on a reading desk and pulled on the overhead light. I thumbed through the leaves, turning them over as I scanned each column. Legs couldn't stand it any longer. "Please . . . what are you looking for?"

I said a nasty word and tapped the bottom of the page.

"But . . ."

"I know. It's gone. Somebody ripped it out."

She said the same nasty word, then asked, "What was it?"

"Beats me, honey. Got any duplicates around?"

"No, we only keep one copy. There's rarely any call for them except from an occasional high school history student who is writing a thesis on something or other."

"Uh-huh." Tearing that spot out wasn't going to do any good. There were other libraries. Somebody was trying to stall me for time. Okay, okay, I have all the time in the world. More time than you have, brother.

I helped her stack the papers back on their shelves before going upstairs. We both ducked into washrooms to get years of dust off our skin, only she beat me out. I half expected it anyway.

When we were walking toward the door I dropped a flyer. "Say, do you know Myra Grange?" Her breath caught and held. "Why . . . no. That is, isn't she the one . . . I mean with Mr. York?"

I nodded. She had made a good job of covering up, but I didn't miss that violent blush of emotion that surged into her cheeks at the mention of Grange's name. So this was why the vanishing lady spent so many hours in the library. "The same," I said. "Did she ever go down there?"

"No." A pause. "No, I don't think so. Oh, yes. She did once. She took the boy . . . Mr. York's son down there, but that was when I first came here. I went with them. They looked over some old manuscripts, but that was all."

"When was she here last?"

"Who are you?" She looked scared.

My badge was in my hand. She didn't have to read it. All she needed was the sight of the shield to start shaking. "She was here . . . about a week ago."

Very carefully, I looked at her. "No good. That was too long ago. Let's put it this way. When did you *see* her last?" Legs got the point. She knew I knew about Myra and guessed as much about her. Another blush, only this one faded with the fear behind it.

"A . . . a week ago, I told you." I thanked her and went out. Legs was lying through her teeth and I couldn't blame her.

The water was starting to bubble now. It wouldn't be long before it started to boil. Two things to do before I went to New York, one just for the pleasure of it. I made my first stop at a drugstore. A short, squat pharmacist came out from behind the glass partition and murmured his greetings. I threw the pills I had taken from Henry's bottle on the counter in front of me.

"These were being taken for aspirin," I said. "Can you tell me what they are?"

He looked at me and shrugged, picking up one in his fingers. He touched a cautious tongue to the white surface, then smelled it. "Not aspirin," he told me. "Have you any idea what they might be?"

"I'd say sleeping pills. One of the barbiturates." The druggist nodded and went back behind his glass. I waited perhaps five minutes before he came back again.

"You were right," he said. I threw two five-dollar bills on the counter and scooped up the rest of the pills. Very snazzy, killer, you got a lot of tricks up your sleeve. A very thorough guy. It was going to be funny when I had that killer at the end of my rod. I wondered if he was thorough enough to try to get rid of me.

Back and forth, back and forth. Like a swing. From kidnapping to murder to petty conniving and back to the kidnapping again. Run, run, run. Shuttle train stuff. Too many details. They were like a shroud that the killer was trying to draw around the original motive. That, there had to be. Only it was getting lost in the mess. It could have been an accident, this eruption of pointless crimes, or they might have happened anyway, or they could have been foreseen by the killer and used to his own advantage. No, nobody could be that smart. There's something about crime that's like a disease. It spreads worse than the flu once it gets started. It already had a good start when Ruston was kidnapped. It seemed like that was months ago, but it wasn't . . . just a few short days.

I reviewed every detail on my way to Wooster, but the answer always came up the same. Either I was dumb or the killer was pretty cagey. I had to find Mallory, I had to find Grange, I had to find the killer if he wasn't one of those two. So far all I found was a play behind the curtain.

Halfway there I gave up thinking and concentrated on the road. With every mile I'd gotten madder until I was chain-smoking right through my deck of butts. Wooster was alive this time. People walked along the streets in noisy contentment, limousines blared indignantly at lesser cars in front of them, and a steady stream of traffic went in and out of the shop doors. There was plenty of room in front of Alice's house. I parked the car and went into the foyer, remembering vividly the crack on my skull.

This time the buzz was a short one. I took the stairs fast, but she was faster. She stood in the door with a smile, ready to be kissed. I said, "Hello, Alice," but I didn't kiss her. Her smile broke nervously.

"What's the matter, Mike?"

"Nothing, kid, nothing at all. Why?"

"You look displeased about something." That was putting it mildly.

I went inside without lifting my hat. Alice went to reach for the decanter, but I stopped her by throwing the envelope on the coffee table. "You were looking for these, I think."

"I?" She pulled one of the pictures out of the wrapper, then shoved it back hastily, her face going white. I grinned.

Then I got nasty. "In payment for last night."

"You can go now."

"Uh-uh. Not yet." Her eyes followed mine to the ashtray. There were four butts there, two of them had lipstick on them and the other two weren't my brand.

Alice tried to scream a warning, but it never got past her lips. The back of my hand caught her across the mouth and she rolled into the sofa, gasping with the sting of the blow. I turned on my heels and went to the bedroom and kicked the door open. William Graham was sitting on the edge of the bed as nice as you please smoking a cigarette. His face was scratched in a dozen places and hunks torn out of his clothes from the briars in the woods.

Every bit of color drained out of his skin. I grabbed him before he could stand up and smashed him right in the nose. Blood spurted all over my coat. His arms flailed out, trying to push me away, but I clipped him again on the nose, and again, until there was nothing but a soggy, pulpy mass of flesh to hit. Then I went to work on the rest of his puss. Slapping, punching, then a nasty cut with the side of my hand. He was limp in my grasp, his head thrown back and his eyes wide open. I let him go and he sagged into a shapeless heap on the floor. It was going to take a thousand dollars worth of surgery to make his face the same.

Alice had seen and heard. When I went into the living room she was crouched in terror behind a chair. That didn't stop me. I yanked her out; her dress split down the middle. "Lie to me, Alice," I warned, "and you'll look just like him. Maybe worse. You put him up to bumping me, didn't you?"

All she could do was nod soundlessly.

"You told him he wasn't in the will, but if he and his brother found the pictures and gave them to you you'd cut them in for your share?"

She nodded again. I pushed her back. "York made the will," I said. "It was his dough and I don't care what he did with it. Take your share and go to hell with it. You probably will anyway. Tell Arthur I'll be looking for him. When I find him he's going to look like his brother."

I left her looking eighty years old. William was moaning through his own blood when I went out the door. Good party. I liked it. There would be no more rides from that enemy camp. The redskins have left, vamoosed, departed.

There was only one angle to the Graham boys that I couldn't cover. Which one of them took the shot at Roxy and why? I'll be damned if I heard a shot. They didn't stop long enough to say boo far less than snap off a quickie. And they certainly would have shot at me, not toward the window. I wasn't sure of anything, but if there was money on the table I'd say that neither one had used a gun at all that night. It was details like that that creased me up. I had to make a choice one way or the other and follow it to a conclusion. All right, it was made. The Graham boys were out. Someone else fired it.

New York was a dismal sight after the country. I hadn't thought the grass and the trees with their ugly bilious color of green could have made such an impression on me. Somehow the crowded streets and the endless babble of voices gave me a dirty taste in my mouth. I rolled into a parking lot, pocketed my ticket, then turned into a chain drugstore on the stem. My first call was back to Sidon. Harvey answered and I told him to keep the kid in the room with Roxy and Billy until I got back and take any calls that came for me. My next dime got Pat Chambers, Captain of Homicide.

"Greetings, chum," I said, "this is Uncle Mike."

"It's about time you buzzed me. I was beginning to think you cooled off another citizen and were on the fly. Where are you?"

"Right off Times Square."

"Coming down?"

"No, Pat. I have some business to attend to. Look, how about meeting me on the steps of the library. West Forty-third Street entrance. It's important."

"Okay. Say in about half an hour. Will that do?"

I told him fine and hung up. Pat was tops in my book. A careful, crafty cop, and all cop. He looked more like a gentleman-about-town, but there it ended. Pat had a mind like an adding machine and a talent for police work backed up by the finest department in the world. Ordinarily a city cop has no truck with a private eye, but Pat and I had been buddies a long time with one exception. It was a case of mutual respect, I guess.

At a stand-up-and-eat joint I grabbed a couple dogs and a lemonade then beat it to the library in time to see Pat step out of a prowl car. We shook hands and tossed some remarks back and forth before Pat asked, "What's the story?"

"Let's go inside where we can talk."

We went through the two sets of doors and into the reading room. Holding my voice down I said, "Ever hear of Rudolph York, Pat?"

"So?" He had.

I gave him the story in brief, adding at the end, "Now I want to see what was attached to the rest of this dateline. It'll be here somewhere, and it's liable to turn up something you can help me with."

"For instance?"

"I don't know yet, but police records go back pretty far, don't they? What I want to know may have happened fourteen years ago. My memory isn't that good."

"Okay, let's see what we can dig up."

Instead of going through the regular library routine, Pat flashed his shield and we got an escort to where the papers were filed. The old gentleman in the faded blue serge went unerringly to the right bin, pulled out a drawer and selected the edition I wanted all on the first try. He pointed to a table and pulled out chairs for us. My hands were trembling with the excitement of it when I opened the paper.

It was there. Two columns right down the side of the page. Two columns about six-inches long with a photo of York when he was a lot younger. Fourteen years younger. A twenty-four-point heading smacked me between the eyes with its implications.

FATHER ACCUSES SCIENTIST OF BABY SWITCH

Herron Mallory, whose wife gave birth to a seven-pound boy that died two days later, has accused Rudolph York, renowned scientist, of switching babies. Mallory alleged that it was York's son, not his, who died. His claim is based on the fact that he saw his own child soon after birth, and recognized it again when it was shown to York, his own having been pronounced dead earlier. Authorities denied that such a mistake could have happened. Head Nurse Rita Cambell verified their denials by assuring both York and Mallory that she had been in complete charge during the two days, and recognized both babies by sight, confirming identification by their bracelets. Mrs. York died during childbirth.

I let out a long, low whistle. The ball had moved up to midfield. Pat suggested a follow-up and we brought out the following day's sheet. On page four was a small, one-column spread. It was stated very simply. Herron Mallory, a small-time petty thief and former bootlegger, had been persuaded to drop the charges against Rudolph York. Apparently it was suspected that he couldn't make any headway against a solid citizen like York in the face of his previous convictions. That was where it ended. At least for the time being.

York had a damn good reason then to turn green when Mallory's name was mentioned. Pat tapped the clipping. "What do you think?"

"It might be the real McCoy . . . then again it might be an accident. I can't see why York would pull a stunt like that."

"There're possibilities here. York was no young man when his son was born. He might have wanted an heir awfully bad."

"I thought of that, Pat, but there's one strike against it. If York was going to pull a switch, with his knowledge of genetics he certainly would have taken one with a more favorable family history, don't you think?"

"Yes, if he made the switch himself. But if it were left up to someone else . . . the nurse, for instance, the choice might have been pretty casual."

"But the nurse stated . . ."

"York was very wealthy, Mike."

"I get it. But there's another side too. Mallory, being a cheap chiseler, might have realized the possibilities in setting up a squawk after his own child died, and picked on York. Mallory would figure York would come across with some hard cash just to keep down that kind of publicity. How does that read?"

"Clever, Mike, very clever. But which one do you *believe*?"

The picture of York's face when he heard the name Mallory flashed across my mind. The terror, the stark terror; the hate. York the strong. He wouldn't budge an inch if Mallory had simply been trying some judicious blackmail. Instead, he would have been the one to bring the matter to the police. I said: "It was a switch, Pat."

"That puts it on Mallory."

I nodded. "He must have waited a long time for his chance. Waited until the kid was worth his weight in gold to York and the public, then put the snatch on him. Only he underestimated the kid and bungled the job. When York went to Grange's place, Mallory followed him, thinking that York might have figured where the kidnapping came from and split his skull."

"Did you try to trace the cleaver, Mike?"

"No, it was the kind you could buy in any hardware store, and it was well handled, besides. A tool like that would be nearly impossible to trace. There was no sense in my fooling around with it. Price will track it down if it's possible. Frankly, I don't think it'll work. What's got me now is why someone ripped out this clipping in the Sidon library. Even as a stall it wouldn't mean much."

"It's bound to have a bearing."

"It'll come, it'll come. How about trying to run down Mallory for me? Think you can find anything on him?"

"We should, Mike. Let's go down to headquarters. If he was pinched at all we'll have a record of it."

"Roger." We were lucky enough to nab a cab waiting for the red light on the corner of Fifth and Forty-second. Pat gave him the downtown address and we leaned back into the cushions. Fifteen minutes later we got out in front of an old-fashioned red brick building and took the elevator to the third floor. I waited in an office until Pat returned bearing a folder under his arm. He cleared off the desk with a sweep of his hand and shook the contents out on the blotter.

The sheaf was fastened with a clip. The typewritten notation read, *Herron Mallory*. As dossiers go, it wasn't thick. The first page gave Mallory's history and record of his first booking. Age twenty in 1927; born in New York City of Irish-Russian parents. Charged with operating a vehicle without a license. That was the starter. He came up on bootlegging, petty larceny; he was suspected of participating in a hijack-killing and a holdup. Plenty of charges, but a fine list of cases suspended and a terse "not convicted" written across the bottom of the page. Mr. Mallory either had a good lawyer or friends where it counted. The last page bore his picture, a profile and front view shot of a dark fellow slightly on the thin side with eyes and mouth carrying an inbred sneer.

I held it under the light to get a better look at it, studying it from every angle, but nothing clicked.

Pat said, "Well?"

"No good, chum. Either I never saw him before or the years have changed him a lot. I don't know the guy from Adam."

He held out a typewritten report. One that had never gotten past a police desk. I read it over. In short, it was the charges that Mallory had wanted filed against York for kidnapping his kid. No matter who Mallory was or had been, there was a note of sincerity in that statement. There was also a handwritten note on hospital stationery from Head Nurse Rita Cambell briefly decrying the charge as absolutely false. There was no doubt about it. Rita Cambell's note was aggressive and assuring enough to convince anyone that Mallory was all wet. Fine state of affairs. I had never participated in the mechanics of becoming a father, but I did know that the male parent was Johnny-the-Glom as far as the hospital was concerned. He saw his baby maybe once for two minutes through a tiny glass plate set in the door. Sure, it would be possible to recognize your child even in that time, but all babies do look alike in most ways. To the nurse actually in charge of the child's entire life, however, each one has the separate identity of a person. It was unlikely that she would make a mistake . . . unless paid for it. Damn, it *could* happen unless you knew nurses. Doubt again. Nurses had a code of ethics as rigid as a doctor's. Any woman who gave her life to the profession wasn't the type that would succumb to a show of long green.

Hell, I was getting all balled up. First I was sure it was a switch, now I wasn't so sure. Pat had seen the indecision in my face. He can figure things, too. "There it is, Mike. I can't do anything more because it's outside my jurisdiction, but if I can help you in any way, say the word."

"Thanks, kid. It really doesn't make much difference whether it was a switch or not. Someplace Mallory figures in it. Before I can go any further I'll have to find either Mallory or Grange, but don't ask me how. If Price turns up Grange I'll get a chance to talk to her, but if Dilwick is the one I'll be out in the cold."

Pat looked sour. "Dilwick ought to be in jail."

"Dilwick ought to be dead. He's a bastard."

"He's still the law, though, and you know what that means."

"Yeah."

Pat started stuffing the papers back in the folder, but I stopped him. "Let me take another look at them, will you?"

"Sure."

I rifled through them quickly, then shook my head.

"Something familiar?"

"No . . . I don't think so. There's something in there that's ringing a bell, but I can't put my finger on it. Oh, nuts, put 'em away."

We went downstairs together and shook hands in the doorway. Pat hailed a cab and I took the next one up to Fifty-fourth and Eighth, then out over to the parking lot. The day was far from being wasted; I was getting closer to the theme of the thing. On top of everything else there was a possible baby switch. It was looking up now. Here was an underlying motive that was as deep and unending as the ocean. The groping, the fumbling after ends that led nowhere was finished. This was meat that could be eaten. But first it had to be chewed; chewed and ground up fine before it could be swallowed.

My mind was hammering itself silly. The dossier. What was in the dossier? I saw something there, but what? I went over it carefully enough; I checked everything against everything else, but what did I forget?

The hell with it. I shoved the key in the ignition and stepped on the starter.

CHAPTER 9

Going back to Sidon I held it down to a slow fifty, stopping only once for a quick bite and a tank of gas. Someday I was going to get me a decent meal. Someday. Three miles from the city I turned off the back road to a cloverleaf, then swung onto the main artery. When I reached the state police headquarters I cut across the concrete and onto the gravel.

For once Price was in when I wanted him.

So was Dilwick.

I said hello to Price and barely nodded to Dilwick.

"You lousy slob!" he muttered softly.

"Shut up, pig."

"Maybe you both better shut up," Price put in quietly. I threw my hat on the desk and pushed a butt between my lips. Price waited until I lit it, then jerked his thumb toward the fat cop.

"He wants words with you, Mike."

"Let's hear 'em," I offered.

"Not here, wise guy. I think you'd do better at the station. I don't want to be interrupted."

That was a nasty dig at Price, and the sergeant took it right up. "Forget that stuff," he barked, "while he's here he's under my jurisdiction. Don't forget it."

For a minute I thought Dilwick was going to swing and I was hoping he would. I'd love to be in a two-way scramble over that guy. The odds were too great. He looked daggers at Price. "I won't forget it," he repeated.

Price led off. "Dilwick says you broke into the Grange apartment and confiscated something of importance. What about it, Mike?"

I let Dilwick have a lopsided grin. "Did I?"

"You know damn well you did! You'd better . . ."

"How do you know it was important?"

"It's gone, that's reason enough."

"Hell."

"Wait a minute, Mike," Price cut in. "What did you take?"

I saw him trying to keep his face straight. Price liked this game of baiting Dilwick.

"I could say nothing, pal, and he couldn't prove a thing. I bet you never found any prints of mine, did you, Dilwick?" The cop's face was getting redder. ". . . and the way you had that building bottled up nobody *should* have been able to get in, should they?" Dilwick would split his seams if I kept it up any longer. "Sure, I was there, so what? I found what a dozen of you missed."

I reached in my pocket and yanked out the two wills. Dilwick reached a shaking hand for them but I passed them to Price. "This old one was in Grange's apartment. It isn't good because this is the later one. Maybe it had better be filed someplace."

Dilwick was watching me closely. "Where did the second one come from?"

"Wouldn't you like to know?"

I was too slow. The back of Dilwick's hand nearly rocked my head off my shoulders. The arm of a chair hit my side and before I could spill over into it Dilwick had my shirt front. Price caught his hand before he could swing again.

I kicked the chair away and pulled free as Price stepped between us. "Let me go, Price!" I yelled.

"Damn it, I said to turn it off!"

Dilwick backed off reluctantly. "I'll play that back to you, Dilwick," I said. Nobody was pulling that trick on me and getting by with it. It's a wonder he had the nerve to start something after that last pasting I gave him. Maybe he was hoping I'd try to use my rod . . . that would be swell. He could knock me off as nice as anything and call it police business.

"Maybe you'll answer the next time you're spoken to, Hammer. You've pulled a lot of shady deals around here lately and I'm sick of it. As for you, Price, you're treating him like he's carrying a badge. You've got me hog-tied, but that won't last long if I want to work on it."

The sergeant's voice was almost a whisper. "One day you're going to go too far. I think you know what I mean."

Evidently Dilwick did. His lips tightened into a thin line and his eyes blazed, but he shut up just the same. "Now if you have anything to say, say it properly."

With an obvious attempt at controlling his rage, Dilwick nodded. He turned to me again. "Where did you get the other will?"

"Wouldn't you like to know?" I repeated.

"You letting him get away with this, Price?"

The trooper was on the spot. "Tell him, Mike."

"I'll tell you, Price. He can listen in. I found it among York's personal effects."

For a full ten minutes I stood by while the two of them went over the contents of the wills. Price was satisfied with a cursory examination, but not so Dilwick. He read every line, then reread them. I could see the muscles of his mouth twitch as he worked the thing out in his mind. No, I was not underestimating Dilwick one bit. There wasn't much that went on that he didn't know about. Twice, he let his eyes slide off the paper and meet mine. It was coming. Any minute now.

Then it was here. "I could read murder into this," he grated.

Price turned sharply. "Yes?"

"Hammer, I think I'm going to put you on the spot."

"Swell. You'd like that. Okay, go ahead."

"Pull up your ears and get a load of this, Price. This punk and the Nichols dame could make a nice team. Damn nice. You didn't think I'd find out about those pictures, did you, Hammer? Well, I did. You know what it looks like to me? It looks like the Nichols babe blackmailed Grange into making York change his will. Let York see those shots and Grange's reputation would be shot to hell, she'd be fired and lose out on the will to boot. At least if she came through on the deal, all she'd lose was the will."

I nodded. "Pretty, but where do I come in?"

"Right now. Grange got hold of those pictures somehow. Only

Nichols pulls a fast one and tells York that Grange was the one who was blackmailing her. York takes off for Grange's apartment in a rage because he had a yen for his pretty little niece, only Grange bumps him. Then Nichols corners you and you bump Grange and get the stuff off her, and the will. Now you turn it up, Nichols comes into a wad of cash and you split it."

It wasn't as bad as I thought. Dilwick had squeezed a lot of straight facts out of somebody, only he was putting it together wrong. Yeah, he had gotten around, all right. He had reached a lot of people to get that much and he'd like to make it stick.

Price said, "What about it, Mike?"

I grinned. "He's got a real sweet case there." I looked at the cop. "How're you going to prove it?"

"Never mind," he snarled, "I will, I will. Maybe I ought to book you right now on what I have. It'll hold up and Price knows it, too."

"Uh-uh. It'll hold up . . . for about five minutes. Did you find Grange yet?"

He said nothing.

"Nuts," I laughed, "no corpus delicti, no Mike Hammer."

"Wrong, Hammer. After a reasonable length of time and sufficient evidence to substantiate death, a corpse can be assumed."

"He's right, Mike."

"Then he's got to shoot holes in my alibi, Price. I have a pretty tight one."

"Where did you go after you left Alice's apartment the other night?" Brother, I should have guessed it. Dilwick had put the bee on the Graham kid and the bastard copped a sneak. It was ten to one he told Dilwick he hadn't seen me.

That's what I get for making enemies. If the Graham kid thought he could put me on the spot he'd do it. So would Alice for that matter.

But there were still angles. "Go ahead and work on my alibi, Dilwick. You know what it is. Only I'll give you odds that I can make your witness see the light sooner than you can."

"Not if you're in the can."

"First get me there. I don't think you can. Even if you did a good lawyer could rip those phonies apart on the stand and you know it. You're stalling, Dilwick. What're you scared of? Me? Afraid I'll put a crimp in your doings?"

"You're asking for it, punk."

Price came back into the argument. "Skip it, Dilwick. If you have the goods on him then present it through the regular channels, only don't slip up. Let you and your gang go too far and there'll be trouble. I'm satisfied to let Mr. Hammer operate unhampered because I'm familiar with him . . . and you, too."

"Thanks, pal."

Dilwick jammed his hat on and stamped out of the room. If I wanted to get anywhere I was going to have to act fast, because my fat friend wasn't going to let any grass grow under his feet finding enough dope to toss me in the clink. When the door slammed I let Price have my biggest smile. He smiled right back.

"Where've you been?"

"New York. I tried to get you before I left but you weren't around."

"I know. We've had a dozen reports of Grange being seen and I've been running them down."

"Any luck?"

"Nothing. A lot of mistaken identities and a few cranks who wanted to see the police in action. What did you get?"

"Plenty. We're back to the kidnapping again. This whole pot of stew started there and is going to end there. Ruston wasn't York's kid at all. His died in childbirth and another was switched to take its place. The father of the baby was a small-time hoodlum and tried to make a complaint but was dissuaded along the line. All very nicely covered up, but I think it's a case of murder that's been brewing for fourteen years."

During the next half hour I gave him everything I knew, starting with my trip to the local library. Price was a lot like Pat. He sat there saying nothing, taking it all in and letting it digest in his mind. Occasionally he would nod, but never interrupted until I had finished.

He said: "That throws the ball to this Mallory character."

"Roger, and the guy is completely unknown. The last time he showed up was a few days after the switch took place."

"A man can change a lot in fourteen years."

"That's what I'm thinking," I agreed. "The first thing we have to do is concentrate on locating Grange. Alive or dead she can bring us further up to date. She didn't disappear for nothing."

"All right, Mike, I'll do my share. I still have men dragging the channel and on the dragnet. What are you going to do?"

"There are a few members of the loyal York clan that I'd like to see. In the meantime do you think you can keep Dilwick off my neck?"

"I'll try, but I can't promise much. Unfortunately, the law is made up of words which have to be abided more by the letter than the spirit therein, so to speak. If I can sidetrack him I will, but you had better keep him under observation if you can. I don't have to tell you what he's up to. He's a stinker."

"Twice over. Okay, I'll keep in touch with you. Thanks for the boost. The way things are I'm going to have to be sharp on my end to beat Dilwick out of putting me up at the expense of the city."

Dusk had settled around the countryside like a gray blanket when I left headquarters. I stepped into the car and rolled out the drive to the highway. I turned toward the full glow that marked the lights of Sidon and pulled into the town at suppertime. I would have gone straight to the estate if I hadn't passed the library, which was still lit up.

It was just an idea, but I've had them before and they'd paid off. I slammed the brakes on, backed up and parked in front of the building. Inside the door I noticed the girl at the desk, but she wasn't the same one I had spoken to before. This one had legs like a bridge lamp. Thinking that perhaps Legs was in one of the reading rooms, I toured the place, but aside from an elderly gentleman, two school-teacher types and some kids, the place was empty.

Just to be sure I checked the cellar, too, but the light was off and I didn't think she'd be down there in the dark even if Grange was with her. Not with that musty-tomb odor anyway.

The girl at the desk said, "Can I help you find something, sir?"

"Maybe you can."

"What book was it?"

I tried to look puzzled. "That is what I forgot. The girl that was here this morning had it all picked out for me. Now I can't find her."

"Oh, you mean Miss Cook?"

"Yeah," I faked, "that's the one. Is she around now?"

This time the girl was the one to be puzzled. "No, she isn't. She went home for lunch this afternoon and never returned. I came on duty early to replace her. We've tried to locate her all over town, but she seems to have dropped from sight. It's so very strange."

It was getting hot now, hotter than ever. The little bells were going off inside my skull. Little bells that tinkled and rang and chimed and beat themselves into shattered pieces of nothing. It was getting hotter, this broth, and I was holding onto the handle.

"This Miss Cook. Where does she live?"

"Why, two blocks down on Snyder Avenue. Shall I call her apartment again? Perhaps she's home now."

I didn't think she'd have any luck, but I said, "Please do."

She lifted the receiver and dialed a number. I heard the buzz of the bell on the other end, then the voice of the landlady answering. No, Miss Cook hadn't come in yet. Yes, she would tell her to call as soon as she did. Yes. Yes. Good night.

"She isn't there."

"So I gathered. Oh, well, she's probably had one of her boy-friends drop in on her. I'll come back tomorrow."

"Very well, I'm sorry I couldn't help you."

Sorry, everybody was being sorry. Pretty soon somebody was going to be so sorry they died of it. Snyder Avenue was a quiet residential section of old brownstone houses that had undergone many a face-lifting and emerged looking the same as ever. On one corner a tiny grocery store was squeezed in between buildings. The stout man in the dirty white apron was taking in some boxes of vegetables as he prepared to close up shop. I drew abreast of him and whistled.

When he stopped I asked, "Know a Miss Cook? She's the librarian. I forgot which house it was."

"Yeah, sure." He pointed down the block. "See that car sitting under the streetlight? Well the house just past it and on the other side is the one. Old Mrs. Baxter is the landlady and she don't like noise, so you better not honk for her."

I yelled my thanks and went up the street and parked behind the car he had indicated. Except for the light in the first floor front, the place was in darkness. I ran up the steps and looked over the doorbell. Mrs. Baxter's name was there, along with four others, but only one bell.

I pushed it.

She must have been waiting for me to make up my mind, because she came out like a jack-in-the-box.

"Well?"

"Mrs. Baxter?"

"That's me."

"I'm looking for Miss Cook. They . . ."

"Who ain't been looking for her. All day long the phone's been driving me crazy, first one fellow then another. When she gets back here I'm going to give her a good piece of my mind."

"May I come in, Mrs. Baxter?"

"What for? She isn't home. If she didn't leave all her things here I'd say she skipped out. Heaven only knows why."

I couldn't stand there and argue with her. My wallet slipped into my palm and I let her see the glint of the metal. Badges are wonderful things even when they don't mean a thing. Her eyes went from my hand to my face before she moistened her lips nervously and stood aside in the doorway.

"Has . . . has there been trouble?"

"We don't know." I shut the door and followed her into the living room. "What time did she leave here today?"

"Right after lunch. About a quarter to one."

"Does she always eat at home?"

"Only her lunch. She brings in things and . . . you know. At night she goes out with her boyfriends for supper."

"Did you see her go?"

"Yes. Well, no. I didn't see her, but I heard her upstairs and heard her come down. The way she always takes the stairs two at a time in those high heels I couldn't very well not hear her."

"I see. Do you mind if I take a look at her room? There's a chance that she might be involved in a case we're working on and we don't want anything to happen to her."

"Do you think . . ."

"Your guess is as good as mine, Mrs. Baxter. Where's her room?"

"Next floor in the rear. She never locks her door so you can go right in."

I nodded and went up the stairs with the old lady's eyes boring holes in my back. She was right about the door. It swung in when I turned the knob. I shut the door behind me and switched on the light, standing there in the middle of the room for a minute taking it all in. Just a room, a nice, neat girl's room. Everything was in its place, nothing was disarranged. The closet was well stocked with clothes including a fairly decent mink coat inside a plastic bag. The drawers in the dresser were the same way. Tidy. Nothing gone.

Son of a bitch, *she* was snatched too! I slammed the drawer shut so hard a row of bottles went over. Why didn't I pick her up sooner? She was Myra Grange's alibi! Of course! And somebody was fighting pretty hard to keep Myra Grange's face in the mud. She didn't skip out on her own . . . not and leave all her clothes here. She went out that front door on her way back to work and she was picked up somewhere between here and the library. Fine, swell. I'd made a monkey of myself by letting things slide just a little longer. I wasn't the only one who knew that she and Grange were on more than just speaking terms. That somebody was either following me around or getting there on his own hook.

A small desk and chair occupied one corner of the room beside the bed. A small letter-writing affair with a flap front was on the desk. I pulled the cover down and glanced at the papers neatly placed in the pigeonholes. Bills, receipted bills. A few notes and some letters. In the middle of the blotter a writing tablet looked at me with a blank stare.

The first three letters were from a sailor out of town. Very factual letters quite unlike a sailor. Evidently a relative. Or a sap. The next letter was the payoff. I breezed through it and felt the sweat pop out on my face. Paragraph after paragraph of lurid, torrid love . . . words of endearment . . . more love, exotic, fantastic.

Grange had signed only her initials at the bottom.

When I slid the letter back I whistled through my teeth. Grange had certainly gone whole hog with her little partner. I would have closed the desk up after rifling through the rest of the stuff if I hadn't felt that squeegy feeling crawling around my neck. It wasn't new. I had had it in Pat's office.

Something I was supposed to remember. Something I was supposed to see. Damn. I went back through the stuff, but as far as I could see there wasn't anything there that I hadn't seen before I came into the room. Or was there?"

Roger . . . there was! It was in my hand. I was staring at Grange's bold signature. It was the handwriting that I had recognized. The first time I had seen it was on some of her papers I had taken from that little cache in her apartment. The next time I had seen it was on the bottom of a statement certifying that Ruston was York's son and not Mallory's, only that time the signature read *Rita Cambell*.

It hit me like a pile driver, hard, crushing. It had been dangling in front of my face all this time and I hadn't seen it. But I wasn't alone with the knowledge, hell no. Somebody else had it too, that's why Grange was dead or missing and Cook on the lam.

Motive, at last the motive. I stood alone in the middle of the room and spun the thing around in my mind. This was raw, bitter motive. It was motive that incited kidnapping and caused murder and this was proof of it. The switch, the payoff. York taking Grange under his wing to keep the thing quiet. Crime that touched off crime that touched off more crime like a string of firecrackers. When you put money into it the thing got bigger and more scrambled than ever.

I had gotten to the center of it. The nucleus. Right on the target were Ruston and Grange. Somebody was aiming at both of them. Winged the kid and got Grange. Mallory, but who the hell was he? Just a figure known to have existed, and without doubt still existing.

I needed bait to catch this fish, yet I couldn't use the kid; he had seen too much already. That is, unless he was willing. I felt like a heel to put it up to him. But it was that or try to track Grange down. Senseless? I didn't know. Maybe a dozen cops *had* dragged the river, and maybe the dragnet *was* all over the state, but maybe they were going at it the wrong way. Sure, maybe it would be best to try for Grange. She was bound to have the story if anyone had, and I wouldn't be taking a chance with the kid's neck either.

Mrs. Baxter was waiting for me at the foot of the stairs, wringing her hands like a nervous hen. "Find anything?" she asked.

I nodded. "Evidence that she expected to come back here. She didn't just run off."

"Oh, dear."

"If anyone calls, try to get their names, and keep a record of all calls. Either Sergeant Price of the state police will check on it or me personally. Under no conditions give out the information to anyone else, understand?"

She muttered her assent and nodded. I didn't want Dilwick to pull another fasty on me. As soon as I left, all the lights on the lower floor blazed on. Mrs. Baxter was the scary type, I guess.

I swung my heap around in a U-turn, then got on the main street and stopped outside a drugstore. My dime got me police headquarters and headquarters reached Price on the radio. We had a brief chitchat through the medium of the desk cop and I told him to meet me at the post in fifteen minutes.

Price beat me there by ten feet and came over to see what was up.

"You have the pictures of Grange's car after it went in the drink?"

"Yeah, inside, want to see them?"

"Yes."

On the way in I told him what had happened. The first thing he did was go to the radio and put out a call on the Cook girl. I supplied the information the best I could, but my description centered mainly about her legs. They were things you couldn't miss. For a few minutes Price disappeared into the back room and I heard him fiddling around with a filing cabinet.

He came out with a dozen good shots of the wrecked sedan. "If you don't mind, tell me what you're going to do with these?"

"Beats me," I answered. "It's just a jumping-off place. Since she's still among the missing she can still be found. This is where she was last seen apparently."

"There've been a lot of men looking for her."

I grinned at him. "Now there's going to be another." Each one of the shots I went over in detail, trying to pick out the spot where it went in, and visualizing just how it turned in the air to land like it did. Price watched me closely, trying to see what I was getting at.

"Price . . ."

"Yes."

"When you pulled the car out, was the door on the right open?"

"It was, but the seat had come loose and was jammed in the

doorway. She would have had some time trying to climb out that way."

"The other door was open too?"

His head bobbed. "The lock had snapped when the door was wrenched open, probably by the force of hitting the water, although being on the left, it could have happened when her car was forced off the road."

"Think she might have gotten out that way?"

"Gotten out . . . or floated out?"

"Either one."

"More like it was the other way."

"Was the car scratched up much?"

The sergeant looked thoughtful. "Not as much as it should have been. The side was punched in from the water, and the front fender partially crumpled where it hit the bottom, but the only new marks were short ones along the bottom of the door and on the very edge of the fender, and at that we can't be sure that they didn't come from the riverbed."

"I get it," I said. "You think that she was scared off the road. I've seen enough women drivers to believe that, even if she was only half a dame. Why not? Another car threatening to slam into her would be reason enough to make her jump the curb. Well, it's enough for me. If she was dead there wouldn't be much sense keeping her body hidden, and if it weren't hidden it would have shown up by now, so I'm assuming that Grange is still alive somewhere and if she's alive she can be found."

I tossed the sheaf of pictures back to Price. "Thanks, chum. No reflection on any of you, but I think you've been looking for Grange the wrong way. You've been looking for a body."

He smiled a bit and we said good night. What had to be done had to wait until morning . . . the first thing in the morning. I tooled my car back to town and called the estate. Harvey was glad to hear from me, yes, everything was all right. Billy had been in the yard with Ruston all day and Miss Malcom had stayed in her room. The doctor had been there again and there was nothing to worry about. Ruston had been asking for me. I told Harvey to tell the kid I'd drop up as soon as I could and not to worry. My last instructions still went. Be sure the place was locked up tight, and that Billy stayed near the kid and Roxy. One thing I did make sure of. Harvey was to tell the gatekeeper what was in the bottle that he thought contained aspirin.

When I hung up I picked up another pack of butts, a clean set of underwear, shirt and socks in a dry goods store, then threw the stuff in the back of the car and drove out around town until I came to the bay. Under the light of the half-moon it was black and shimmering, an oily, snaky tongue that searched the edges of the shore with frightened, whimpering sounds. The shadows were black as pitch, not a soul was on the streets. Three-quarters of a mile down the road one lone window winked with a yellow, baleful eye.

I took advantage of the swath Grange had cut in the restraining wire and pulled up almost to the brink of the drop-off, changed my mind, pulled out and backed in, just in case I had to get out of there in a hurry. When I figured I was well set I opened my fresh deck of butts, chain-smoked four of them in utter silence, then closed up the windows to within an inch of the top, pulled my hat down over my eyes and went to sleep.

The sun was fighting back the night when I woke up. Outside the steamed-up windows a gray fog was drifting up from the waters, coiling and uncoiling until the tendrils blended into a low-hanging blanket of haze that hung four feet over the ground.

It looked cold. It was cold. I was going to be kicking myself a long time if nothing came of this. I stripped off my clothes, throwing them into the car until I was standing shivering in my underwear. Well, it was one way to get a bath, anyway. I could think of better ways.

A quick plunge. It had to be quick or I would change my mind. I swam out to the spot I had fixed in my mind; the spot where Grange's car had landed. Then I stopped swimming. I let myself go as limp as possible, treading water just enough to keep my head above the surface. You got it. I was supposed to be playing dead, or almost dead. Half knocked out maybe. The tide was the same, I had checked on that. If this had been just another river it wouldn't have mattered, but this part was more an inlet than anything else. It emptied and filled with the tides, having its own peculiarities and eddies. It swirled and washed around objects long sunk in the cove of the bottom. I could feel it tug at my feet, trying to drag me down with little monkey hands, gentle, tugging hands that would mean nothing to a swimmer, but could have a noticeable effect on someone half dazed.

Just a few minutes had passed and I was already out of sight of the car around the bend. Here the shores drew away as the riverbed widened until it reached the mouth of the inlet opening into the bay. I thought that I was going to keep right on drifting by, and had about made up my mind to quit all this damn foolishness when I felt the first effect of the eddy.

It was pulling me toward the north shore. A little thrill of excitement shot through me, and although I was numb I felt an emotional warmth dart into my bones. The shore was closer now. I began to spin in a slow, tight circle as something underneath me kicked up a fuss with the water. In another moment I saw what was causing the drag. A tiny U-bend in the shoreline jutted out far enough to cause a suction in the main flow and create enough disturbance to pull in anything not too far out.

Closer . . . closer . . . I reached out and got hold of some finger-thick reeds and held on, then steadied myself with one hand in the mud and clambered up on the shore. There were no tracks save mine, but then again there wouldn't be. Behind me the muck was already filling in the holes my feet had made. I parted the reeds, picking my way through the remains of shellfish and stubble. They were tough reeds, all right. When I let them go they snapped back in place like a whip. If anyone had come out of the river it would have been here. It *had* to be here!

The reeds changed into scrub trees and thorny brush that clawed at my skin, raking me with their needlepoints. I used a stick as a club and beat at them, trying to hold my temper down. When they continued to eat their way into my flesh I cursed them up and down.

But the next second I took it all back. They were nice briars. Beautiful briars. The loveliest briars I had ever seen, because one of them was sporting part of a woman's dress.

I could have kissed that torn piece of fabric. It was stained, but fresh. And nobody was going to go through those reeds and briars except the little sweetheart I was after. This time I was gentler with the bushes and crawled through them as best I could without getting myself torn apart. Then the brush gave way to grass. That green stuff felt better than a Persian rug under my sore feet. I sat down on the edge of the clearing and picked the thorns out of my skin.

Then I stood up and shoved the tail end of my T-shirt down into my shorts. Straight ahead of me was a shack. If ever there was an ideal hiding place, this was it, and as long as I was going to visit its occupant I might as well look my charming best.

I knocked, then kicked the door open. A rat scurried along the edge of the wall and shot past my feet into the light. The place was as empty as a tomb. But it *had* been occupied. Someone had turned the one room into a shambles. A box seat was freshly splintered into sharp fragments on the floor, and the makeshift stove in the middle of the room lay on its side. Over in the corner a bottle lay smashed in a million pieces, throwing jagged glints of light to the walls. She had been here. There was no doubt of it. Two more pieces of the same fabric I held in my hand were caught on the frayed end of the wooden table. She had put up a hell of a fight, all right, but it didn't do her any good.

When the voice behind me said, "Hey, you!" I pivoted on my heel and my hand clawed for the gun I didn't have. A little old guy in baggy pants was peering at me through the one lens of his glasses, wiping his nose on a dirty hunk of rag at the same time.

"That's not healthy, Pop."

"You one of them there college kids?" he asked.

I eased him out the door and came out beside him. "No, why?"

"Always you college kids what go around in yer shorts. Seed some uptown once." He raised his glasses and took a good look at my face. "Say . . . you ain't no college kid."

"Didn't say I was."

"Well, what you guys joining? I seed ya swimming in the crick, just like the other one."

I went after that *other one* like a bird after a bug. "What other one?" My hands were shaking like mad. It was all I could do to keep my hands off his shirt and shake the facts out of him.

"The one what come up t'other day. Maybe it was yesterday. I disremember days. What ya joining?"

"Er . . . a club. We have to swim the river then reach the house without being seen. Guess they won't let me join now that somebody saw me. Did you see the other guy too?"

"Sure. I seed him, but I don't say nothing. I seed lotta funny things go on and I don't ask no questions. It's just that this was kinda funny, that's all."

"What did he look like?"

"Well, I couldn't see him too good. He was big and fat. I heered him puffing plenty after he come out of the weeds. Yeah, he was a big feller. I didn't know who he was so I went back through the woods to my boat."

"Just the other guy, that's all you saw?"

"Yep."

"Nobody else?"

"Nope."

"Anybody live in that shack?"

"Not now. Comes next month and Pee Wee'll move in. He's a tramp. Don't do nothing but fish and live like a pig. He's been living there three summers now."

"This other one you saw, did he have a mean-looking face, sort of scowling?"

"Ummmm. Now that you mention it, he looked kinda mad. Guess that was one reason why I left."

Dilwick. It was Dilwick. The fat slob had gotten the jump on me again. I knew he was smart . . . he had to be to get along the way he did, but I didn't think he was that smart. Dilwick had put the puzzle together and come out on top. Dilwick had found Grange in the shack and carted her off. Then why the hell didn't he produce her? Maybe the rest of the case stunk, but this part raised a putrid odor to high heaven. Everybody under the sun wanted in on the act, now it was Dilwick. Crime upon crime upon crime upon crime. Wasn't it ever going to end? Okay, fat boy, start playing games with me. You think you pulled a quickie, don't you? You think nobody knows about this . . . T.S., junior, I know about it now, and brother, I think I'm beginning to see where I'm going.

"How can I get back to the bridge without swimming, Pop?"

He pointed a gnarled finger toward the tree line. "A path runs through there. Keeps right along the bank, but stick to it and nobody'll see ya in ya jeans. Hope they let ya join that club."

"I think I can fix it." I batted away the bugs that were beginning to swarm around me and took off for the path. Damn Dilwick anyway.

CHAPTER 10

Going back was rough. My feet were bleeding at the end of the first hundred yards and the blue-tailed flies were making my back a bas-relief of red lumps. Some Good Samaritan had left a dirty burlap bag that reeked of fish and glinted with dried scales in the path and I ripped it in half and wrapped the pieces over my instep and around my ankles. It wasn't so bad after that.

By the time I reached the bridge the sun was hanging well up in the sky and a few office workers were rolling along the road on their way to town. I waited until the road was clear, then made a dash across the bridge to the car and climbed into some dry clothes. My feet were so sore I could hardly get into my shoes, but leaving the laces open helped a little. I threw the wet shorts in the back with the rest of the junk and reached for a butt. There are times when a guy wants a cigarette in the worst way, and this was one of them.

I finished two, threw the car in gear and plowed out to the concrete. Now the fun began. Me and Dilwick were going to be as inseparable as clamshells. Grange was the key to unlock this mess. Only Dilwick had Grange. Just to be certain I pulled into a dog wagon and went to the pay phone. Sergeant Price was in again. It was getting to be a habit.

I said hello, then: "Get a report on Grange yet, Sergeant?"

He replied in the negative.

"How about the city cops?"

"Nothing there either. I thought you were looking for her?"

"Yeah . . . I am. Look, do me a favor. Buzz the city bulls and see if they've turned up anything in the last few hours. I'll hold on."

"But they would have called me if . . ."

"Go on, try it anyway."

Price picked up another phone and dialed. I heard him ask the cop on the desk the question, then he slammed the receiver down. "Not a thing, Mike."

"Okay, that's all I want to know." I grinned to myself. It was more than a feud between the city and the state police; it was monkey business. But it was all right with me. In fact, I was happier about it than I should have been. I was looking forward to kicking Dilwick's teeth right down his big fat yap.

But before I did anything I was going to get some breakfast. I went through my first order, had seconds, then went for another round. By that time the counterman was looking at the stubble of the beard on my face and wondering whether or not I was a half-starved tramp filling my belly then going to ask to work out the check.

When I threw him a ten his eyes rolled a little. If he didn't check the serial number of that bill to see if it was stolen I didn't know people. I collected my change and glanced at the time. Ten fifteen. Dilwick would be getting to his office about now. Swell.

This time I found a spot on the corner and pulled in behind a pickup truck. I shut off the motor then buried my nose in a magazine with one eye on the station house across the street. Dilwick came waddling up five minutes later. He disappeared inside and didn't show his face for two hours. When he did come out he was with one of the boys that had worked over Billy that night.

The pair stepped into an official car and drove down the street, turning onto Main. I was two cars behind. A half mile down they stopped, got out and went into a saloon. I took up a position where I could cover the entrance.

That was the way the day went: from one joint to another. By five o'clock I was dying for a short beer and a sandwich, and the two decided to call it quits. Dilwick dumped his partner off in front of a modern, two-story brick building, then cut across town, beating out a red light on the way. By the time I had caught up with him he was locking the car up in front of a trim duplex. He never saw me, not because I slouched down in my seat as I shot by, but because he was waving to a blonde in the window.

I only got a glimpse of her well-rounded shoulders and ample bust, but the look on her face told me that I had might as well go home because this was going to be an all-night affair.

No sense taking any chances. I bought a container of coffee and some sandwiches in a delicatessen then circled the block until I eased into the curb across the street and fifty yards behind the police buggy. The sandwiches went in a hurry. On top of the dash I laid out my cigs and a pack of matches, then worked the seat around until I was comfortable. At nine o'clock the lights went out in the duplex. Twenty cigarettes later they were still out. I curled up on the seat and conked off.

I was getting to hate the morning. My back ached from the swim yesterday and the cramped position behind the wheel. I opened the door and stretched my legs, getting a peek at myself in the rear-vision mirror. I didn't look pretty. Dilwick's car was still in front of the duplex.

"Have a rough night?"

I raised my eyebrows at the milkman. He was grinning like a fool.

"See a lot of you guys around this morning. Want a bottle of milk? It's good and cold."

"Hell yeah, hand one over." I fished in my pocket and threw him a half.

"Someday," he said, "I'm going to sell sandwiches on this route. I'll make a million."

He walked off whistling as I yanked the stopper out and raised the bottle to my lips. It was the best drink I ever had. Just as I reached the bottom the door opened in the duplex. A face came out, peered around, then Dilwick walked out hurriedly. I threw the empty bottle to the grass beside the curb then waited until the black sedan had turned the corner before I left my position. When I reached the intersection Dilwick was two blocks ahead. Tailing him was too easy. There were no cars out that early to screen me. When he stopped at a diner I kept right on going to the station house and got my old spot back, hoping that I hadn't made a mistake in figuring that Dilwick would come back to his castle after he had breakfast.

This time I was lucky. He drove up a half hour later.

Forcing myself to be patient was brutal. For four solid hours Dilwick went through the saloon routine solo, then he picked up his previous companion. At two in the afternoon he acquired another rummy and the circus continued. I was never far behind. Twice, I hopped out and followed them on foot, then scrambled for my heap when they came out of a joint. Six o'clock they stopped in a chop suey joint for supper and I found a chance to get a shave and watch them at the same time from a spot on the other side of the avenue. If this kept up I'd blow my top. What the hell was Dilwick doing with Grange anyway? What goes on in a town where all the cops do is tour the bars and spend their nights shacking up with blondes? If Grange was such a hot potato why wasn't Dilwick working on her? Or did he have her stashed away somewhere . . . ? Or what could be worse, maybe I was all wet in thinking Dilwick had her in the first place.

Nuts.

I had a coffee and was two cigarettes to the good when the trio came out of the restaurant, only this time they split up in front of the door, shaking hands all around. Dilwick got in the car, changed his mind and walked down to a liquor store. When he came out with a wrapped bottle under his arm the other two were gone. Good, this was better. He slid under the wheel and pulled out. I let a convertible get between us and went after him. No blonde tonight. Dilwick went through town taking his time until he reached the highway, stopped at one of those last chance places for a beer while I watched from the spacious driveway, unwrapped his bottle before he started again and had a swig.

By the time he was on the highway it was getting dark. What a day. Five miles out of Sidon he turned right on a black macadam road that wound around the fringes of some good-sized estates and snapped on his lights. I left mine off. Wherever he was going, he wasn't in a hurry. Apparently the road went nowhere, twisting around hills and cutting a swath through the oaks lining the roads.

After a while the estates petered out and the countryside, what was visible of it, became a little wild.

Ahead of me his taillight was a red eye, one that paced itself at an even thirty-five. On either side of me were walls of Stygian blackness, and I was having all I could do to stay on the road. I had to drive with one eye on the taillight and the other on the macadam, but Dilwick was making it easy for me by taking it slow.

Too easy. I was so busy driving I didn't see the other car slide up behind me until it was too late. They had their lights out too.

I hit the brakes as they cut across my nose, my hand fumbling for my rod. Even before I stopped the guy had leaped out of the car and was reaching through my window for me. I batted the hand away from my neck then got slammed across my eyes with a gun barrel. The door flew open. I kicked out with my feet and somebody grunted. Somehow I got the gun in my hand, but another gun lashed out of the darkness and smashed across my wrist.

Damn, I was stupid! I got mousetrapped! Somehow I kicked free of the car and swung. A formless shape in front of me cursed and grunted. Then a light hit me full in the face. I kicked it out of a hand, but the damage had been done. I couldn't see at all. A fist caught me high on the head as a pair of arms slipped around my waist and threw me into a fender. With all my strength I jerked my head back and caught the guy's nose. The bone splintered and hot blood gushed down my collar.

It was kick and gouge and try to get your teeth in something. The only sounds were of fists on flesh and feet on the road. Heavy breathing. I broke free for a moment, ducked, and came in punching. I doubled one up when I planted my knuckles in his belly up to the wrist. A billy swooshed in the air, missed and swooshed again. I thought my shoulder was broken. I got so damn mad I let somebody have it in the shins and he screamed in pain when I nearly busted the bone with my toe. The billy caught me in the bad shoulder again and I hit the ground, stumbling over the guy who was holding his leg. He let go long enough to try for my throat, but I brought my knee up and dug it in his groin.

All three of us were on the ground, rolling in the dirt. I felt cold steel under my hand and wrapped my fingers around a gun butt as a foot nearly ripped me in half. The guy with the billy sent one tearing into my side that took the breath out of my lungs. He tried again as I rolled and grazed me, then landed full on my gut with both his knees. Outlined against the sky I could see him straddling me, the billy raised in the air, ready to crush in my skull. Little balls of fire were popping in my brain and my breath was still a tight knot in my belly when that shot-weighted billy started to come down.

I raised the gun and shot him square in the face, blowing his brains all over the road.

But the billy was too much to stop. It was pulled off course yet it managed to knock me half senseless when it grazed my temple. Before I went completely out I heard feet pounding on the road and an engine start up. The other guy wasn't taking any chances. He was clearing out.

I lay there under a corpse for three-quarters of an hour before I had enough strength to crawl away. On my hands and knees I reached my car and pulled myself erect. My breath came in hot, jerky gasps. I had to bend to one side to breathe at all. My face felt like a truck went over it and I was sticky with blood and guts, but I couldn't tell how much of it was my own. From the dash I pulled a flashlight and played its beam over the body in the road. Unless he had some identifying scars, nobody would ever be able to tell who he was. Ten feet away from his feet his brainpan lay like a gooey ashtray on the road.

His pockets held over a hundred bucks in cash, a wallet with a Sidon police shield pinned to it and a greasy deck of cards. The billy was still in his hand. I found my own gun, cleaned off the one I had used and tossed it into the bushes. It didn't matter whether they found it or not. I was going to be number-one client in a murder case.

Lousy? It was stinking. I was supposed to have been rubbed out. All very legal, of course. I was suspiciously tailing a cop down a dark road with my lights out, and when ordered to halt put up a fight and during it got myself killed. Except it didn't happen that way. I nailed one and the other got away to tell about it. Maybe Dilwick would like it better this way.

So they caught me. They knew I was trailing them all day and laid a lot of elaborate plans to catch me in the trap. I had to get out of there before that other one got back with reinforcements. I let the body stay as it was, then crawled under the wheel and drove onto the grass, swinging around the corpse, then back on the highway. This time I used my lights and the gas pedal, hightailing it away as fast as I could hold the turns. Whenever I reached an intersection I cut off on it, hoping it wasn't a dead end. It took me a good two hours to circle the town and come out in the general vicinity of York's place, but I couldn't afford using the highway.

The car was in my way now; it could be spotted too easily. If they saw me it would be shoot to kill and I didn't have the kind of artillery necessary to fight a gang war. Dilwick would have every cop in town on the lookout, reporting the incident to Price only after they cornered me somewhere and punched me full of holes, or the death of the cop was printed in the papers.

There was only one reason for all the hoodah . . . Grange was still the key, and Dilwick knew I knew he had her.

Trusting luck that I wasn't too far from home, I ran the car off the road between the trees, pulling as far into the bushes as I could get. Using some cut branches for camouflage I covered up the hood and any part that could be seen by casual observation from the road. When I was satisfied I stepped out and began walking in a northerly direction.

A road finally crossed the one I was on with phone wires paralleling it. A lead from a pole a hundred yards down left the main line and went into the trees. When I reached it I saw the sleepy little bungalow hidden in the shadows. If my feet on the pavement didn't wake the occupants, my sharp rapping did.

Inside someone said, "George . . . the door."

Bedsprings creaked and the guy mumbled something then crossed the room to the door. A light went on overhead and when the guy in the faded bathrobe took a look at me he almost choked.

"I had an accident. Do you have a phone?"

"Accident? Yeah . . . yeah. Come in."

He gulped and, glancing at me nervously, called, "Mary. It's a man who's had an accident. Anything I can do for you, mister? Anybody else hurt?"

The guy back there would never feel anything again. "No, nobody else is hurt."

"Here's the phone." His wife came out while I dialed Price's number. She tried to fuss around with a wet rag, wiping the blood off my face, but I waved her off. Price wasn't there, but I got his home number. He wasn't there, either, he had left for headquarters. The woman was too excited. I insisted that I didn't need a doctor, but let her go over my battered face with the rag, then dialed headquarters again.

Price was there. He nearly exploded when he heard my voice. "What the hell happened? Where are you?"

"Out of town. What are you doing up at this hour?"

"Are you kidding? A police reporter slipped me the news that a cop was killed south of town. I got the rest from Dilwick. You're in a jam now."

"You're not telling me anything new," I said. "Has he got the police combing the town for me?"

"Everyone on the force is out. I had to put you on the Teletype myself. All the roads are blocked and they have a cordon around York's house. Are you giving yourself up?"

"Don't be silly. I'd be sticking my head in a noose. As far as Dilwick is concerned I have to be knocked off. It's a screw pitch, pal, and I'm in it deep, but don't believe all you hear."

"You killed him, didn't you?"

"You're damn right. If I hadn't it would have been me lying back there with my head in sections all over the ground. They squeezed me good. I was tailing Dilwick, but they got wise and tailed me. Like a damn fool I let Dilwick lead me out in the sticks and they jumped me. What was I supposed to do, take it lying down? They didn't have orders to pick me up, they were supposed to knock me off."

"Where are you? I'll come out and get you."

"No dice, buddy, I have work to do."

"You'd better give yourself up, Mike. You'll be safer in the custody of the law."

"Like hell. Dilwick will have me held under his jurisdiction and that's what he wants. He'll be able to finish the job then."

"Just the same, Mike . . ."

"Say, whose side are you on?"

He didn't say a word for a full minute. "I'm a policeman, Mike. I'll have to take you in."

He was making it hard for me. "Listen, don't be a sap, Price, something's come up that I have to follow."

"What?"

I glanced at the two faces that were taking in every word. "I can't tell you now."

"The police can handle it."

"In a pig's eye. Now listen. If you want to see this case solved you'll have to stay off my back as much as you can. I know something that only the killer knows and I have to use it while it's hot. If you take me in it'll be too late for both of us. You know what Dilwick and his outfit are like. So I shot one of them. That's hardly killing a cop, is it? Then don't get so upset about me blasting a cheap crook. Do you want to see this case wrapped up or not?"

"Of course."

"Then keep your boys out of this. I'm not worried about the rest."

There was another silent period while he thought it over, then he spoke. "Mike, I shouldn't do this; it's against all rules and regulations. But I know how things stand and I still want to be a good cop. Sometimes to do that you have to fall in line. I'll stay off you. I don't know how long it will be before the pressure gets put on me, but until then I'll do what I can."

"Thanks, pal. I won't run out on you."

"I know that."

"Expect to hear from me every once in a while. Just keep the calls under your hat. If I need you I'll yell for help."

"I'll be around, Mike. You'd better steer clear of York's place. That place is alive with city cops."

"Roger . . . and thanks again."

When I cradled the phone I could see a thousand questions getting ready to come my way. The guy and his wife were all eyes and ears and couldn't make sense out of my conversation. It had to be a good lie to be believed.

I shoved my badge under their noses. "You've overheard an official phone conversation," I said brusquely. "Under no circumstances repeat any part of it. A band of thieves has been operating in this neighborhood under the guise of being policemen and we almost got them. Unfortunately one got away. There's been difficulty getting cooperation from the local police, and we have been operating undercover. In case they show up here you saw nothing, heard nothing. Understand?"

Wide-eyed, their heads bobbed in unison and I let myself out through the door. If they believed that one they were crazy.

As soon as I was in the shadows I turned up the road toward York's estate. Cops or no cops I had to get in there someway. From the top of a knoll I looked down the surrounding countryside. In the distance the lights of Sidon threw a glow into the sky, and here and there other lights twinkled as invisible trees flickered between us in the night breeze. But the one I was interested in was the house a bare mile off that was ablaze with lights in every window and ringed with the twin beams of headlights from the cars patroling the grounds. Occasionally one would throw a spotlight into the bushes, a bright finger of light trying to pin down a furtive figure. Me.

The hell with them. This was one time I couldn't afford a run-in with the bulls. I cut across the fields until the dark shape of a barn loomed ahead. Behind it was a haystack. It was either one or the other. I chose the stack and crawled in. It would take longer for the cows to eat me out than it would for some up-with-the-sun farmer to spot me shacking up with bossy. Three feet into the hay I shoved an armload of the stuff into the tunnel I had made, kicked my feet around until I had a fair-sized cave and went to sleep.

The sun rose, hit its midpoint then went down before I moved. My belly was rumbling with hunger and my tongue was parched from breathing chaff. If a million ants were inside my shirt I couldn't have felt more uncomfortable. Keeping the stack between me and the house, I crawled through the grass to the watering trough and brushed away the dirt that had settled on top of the water. If I thought that last bottle of milk was the best drink I ever had, I was wrong. When I could hold no more I splashed my face and neck, letting it soak my shirt, grinning with pleasure.

I heard the back door of the house slam and took a flying dive to the other side of the trough. Footsteps came closer, heavy, boot-shod feet. When I was getting set to make a jump I noticed that the steps were going right on by. My breath came a little easier. Sticking my head out from behind the trough I saw the broad back of my host disappearing into the barn. He was carrying a pail in either hand. That could mean he was coming over to the trough. I had it right then. Trying to step softly, I ducked into a crouch and made a dash for the darkness of the tree line.

Once there I stripped to the skin and dusted myself off with my shirt. Much better. A bath and something to eat and I would feel almost human. Sometime during the night my watch had stopped and I could only guess at the time. I put it at an arbitrary nine thirty and wound it up. Still too early. I had one cigarette left, the mashed, battered remains of a smoke. Shielding the match I fired it up and dragged it down to my fingernails. For two hours I sat on a stump watching a scud of clouds blot out the stars and feeling little crawling things climb up my pants leg.

The bugs were too much. I'd as soon run the risk of bumping into a cordon of Dilwick's thugs. When my watch said ten after eleven I skirted the edge of the farm and got back on the road. If anyone came along I'd see them a mile away. I found my knoll again. The lights were still on in York's house, but not in force like they had been. Only one pair of headlights peered balefully around the grounds.

An hour later I stood opposite the east wall leaning over the edge of a five-foot drainage ditch with my watch in my hands. At regular six-minute intervals the outlines of a man in a slouch hat and raincoat would drift past. When he reached the end of the wall he turned and came back. There were two of them on this side. Always, when they met at the middle of the wall, there would be some smart retort that I couldn't catch. But their pacing was regular. Dilwick should have been in the Army. A regular beat like that was a cinch to sneak through. Once a car drove by checking up on the men and tossing a spot into the bushes, but from that angle the ditch itself was completely concealed by the foot-high weeds that grew along its lip.

It had to be quick. And noiseless.

It took the guy three minutes to reach the end of the wall, three minutes to get back to me again. Maybe three-quarters of a minute if he ran. When he passed the next time I checked my watch, keeping my eyes on the second hand. One, two, two and a half. I gripped the edge of the ditch. Ten seconds, five . . . I crouched . . . now! Vaulting the ditch I ducked across the road to the wall. Ten feet away, the tree I had chosen waved to me with leafy fingers. I jumped, grabbed the lowest limb and swung up, then picked my way up until I was even with the wall. My clothes caught on spike-like branches, ripped loose, then caught again.

Feet were swishing the grass. Feet that had a copper over them. This was the second phase. If he looked up and saw me outlined against the sky I was sunk. I palmed the .45 and threw the safety off, waiting. They came closer. I heard him singing a tuneless song under his breath, swearing at briars that bit at his ankles.

He was under the tree now, in the shadows. The singing stopped. The feet stopped. My hand tightened around the butt of the gun, aiming it where his head would be. If he saw me he was held in his tracks. I would have let one go at him if I didn't see the flare of the match in time. When his butt was lit he breathed the smoke in deeply then continued on his rounds. I shoved the gun back and put the watch on him again until it read another three minutes.

Button your coat . . . be sure nothing was going to jingle in your pockets . . . keep your watch face blacked out . . . hold tight . . . get ready . . . and jump. For one brief moment I was airborne before my fingers felt the cold stone wall. The corner caught me in the chest and I almost fell. Somehow I kicked my feet to the top and felt broken glass cemented in the surface shatter under my heels. Whether or not anybody was under me, I had to jump, I was too much of a target there on the wall. Keeping low I stepped over the glass and dropped off.

I landed in soft turf with hardly a sound, doubled up and rolled into a thorny rosebush. The house was right in front of me now; I could pick out Roxy's window. The pane was still shattered from the bullet that had pierced it and nicked her.

Ruston's window was lit, too, but the shade was drawn. Behind the house the police car stopped, some loud talking ensued, then it went forward again. No chance to check schedules now. I had to hope that I wasn't seen. Just as soon as the car passed I ran for the wall of the building, keeping in whatever cover the bushes and hedgerows afforded. It wasn't much, but I made the house without an alarm going off. The wrist-thick vine that ran up the side wasn't as good as a ladder, but it served the purpose. I went up it like a monkey until I was just below Roxy's window.

I reached up for the sill, grabbed it and as I did the damn brick pulled loose and tumbled down past me, landing with a raucous clatter in the bushes below and then bounced sickeningly into other bricks with a noise as loud as thunder in my ears. I froze against the wall, heard somebody call out, then saw a bright shaft of light leap out from a spot in someone's hand below and watched it probe the area where the brick had landed.

Whoever he was didn't look up, not expecting anyone above him. His stupidity was making me feel a little better and I figured I had it made. I wasn't that lucky. There was too much weight on the vine and I felt it beginning to pull loose from wherever it was anchored in the wall above my head.

I didn't bother trying to be careful. Down below a couple of voices were going back and forth and their own sounds covered mine. I scrambled up, reached and got hold of an awning hook imbedded in the concrete of the exterior frame of the window and hung on with one hand, my knee reaching for the sill before I could pull the hook out of the wall.

Down below everybody was suddenly satisfied and the lights went out. In the darkness I heard feet taking up the vigil again. I waited a full minute, tried the window, realized that it was locked then tapped on the pane. I did it again, not a frantic tapping, but a gentle signaling that got a response I could hear right through the glass. I hoped she wouldn't scream, but would think it out long enough to look first.

She did.

There was enough reflected light from a bed lamp to highlight my face and I heard her gasp, reach for the latch and ease the window up. I rolled over the sill, dropped to the floor and let her shut the window behind me and pull down the blind. Only then did she snap on the light.

"Mike!"

"Quiet, kid, they're all over the place downstairs."

"Yes, I know." Her eyes filled up suddenly and she half ran to me, her arms folding me to her.

486 • THE MIKE HAMMER COLLECTION

Behind us there was a startled little gasp. I swung, pushed Roxy away from me, then grinned. Ruston was standing there in his pajamas, his face a dead white. "Mike!" he started to say, then swayed against the doorjamb. I walked over, grabbed him and rubbed his head until he started to smile at me.

"You take it easy, little buddy . . . you've had it rough. How about letting me be the only casualty around here? By the way, where is Billy?"

Roxy answered. "Dilwick took him downstairs and is making him stay there."

"Did he get rough with him?"

"No . . . Billy said he'd better lay off or he'd get a lawyer that would take care of that fat goon and Dilwick didn't touch him. For once Billy stood up for himself."

Ruston was shaking under my hand. His eyes would dart from the door to the window and he'd listen attentively to the heavy footsteps wandering down in the rooms below. "Mike, why did you come? I don't want them to see you. I don't care what you did, but you can't let them get you."

"I came to see you, kid."

"Me?"

"Uh-huh."

"Why?"

"I have something big to ask you."

The two of them stared at me, wondering what could be so great as to bring me through that army of cops. Roxy, quizzically; Ruston with his eyes filled with awe. "What is it, Mike?"

"You're pretty smart, kid, try to understand this. Something has come up, something that I didn't expect. How would you like to point out the killer for me? Be a target. Lead the killer to you so I can get him?"

"Mike, you can't!"

I looked at Roxy. "Why not?"

"It isn't fair. You can't ask him to do that!"

I slumped in a chair and rubbed my head. "Maybe you're right. It is a lot to expect."

Ruston was tugging at my sleeve. "I'll do it, Mike. I'm not afraid."

I didn't know what to say. If I missed I'd never be able to look at myself in the face again, yet here was the kid, ready and trusting me not to miss. Roxy sank to the edge of the bed, her face pale, waiting for my answer. But I couldn't let a killer run around loose.

"Okay, Lancelot, it's a deal." Roxy was hating me with her eyes. "Before we go over it, do you think you can get me something to eat?"

"Sure, Mike. I'll get it. The policemen won't bother me." Ruston smiled and left. I heard him going down the stairs, then tell the cop he was hungry and so was his governess. The cop growled and let him go.

Roxy said, "You're a louse, Mike, but I guess it has to be that way. We almost lost Ruston once, and it's liable to happen again if somebody doesn't think of something. Well, you did. I just hope it works, that's all."

"So do I, kid."

Ruston came running up the stairs and slipped into the room, bearing a pair of enormous sandwiches. I all but snatched them out of his hand and tore into them wolfishly. Once, the cop came upstairs and prowled past the door and I almost choked. After he went by, the two of them laughed silently at me standing there with my rod in my hand and the remains of a sandwich sticking out of my mouth.

Roxy went over and pressed her ear to the door, then slowly turned the key in the lock. "I suppose you'll leave the same way you came in, Mike, so maybe that'll give you more time if you have to go quickly."

"Gee, I hope nothing happens to you, Mike. I'm not afraid for myself, I'm just afraid what those policemen will do. They say you shot a cop and now you have to die."

"Lancelot, you worry too much."

"But even if you find out who's been causing all the trouble the police will still be looking for you, won't they?"

"Perhaps not," I laughed. "They're going to be pretty fed up with me when I bust this case."

The kid shuddered, his eyes closed tightly for a second. "I keep thinking of that night in the shack. The night you shot one of those men that kidnapped me. It was an awful fight."

I felt as though a mule had kicked me in the stomach. "What did you say?"

"That night . . . you remember. When you shot that man and . . ."

I cut him off. "You can get off that target, Ruston," I said softly. "I won't need you for a decoy after all."

Roxy twisted toward me, watching the expression in my eyes. "Why, Mike?"

"I just remembered that I shot a guy, that's why. I had forgotten all about it." I jammed on my hat and picked up a pack of Roxy's butts from the dresser. "You two stay here and keep the door locked. I can get the killer, now, by damn, and I won't have to make him come to me either. Roxy, turn that light off. Give me five minutes after I leave before you turn it on again. Forget you ever saw me up here or Dilwick will have your scalp."

The urgency in my voice moved her to action. Without a word in reply she reached out for the light and snapped it off. Ruston gasped and moved toward the door, with the slightest tremor of excitement creeping into his breathing. I saw him silhouetted there for an instant, a floor lamp right in front of him. Before I could caution him the shade struck him in the face. His hand went out . . . hit the lamp and it toppled to the floor with the popping of the bulb and the crash of a fallen tree. Or so it seemed.

Downstairs a gruff voice barked out. Before it could call again I threw the window up and went out, groping for the vine. Someplace in the house a whistle shrilled and angry fists beat at the door. Half sliding, half climbing, I went down the side of the building. Another whistle and somebody got nervous and let a shot blast into the confusion. From every side came the shouts and the whistles. Just before I reached the ground a car raced up and two figures leaped out. But I was lucky. The racket was all centered on the inside of the house and the coppers were taking it for granted that I was trapped there.

As fast as I could go, I beat it across the drive to the lawn, then into the trees. Now I knew where I was. One tree ahead formed the perfect ladder over the wall. I had my gun out now in case that patrol was waiting. There would be no command to halt, just a volley of shots until one of us dropped. All right, I was ready. Behind me a window smashed and Roxy screamed. Then there was a loud "There he goes!" and a pair of pistols spit fire. With the trees in the way and the distance opening between us, I wasn't concerned about getting hit.

The tree was a godsend. I went up its inclined trunk thanking whatever lightning bolt had split it in such a handy fashion, made the top of the wall and jumped for the grass. The sentries weren't there anymore. Probably trying to be in on the kill.

A siren screamed inside the wall and the chase was on, but it would be a futile chase now. Once in the tree line on the other side of the road I took it easy. They'd be looking for a car and the search would be along the road. So long, suckers!

CHAPTER 11

I slept in my car all night. It wasn't until noon that I was ready to roll. Now the streets would be packed with traffic and my buggy would be just another vehicle. There were hundreds like it on the road. Superficially it was a five-year-old heap that had seen plenty of service, but the souped-up motor under the hood came out of a limousine that had packed a lot of speed and power. Once on the road nothing the city cops had was going to catch me.

Good old Ruston. If my memory had been working right I wouldn't have forgotten my little pal I plugged. Guys who are shot need doctors, and need them quick, and in Sidon there wouldn't be that many medics that I couldn't run them all down. A crooked doc, that's what I wanted. If a gunshot had been treated Price would have known about it and told me, but none had been entered in the books. Either a crooked doc or a threatened doc. He was the one to find.

I stripped the branches from the fenders and cleared a path to the road, and then eased out onto the macadam. At the first crossroad a sign pointed to the highway and I took the turn. Two miles down I turned into a stream of traffic, picked out a guy going along at a medium clip and nosed in behind him.

We both turned off into the city, only I parked on a side street and went into a candy store that had a public phone. Fiddling through the Yellow Pages, I ripped out the sheet of doctors listed there, and went through the motions of making a phone call. Nobody bothered to so much as glance at me.

Back in the car I laid out my course and drove to the first on my list. It wasn't an impressive list. Seven names. Dr. Griffin was stepping out of his car when I pulled in.

"Doctor . . ."

"Yes?"

His eyes went up and down the ruin of my suit. "Don't mind me," I said. "I've been out all night chasing down the dick that shot that cop. I'm a reporter."

"Oh, yes, I heard about that. What can I do for you?"

"The police fired several shots at him. There's a chance that he might have been hit. Have you treated any gunshot wounds lately?"

He drew himself up in indignant pride. "Certainly not! I would have reported it immediately had I done so."

"Thank you, Doctor."

The next one wasn't home, but his housekeeper was. Yes, she knew all about the doctor's affairs. No, there had been no gunshot wounds since Mr. Dillon shot himself in the foot like a silly fool when loading his shotgun. Yes, she was very glad to be of service.

Dr. Pierce ushered me into his very modern office personally. I pulled the same reporter routine on him. "A gunshot wound, you say?"

"Yes. It wasn't likely that he'd treat it himself."

He folded his hands across his paunch and leaned back in his chair. "There was one the day before yesterday, but I reported that. Certainly you know about it. A .22-caliber bullet. The man was hit while driving out in the country. Said he didn't know where it came from."

I covered up quickly. "Oh, that one. No, this would have been a larger shell. The cops don't pack .22's these days."

"I expect not," he laughed.

"Well, thanks anyway, Doctor."

"Don't mention it."

Four names left. It was past three o'clock. The next two weren't home, but the wife of one assured me that her husband would not have treated any wounds of the sort because he had been on a case in the hospital during the entire week.

The other one was in Florida on a vacation.

Dr. Clark had offices a block away from police headquarters, a very unhealthy place right now. Cars drove up and away in a constant procession, but I had to chance it. I parked pointing away from the area, making sure I had plenty of room to pull out, my wheels turned away from the curb. A woman came out of the office holding a baby. Then a man walking on a cane. I didn't want to enter an office full of people if I could help it, but if he didn't get rid of his patients in a hurry I was going to have to bust in anyway. A boy went in crying, holding his arm. Damn it, I was losing time!

As I went to reach for the ignition switch another guy came out, a four-inch wide bandage going from the corner of his mouth to his ear. The bells again. They went off all at once inside my skull until I wanted to scream. The bandage. The hell with the gunshot wound, he was probably dead. The bandage. My fingers hooking in a mouth and ripping the skin wide open. Of course, he'd need a doctor too! You wouldn't find two freak accidents like that happening at once. He was a ratty-looking guy dressed in a sharp gray suit with eyes that were everywhere at once. He went down the steps easily and walked to a car a couple ahead of me. I felt my heart beginning to pound, beating like a heavy hammer, an incredible excitement that made my blood race in my veins like a river about to flood.

He pulled out and I was right behind him, our bumpers almost touching. There was no subtlety about this tail job, maybe that's why I got away with it so long. He didn't notice me until we were on the back road six miles out of town ripping off seventy miles an hour. Just the two of us. We had left all other traffic miles behind. I saw his eyes go to the rear-vision mirror and his car spurted ahead. I grinned evilly to myself and stepped down harder on the accelerator until I was pushing him again.

His eyes hardly left the mirror. There was fright in them now. A hand went out and he signaled me to pass. I ignored it. Eighty-five now. A four-store town went by with the wind. I barely heard the whistle of the town cop blast as I passed him. Eighty-seven. The other car was having trouble holding the turns. It leaned until the tires screamed as the driver jerked it around. I grinned again. The frame of my car was rigged for just such emergencies. Ninety. Trees shot by like a huge picket fence. Another town. A rapid parade of identical billboards advertising a casino in Brocton. Ninety-five. A straightaway came up lined with more billboards. A nice flat stretch was ahead, he would have opened up on it if he could have, but his load was doing all it could. At the end of the straightaway was the outline of a town.

My little friend, you have had it, I said to myself. I went down on the gas, the car leaped ahead, we rubbed fenders. For a split second I was looking into those eyes and remembering that night, before I cut across his hood. He took to the shoulder, fought the wheel furiously but couldn't control it. The back end skidded around and the car went over on its side like a pinwheel. I stood on the brake, but his car was still rolling as I stopped.

I backed up and got out without shutting the engine off. The punk was lucky, damn lucky. His car had rolled but never up-ended, and those steel turret top jobs could take it on a roll in soft earth. He was crawling out of the door reaching under his coat for a rod when I jumped him. When I slapped him across that bandage he screamed and dropped the gun. I straddled him and picked it up, a snub-nosed .38, and thrust it in my waistband.

"Hello, pal," I said.

Little bubbles of pink foam oozed from the corners of his mouth. "Don't . . . don't do nothing . . ."

"Shut up."

"Please . . ."

"Shut up." I looked at him, looked at him good. If my face said anything he could read it. "Remember me? Remember that night in the shack? Remember the kid?"

Recognition dawned on him. A terrible, fearful recognition and he shuddered the entire length of his body. "What're ya gonna do?"

I brought my hand down across his face as hard as I could. He moaned and whimpered, "Don't!" Blood started to seep through the bandage, bright red now.

"Where's the guy I shot?"

He breathed, "Dead," through a mouthful of gore. It ran out his mouth and dribbled down his chin.

"Who's Mallory?"

He closed his eyes and shook his head. All right, don't talk. Make me make you. This would be fun. I worked my nails under the adhesive of the bandage and ripped it off with one tug. Clotted blood pulled at his skin and he screamed again. A huge half-open tear went from the corner of his mouth up his jawline, giving him a perpetual grin like a clown.

"Open your eyes." He forced his lids up, his chest heaved for air. Twitches of pain gripped his face. "Now listen to me, chum. I asked you who Mallory was. I'm going to put my fingers in your mouth and rip out those stitches one by one until you tell me. Then I'm going to open you up on the other side. If you'd sooner look like a clam, don't talk."

"No! I . . . I don't know no Mallory."

I slapped him across the cheek, then did as I promised. More blood welled out of the cut. He screamed once more, a short scream of intolerable agony. "Who's Mallory?"

"Honest . . . don't know . . ."

Another stitch went. He passed out cold.

I could wait. He came to groaning senselessly. I shook his head until his eyes opened. "Who do you work for, pal?"

His lips moved, but no sound came forth. I nudged him again. "The boss . . . Nelson . . . at the casino."

Nelson. I hadn't heard it before. "Who's Mallory?"

"No more. I don't know . . ." His voice faded out to nothing and his eyes shut. Except for the steady flow of blood seeping down his chin he looked as dead as they come.

It was getting dark again. I hadn't noticed the cars driving up until the lights of one shone on me. People were piling out of the first car and running across the field, shouting at each other and pointing to the overturned car.

The first one was all out of breath when he reached me. "What happened, mister? Is he dead? God, look at his face!"

"He'll be all right," I told him. "He just passed out." By that time the others were crowded around. One guy broke through the ring and flipped his coat open to show a badge.

"Better get him to a hospital. Ain't none here. Nearest one's in Sidon." He yanked a pad out of his pocket and wet the tip of a pencil with his tongue. "What's your name, mister?"

I almost blurted it out without thinking. If he heard it I'd be under his gun in a second, and there wasn't much I could do with this mob around. I stood up and motioned him away from the crowd. On the other side of the upturned car I looked him square in the eye.

"This wasn't an accident," I said, "I ran him off the road."

"You what?"

"Keep quiet and listen. This guy is a kidnapper. He may be a killer. I want you to get to the nearest phone and call Sergeant Price of the state police, understand? His headquarters is on the highway outside of Sidon. If you can't get him, keep trying until you do."

His hands gripped my lapels. "Say, buster, what are you trying to pull? Who the hell are you, anyway?"

"My name is Mike . . . Mike Hammer. I'm wanted by every crooked cop in this part of the state and if you don't get your paws off me I'll break your arm!"

His jaw sagged, but he let go my coat, then his brows wrinkled. "I'll be damned," he said. "I always did want to meet you. Read all the New York papers y' know. By damn. Say, you *did* kill that Sidon cop, didn't you?"

"Yes, I did."

"By damn, that's good. He put a bullet into one of our local lads one night when he was driving back from the casino. Shot him while he was dead drunk because he didn't like his looks. He got away with it too, by damn. What was that you wanted me to tell the police?"

I breathed a lot easier. I never thought I'd find a friend this far out. "You call Price and tell him to get out to the casino as fast as his car will bring him. And tell him to take along some boys."

"Gonna be trouble?"

"There's liable to be."

"Maybe I should go." He pulled at his chin, thinking hard. "I don't know. The casino is all we got around here. It ain't doing us no good, but the guy that runs it runs the town."

"Stay out of it if you can help it. Get an ambulance if you want to for that guy back there, but forget the hospital. Stick him in the cooler. Then get on the phone and call Price."

"Okay, Mike. I'll do that for you. Didn't think you shot that cop in cold blood like the notices said. You didn't, did you?"

"He was sitting on top of me about to bash my brains out with a billy when I shot the top of his head off."

"A good thing, by damn."

I didn't hang around. Twenty pairs of eyes followed me across the field to my car, but if there was any explaining to be done the cop was making a good job of it. Before I climbed under the wheel he had hands helping to right the car and six people carrying the figure of The Face to the road.

Nelson, the Boss. Another character. Where did he come in? He wasn't on the level if rat-puss was working for him. Nelson, but no Mallory. I stepped on the starter and ran the engine up. Nelson, but no Mallory. Something cold rolled down my temple and I wiped it away. Sweat. Hell, it couldn't be true, not what I was thinking, but it made sense! Oh, hell, it was impossible, people just aren't made that way! The pieces didn't have to be fitted into place any longer . . . they were being drawn into a pattern of murder as if by a magnet under the board, a pattern of death as complicated as a Persian tapestry, ugly enough to hang in Hitler's own parlor. Nelson, but no Mallory. The rest would be only incidental, a necessary incidental. I sweated so freely that my shirt was matted to my body.

I didn't have to look for the killer any longer. I knew who the killer was now.

The early crowd had arrived at the casino in force. Dozens of cars with plates from three states were already falling into neat rows at the direction of the attendant and their occupants in evening dress and rich business clothes were making their way across the lawn to the doors. It was an imposing place built like an old colonial mansion with twenty-foot pillars circling the entire house. From inside came the strains of a decent orchestra and a lot of loud talk from the bar on the west side. Floodlights played about the grounds, lighting up the trees in the back and glancing off the waters of the bay with sparkling fingers. The outlines of a boathouse made a dark blot in the trees, and out in the channel the lights from some moored yachts danced with the roll of the ships.

For five minutes I sat in the car with a butt hanging between my lips, taking in every part of the joint. When I had the layout pretty well in my mind I stepped out and flipped the attendant a buck. The guy's watery eyes went up and down my clothes, wondering what the hell I was doing there.

"Where'll I find Nelson, friend?"

He didn't like my tone, but he didn't argue about it. "What do you want him for?"

"We got a load of special stuff coming in on a truck and I want to find out what he wants done with it."

"Booze?"

"Yeah."

"Hell, ain't he taking the stuff off Carmen?"

"This is something special, but I'm not jawing about it out here. Where is he?"

"If he ain't on the floor he'll be upstairs in his office."

I nodded and angled over to the door. Two boys in shabby tuxedos stood on either side throwing greetings to the customers. They didn't throw any to me. I saw them exchange glances when they both caught the outlines of the rod under my coat. One started drifting toward me and I muttered, "I got a truckload of stuff for the boss. When it comes up get it around the back. We had a police escort all the way out of Jersey until we lost them."

The pair gave me blank stares wondering what I was talking about, but when I brushed by them they fingered me an okay thinking I was on the in. Bar noises came from my left, noises you couldn't mistake. They were the same from the crummiest joint in the Bronx to the swankiest supper club uptown. I went in, grabbed a spot at the end and ordered a brew. The punk gave me a five-ounce glass and soaked me six bits for it. When he passed me my change I asked for the boss.

"Just went upstairs a minute ago." I downed the drink and threaded my way out again. In what had been the main living room at one time were the bobbing heads of the dancers, keeping time to the orchestra on the raised dais at one end. Dozens of white-coated waiters scurried about like ants getting ready for winter, carrying trays loaded to the rims with every size glass there was. A serving bar took up one whole end of the corridor with three bartenders passing out drinks. This place was a gold mine.

I went up the plush-carpeted stairs with traffic. It was mostly male. Big fat guys chewing on three-buck cigars carrying dough in their jeans. An occasional dame with a fortune in jewelry dangling from her extremities. At the top of the landing the whir of the wheels and the click of the dice came clearly over the subdued babble of tense voices seated around the tables. Such a beautiful setup. It would be a shame to spoil it. So this was what Price had referred to. Protected gambling. Even with a hundred-way split to stay covered the boss was getting a million-dollar income.

The crowd went into the game rooms, but I continued down the dimly lit hallway past the rest rooms until I reached another staircase. This one was smaller, less bright, but just as plush and just as well used. Upstairs someone had a spasm of coughing and water splashed in a cooler.

I looked around me, pressing flat against the wall, then ducked around the corner and stood on the first step. The gun was in my hand, fitting into its accustomed spot. One by one I went up the stairs, softly, very softly. At the top, light from a doorway set into the wall threw a yellow light on the paneling opposite it. Three steps from the landing I felt the board drop a fraction of an inch under my foot. That was what I was waiting for.

I hit the door, threw it open and jammed the rod in the face of the monkey in the tux who was about to throw the bolt. "You should have done that sooner," I sneered at him.

He tried to bluff it out. "What the hell do you think you're doing?"

"Shut up and lay down on the floor. Over here away from the door."

I guess he knew what would happen if he didn't. His face went white right down into his collar and he fell to his knees then stretched out on the floor like he was told. Before he buried his map in the nap of the carpet he threw me one of those "you'll-be-sorry" looks.

Like hell I'd be sorry. I wasn't born yesterday. I turned the gun around in my hand and got behind the door. I didn't have long to wait. The knob turned, a gun poked in with a guy behind it looking for a target, a leer of pure sadistic pleasure on his face. When I brought the butt of the .45 across his head the leer turned to amazement as he spilled forward like a sack of wet cement. The skin on his bald dome was split a good three inches from the thong hook on the handle and pulled apart like a gaping mouth. He would be a long time in sleepy town.

"You ought to get that trip fixed in the stairs," I said to the fancy boy on the floor. "It drops like a trapdoor."

He looked back at me through eyes that seemed to pulse every time his heart beat. Both his hands were on the floor, palms down, his body rising and falling with his labored breathing. Under a trim moustache his chin fell away a little, quivering like the rest of him. A hairline that had once swept across his forehead now lay like low tide on the back of his head, graying a little, but not much. There was a scar on one lip and his nose had been twisted out of shape not too long ago, but when you looked hard you could still see through the wear of the years.

He was just what I expected. "Hello, Mallory," I said, "or should I say Nelson?"

I could hardly hear his voice. "W . . . who are you?"

"Don't play games, sucker. My name is Mike Hammer. You ought to know me. I bumped one of your boys and made a mess of the other awhile back. You should see him now. I caught up with him again. Get up."

"What . . . are you going . . . to do?" I looked down at the .45. The safety was off and it was the nastiest-looking weapon in existence at that moment. I pointed it at his belly.

"Maybe I'll shoot you. There." I indicated his navel with the muzzle.

"If it's money you want, I can give it to you, Hammer. Please, get the rod off me."

Mallory was the tough guy. He edged away from me, holding his hands out in a futile attempt to stop a bullet if it should come. He stopped backing when he hit the edge of the desk. "I don't want any of your dough, Mallory," I said, "I want you." I let him look into the barrel again. "I want to hear something you have to say."

"I . . ."

"Where's Miss Grange . . . or should I say Rita Cambell?"

He drew his breath in a great swallow and before I could move swung around, grabbed the pen set from the desk and sent the solid onyx base crashing into my face.

Fingers clawed at my throat and we hit the floor with a tangle of arms and legs. I brought my knee up and missed, then swung with the gun. It landed on the side of his neck and gave me a chance to clear my head. I saw where the next punch was going. I brought it up from the floor and smacked him as hard as I could in the mouth. My knuckles pushed back his lips and his front teeth popped like hollow things under the blow.

The bastard spit them right in my face.

He was trying to reach my eyes. I tossed the rod to one side and laughed long and loud. Only for that one moment did he possess any strength at all, just that once when he was raging mad. I got hold of both his arms and pinned them down, then threw him sideways to the floor. His feet kicked out and kicked again until I got behind him. With his back on the floor I straddled his chest and sat on his stomach, both his hands flat against his sides, held there by my legs. He couldn't yell without choking on his own blood and he knew it, but he kept trying to spit at me nevertheless.

With my open palm I cracked him across the cheek. Right, left, right, left. His head went sideways with each slap, but my other hand always straightened it up again. I hit him until the palms of my hands were sore and his cheek split in a dozen places from my ring. At first he flopped and moaned for me to stop, then fought bitterly to get away from the blows that were tearing his face to shreds. When he was almost out, I quit.

"Where's Grange, Mallory?"

"The shed." He tried to plead with me not to hit him, but I cracked him one anyway.

"Where's the Cook girl?"

No answer. I reached for my rod and cradled it in my hand.

"Look at me, Mallory."

His eyes opened halfway. "My hand hurts. Answer me or I use this on you. Maybe you won't live through it. Where's the Cook girl?"

"Nobody else. Grange . . . is the . . . only one."

"You're lying, Mallory."

"No . . . just Grange."

I couldn't doubt but what he was telling the truth. After what I gave him he was ready to spill his guts. But that still didn't account for Cook. "Okay, who does have her then?"

Blood bubbled out of his mouth from his split gums. "Don't know her."

"She was Grange's alibi, Mallory. She was with the Cook dame the night York was butchered. She would have given Grange an out."

His eyes came open all the way. "She's a bitch," he mouthed. "She doesn't deserve an alibi. They kidnapped my kid, that's what they did!"

"And you kidnapped him back . . . fourteen years later."

"He was mine, wasn't he? He didn't belong to York."

I gave it to him slowly. "You didn't really want him, did you? You didn't give a damn about the kid. All you wanted was to get even with York. Wasn't that it?"

Mallory turned his head to one side. "Answer me, damn you!"

"Yes."

"Who killed York?"

I waited for his answer. I had to be sure I was right. This was one time I had to be sure. "It . . . it wasn't me."

I raised the gun and laid the barrel against his forehead. Mallory was staring into the mouth of hell. "Lie to me, Mallory," I said, "and I'll shoot you in the belly, then shoot you again a little higher. Not where you'll die quick, but where you'll wish you did. Say it was you and you die fast . . . like you don't deserve. Say it wasn't you and I may believe you and I may not . . . only don't lie to me because I know who killed York."

Once more his eyes met mine, showing pain and terror. "It . . . wasn't me. No, it wasn't me. You've got to believe that." I let the gun stay where it was, right against his forehead. "I didn't even know he was dead. It was Grange I wanted."

Even with his shattered mouth the words were coming freely as he begged for his life. "I got the news clipping in the mail. The one about the trouble in the hospital. There was no signature, but the letter said that Grange was Rita Cambell and she was a big shot now and if I kidnapped the kid, instead of ransom I could get positive information from York that his kid was my son. I wouldn't have snatched him if it wasn't so easy. The letter said the watchman on the gate would be drugged and the door to the house open on a certain night. All I had to do to get the kid was go in after him. I was still pretty mad at York and the letter made it worse. I wanted Myra Grange more than the old man, that's why when those crazy lugs I sent after the kid lost him I made a try for her. I followed her from her house to another place then waited for her to come out before I grabbed her. She was in there when York was killed and I was waiting outside. Honest, I didn't kill him. She didn't know who I was until I told her. Ever since that time when York stole my kid I used the name Nelson. She started to fight with me in the car and hit me over the head with the heel of her shoes. While I was still dizzy she beat it and got in her car and scrammed. I chased her and forced her off the road by the river and she went in. I thought she was dead . . ."

The footsteps coming up the stairs stopped him. I whipped around and sent a shot crashing through the door. Somebody swore and yelled for reinforcements. I prodded Mallory with the tip of the rod. "The window and be quick."

He didn't need any urging. The gun in his back was good incentive. That damn warning trip. Either it went off someplace else or the boys on the doors got suspicious. Egghead was starting to groan on the floor. "Get the window up."

Mallory opened the catch and pushed. Outside the steel railings of the fire escape were waiting. I thanked the good fathers who passed the law making them compulsory for all three-story buildings. We went out together, then down the metal stairs without trying to conceal our steps. If I had a cowbell around my neck I couldn't have made more noise. Mallory kept spitting blood over the side, trying to keep his eyes on me and the steps at the same time. Above us heavy bodies were ramming the door. The lock splintered and someone tripped over the mug on the floor, but before they could get to the window we were on the ground.

"The boathouse. Shake it, Mallory, they won't care who they hit," I said.

Mallory was panting heavily, but he knew there was wisdom in my words. A shot snapped out that was drowned in a sudden blast from the orchestra, but I saw the gravel kick up almost at my feet. We skirted the edge of cars and out in between the fenders, then picked an opening and went through it to the boathouse. The back of it was padlocked.

"Open it."

"I . . . I don't have the key."

"That's a quick way to get yourself killed," I reminded him.

He fumbled for a key in his pocket, brought it out and inserted it in the padlock. His hands were shaking so hard that he couldn't get it off the hasp. I shoved him away and ripped it loose myself. The door slid sideways, and I thumbed him in, closing the door behind us. With the gun in the small of his back I flicked a match with my fingernail.

Grange and Cook were lying side by side in a pile of dirt at the far end of the boathouse. Both were tied up like Thanksgiving turkeys with a wad of cloth clamped between their jaws. They were out cold. Mallory's mouth dropped to his chin and he pointed a trembling finger at Cook. "She's here!"

"What the hell did you expect?"

His face grew livid until blood flowed afresh from his mouth. Mallory might have said something in anger if the match had not scorched my finger. I dropped it and cursed. He pulled away from the gun at the same time and ran for it. I took four steps toward the door, my arms outstretched to grab him, but he wasn't there. At the other end of the room one of the girls started to moan through her gag. A knob turned and for a second I saw stars in the sky at the side of the wall. My first shot got him in the leg and he fell to the floor screaming. In the half-light of the match I hadn't seen that side door, but he knew it was there. I ran over and yanked him back by the foot, mad enough to send a bullet into his gut.

I never had the chance. There was a blast of gunfire and my rod was torn from my grasp. The beam of a spotlight hit me in the eyes as Dilwick's voice said, "Freeze, Hammer. You make one move and I'll shoot hell out of you."

The light moved over to the side, never leaving me. Dilwick snapped on the overhead: one dim bulb that barely threw enough light to reach both ends. He was standing there beside the switch with as foul a look as I ever hope to see on a human face and murder in his hands. He was going to kill me.

It might have ended then if Mallory hadn't said, "You lousy rat. You stinking, lousy rat. You're the one who's been bleeding me. You son of a bitch."

Dilwick grinned at me, showing his teeth. "He's a wise guy, Hammer. Listen to him bawl."

I didn't say a word.

Dilwick went over and got my gun from the floor, using his handkerchief on the butt, never taking his eyes from either of us. He looked at me, then Mallory, and before either of us could move sent a shot smashing into Mallory's chest from my .45. The guy folded over in a quarter roll and was still. Dilwick tossed the still-smoking gun down. "It was nice while it lasted," he said, "but now it will be even better."

I waited.

"The boss had a swell racket here. A perfect racket. He paid us off well, but I'm going to take over now. The hell with being a cop. It'll make a pretty story, don't you think? I come in here and see you shoot him, then shoot you. Uh-huh, a very pretty story and nobody will blame me. You'll be wrapped up cold for a double murder, first that copper and now him."

"Sure," I said, "but what are you going to do about Grange and her pal?"

Dilwick showed his teeth again. "She's wanted for York's murder, isn't she? Wouldn't it be sweet if they were found dead in a love tryst? The papers would love that. Boy, what a front-page story if *you* don't crowd them off. Grange and her sweetie doing the double Dutch in the drink instead of her cooking for the York kill. That would put a decent end to this mess. I got damn sick and tired of trying to cover up for the boss anyway, and you got in my hair, Hammer."

"Did I?"

"Don't get smart. If I had any sense I would have taken care of you myself instead of letting that dumb bunny of a detective bollix up things when you were tailing me on that back road."

"You wouldn't have done any better either," I spat out.

"No? But I will now." He raised the gun and took deliberate aim at my head.

While he wasted time thumbing back the hammer I tugged the snub-nosed .38 from my waistband that I had taken from the punk with the wrecked face and triggered one into his stomach. His face froze for an instant, the gun sagged, then with all the hatred of his madness he stumbled forward a step, raising his gun to fire.

The .38 roared again. A little blue spot appeared over the bridge of his nose and he went flat on his face.

Mine wasn't the only gun to speak. Outside there was a continual roar of bullets; screams from the house and commands being shouted into the dark. A car must have tried to pull away and smashed into another. More shots and the tinkling of broken glass. A man's voice screamed in agony. A tommy went off in short burps blasting everything in its path. Through the door held open by Mallory's body the brilliant white light of a spotlight turned the night to day and pairs of feet were circling the boathouse.

I shouted, "Price, it's me, Mike. I'm in here!"

A light shot in the door as hands slid the other opening back. A state trooper with a riot gun pointed at me slid in and I dropped the .38. Price came in behind him. "Damn, you still alive?"

"I look it, don't I?" Laughing almost drunkenly I slapped him on the shoulder. "Am I glad to see you! You sure took long enough to get here." Price's foot stretched out and pushed the body on the floor.

"That's . . ."

"Dilwick," I finished. "The other one over there is Mallory."

"I thought you were going to keep me informed on how things stood," he said.

"It happened too fast. Besides, I couldn't be popping in places where I could be recognized."

"Well, I hope your story's good, Mike. It had better be. We're holding people out there with enough influence to swing a state legislature, and if the reason is a phony or even smells like one, you and I are both going to be on the carpet. You for murder."

"Nuts, what was all the shooting about outside?"

"I got your message such as it was and came up here with three cars of troopers. When we got on the grounds a whole squad of mugs with guns in their hands came ripping around the house. They let go at us before we could get out of the cars and there was hell to pay. The boys came up expecting action and they got it."

"Those mugs, chum, were after me. I guess they figured I'd try to make a break for it and circled the house. Dilwick was the only one who knew where we'd be. Hell, he should have. I was after Grange and the Cook girl and he had them in here."

"Now you tell me. Go on and finish it."

I brought him up to date in a hurry. "Dilwick's been running cover for Mallory. When you dig up the books on this joint you're going to see a lot of fancy figures. But our boy Dilwick got ideas. He wanted the place for himself. He shot Mallory with my gun and was going to shoot me, only I got him with the rod I took off the boy whose car I flipped over. Yeah. Dilwick was a good thinker all right. When Grange didn't show up he did what I did and floated down the river himself and found how the eddies took him to the shore. At that time both he and Mallory were figuring on cutting themselves a nice slice of cash from the York estate. Grange was the only one who knew there was evidence that Ruston wasn't York's son and they were going to squeeze it out of her or turn her over to the police for the murder of York."

Price looked at the body again, then offered me a cigarette. "So Grange really did bump her boss. I'll be a so-and-so."

I lit the butt slowly, then blew the smoke through my nostrils. "Grange didn't bump anybody."

The sergeant's face wrinkled. He stared at me queerly.

"This is the aftermath, Price," I reflected. "It's what happens when you light the fuse."

"What the hell are you talking about?"

I didn't hear him. I was thinking about a kidnapping. I was thinking about a scientist with a cleaver in his skull and the chase on for his assistant. I was thinking about Junior Ghent rifling York's office and coming up with some dirty pictures, and then getting beat up. I was thinking about a shot nicking Roxy and a night with Alice Nichols that might have been fun if it hadn't been planned so my clothes could be searched and my skull cracked afterward. I was thinking about a secret cache in the fireplace, a column in the paper, a cop trying to kill me and some words Mallory told me. I was thinking how all this might have been foreseen by the killer when the killer planned the first kill. I was thinking of the face of the killer.

It was a mess. I had said that a hundred times now, but what a beautiful mess it was. There had never been a mess as nasty as this. Nope, not a dull moment. Every detail seemed to overlap and prod something bigger to happen until you were almost ready to give up, and the original murder was obscured by the craziest details imaginable. Rah, rah, sis boom bah, with a fanfare of trumpets as the police come in and throw bullets all over the place. Was it supposed to end like this? I knew one thing. I was supposed to have died someplace along the line. The killer must be fuming now because I was very much alive. What makes people think they can get away with murder? Some plan it simple, some elaborately extreme, but this killer let things take care of themselves and they wound up better than anyone could have hoped for.

"Don't keep secrets, Mike, who did it?"

I threw the butt down, stamped on it. "I'll tell you tomorrow, Price."

"You'll tell me now, Mike."

"Don't fight me, kid. I appreciate all that you did for me, but I don't throw anyone to the dogs until I'm sure."

"You've killed enough people to be sure. Who was it?"

"It still goes. I have to check one little detail."

"What?"

"Something that makes a noise like a cough."

Price thought I was crazy. "You tell me now or I'll hold you until you do. I can't stick my neck out any further. I'll have hot breaths blowing on my back too, and they'll be a lot hotter if I can't explain this mix-up!"

I was tired. I felt like curling up there with Dilwick and going to sleep. "Don't squeeze, Price. I'll tell you tomorrow. When you take this little package home . . ." I swept my hand around the room, ". . . you'll get a commendation." Over in the corner a trooper was taking the bonds from the girls. Grange was moaning again. "You can get her side of the story anyway, and that will take care of your superiors until you hear from me."

The sergeant waited a long moment then shrugged his shoulders. "You win. I've waited this long . . . I guess tomorrow will be all right. Let's get out of here."

We carried Grange out together with the other trooper lugging the Cook girl over his shoulder. Myra Grange's pupils were big black circles, dilated to the utmost. She was hopped up to the ears. We got them into one of the police cars then stood around until the casino gang was manacled to each other and the clientele weeded out. I grinned when I spotted a half-dozen Sidon cops in the group. They had stopped bellowing long ago, and from the worried looks being passed around it was going to be a race to see who could talk the loudest and the fastest. There would be a new police force in Sidon this time next week. The public might be simple enough to let themselves be bullied around and their government rot out from underneath them, but it would only go so far. An indignant public is like a mad bull. It wouldn't stop until every tainted employee on the payroll was in a cell. Maybe they'd even give me a medal. Yeah, maybe.

I was sick of watching. I called Price over and told him I was going back. His face changed, but he said nothing. There was a lot he wanted to say, but he could tell how it was with me. Price nodded and let me climb into my car. I backed it up and turned around in the drive. Tomorrow would be a busy day. I'd have to prepare my statements on the whole affair to hand over to a grand jury, then get set to prove it. You don't simply kill people and walk away from it. Hell, no. Righteous kill or not the law had to be satisfied.

Yes, tomorrow would be a busy day. Tonight would be even busier. I had to see a killer about a murder.

CHAPTER 12

It was ten after eleven when I reached the York estate. Henry came out of his gatehouse, saw me and gaped as though he were looking at a ghost. "Good heavens, Mr. Hammer. The police are searching all over for you! You . . . you killed a man."

"So I did," I said sarcastically. "Open the gates."

"No . . . I can't let you come in here. There'll be trouble."

"There will if you don't open the gates." His face seemed to sag and his whole body assumed an air of defeat. Disgust was written in the set of his mouth, disgust at having to look at a man who shot a fellow man. I drove through and stopped.

"Henry, come here."

The gatekeeper shuffled over reluctantly. "Yes, sir?"

"I'm not wanted any longer, Henry. The police have settled the matter up to a certain point."

"You mean you didn't . . ."

"No, I mean I shot him, but it was justified. I've been cleared, understand?"

He smiled a little, not quite understanding, but he breathed a sigh of relief. At least he knew he wasn't harboring a fugitive in me. I pulled up the driveway to the house, easing around the turns until the beams of my brights spotlighted the house. Inside I saw Harvey coming to the door. Instead of parking in front of the place I rolled around to the side and nosed into the open door of the garage. A big six-car affair, but now there were only two cars in it, counting mine. A long time ago someone started using it for a storeroom and now one end was cluttered with the junk accumulated over the years. Two boys' bicycles were hanging from a suspension gadget set in the ceiling and underneath them a newer model with a small one-cylinder engine built into the frame. Hanging from a hook screwed into an upright were roller skates and ice skates, but neither pair had been used much. Quite a childhood Ruston had.

I shut the door of the garage and looked up. The rain had started. The tears of the gods. Of laughter or sorrow? Maybe the joke was on me, after all.

Harvey was his usual, impeccable, unmoving self as he took my hat and ushered me into the living room. He made no mention of the affair whatsoever, nor did his face reveal any curiosity. Even before he announced me, Roxy was on her way down the stairs with Ruston holding her arm. Billy Parks came out of the foyer grinning broadly, his hand outstretched. "Mike! You sure got your nerve. By gosh, you're supposed to be Public Enemy Number One!"

"Mike!"

"Hello, Lancelot. Hello, Roxy. Let me give you a hand."

"Oh, I'm no cripple," she laughed. "The stairs get me a little, but I can get around all right."

"What happened, Mike?" Ruston smiled. "The policemen all left this evening after they got a phone call and we haven't seen them since. Golly, I was afraid you'd been shot or something. We thought they caught you."

"Well, they came close, kid, but they never even scratched me. It's all finished. I'm in the clear and I'm about ready to go home."

Billy Parks stopped short in the act of lighting a cigarette. His hands began to tremble slightly and he had trouble finding the tip of the butt.

Ruston said, "You mean the police don't want you any longer, Mike?" I shook my head. He gave a little cry of gladness and ran to me, throwing his arms about me in a tight squeeze. "Gee, Mike, I'm so happy."

I patted his arm and smiled crookedly. "Yep, I'm almost an honest man again."

"Mike . . ."

Roxy's voice was the hoarse sound of a rasp on wood. She was clutching the front of her negligee with one hand, trying to push a streamer of hair from her eyes with the other. A little muscle twitched in her cheek. "Who . . . did it, Mike?"

Billy was waiting. Roxy was waiting. I heard Harvey pause outside the door. Ruston looked from them to me, puzzled. The air in the room was charged, alive. "You'll hear about it tomorrow," I said.

Billy Parks dropped his cigarette.

"Why not now?" Roxy gasped.

I took a cigarette from my pocket and stuffed it between my lips. Billy fumbled for his on the floor and held the lit tip to mine. I dragged the smoke in deeply. Roxy was beginning to go white, biting on her lip. "You'd better go to your room, Roxy. You don't look too good."

"Yes . . . yes. I had better. Excuse me. I really don't feel too well. The stairs . . ." She let it go unfinished. While Ruston helped her up I stood there in silence with Billy. The kid came down again in a minute.

"Do you think she'll be all right, Mike?"

"I think so."

Billy crushed his cig out in an ashtray. "I'm going to bed, Mike. This day has been tough enough."

I nodded. "You going to bed, too, Ruston?"

"What's the matter with everybody, Mike?"

"Nervous, I guess."

"Yes, that's it, I suppose." His face brightened. "Let me play for them. I haven't played since . . . that night. But I want to play, Mike. Will it be all right?"

"Sure, go ahead."

He grinned and ran out of the room. I heard him arrange the seat, then lift the lid of the piano, and the next moment the heavy melody of a classical piece filled the house. I sat down and listened. It was gay one moment, serious the next. He ran up and down the keys in a fantasy of expression. Good music to think by. I chain-lit another cigarette, wondering how the music was affecting the murderer. Did it give him a creepy feeling? Was every note part of his funeral theme? Three cigarettes gone in thought and still I waited.

The music had changed now, it was lilting, rolling in song. I put the butt out and stood up. It was time to see the killer.

I put my hand on the knob and turned, stepped in the room and locked the door behind me. The killer was smiling at me, a smile that had no meaning I could fathom. It was a smile of neither defeat nor despair, but nearer to triumph. It was no way for a murderer to smile. The bells in my head were rising in a crescendo with the music.

I said to the murderer, "You can stop playing now, Ruston."

The music didn't halt. It rose in spirit and volume while Ruston York created a symphony from the keyboard, a challenging overture to death, keeping time with my feet as I walked to a chair and sat down. Only when I pulled the .45 from its holster did the music begin to diminish. My eyes never left his face. It died out in a crashing maze of minor chords that resounded from the walls with increased intensity.

"So you found me out, Mr. Hammer."

"Yes."

"I rather expected it these last few days." He crossed his legs with complete nonchalance and barely a glance at the gun in my hand. I felt my temper being drawn to the brink of unreason, my lips tightening.

"You're a killer, little buddy," I said. "You're a blood-crazy, insane little bastard. It's so damn inconceivable that I can hardly believe it myself, but it's so. You had it well planned, chum. Oh, but you would, you're a genius. I forgot. That's what everyone forgot. You're only fourteen but you can sit in with scientists and presidents and never miss a trick."

"Thank you."

"You have a hair-trigger mind, Ruston. You can conceive and coordinate and anticipate beyond all realm of imagination. All the while I was batting my brains out trying to run down a killer you must have held your sides laughing. You knew pretty well what killing York would expose . . . a series of crimes and petty personalities scrambled together to make the dirtiest omelet ever cooked. But *you'd* never cook for it. Oh, no . . . not you. If . . . if you were found out the worst that could happen would be that you'd face a juvenile court. That's what you thought, didn't you? Like hell.

"Yes, you're only a child, but you have a man's mind. That's why I'm talking to you like I would to a man. That's why I can kill you like I would a man."

He sat there unmoving. If he knew fear he showed it only in the tiny blue vein that throbbed in his forehead. The smile still played around his mouth. "Being a genius, I guess you thought I was stupid," I continued. With every word my heart beat harder and faster until I was filled with hate. "It was getting so that I thought I was stupid myself. Why wouldn't I? Every time I turned around something would happen that was so screwy that it didn't have any place in the plot, yet in a way it was directly related. Junior Ghent and Alice. The Graham boys. Each trying to chop off a slice of cash for themselves. Each one concerned with his own little individual problem and completely unknowing of the rest. It was a beautiful setup for you.

"But please don't think I was stupid, Ruston. The only true stupidity I showed was in calling you Lancelot. If I ever meet the good knight somewhere I'll beg him to forgive me. But I wasn't so stupid otherwise, Ruston. I found out that Grange had something on York . . . and that something was the fact that she was the only one who knew that he was a kidnapper in a sense. York . . . an aging scientist who wanted an heir badly so he could pass on his learning to his son . . . but his son died. So what did he do? He took a kid who had been born of a criminal father and would have been reared in the gutter, and turned him into a genius. But after a while the genius began to think and hate. Why? Hell, only you know that.

"But somewhere you got hold of the details concerning your birth. You knew that York had only a few years to live and you knew, too, that Grange had threatened to expose the entire affair if he didn't leave his money to her. Your father (should I call him that?) was a thinker too. He worked out a proposition with Alice to have an affair with his lesbian assistant and hold that over her head as a club, and it worked, except that Junior Ghent learned of the affair when his sister told him that York had proposed the same deal to her, too, and Junior wanted to hold that over Grange's head, and Alice's, too, so that he could come in for part of the property split. Man, what a scramble it was after that. Everybody thought I had the dope when it was lying beside the wall out there. Yeah, the wall. Remember the shot you took at Roxy? You were in your room. You tossed that lariat that was beside your bed around the awning hook outside her window, swung down and shot at her through the glass. She had the light on and couldn't see out, but she was a perfect target. You missed at that range only because you were swinging. That really threw me off the track. Nice act you put on when I brought the doctor in. You had him fooled too. I didn't get that until a little while ago.

"Now I know. You, as an intelligent, emotional man, were in love. What a howl. In love with your nurse." His face darkened. The vein began to throb harder than ever and his hands clenched into a tight knot. "You shot at her because you saw me and Roxy in a clinch and were jealous. Brother, how happy you must have been when the cops were on my back with orders to shoot to kill. I thought you were simply surprised to see me when I climbed in the window that time. Your face went white, remember? For one second there you thought I came back to get you. That was it, wasn't it?"

His head nodded faintly, but still he said nothing. "Then you saw your chance of bringing the cops charging up by knocking over the lamp. Brilliant mind again. You knew the bulb breaking would sound like a shot. Too bad I got away, wasn't it?

"If I wasn't something of a scientist myself I never would have guessed it. Let me tell you how confounded smart I am. Your time doesn't matter much anyway. I caught up with one of your play-mates that snatched you. I beat the living hell out of him and would have done worse to make him talk and he knew it. I'm a scientist at that kind of stuff. He would have talked his head off, only he didn't have anything to say. You know what I asked him? I asked him who Mallory was and he didn't know any Mallory. Good reason too, because ever since you were yanked out of his hands, your father went by the name of Nelson.

"No, he didn't know any Mallory, yet you came home after the kidnapping and said . . . you . . . *heard* . . . *the* . . . *name* . . . *Mallory* . . . mentioned. When I finally got it I knew who the killer was. Then I began to figure how you worked it. Someplace in the house, and I'll find it later, you have the information and Grange's proof that you were Mallory's son. Was it a check that York gave Myra Grange? Somehow you located Mallory and sent him the clipping out of the back issue in the library and the details on how to kidnap you. That was why the clipping was gone. You set yourself up to be snatched hoping that the shock would kill York. It damn near did. You did it well, too, even to the point of switching Henry's aspirins to sleeping tablets. You set yourself up knowing you could outthink the ordinary mortals on the boat and get away. You came mighty close to failing, pal. I wish you had.

"But when that didn't do it you resorted to murder . . . and what a murder. No sweeter deal could have been cooked up by anyone. You knew that when York heard Mallory's name brought into it he'd think Grange had spilled the works and go hunting up his little pet. You thought correctly. York went out there with a gun, but I doubt if he intended to use it. The rod was supposed to be a bluff. Billy heard York leave, and he heard me leave, but how did you reach the apartment? Let me tell you. Out in the garage there's a motorbike. Properly rigged they can do sixty or seventy any day. The noise like a cough that Billy heard was you, Ruston. The sound of the motorbike, low and throaty. I noticed it had a muffler on it. Yeah, York had a gun, and you had to take along a weapon too. A meat cleaver. When I dreamed up all this I wondered why nobody spotted you going or coming, but it wouldn't be too hard to take to the back roads.

"Ruston, you were born under an evil, lucky star. Everything that happened after you surprised York in that room and split his skull worked in your favor. Hell seemed to break loose with everybody trying to cut in on York's dough. Even Dilwick. A crooked copper working for Mallory. Your real father needed that protection and Dilwick fitted right in. Dilwick must have guessed at part of the truth without ever really catching on, and he played it to keep Mallory clear and in a good spot to call for a rake-off, but he got too eager. Dilwick's dead and the rest of his lousy outfit are where they're supposed to be, cooling their heels in a cell.

"But where are you? You . . . the killer. You're sitting here listening to me spiel off everything you already know about and you're not a bit worried. Why should you be? Three or four years in an institution for the criminally insane . . . then prove yourself normal and go back into the world to kill again. You have ethics like Grange. There was a woman who probably loved her profession. She loved it so much she saw a chance to further her career by aiding York, then using it as a club to gain scientific recognition for herself.

"But you on . . . hell." I spit the word out. "You banked on getting away scot-free first, then as a second-best choice facing a court. Maybe you'd even get a suspended sentence. Sure, why not? Any psychiatrist would see how that could happen. Under the pressure of your studies your mind snapped. Boy, have you got a brain! No chair, not for you. Maybe a couple of years yanked from your life span, but what did it matter? You were twenty years ahead of yourself anyway. That was it, wasn't it? Ha!

"Not so, little man. The game just doesn't go that way. I hate to go ex post facto on you, but simply because you're nicely covered by the law doesn't mean you'll stay that way. I'm making up a new one right now. Know what it is?"

He still smiled, no change of expression. It was almost as if he were watching one of his experiments in the rabbit cage.

"Okay," I said, "I'll tell you. All little geniuses . . . or is it genii? . . . who kill and try to get away with it get it in the neck anyway."

Very deliberately I let him see me flick the safety catch on the .45. His eyes were little dark pools that seemed to swim in his head.

I was wondering if I was going to like this.

I never killed a little genius before.

For the first time, Ruston spoke. "About an hour ago I anticipated this," he smiled. I tightened involuntarily. I didn't know why, but I almost knew beforehand what he'd say.

"When I threw my arms around you inside there feigning happiness over your miraculous reappearance, I removed the clip from your gun. It's a wonder you didn't notice the difference in weight."

Did you ever feel like screaming?

My hand was shaking with rage. I felt the hollow space where the clip fitted and swore. I was so damn safety conscious I didn't jack a shell into the chamber earlier either.

And Ruston reached behind the music rack on the piano and came out with the .32.

He smiled again. He knew damn well what I was thinking. Without any trouble I could make the next corpse. He fondled the gun, eyeing the hammer. "Don't move too quickly, Mike. No. I'm not going to shoot you, not just yet. You see, my little knowledge of sleight of hand was quite useful . . . as handy as to know how to open locks. The Normanic sciences weren't all I studied. Anything that presented a problem afforded me the pleasure of solving it in my spare time.

"Move your chair a little this way so I can see you to the best advantage. Ah . . . yes. Compliments are in order, I believe. You were very right and very clever in your deductions. Frankly, I didn't imagine anyone would be able to wade through the tangle that the murder preceded. I thought I did quite well, but I see I failed, up to a certain point. Look at it from my point of view before you invite any impetuous ideas. If you turned me over to the police and proved your case, I would, as you say, stand before a juvenile court. Never would I admit my actual adulthood to them, and I would be sent away for a few years, or perhaps not at all. You see, there's a side to my story too, one you don't know about.

"Or, Mike, and this is an important 'or' . . . I may kill you and claim self-defense. You came in here and in a state of extreme nervous tension hit me. I picked up a gun that dropped out of your pocket"—he held up the .32—"and shot you. Simple? Who would disbelieve it, especially with your temperament . . . and my tender years. So sit still and I don't think I'll shoot you for a little while, at least. Before I do anything, I want to correct some erroneous impressions you seem to have.

"I am not a 'few' years ahead of my time . . . the difference is more like thirty. Even that is an understatement. Can you realize what that means? Me. Fourteen years old. Yet I have lived over fifty years! God, what a miserable existence. You saw my little, er, schoolhouse, but what conclusion did you draw? Fool that you were, you saw nothing. You saw no electrical or mechanical contrivances that had been developed by one of the greatest scientific minds of the century. No, you merely saw objects, never realizing what they were for." He paused, grinning with abject hatred. "Have you ever seen them force-feed ducks to enlarge their livers to make better sausages? Picture that happening to a mind. Imagine having the learning processes accelerated through pain. Torture can make the mind do anything when properly presented.

"Oh, I wasn't supposed to actually feel any of all that. It was supposed to happen while I was unconscious, with only the sub-conscious mind reacting to the incredible pressures being put upon it to grasp and retain the fantastic array of details poured into it like feed being forced through a funnel down a duck's gullet into its belly whether it wants it or not.

"Ah, but who is to say what happens to the mind when such a development takes place? What may happen to the intricate mech-anism of the human mind under such stimulation? What new reac-tions will it develop . . . what new outlets will it seek to repel the monster that is invading it?

"That is how I became what I am . . . but what I learned! I went even farther than was expected of me . . . much farther than the simple sciences and mathematics *he* wanted me to absorb. I even delved into criminology, Mr. Hammer, going over thousands of case histories of past crimes, and when this little . . . circumstance . . . came to my attention, I knew what I had to do . . . then figured out how I could do it.

"I researched, studied and very unobtrusively collected my data, putting myself not *ahead* of you in the commission and solution of criminal actions, but on an approximate level. With your mind highly tuned to absorb, analyze and reconstruct criminal ways, your close association with the police and past experience, you have been able to run a parallel course with me and arrive at the destina-tion at the same time."

He gave me a wry grin. "Or should I say a little behind me?" With his head he indicated the gun in his hand, ". . . seeing that at present I hold the most advantageous position."

I started to rise, but his gun came up. "Remain seated, please. I only said I didn't *think* I would shoot you. Hear me out."

I sat down again.

"Yes, Mr. Hammer, if I had but given it a few days more study your case would have been a hopeless one. Yet you did find me out with all my elaborate precautions, but I still have a marvelous chance to retain my life and liberty. Don't you think?"

I nodded. He certainly would.

"But what good would it do me? Answer me that? What good would it do me? Would I ever have the girl I love . . . or would she have me? She would vomit at the thought. Me, a boy with an adult mind, but still a boy's body. What woman would have me? As the years passed my body would become mature, but the power of my mind would have increased tenfold. Then I would be an old man within the physical shell of a boy. And what of society? You know what society would do . . . it would treat me as a freak. Perhaps I could get a position as a lightning calculator in a circus. That's what that man did to me! That's what he did with his machines and brilliant thoughts. He crumpled my life into a little ball and threw it in the jaws of science. How I hated him. How I wish I could have made him suffer the way he made me suffer!

"To be twisted on the rack is trivial compared to the way one can be tortured through the mind. Has your brain ever been on fire? Have you ever had your skull probed with bolts of electrical energy while strapped to a chair? Of course not! You can remain smug and commonplace in your normal life and track down criminals and murderers. Your one fear is that of dying. Mine was of not dying soon enough!

"You can't understand how much the human body can suffer punishment. It's like a giant machine that can feed itself and heal its own wounds, but the mind is even greater. That simple piece of sickly gray matter that twists itself into gentle shapes under a thin layer of bone and looks so disarming lying in a bottle of formaldehyde is a colossus beyond conception. It thinks pain! Imagine it . . . it thinks pain and the body screams with the torture of it, yet there is nothing you can call physical in the process. It can conceive of things beyond normal imagination if it is stirred to do so. That is what mine did. Things were forced into it. Learning, he called it, but it might as well have been squeezed into my brain with a compressor, for it felt that way. I knew pain that was not known by any martyr . . . it was a pain that will probably never be known again.

"Your expression changes, Mr. Hammer. I see you believe what I say. You should . . . it is true. You may believe it, but you will never understand it. Right now I can see you change your mind. You condone my actions. I condone them. But would a jury if they knew? Would a judge . . . or the public? No, they couldn't visualize what I have undergone."

Something was happening to Ruston York even as he was speaking. The little-boy look was gone from his face, replaced by some strange metamorphosis that gave him the facial demeanor I had seen during the wild mouthings of dictators. Every muscle was tense, veins and tendons danced under the delicate texture of his skin and his eyes shone with the inward fury that was gnawing at his heart.

He paused momentarily, staring at me, yet somehow I knew he wasn't really seeing me at all. "You were right, Mr. Hammer," he said, a new, distant note in his voice now. "I was in love with my nurse. Or better . . . I am in love with . . . Miss Malcom. From the moment she arrived here I have been in love with her."

The hard, tight expression seemed to diminish at the thought and a smile tugged faintly at the corners of his mouth. "Yes, Mr. Hammer, love. Not the love a child would give a woman, but a man's love. The kind of love you can give a woman . . . or any other normal man."

Suddenly the half smile vanished and the vacant look came back again. "That's what that man did to me. He made an error in his calculations, or never expected his experiment to reach such a conclusion, but that man did more than make me a mental giant. He not only increased my intellectual capacity to the point of genius . . . but in the process he developed my emotional status until I was no longer a boy.

"I am a man, Mr. Hammer. In every respect except this outer shell, and my chronological age, I am a man. And I am a man in love, trapped inside the body of a child. Can you imagine it? Can you think of me presenting my love to a woman like Roxy Malcom? Oh, she might understand, but never could she return that love. All I would get would be pity. Think of that . . . pity. That's what that bastard did to me!"

He was spitting the words out now, his face back in the contours of frustration and hatred, his eyes blankly looking at me, yet through me. It had to be like this, I thought, when he was on the

brink of the deep end. It was the only chance I had. Slowly, I tucked my feet under me, the movement subtle so as not to distract him. I'd probably take a slug or two, but I'd lived through them before and if I managed it right I might be able to get my hands on his gun before he could squeeze off a fatal one. It was the only chance I had. My fingers were tight on the arms of the chair, the muscles in my shoulders bunched to throw myself forward . . . and all the time my guts were churning because I knew what I could expect before I could get all the way across that room to where he was sitting.

"I have to live in a world of my own, Mr. Hammer. No other world would accept me. As great a thing, a twisted thing that I am, I have no world to live in."

The blankness suddenly left his eyes. He was seeing me now, seeing what I was doing and knowing what I was thinking. His thumb pulled back the hammer on the .32 to make it that much easier to trigger off. Behind the now almost colorless pupils of his eyes some crazy thought was etching itself into his mind.

Ruston York looked at me, suddenly with his boy face again. He even smiled a tired little smile and the gun moved in his hand. "Yes," he repeated, "as great as I am, I am useless."

Even while he had talked, he had done something he had never done before. He exposed himself to himself and for the first time saw the futility that was Ruston York. Once again he smiled, the gun still on me.

There was no time left at all. It had to be now, *now*! Only a second, perhaps, to do it in.

He saw me and smiled, knowing I was going to do it. "Sir Lancelot," he said wistfully.

Then, before I could even get out of the chair, Ruston York turned the gun around in his hand, jammed the muzzle of it into his mouth and pulled the trigger.

About the Author

A bartender's son, **Mickey Spillane** was born in Brooklyn, New York, on March 9, 1918. An only child who swam and played football as a youth, Spillane got a taste for storytelling by scaring other kids around the campfire. After a truncated college career, Spillane—already selling stories to pulps and slicks under pseudonyms—became a writer in the burgeoning comic-book field, a career cut short by World War II. Spillane, who had learned to fly at airstrips as a boy, became an instructor of fighter pilots.

After the war, Spillane converted an unsold comic-book project—"Mike Danger, Private Eye"—into a hard-hitting, sexy novel. The thousand-dollar advance was just what the writer needed to buy materials for a house he wanted to build for himself and his young wife on a patch of land in New Jersey.

The 1948 Signet reprint of his 1947 E. P. Dutton hardcover novel *I, the Jury* sold in the millions, as did the six tough mysteries that soon followed; all but one featured hard-as-nails P.I. Mike Hammer. The Hammer thriller *Kiss Me, Deadly* (1952) was the first private eye novel to make the *New York Times* bestseller list.

Mike Hammer's creator claimed to write only when he needed the money, and in periods of little or no publishing, Spillane occupied himself with other pursuits: flying, traveling with the circus, appearing in motion pictures, and nearly twenty years spoofing himself and Hammer in a lucrative series of Miller Lite beer commercials.

The controversial Hammer has been the subject of a radio show, a comic strip, two television series, and numerous gritty movies, notably director Robert Aldrich's seminal film noir *Kiss Me Deadly*

(1955), and *The Girl Hunters* (1963), starring Spillane as his famous hero.

Spillane was honored by the Mystery Writers of America with the Grand Master Award, and with the Private Eye Writers of America "Eye" Lifetime Achievement Award; he was also a Shamus Award winner. The creator of Mike Hammer died in 2006. His wife, Jane, and his friend and collaborator Max Allan Collins are working together to bring Mickey Spillane's unpublished (and at times unfinished) fiction to fruition.